A Prince In Need
Volume 2 in the Myrridian Cycle

Debra Killeen

A Prince In Need

Helm Publishing

For information address:
Helm Publishing
3923 Seward Ave.
Rockford, IL 61108
815-398-4660
www.publishersdrive.com

ISBN 978-0-9801780-5-0

Printed in the United States of America

Dedication

This book is dedicated to my aunts and uncles: Anne, Diane, Diann, Tom, and TC. DiDi, you have gone above and beyond, and AA, welcome to the ranks!

Acknowledgements

First and foremost, THANK YOU to my trusted first reader and editor extraordinaire, another Diane, who continues to keep my writing, and the characters, honest. I wouldn't be where I am now without your input.

Also, thank you to the fine residents, schoolteachers and educators of Indian River County, Florida. A special mention to the Honors English students at Vero Beach High School – you ROCK!

Special thanks to my early readers, especially to Will and Adam, for your superb critical suggestions and encouraging feedback. In addition, thanks to Janet, Mary Ann, Jessica, Debbie M., Debbie G., Terry, Pam C., Karen K., Victoria, Brenda – your comments are all taken seriously.

Thank you to Brian, for keeping up the website and to Vin for another terrific cover. Thank you to Dianne Helm for continuing to believe in me and the books – we're going places, lady!

Thank you to Meade, Kate, Kim, Pat, Steve, Doug, Jim, G Kay, Arnold, Jerry – you are the best writing group, providing much-needed feedback and support.

Thank you to the fine folks at PharmaLinkFHI and POZEN, for your support and flexibility regarding my second job.

Thanks to Ethel and Jack for the continued use of your name as well as your support.

Scott gets an honorable mention, as the nameless stable cat at Rhennsbury Castle.

Reviews

"A Prince In Need is wonderful. All the likeable characters are back plus a few more. The compelling plot carries you along, and gradually reveals a profound healing sanity. The imagined world is vivid and believable. The 'young adult' part of me refuses to put the book down! But the 'adult' part of me insists there are other things to do…but then resists doing them. I just want to stay in this story!"
Alexa Wolf, author of *My Mother's House,* a memoir

"Debra Killeen's *A Prince in Need*, Volume Two of her Myrridia Cycle, is an entertaining tale of magick, mayhem, dark deeds and vengeance, as the valiant time-travelers of Volume One, *An Unlikely Duke*, find themselves embroiled in new adventures in an intriguing and perilous world."
Kate Betterton, author of *Where the Lake Becomes the River*

"Debra Killeen's writing style is full of character development and excitement…"A Prince in Need" [has] plenty of romance, plot twists and feminist humor."
Ian McCurley, reviewer for Reader Views

Prologue

"Are you sure you want to do this?" Angelita Martinez asked the two women sitting with her at a small table in a Boston coffee shop.

"I wouldn't be here talking to you if I weren't," one of the women asserted, her jaw set with stubbornness.

The other woman was quiet for several seconds. "I have to see Chris again," she said. "I can't explain it. I'm usually more...I don't know...practical than this, but there're just too many..." She broke off, and her eyes met Angelita's. "You tell me that Chris is in this other place, but none of us, even you, have any real idea of what's happening there, what things are like."

"Perhaps not," Angelita replied. "But he and Elijah have had a number of chances to return to our world. So far, they choose to remain in Myrridia." She shrugged. "I will attempt to open the window to this world again tonight. But you should know - I may not be able to do so."

"What!" The first woman kept her voice down with an effort, but she stood, her hands gripping the table. "You'd better," she added, her eyes narrowed.

The second woman had paled. "What you're not saying is that there's an equal, or greater, chance that you might not be able to do it next month, when we're ready to return here, and we could be stuck there, forever." She glanced at her companion, seeing a frown of worry pass fleetingly across the woman's brow. She swallowed hard.

"It could happen," Angelita agreed. She stood. "My advice, ladies, is to think about your decision carefully. You still have a few hours. I will be at St. Magdalene's Church at eight, whether you come or not." She glanced at each one, running her gaze down their garments. "I suggest you go shopping for some more historically accurate clothing."

The two women exchanged glances after Angelita had gone. The first woman stared down at her jeans. "I don't think so," she said, smiling. "I want to have something I know is comfortable. I'm not planning to go native."

"But if we're going to be there for a whole month, shouldn't we try to fit in?" the other woman asked. She was wearing a long rayon skirt, boots with sturdy, 1-inch heels, and a long-sleeved tunic-style cotton sweater. "Okay, the fabrics are all wrong, but at least my ankles aren't showing."

"And it's not like we're going to the Middle East, with those burqa things," the first woman agreed. "What does this Angelita know about anything?"

"Probably a lot more than she's saying. I mean, she is a bona fide psychic, right? If you believe in that sort of thing." She took a deep breath. "Maybe I should stay back. I could be opening up a lot of old wounds better left…"

"Sure, and then you'll never get any answers. And a week from now you'll be kicking yourself for backing out." The woman picked up her half-full latte. "I'm going. Let's go find some place to hang out for a few hours. Isn't there a big museum here?"

Shortly before eight that evening, in the sanctuary of St. Magdalene's Church, Angelita put the finishing touches on her preparations for her Magical Working. She was relieved that the two women had not appeared yet, hoping they'd changed their minds. Nearly a year prior, she'd aided Drs. Chris McCabe and Elijah Holmes in traveling to Myrridia via this same window. Those two men had a definite mission, while these two women did not, which meant this trip could end in real disaster.

She lit the four lavender-scented candles she'd placed at the four cardinal points of the circle she'd drawn in chalk on the floor near the altar. Kneeling, she focused her mind on the Working ahead, praying quietly in Spanish. As she finished the prayer, she heard voices and turned to see that the two women had arrived. Both glanced around the interior of the church.

The woman in jeans arched an eyebrow. "I still have trouble believing in this whole magical business." She lowered her backpack to the floor. The other woman carried a cloth overnight bag.

"Then I suspect your opinion is about to change," Angelita noted. "Please join me in the Circle, and think of something calming." After a brief pause the women obeyed.

Angelita began a ritual prayer as she slipped into trance, smiling as she recognized the features of the priest on the other side of the window that had appeared a couple of feet in front of them. Angelita stood and passed a note to him, ignoring the tingling in her arm. He passed a piece of parchment to her, glanced at her note, and stared at her in puzzlement. He raised his hand, a nonverbal request for her to wait.

She nodded.

"So?" one of the women asked.

The other stared, openmouthed, at the flickering opening between two worlds.

"We wait. If they say 'no,' you stay here," Angelita replied.

The woman looked her over. "You can't really stop me," she said quietly.

The other woman shushed her. "Nobody came here to cause trouble. Let's wait and see what happens."

After a short delay, the women were given permission to cross over. They stepped through the window.

Chapter One

While May Day revels continued well past nightfall in Rhennsbury, the capital of the kingdom of Myrridia, the thoughts of her king, Reginald Claybourne, were on his son and heir, Robert, and they were far from happy. Robert had turned seventeen a couple of months ago, and in Reginald's opinion, it was high time the youth took a woman to bed. An hour before, he'd sent one of his men-at-arms to his favorite brothel to make arrangements for his and Robert's entertainment, knowing the establishment would likely be crowded with those still celebrating the holiday. He also knew that, as the king, his request would take precedence. He'd given many of the castle's servants the night off by not dining in the Great Hall, and his wife Margaret had left the castle early in January to retire to a convent, so she was no longer there to criticize his decisions.

Reginald scowled at the memory of his wife. She'd admitted to him that she'd ordered the death of one of his most trusted advisers, the Duke of Saelym, because the man had threatened the virtue of Reginald's daughter, Allyson. Reginald didn't believe a word of the tale; as far as he was concerned, the duke would never have considered such an act of treason, so he never asked his daughter to corroborate Margaret's words. The duke's murder had left Reginald with a personal as well as political void, and though a stranger to Myrridia, Christopher McCabe, had stepped in for the slain duke, the man was no friend to Reginald. The king suppressed a sigh; he'd just sent out summonses to all of his ranking nobles, including Chris, to come to Rhennsbury to prepare for war, though he had no idea how the man would argue in council about the situation.

Reginald shook his head to clear his thoughts and looked around his private bedchamber, to see if he'd forgotten anything for his upcoming foray into the city. He glanced into the looking-glass, nodding at his reflection. Though he was forty, his shoulders were still powerful, as evidenced from an ill-fitting and wrinkled tunic, thanks to his many years of warring. He frowned at the gray streaks in his brown hair. Shrugging that off, he fidgeted with his royal blue tunic, leaving his chamber to go a short way down the hall. Rapping firmly at his son's door, Reginald let himself into the sitting room without waiting for a reply.

Robert looked up guiltily, and his eyes widened in dismay. He was on his knees before a shelf of books, a small volume in his hands. His squire, Paul, entered from the dressing room, to answer the door, and he stopped in his tracks to see Reginald already in the chamber and bowed hastily, flushing in irritation. Robert put the book back on the shelf and stood quickly, fighting the urge to straighten his tunic. Paul glanced at Robert and raised an eyebrow in silent query. Robert ignored him and faced his Father, schooling his features into their usual neutral expression.

"Yes, Sire? May I be of assistance?" Robert asked.

Reginald had scowled when he saw Robert with a book in his hands; he, the King, had no time for scholarly nonsense. If his son were truly a man, he'd have disguised himself, sneaked into the city, and joined the holiday revelers. Reginald now studied his son's appearance critically. Robert had added perhaps an inch to his height over the winter, but still hadn't filled out, though he was now a couple of inches taller than his father. His hair nearly matched Reginald's, and his eyes were of a slightly darker blue. He was dressed in plain black woolen trousers, with a royal blue wool tunic over his unbleached linen shirt. His black boots were worn. He didn't look like a prince and the heir to the throne at the moment, but Reginald decided that with his destination in mind, it was a good thing.

"Get your cloak, Robert. We are going into the city," Reginald commanded.

"Into the city?" Robert repeated. "At this time of night?"

"Aye. No questions, now. I have a surprise for you. We are celebrating the holiday."

Reginald's words made Robert reluctant to accompany his father. He suspected the surprise was not going to be to his liking, but he obediently collected his oldest black wool cloak, fastening it with a nondescript silver brooch. Paul offered to help him, but Robert declined his aid, and, with another glance at his father, told his squire not to wait up. Paul bit back an argument, instead wishing his young lord well. Robert sensed the change and fleetingly smiled at Paul. He had more things on his mind than whatever entertainment his father had planned. He needed to talk to his sister Allyson, and soon.

Reginald led his son through the castle, leaving via a postern gate rather than the main one. They rode along the cobbled road leading into the city proper. Their progress was slowed by crowds of people traveling to and from the bonfire outside the city. Reginald made small talk about his battle plans for the spring and summer, but Robert spoke little. He barely noticed the sounds of music and voices, distracted by his own swirling thoughts. He was not relieved when his father turned off the city's main street into a dark alleyway and he saw the red lanterns hanging above several doorways.

"Father, we are not -" he began as Reginald dismounted awkwardly

"No protests, Robert. I am determined to make a man out of you tonight if it kills us both," Reginald stated. He handed his reins to a man who appeared out of nowhere, following them with a copper coin. He moved to Robert's mount. "Get down. *Now.*"

"But, sir…" Robert tried to protest again.

"Quiet!" Reginald roared. Once his son was on the ground, he grasped Robert by one arm. Robert frowned and jerked his arm away. Reginald glowered at his son, pushing him towards a red-painted door, on which he knocked firmly. Laughter could be heard from within, and the door was quickly opened. A busty, half-dressed young woman invited them in, proceeding to drape herself across Reginald's chest.

"Oh, welcome, Sire! A pleasure, as always," a sultry, deep throated voice sang.

"And who is your young friend, Majesty?" another young woman asked, dressed - or undressed - like the one who had opened the door.

Then the establishment's proprietress, Lenore Fitzallen, came into the common room. Upon seeing her royal guests, she hurriedly poured wine into two goblets, handing one to Reginald, but hesitating before Robert.

The young prince was blushing to his hairline. He was still a virgin, but it wasn't from lack of opportunity. Most of the younger serving women in the castle would have been happy to oblige his physical needs, indeed, several had already approached him. He had refused all of the offers, partly out of embarrassment but also partly out of the fear of becoming like his father. He was completely uncomfortable now. Most of the young women were giving him appraising glances. Reginald was introducing him to a number of them. He remembered none of their names and barely glanced at their faces.

"Father, I do not…" Robert began again.

"Nonsense. You are here. I am paying for the service, and we are not going back to the castle until you have proven yourself."

Reginald's tone allowed no room for argument, and Robert's heart sank. He swallowed hard, reaching for the wine now being offered to him by Lenore. She studied him, her eyes raking him from head to toe as though he were a horse she was considering purchasing. To his humiliation and the women's amusement, his hand shook.

"Mary will do for His Highness, methinks," Lenore stated, nodding to herself. A young woman stepped up to Robert, taking his free hand and smiling at him. She was wearing a pale blue silk dressing gown over her linen shift, leaving her body somewhat to the imagination. Her long blond hair flowed freely over her shoulders. She had pretty, delicate features and wore little makeup. Robert guessed she was close to his own age, perhaps a year or two younger, but her eyes seemed far older. He tried to avoid shuddering as she led him up the staircase. It took all of his willpower not to look back toward the common room. There was no sympathy to be had there, from his father or, he suspected, any of the women.

Mary led him into an empty room containing only a bed, a small table, and two stools. The bed was draped in pale green silk cloth, and the bedding seemed to be made of silk as well. Robert noted a tapestry on one wall that showed a bacchanalian revel with naked satyrs and scantily clad nymphs. He looked away from it quickly. He thought, in an effort to keep his mind distracted, that the establishment must be doing well, to afford silk bed linens; maybe it was all of the royal patronage. Mary took the wine from him, glanced into the goblet, and saw he hadn't touched the drink

"You are uncomfortable, my lord?" she asked in a voice deeper than Robert expected.

"I...does it show?" Robert walked over to the fireplace, turning his back to the fire and facing Mary. "I really do not want to do this." He gestured toward the bed.

"Have you ever lain with a woman, Highness?" Mary's tone was neutral. Robert didn't know if she were asking out of curiosity or calculating her next move.

"No, but that is not the problem," Robert said, trying to explain himself. "I...I am not like my father. No offense, but I would rather that Rhennsbury did not have such a flourishing -" He floundered, unable to find the word he wanted.

Mary laughed. It sounded genuine. "You would put me out of work, then?" she asked in a saucy tone, her hands on her hips. Her smile was wide.

Robert looked at her, disconcerted. *Did the young woman get pleasure from her profession?* "Do you enjoy this line of work, Mary?" he countered, voicing his thought.

Her smile disappeared in her confusion. Men never called her by name. They rarely talked before using her, for that matter. Most of them never talked afterwards. She looked down for a moment, then met Robert's gaze without flinching. Robert now had to force himself to continue to meet her eyes, surprised by her directness.

"It matters not, my lord. It is simply what I do." There was no bitterness in Mary's tone. Before Robert could reply or ask any more questions, she spoke again. "If all you wish is to talk, I am at your service. But I assure you, it would be more fun to skip the talk and get into the bed. Have you ever slept on silken sheets, Highness?"

Robert hadn't thought he could feel any more uncomfortable, but he was wrong. Feeling no shyness toward his social position, Mary crossed the few feet separating them and put her hands behind his head, pressing her body against him. She stood on her toes and brushed her lips against his. Despite his intentions otherwise, his body reacted to the contact, and he returned the kiss, putting his arms around her awkwardly. With a smile, Mary released him and stepped back, assuming she had caused him to change his mind. She now removed her dressing gown and shift, then climbed onto the bed, her movements slow enough to display her entire body. Her breasts were small, her hips narrow but rounded.

Robert felt his face warm. He couldn't help but admire her for a few heartbeats, but he forced himself to turn away. He took a deep breath, trying to control his adolescent body. He had never seen a naked, pretty young woman before, nor had he ever been kissed. Robert didn't want his first experience to be with a professional and wished he could leave the room, the brothel. He pinched himself in a vain hope that he was having a nightmare and he would wake up at his writing table or, better yet, safe in his bed, alone. He closed his eyes, but when he reopened them, he was still in the brothel. He turned to face the bed again. Mary had lain back, her eyes half-closed; she was smiling at him as she moved her hands around on the sheets in welcome. The movement caused a quiet rustling noise. "Come to me, my lord, and I will help you relax," she murmured, not quite purring.

"I doubt that," Robert muttered. Seeing no other option available, he sat down on one of the stools, not looking at Mary or the bed. He knew it was rude to turn his back on her, but if he kept looking at her, he was afraid of what would happen. He remembered the brief kiss and was terrified of things getting out of control. He heard a deep sigh from the bed before the wooden frame creaked as Mary shifted position.

"A pity," Mary said loudly. "I get a nice, handsome young man, who does not have any horrible disease, and he has no wish to bed me. Sweet Mother, where did I go wrong?"

Robert turned to face her, and quickly dropped his gaze to the floor. She had crossed her arms over her chest. The small breasts now looked more rounded. "I apologize, Mary. 'Tis not you, it is me. I do not wish to take you like this." He was frustrated at his inability to say what he meant. "It is nothing personal. Oh, bloody - I can tell off members of the nobility with eloquence enough, but I am not able to say 'no' to you gently!"

Mary smiled as she rose from the bed, picked up her discarded dressing gown, and donned it. Gentleness was not something with which she was familiar. She cinched the sash about her waist as she walked over to stand behind Robert. He turned to look up at her, but she gently turned his face away from her again. Mary touched his cheek for a moment, then placed her hands on his shoulders and began to massage them. In spite of his desire not to relax his guard, Robert felt the tension passing out of his shoulders and neck.

"I...that feels nice, Mary," he said after several moments. His tone was hesitant.

Mary's smile widened a little, sensing that part of his discomfort was due to shyness around women. "I knew I could find something that would please you, my lord, since you do not seem to find my body attractive," she replied without rancor.

"It is not your body. I...I found your body beautiful to look upon." Robert was not used to having this type of conversation.

"Truly, Highness?"

"Truly." Mary stopped kneading, and Robert once more turned to look at her. "I have never seen a woman like that before, but you were - well, I have nothing to compare it to - but you were stunning." Robert had reddened again, but he forced himself to finish the statement. He knew the young woman, or girl, before him was a prostitute, but he saw no reason to be dishonest. "Mary, how old are you?"

Mary looked away from him, but he reached up and took one of her hands. The gesture surprised them both, but she didn't withdraw. She shrugged. "I do not know, my lord. I was orphaned when I was a small child and taken in by relations. When I was old enough to earn my keep, a couple of winters ago, my aunt left me here."

"Your aunt?" Robert tried not to show the shock he felt, but the words slipped out. He was a prince and therefore not supposed to show his emotions, but this was completely outside the realm of his experience. "I am sorry; it is not my affair." He was still holding her hand.

"Perhaps not, but 'twould seem you would rather talk, than..." she glanced meaningfully toward the bed. "I do not know how to properly entertain a fine prince such as yourself."

"An accident of birth, Mary," Robert said soberly. "I think I know very little of the world if a story such as yours comes as a surprise to me. I am sure it is a common enough tale."

Mary shrugged. "Things do not always work out as we plan."

"What would you rather do, if you had a choice in the matter?" Robert didn't know if he could do anything to help her, but he could try.

Mary laughed for several moments, and then, to Robert's surprise, she started to cry. Robert was totally unprepared for this. He decided that the young woman must be much younger than he was, and he was probably the first person in a long time to offer her a kind word. He offered his sleeve for her to dry her eyes and blow her nose.

"I-I am sorry, my lord. I will be punished for this."

"Why should you be punished? The fault is mine; I insisted we talk. I do not plan to tell your mistress about it." Robert stood and guided Mary to the other stool, then crouched next to her. She met his gaze without flinching.

"I would like to become a midwife and herbalist," she said suddenly. "I have aided my cousins in delivering their babes in the past, and I have done well at it. I have also helped a few of the women here in that capacity, though one woman, a friend, was not fortunate enough to survive a difficult birth." She began crying again.

Robert had gotten more than he'd bargained for. He had little knowledge of the birthing process, except what he'd seen amongst the dogs and cats living in and around the castle. When it came to women, all that his father had told him, and at great length, was about getting women with child. He was hardly following his father's advice at the moment. "Mary," he said quietly. He was trying to think of something he could do to help her and other women like her. He lacked experience, and he had no real authority in matters of policy, despite being a year past legal age.

Mary slowed her crying, and gave him a weak smile. "Thank you for listening, Prince Robert. You are a prince, indeed. I think Myrridia might be a far different place in the future," she said. Then they both stiffened as a woman screamed somewhere else on the floor.

* * *

Reginald had gone upstairs with one of his favorite women, Vivian. He liked to sport with her regularly, and she never complained. She was an older woman of the house, in her early twenties, and voluptuous, with long wavy red hair, bright green eyes, and porcelain skin. She had borne three children, though two had died of illness, but she regained her figure after each pregnancy from regular exercise. She ran errands for the establishment all over the city most afternoons.

Vivian escorted Reginald to his usual room, the most opulent one in the brothel. It was decorated with tapestries depicting Jove's exploits on three of the room's walls. One tapestry showed the god embracing Io on one side and Io transforming into a heifer on the other, an angry Juno looking on from Olympus. Another showed Juno changing Callisto from nymph to bear after the nymph made love to Jove. The final arras was of Europa riding Jove when he wore the guise of a bull on one side and the god making love to her on the other.

The bed draperies were red and black silk. The bed was covered with red and black silk cushions, red silk sheets, and several high-quality sable furs. Vivian's shift was off moments after the door was shut behind them, and she proceeded in removing his boots and trousers.

Reginald did not realize his regular bouts of impotence were directly related to his increased drinking. He blamed it instead on the women he tried to bed. It had never happened with Vivian before, though, so he was at once angry and frustrated when it happened this evening. He shifted some of the blame to Robert, thinking he would not be here tonight, save for his son's lack of masculine ambition. Reginald punched a couple of the cushions to release some of his anger.

Vivian started stroking his thigh, moving in circles, closer to his groin. "'Tis no matter, Reginald," she purred. "I will have you up and going anon. You have never failed to please me yet." Reginald's brain was starting to spin in faster and faster circles, but his organ remained lifeless. He rolled over, away from her.

"Bring me some wine," he ordered. Vivian climbed over him, showing him her thighs and womanhood, scampering off to bring him back a brimming goblet.

"Your favorite vintage, Sire," she said. He drained the goblet in a few swallows, pushing it towards her for a refill. She retrieved the decanter, and poured more for him. After draining the goblet a third time, Reginald wiped his mouth, suggesting they try again. When his member failed to harden this time, Reginald hit Vivian in his frustration, blaming her.

She wiped the drops of blood from the side of her mouth, saying not a word. Getting out of the bed, Vivian gave him more wine, donning her shift. "I will return shortly, Majesty," she said, going out of the room.

Reginald leaned back against the cushions, sipping the wine. After a short while, Vivian having still not returned, he fell asleep, snoring loudly. He hadn't noticed the bitter taste of the poppy juice that had been added to the wine.

Vivian reentered the room when she heard the snoring. A tall man dressed completely in black accompanied her. Her lip curled in the disgust she felt, but couldn't show, toward Reginald.

"He is yours, my lord," she said to her companion.

"So simple, after so much time," he said. He silently removed his sword from its sheath. The sheath was well worn, as were his clothes, as if both sword and man had seen a great deal of action. The sword was unremarkable, with a plain iron hilt, but it had been recently sharpened. The man's first cut was a test, near Reginald's groin, to wake the king. Reginald stirred, opening his eyes, but he had little time to take in what was happening to him. He did not get the chance to cry out as the man stabbed him in the chest. His lung collapsed and his chest cavity began to fill with blood, causing him to slowly drown, unable to get the air his body required. Vivian and the man were silent, watching his unsuccessful struggle to rise. A small amount of blood leaked out of Reginald's mouth.

When Reginald's eyes finally glazed over, Vivian went to the window, to check the alley below. She turned to face her companion. "Prince Robert is here as well," she noted.

The man glanced at her and had to mask his surprise. "I have no quarrel with the prince," he stated. He gestured toward the window. "Will I fit?"

"You would not be the first man who needed to make a quick exit," Vivian replied tartly.

"Aye, but maybe the first without an angry woman behind him." He smiled fleetingly, kissing Vivian on the mouth, hard, adding, "My thanks, Vivian. A great evil has been avenged this night."

Vivian waited several minutes before silently returning to the corridor, checking to make sure it was empty. She then rapped quietly on the door and reentered the chamber. She barely glanced at Reginald's body on the bed and screamed, flinging the door open again and falling into the arms of the first prostitute drawn by the noise. As she began weeping hysterically, the doors of all of the occupied rooms opened, with women and men in varying states of undress wondering what all the commotion was about. Lenore was climbing the stairs while Robert and Mary had joined Vivian, who was leaning heavily on another woman.

Robert looked into the open bedroom and almost fainted at the sight of his father. He clutched the doorjamb for support. Lenore came up behind him and entered the room. She called for Vivian.

Swallowing bile, Robert entered the room and approached the bed, unsure he would be able to touch his father's body. He averted his gaze briefly, but then with shaking hands, he covered the body with one of the furs that had been flung aside before Vivian and Reginald had gotten into the bed. He forced himself to check his father's neck for a pulse, and finding none he dropped to his knees. His emotions were in turmoil...shock, anger, humiliation. Summoning his reserves of strength after several heartbeats, he rose to his feet, turning to face the gaping onlookers.

Having stopped just within the doorway, Lenore was unable to meet his gaze. "I...I am sorry, Your Highness, I have no idea what transpired here."

Vivian came in, still supported by the other woman. She looked at the bed, blanched, and began weeping again. "I-I do not know - h-he was fine when I left the room. I-I was only gone for a moment - he had asked for more wine." Her voice faltered. She curtseyed to Lenore and Robert, and then crumbled to the floor. "Please, please forgive me. H-he was alive when I left." She was playing her part as instructed, having no idea what Robert would do.

Robert had no idea what to do. He was aghast - it had not even dawned on him yet that he was now king. He was a frightened teen, humiliated at the situation his father had put him in by bringing him to an alien environment, surrounded by strangers, several of whom were now gawking at the sight on the bed. Robert turned around to face the bed again, crossed himself, and walked over to Lenore. "Let us leave this room...give him some privacy," he whispered. "I...Something will have to be done, but can we discuss it - downstairs?"

"Aye, my lord." Lenore's tone had turned respectful toward him. "The gossips will be spreading this all over the city by morning as it is." She called for a strapping male worker, employed to discourage men of the merchant class who got out of hand with her women, and instructed him to stand guard outside the room. "Let no one enter without me or the prince," she ordered.

He nodded, folding his arms across his chest, glaring at the people in the corridor. Most of them returned to their rooms to dress, escape, and spread the tale.

Lenore led Robert to her study on the ground floor. It was a sparsely furnished room, containing two chairs and a writing table. There were several parchments on a shelf on one wall, and a small window on another, facing a garden. Lenore pointed at a chair behind the table for Robert. He sat down, his knees giving out. He put his arms down on the tabletop, then lowered his head. Lenore let the silence build. Then she sat down.

Robert used the quiet to get his emotions under control. "I am at a loss," he admitted after several moments. "I did not want to come here this evening, and now...and now..." He was unable to continue. He continuously saw the image of his father's naked, bloody body sprawled on the bed. Reginald's death did not appear to have been an easy one, and Robert, even though he did not have a good relationship with his father, was still overwhelmed by it all. He forced himself to remember his position as a prince and regain his composure again. But he faltered at the thought - he wasn't a prince any more, he was the king. "Good God," he said, as the situation fully dawned on him.

He turned to Lenore and was able to meet her gaze evenly. She sensed the change in him as well. "What does Your Majesty will?" she asked.

"Send for several castle guards to move my...his body, and summon Bishop Edward Fitzroy at once. I believe he is in the city." If Robert were honest with himself, Edward was the last man he wanted to see right now, but if Reginald's body was going to tell them anything about his last moments, Edward was the person most qualified to uncover the information.

"It will be done as you command, Sire," Lenore said, standing and dropping Robert a deep curtsey. "I will send him to you as soon as he arrives. In the meantime, you will not be disturbed." She left the room.

"Thank you," Robert whispered, feeling like anything but a king.

Chapter Two

Edward Fitzroy, Bishop of Belgravia, was not pleased at being rousted from a sound sleep in the small hours of the night. He was in Rhennsbury instead of Belgravia because of his superior's poor health. Myrridia's archbishop, Francis McHenry, had a severe attack of bronchitis over the winter and was only recently starting to recover his health. Edward suspected his superior would not survive many more Myrridian winters. Edward's first thought now when his assistant, Father Ambrose Spenser, woke him, was that something had happened to the archbishop. He was relieved when Ambrose replied to his question in the negative.

"The summons is from Prince Robert Claybourne, Excellency, by way of a Mistress Lenore Fitzallen, of an establishment of dubious reputation. There is someone waiting to escort you," Ambrose concluded.

"Who? What? Speak up, man!" Edward was now fully awake, his momentary relief rapidly disappearing.

"The p-prince requires your presence at a local br-brothel," Ambrose replied while crossing himself. "He sends no explanation with the summons."

Edward stared at his assistant openmouthed for several heartbeats before recovering his aplomb and frowning. "Well, do not just stand there, help me dress. I think I will wear just the cassock and a cloak. There is no sense in announcing my identity," Edward stated, as much to himself as to his assistant.

With Ambrose's help, Edward dressed quickly and set off through the still-bustling city streets with his escort, a well-muscled man. On normal nights, the city had a curfew after midnight, but many of the city's lower elements disregarded the order, knowing it was seldom enforced. To Edward, it seemed as though everyone ignored it tonight.

Edward walked quickly and purposefully, cloaking himself in an aura of Magic to intimidate any potential pickpockets or cutthroats. His companion appeared well able to defend them in a fight, but Edward was taking no chances. When they arrived at the brothel, Edward crossed himself before stepping over the threshold. Reginald, as Edward's half-brother, had often asked him to visit such places when they were younger men, but Edward had always refused. He was unhappy to be visiting such a place now, and dark thoughts centered on why Robert had summoned him here.

At his entrance, several of the half-dressed women in the common room fled up the stairs. An older woman approached Edward. She was dressed, though not decently. Her dress was cut low across the bosom, showing ample cleavage. She had a narrow waist that only accentuated her wide, rounded hips. Her makeup was understated. She curtseyed deeply to Edward, kissing his ring and ignoring his look of distaste.

"This way, Excellency," she said. She led him down a short hallway to a small study, opening the door and motioning him inside. "Bishop Edward Fitzroy, Your Majesty," she said from the doorway before closing the door behind Edward.

Edward froze just inside the chamber. That honorific belonged to Reginald, not Robert. The prince had his back to the door, and Edward thought his nephew's shoulders looked tense. Robert turned around as Lenore finished her announcement. His lips were set in a straight line, and his eyes flashed with strong emotion.

"What has happened, Robert? What are you doing in such a place as this? Why did she just call you -?" Edward demanded. He didn't try to hide his disgust at their surroundings or his confusion and impatience.

Robert turned back to the window, making it impossible for Edward to note any change in expression on his face. "It was Father's idea to come here, not mine." Edward noticed Robert's dispassionate tone. He debated reaching outward with his mind, to read the emotional currents coming from his nephew. "He wanted to make a man out of me tonight, though I'm sure he intended for it to turn out differently." He paused for several moments for effect, and Edward's impatience intensified. Robert turned to face him, and the anger was clear in his features, "Father is dead. Someone murdered him." Irritation had crept into his voice by the time he finished speaking. "We have to straighten out this mess."

Edward paled and swayed on his feet. "Reginald is dead?" he repeated. He'd expected to hear any news but this, despite the brothel proprietress's words to Robert. "How? Who?"

"If I knew that, I would not have needed to send for you, would I?" Robert retorted. He took a deep breath and willed himself to regain some semblance of calm. "I could have arrested the guilty party and had him or her hanged at dawn, or beheaded, or whatever." His calm dissipated as quickly as it came. "Can you think of a more humiliating way for a king to die than in a whorehouse, stabbed to death?" He strode to the chair behind the table and flung himself into it.

Edward focused on the small piece of information. "Stabbed?"

Robert closed his eyes as his hands clenched reflexively. He vainly tried to put the memory of his father's body aside. "Aye, in his chest. It was a mortal blow. He may have had other injuries, but I hardly noticed." He opened his eyes and stared at Edward. "Can you...learn anything from him...from his body?"

Edward took a steadying breath, then met his nephew's gaze evenly. "I can try. Take me to him."

Robert stood and led Edward out of the study. Edward was struck with his nephew's ability to ignore the looks directed at them from the women who had gathered again in the common room. There were looks of scorn from some and pity from others. One blond young woman looked sad.

Robert led Edward up the stairs, passing by several rooms before stopping in front of a man standing guard outside one of them. The man had not changed his position, and he met Robert's eyes briefly before stepping aside.

"Thank you," Robert said to him. The man looked surprised for a moment, and then bowed his head to the prince. Robert paused as he put his hand on the knob and took a deep breath before opening the door. "'Tis bad," he warned Edward. He eased the door open and stepped into the chamber, Edward on his heels. The candles in the room were still burning, but the fire had nearly gone out. The room was dim, but not dim enough to hide the body on the bed.

Edward summoned a sphere of light as he approached the bed. Robert remained near the door, his face pale but his expression resolute. Robert looked about the room as he tried to take in more details, though he avoided looking at the bed. Edward stopped short of the bed and stared at Reginald's face for a moment. His half-brother had not died easily.

Edward removed the fur covering the body. The body was sprawled across the bed. There was a short cut in Reginald's groin area, which had bled some, and there was a trickle of blood from one side of his mouth. His chest was covered in blood, and the wound looked deep.

Edward perched on the bed and went into trance. He touched the chest wound with his left hand, easing out a breath and closing his eyes. The wound was as deep as it appeared. Edward opened his eyes and noticed the blood stain on the silk sheets that had spread from the underside of the body. The sword thrust had passed through Reginald's torso.

Grateful that he hadn't eaten for several hours, Edward moved his hands to Reginald's temples and attempted to retrieve memories of the king's last moments. Edward gained a sense of drugged consciousness, then a feeling of pain from the groin. He reached back a little further, experiencing Reginald's frustration from his impotence and subsequent drinking. Edward could sense the drug in the wine, taste the bitterness of it as if he were drinking it himself. He steeled himself to experience the wounds as they occurred, gasping as his own chest felt Reginald's stabbing. He quickly withdrew his contact and sat back, trying to steady his nerves.

Robert had silently joined him and stared down at his father. He touched Edward lightly on the shoulder; he suspected that what Edward had just experienced had to be horrible, worse than the mere sight of the body. Edward jumped, startled, and grasped Robert's hand in an uncharacteristic show of weakness for a moment, confirming Robert's suspicions. Edward took a deep breath, in preparation to perform the Last Rites for his slain half-brother. Robert kept quiet during the ritual, crossing himself and murmuring "Amen," when Edward had finished. Edward stood up on shaky legs. Leading Robert out of the room, he leaned against the wall before speaking. "Aye, 'twas not an easy death, and I discovered little of his killer. Reginald was drugged beforehand, with the wine."

Robert's eyes flashed. "Then the woman who was with Father must have been involved," he noted. "She said, afterwards, that she had gone for more wine. She said that Father had -" Robert stopped speaking suddenly as the cold-bloodedness of the deed hit him fully. He took a step back. Recovering slightly, he asked, "But why, Edward? And who?"

Edward had difficulty following all of Robert's words. "I do not know. Reginald did see a man, and a woman, but the only impression I could glean between the wine, the drug and his pain was that the man was clad in dark clothing. He had a sword, but beyond that I could 'see' nothing. I think it may be difficult to find Reginald's killer. As for why, your father had many enemies. We will make inquiries, but we should keep some details of his death private."

"'Tis too late for that, Edward," Robert observed. He felt his body stiffen with memory. "These women will talk. There were men here earlier, too, and some of them stared into the room after Vivian, the woman with him, screamed. This tale will spread throughout the city, and likely get worse with each telling." His control broke. "By the saints, this is humiliating!"

Robert motioned impatiently toward the stairs as he fought to rein in his emotions again, and the two of them descended. Men-at-arms from the castle had arrived, and their sergeant, Ian, caught Robert's eye. Robert spoke with him quietly, and the sergeant's eyes widened. He motioned to his men and headed up the stairs, with Lenore ahead of them. Robert led Edward back to the study. Edward sat while Robert paced. "They will get Father to the castle," Robert said.

There were several moments of silence. "Why would a prostitute want to kill Father?" Robert asked suddenly. "Did he abuse her? I never understood him." He sucked in a breath. "I guess now I never will." He stopped pacing and stared at Edward. "You are his brother. What was he thinking? How did this other man even know Father would be here? I did not know we would be here until we arrived. Bloody -!" Robert turned away and faced the window, trying to control his temper.

"Calm down, Robert," Edward ordered. Robert turned back to him, an angry retort on his lips. Edward held up a hand. "The timing must have been fortuitous. The whore went to her partner and told him of Reginald's presence. She brought drugged wine, and this man came to the room and murdered Reginald."

"Edward, this is embarrassing. Forgive me, but how could Father let this happen to him, to me? And what about Myrridia's reputation?" Robert's tone was less vehement now, but his anger and humiliation were still reflected in his eyes.

20

Edward sensed Robert's turmoil, so he chose his next words with care, "Reginald came here often enough, or to other similar establishments. None will fault you for being upset about his death in such a place."

"I am not upset!" Robert clapped a hand over his mouth - he'd nearly shouted the words. He stared up at the ceiling for several moments, then shook his head and lowered his hand. "I am way beyond upset - I am angry, and, and mortified." Robert gulped for air. "I am trying to salvage Father's dignity here, but it may be impossible." He changed the subject. "I think it is time we spoke with Vivian."

At Edward's nod, Robert crossed the room and opened the door. Lenore was standing several paces up the hall and turned to face him. "Pl - Bring Vivian here," Robert ordered, catching himself. "At once."

"Aye, Majesty." Lenore curtseyed and fetched Vivian herself. Vivian entered the study several moments later, her expression fearful. Her fear deepened when she recognized Edward.

"M-my lords?" She curtseyed deeply.

"Rise, woman," Edward said impatiently. "We can do this easily or with difficulty; it makes no difference to me. You were the last person to see the king alive. I am certain you were privy to his death. The wine that you gave him was tainted."

Vivian cowered. She, like many in Myrridia, was terrified of Edward Fitzroy. No longer acting, she threw herself at his feet and pleaded. "'Twas no fault of mine, Excellency. Th-the man - i-it was his idea - h-he forced me…"

Robert watched her grovel.

Edward's eyes narrowed. "Then you have nothing to fear if I probe your memories," he said quietly.

Still on her knees, Vivian backed away from Edward, "No, Excellency, please. I-I know nothing of this man. I-it is my job to do as men will. H-he promised me a horrible death if I refused to help him." She turned to Robert. "Please, Your Highness. M-mercy," she whispered.

"You showed none," Edward snapped. Robert was about to agree with him, then he stepped between Edward and Vivian. He didn't feel right in his conscience about letting Edward learn what he could, regardless of the cost to her.

"Wait a moment, Edward." Edward's eyebrows shot up in stunned surprise. Ignoring him, Robert turned to Vivian. "You can tell us all you know about my father's, your king's, death, and your own death will be easier. Know one thing, Vivian. I can tell if you are lying. You lied just now. You were a willing participant."

Vivian stared at Robert. "If I will not talk, what will happen to me?" She raised her chin in defiance.

"I shall let the bishop do as he wishes," Robert replied.

Vivian paled and her shoulders sagged in defeat. She looked from one to the other. Edward glared at her, though part of his anger was also directed at his nephew. How dare Robert show mercy to this woman? Vivian chose quickly. She met Robert's gaze briefly before staring at the floor.

"I do not know his name, that is the truth. He has come here before, and asks for me by name. He always dresses in black. He treats me better than most of the men and pays well. I have no idea if he is highborn or low." Vivian was wringing her hands as she spoke.

"One night a few weeks ago, he asked me why I had bruises on my face and neck. I-I answered him honestly, telling him that the king could be rough with me. I was not complaining; I have a job to do and I do it without question. I was only replying to him matter-of-factly. This other man listened, and his eyes hardened. I flinched, thinking he would strike me for speaking critically of another man, my sovereign." Vivian didn't notice Robert's hands clench, and he forced himself to keep his eyes on her face.

"Instead, this man kissed me tenderly and told me he would take care of my troubles. He did not tell me what he meant, and I did not ask. He gave me the poppy juice a few days ago and asked me to guard it until he had opportunity to use it. He had been with me earlier this evening, but he must have seen the king's man come to make arrangements. He slipped back inside and told me he would finish things tonight. I gave the king the drugged wine when he requested a drink, and I let the man into the chamber while the corridor was empty. He escaped through the chamber's window." Vivian continued to stare at the floor after she'd finished her recitation.

"You freely admit your guilt?" Robert asked.

"Yes, Sire." She looked up finally and locked gazes with him. "I also admit I bore no love for Reginald Claybourne. I am not sorry that he is dead!" she concluded, defiant again for a moment.

Edward's expression said, *I told you so.* "You speak treason, woman!" he exclaimed aloud.

"Aye, honest treason as opposed to hypocrisy," Robert agreed, ignoring Edward's expression. Like Edward, he was angered by her words about his father, but his anger was directed *at* his father. Reginald's murder could be revenge for a personal affront he had committed against a noblewoman, one of Rhennsbury's merchants' wives or daughters, or even a commoner's. Robert knew it wasn't unheard of - his father had always behaved boorishly with women, beginning with his own wife.

Edward turned on him. "Do you not care that your father has been brutally murdered and that this whore has no remorse? She helped someone slay Myrridia's king!" Edward had to make a conscious effort to keep from shouting.

Robert rubbed his eyes, fatigue and reaction overtaking him. "I care very much," he replied quietly. "I can also understand being provoked beyond endurance." *Father provoked me and I provoked him often enough,* he thought. "She will be punished." He turned to Vivian. "Can you describe this man?"

"He is taller than average, as tall as the bishop," she said, pointing toward Edward. "His hair is black and unruly, his eyes blue, and he keeps his mustache and beard trimmed. He is strong and has a deep voice. I-I suppose he is around my age, in his twenties. Like I said earlier, he was gentler than most of the men I serve. He said tonight that he was working with others, and his plans suffered at Christmas. I have no idea what he meant."

Vivian stopped speaking and bowed her head, awaiting Robert's judgment.

Robert was jolted into silence. Christmas? Someone had tried to kill *him* at Christmas, not his father. He felt a momentary weakness in his knees. He and Christian Lattimore, the Duke of Saelym, had each been targets at that time, though Chris McCabe had told him that he'd thought the plan had been to discredit Christian. The duke would not have gone out of his way to save Robert from injury. Robert now wondered if his father's killer was a mutual enemy of Reginald's and Christian's. He roused from his reverie as Edward spoke.

"She has to die," the bishop said flatly. "As does this man when we discover his identity."

"I agree. The law is the law." Robert forced his thoughts to the matter at hand. Speculation about his father's murderer could wait. "However, as king, I have the right to temper justice with mercy."

"You are not serious!" Edward snapped.

Robert looked at him sharply, as though to say, *Remember your place.* Edward had opened his mouth to continue, but it now snapped shut. His blue eyes continued to blaze as Robert gave his attention to Vivian.

"Vivian, you have until dawn to leave the city and a fortnight to leave Myrridia forever. Should you return, you will immediately be arrested and hanged. Unless you prefer to hang at first light?"

Vivian glanced at Edward, who stared at her with open loathing. "Your Highness, I go to my death without fear. I would gladly leave Myrridia, but as a whore, my choices are limited." Edward's countenance didn't alter. "I thank you for the offer. A lesser man would not have given me the option." She rose shakily, but managed a deep, graceful curtsey. Edward knew he'd just been insulted, and his expression darkened.

Robert called Lenore back into the room and explained to her that Vivian had played a role in the death of the king. Lenore blanched as Robert stated Vivian's punishment. "She will return with us to the castle, and the sentence will be carried out in the morning," Robert concluded.

"My lord, you do not question our loyalty -" she began, her tone now all business. She had been receiving royal largesse for several years and feared the effect rumors of treason would have on her establishment.

Robert fought down his disgust and glanced at Edward. The bishop's expression had still not softened. Robert ignored her statement. "I think it is time to return to the castle. The guards will have already left with Father." Robert led Vivian out of the office. Ian had waited in the common room for him, surrounded by a number of women, and now stood quickly at Robert's entrance.

"Highness, the other men have taken the king to the castle. I took the liberty of instructing them to take him to his apartment," he said after bowing.

"Thank you, sergeant." Robert handed Vivian over to him. "We are escorting this woman to the castle as well. She will need to be left under guard until dawn, when she is to be hanged for treason." Ian's eyebrows rose, but he made no comment. He tightened his grip on Vivian's arm.

"As you will, Sire," he said.

Robert turned to Lenore. "'Tis no offense to you, mistress, but I hope we never meet again," he said in parting. "I hope one day to make places like this unnecessary in Rhennsbury, but I also want to make sure these women are not left on the street to beg and starve." He then exited the establishment, his carriage straight. Robert led Ian and Vivian to the tethered mounts he and Reginald had arrived with. Edward was on their heels. Robert held Vivian while Ian mounted Reginald's horse, then handed her up to the sergeant. She'd not spoken since leaving the study. Robert swung into his saddle.

"Edward, go back to your residence. There is no need for you to come to the castle now. Try to get some sleep if you are able."

Edward nodded, watching as his nephew set spurs to his horse and began cantering toward the castle. He decided that Robert's assertiveness over the past couple of hours was alarming, and he felt thwarted of an opportunity to learn more about the man who'd murdered Reginald.

Robert maintained his calm until they arrived at the castle. He noticed that the eastern sky was turning light. *Was it nearly dawn already?* he wondered. He felt exhaustion steal over him at the thought.

Ian dismounted, assisting Vivian in alighting. "My lord, she should be given opportunity to make confession. Shall I take her to the chapel where the chaplain can take care of her spiritual needs?"

"Aye, sergeant. Thank you." Robert debated between going to his sister's apartment or his father's. He decided that if Allyson were asleep, there was no need to wake her. He climbed wearily to the royal chambers. As he passed his sister's quarters, he left word with her maid to inform him when Allyson wakened.

Robert let himself into his father's chambers and walked through the sitting room to the bedchamber, noting the room's untidiness. A goblet of wine and the remains of Reginald's supper were on a tray set on the floor near the door. Reginald had been laid out on his bed, his body cleaned up and covered with one of the sleeping furs. Reginald's squire, Adam, was in the dressing room collecting the king's state robes. He stepped into the bedroom and was startled at Robert's presence. "Your Highness, I did not realize you were here," he said.

Robert shook his head. "Nay, I just arrived. It has been an appalling night." He turned toward the room's entrance as Ian stepped into the chamber.

"My lord, the woman is giving confession now. I left two castle guards to keep an eye on her until it is time for her execution."

Robert thanked him and sat heavily in one of the room's chairs. He closed his eyes in fatigue as Adam, with the aid of two remaining men-at-arms, dressed Reginald in his finest clothes of royal blue and gold velvet. Robert opened his eyes after several moments and was about to go to the bedside to utter a prayer when

Ian came to his chair. The sergeant knelt at his elbow and handed Reginald's signet ring to Robert. Robert stared at the sapphire stone and gold griffin etched into the gem, incredulous at first, eyes wide open.

Ian said quietly, "The King is dead, long live the King."

His hands shaking, Robert solemnly put the ring on his own finger. The ring was still loose on his middle finger. He looked at it for a few moments, and then held the hand out to Ian hesitantly. With no hesitation on his part, Ian took the hand and swore an informal fealty to Robert, promising to serve the son as he had served the father.

A man-at-arms came over and asked Ian if they should close Reginald's eyes. Robert sat back, shocked, and Ian glared at the man before hissing, "Aye, fool." He turned back to Robert. "I am sorry, my lord. You need not remain here if you would prefer to be elsewhere. Your own chamber? Curse me for an idiot as well." He motioned Adam over. "Go fetch His Highness's squire. Now."

Paul arrived on Adam's heels, having hastily donned his trousers and boots after being awakened. He took in Robert's hollow-eyed appearance, and glanced at Reginald's body lying in state on the bed. Adam had told him what had happened, but he still wasn't prepared for the reality of it. He was a few years older than Robert and had served him for about three years, but he respected the prince and genuinely liked him. He had no idea what Robert was going through at the moment, but he'd provide whatever support the younger man needed. Robert stood and let Paul lead him out of the apartment.

As Paul began to escort him to his chambers, Robert stopped him. "Nay, Paul, I need to speak to Allyson as soon as she wakens. I can wait in her sitting room. If anyone should need me, you can find me there." As he finished speaking, a page ran up to them.

"'Tis dawn, Highness. The guards are requesting your presence in the entry yard."

Robert sagged against Paul, who placed an unobtrusive arm around him to support him. "God, will this night never end?" he asked after a moment, pulling away. "I must watch justice being meted out." Paul agreed and they descended through the castle to emerge from the main entrance and walked to the entry yard.

A temporary wooden gallows had been set up in the yard since Robert's return to the castle, and Vivian was being led to it as he and Paul entered the area. Father Timothy, the castle chaplain, walked a few steps behind her.

Vivian stared at the noose for several heartbeats, her eyes wide and frightened. Then she squared her shoulders and climbed the dozen steps. Her wrists were bound behind her back and the noose placed around her neck. Her gaze met Robert's briefly, then moving off toward the castle's gate. Father Timothy administered the Last Rites to her, retreating slowly down the steps. At a gesture from Robert, the trapdoor beneath Vivian opened, and she fell, the noose tightening efficiently.

Robert forced himself to watch the sentence being carried out, but his gaze focused on the distance once Vivian's body hung lifelessly. Paul squeezed his shoulder surreptitiously, and after a few moments, Robert focused again on his immediate surroundings.

"'Tis not over," he said quietly to his squire before returning to the castle and climbing to his sister's chambers.

Her maid, Diana, was in the sitting room when Robert and Paul arrived. "Your Highness, my lady Allyson is awake," the maid said after curtseying.

"Please tell her that I am here, and the matter is urgent," Robert requested.

Diana entered the bedchamber, and Allyson came into the sitting room after a few moments. She was a few weeks shy of her nineteenth birthday. Her coloring favored her mother's - thick auburn hair and green eyes. Her hair was still braided for sleep, but she had donned a dark green dress over her unbleached linen shift. She took in her brother's appearance - the bruised look around his eyes, the skin gray with fatigue. His clothes looked like he'd not changed them since yesterday, and he looked several years older.   Allyson's expression changed from curiosity to concern. She motioned him to a chair.

"What has happened?" she asked.   Before replying, Robert helped her into the chair, and sagged onto a stool Paul supplied. She gave her brother her full attention.

He looked away from her. "I - God, there is no way to say it that is not awful," Robert began.

"Then be blunt."   Allyson willed herself to remain calm no matter what Robert had to tell her.

"Father took me to a brothel last night," Robert began.

"What!"   Allyson bit her lip to prevent a profanity. So much for her attempt at calm.

"Wait, 'tis worse. He - he was murdered there last night. He is laid out in his quarters -" Robert buried his face in his hands, unable to keep his tumultuous emotions in check any longer. When he looked up again, he was dry-eyed. "My apologies, sister," he said. "I-it has been a dreadful night."

"Mother of God," Allyson breathed, crossing herself. She stood and went over to her brother, putting her arms around him. He leaned into her, grateful to be able to lean on someone, even for just a little while. "Is there more?"

"Yes. The prostitute he was with assisted in his death, and she - I ordered that she be hanged at dawn this morning. I just - I cannot think straight. I am still angry, humiliated, exhausted." He paused. "Do you want to see him?"

No, was her immediate thought, but it came out as, "Of course."

Robert led the way to Reginald's apartment. Allyson knelt at the bedside and said a quick prayer for his soul. She waited several moments before rising, requesting Robert accompany her to the castle chapel. Bewildered, he followed. Allyson directed him to a pew. "We will not be disturbed here. I want you to share everything from last night, so I can pass it along to Lady Helen and Duke Chris in a little while." She indicated the Magical workroom adjacent to the chapel, smiling slightly in apology. "I realize you are past exhaustion, but we really should not wait."

"Not quite everything," Robert countered, remembering his own embarrassing scene with Mary. "We can start with when Vivian screamed."

Allyson raised an eyebrow, but agreed. She stood behind her brother and placed her fingers lightly on Robert's temples. "Close your eyes and breathe slowly." The two of them had performed similar actions over the past few years as Allyson's Magical abilities began to manifest. Robert's talents were more limited, accounting for his ability to accurately read people's intentions. He'd felt an immediate closeness with Chris, a reaction all the more ironic because of his poor relationship with Christian Lattimore, to whom Chris was eerily identical physically. It had certainly driven home to him the lesson of not judging people by their appearances.

He now complied with Allyson's directions, relaxing his mind a little. Robert focused on hearing Vivian's scream, and then he let memories play out as the events had unfolded. He felt his sister tense several times. She finally broke the contact with a sigh.

He stood and turned to face her. "Sit," he ordered. Allyson sat. After a few moments, she met his gaze.

"You did well. I do not know how you managed it, but congratulations on standing up to Edward in such a situation. Most people would have caved in to him. That was very good judgment on your part."

"Vivian was guilty, but she was also used," Robert noted.

"I agree. You had no choice, though, but to have her executed. 'Twas commendable to offer her the opportunity to flee. Many men in your position would not have acted thus." Allyson stood, testing to see if her legs would support her. They did. "I am going to try to contact Helen now. She and Chris need to hear about this as soon as possible, since Father's summons just went out."

Robert followed her into the workroom. Allyson removed the ivory linen cloth covering the castle's communication mirror, showing her reflection. She asked Robert to stand with her, while she began to visualize Helen and the workroom in Saelym. The mirror's image changed to a swirling fog, which cleared quickly to show Saelym's workroom.

"Hello? Is anyone there?" Allyson called.

A surprised Father Michael Pembroke appeared in the mirror. "Your Highnesses," he said as he bowed. "I will go fetch Helen. A moment." He fled the room

Allyson and Robert exchanged startled looks. What was happening in Saelym? A short while later Helen and Chris entered the workroom, both looking tired and strained, but curious. Michael was right behind them. Helen and Chris's eyes widened at Robert's appearance. "What has happened, my dears?" Helen asked.

"'Tis horrible news, Lady Helen. You both may want to sit down," Allyson said.

Chris got a chair for Helen. He helped her sit, and then stood behind her. Touching her on one shoulder, he felt her tense before she put her hand on his.

Allyson closed her eyes for a moment, trying to step back from the events she was to relate. She had learned of things secondhand, but they still affected her personally. Opening her eyes, she told Chris and Helen what had happened to Reginald in the brothel and its aftermath, sparing little detail. Helen's hand went to her mouth, stifling a scream early in the telling. Chris's eyes registered shock and disbelief as the story unraveled. At one point Chris found himself tightening his grip on Helen's shoulder but stopped before he hurt her. His other hand clenched into a fist. Michael crossed himself and began to murmur a prayer.

"We shall leave for Rhennsbury at once. We will be there as soon as possible," Helen promised. "We will get to the bottom of the matter." Chris murmured agreement.

Robert and Allyson spoke in unison. "Thank you." Allyson broke the contact then turned to face Robert. "So what was all that about, I wonder?" They left the workroom and returned to the chapel. Robert shook his head. "I have no idea." Answers would have to wait until Helen and Chris got to Rhennsbury.

31

Chapter Three

The previous evening had been far from calm in the Duchy of Saelym as well. It had begun quietly enough, with Helen Lattimore and Chris McCabe enjoying a private supper in Chris's chambers. They'd put Helen's children, Reginald and Eleanor, to bed before the meal. The children had been excited for most of the day, watching from the castle's windows some of the revelries taking place in and out of the town for the spring holiday. Women had danced around a Maypole set up in the meadow between castle and town.

Late in the afternoon, Eleanor had shared with her parents a piece of string that her kitten Grimalkin had brought her for approval of his hunting skills. Helen told her to keep the string in a special place, but requested that her daughter not do the same when the cat brought her pieces of once-living creatures. Eleanor made a face and told her mother with five-year-old dignity that she wasn't touching anything dead, that she would come to her father to take care of that. Chris smiled and hugged the girl, assuring her that he would be glad to handle those sorts of "gifts." Eleanor gave him a shy kiss. Chris was still amazed that Eleanor had taken to him so quickly. Helen had told him some months before that if he didn't turn into Christian, he and Eleanor would be friends forever.

A page knocked and hurried into the room, not waiting for Chris or Helen to reply. He bowed. "Father Michael says to come to the chapel workroom immediately, your Graces!" he exclaimed.

Helen and Chris exchanged confused glances before hurrying to the workroom. The abrupt summons wasn't like Michael, but both knew the priest was contacting a Magical practitioner from Chris's native world. Chris stopped short when he saw the window glowing in the middle of the room, but recovered quickly.

Helen looked at her cousin, noting the strain on his face. He handed her a note and pointed to the window. Helen read the note quickly and handed it to Chris. "Naomi Holmes is Elijah's relation, yes?" she asked.

"She is his younger sister," Chris confirmed.

"Who is Nicole Carpenter?"

Chris paled. "Nicole Carpenter?" he repeated, glancing at the small piece of paper before staring at Helen. "I - She and I were, oh, God, this cannot be happening!" Helen stared back at him, a sick feeling beginning in the pit of her stomach.

"Chris, who is she?" She kept her tone neutral.

Chris looked at the floor, took a deep breath, and looked back at Helen. "We were engaged to be married once, a number of years ago. She got impatient with me, and left me. I thought I was in love with her - it took me a couple of years to get over her leaving me." He paused. "Helen, I honestly have no idea what she wants with me now."

"Helen, you and Chris need to decide what you want to do...soon," Michael said, wiping his sweaty brow with his cassock's sleeve. "Mistress Angelita and I cannot keep this window open much longer." The lines of strain on his forehead intensified as he increased his concentration on the window and the women beyond it.

"I think letting them come is a bad idea -" Chris began.

"As do I." Helen sighed. "Methinks I will regret this ere long, but perhaps 'tis better to find out what they want." Helen turned to face Angelita Martinez, a Boston Magical practitioner, who was on the other side. Helen nodded once.

A few moments later, two young women had joined them in the workroom. One immediately doubled over with nausea; the other stoically remained upright. She was a young, attractive dark-skinned woman, with the same brown eyes and stubborn square chin as her brother, Elijah. She had high, sculpted cheekbones. She was nearly a foot shorter than her brother, but still tall for a woman, about five feet, eight inches. She was several inches taller than Helen. Her expression changed to surprise, then recognition, then curiosity, as her discomfort began to ease.

The other woman was slightly taller than Helen. She had dark hair and brown eyes, pale skin, and a scattering of freckles. She wore eyeglasses. Helen noticed she looked several years younger than herself, with a young, trim body.

Helen forced herself to go over to Nicole and helped her onto a stool. "The nausea will pass soon," she assured her. Nicole murmured her thanks. Chris hadn't moved.

"Nicole, what are you doing here?" he asked finally, keeping his hands open and non-threatening at his side with an effort. He wanted to point an accusing finger at her, or at least have his hands on his hips.

Naomi and Nicole were both startled to hear him speak in a British accent. The last time Naomi had seen him, before he and Elijah had traveled to Myrridia nearly a year ago, he'd spoken with his normal, upstate New York accent. She looked from his face to the woman near Nicole. The woman was dressed in a simple but elegant long green dress, which suited her hazel eyes. Naomi couldn't tell what her hair color was; it was covered in some kind of veil. In her opinion, the woman was holding back her emotions, barely. Uncharacteristically, she decided to remain quiet for a few minutes.

Nicole was recovering her wits. She glanced at Chris for a moment, then around the room. There was a mirror on the wall to her left, and a marble altar a few feet in front of her. As Chris spoke, her gaze flew back to him. This time she took in his medieval garb. She decided it suited him. "You look wonderful, Chris. I came looking for you, to -" She stood and took a step toward him, but he stepped back. Helen looked from Chris to Nicole, then back to Chris, her expression darkening.

Naomi thought, *Uh oh.* She took a step toward Nicole.

"What exactly did you come here for, Mistress Nicole?" Helen asked her.

"I-I-" Nicole's voice faltered as she looked from Helen's angry expression to Chris's perplexed one. "Oh, God," she said.

Helen was now silent. She had never experienced jealousy during her years of marriage to Christian. He had been unfaithful, but she had not loved him, so it had mattered little to her. At this moment she was having difficulty breathing and felt a pain in her heart. Chris reached a tentative hand toward her, but her look of betrayal stopped him. Chris stepped back as though he'd been slapped.

Nicole spoke into the growing silence. "Chris, what's going on?"

Chris raised his eyes to the ceiling for spiritual strength. *Great, I get to hurt two women in one evening*, he thought. "Nicole, this is Duchess Helen Lattimore. She and I were married a few weeks ago."

"What?" Nicole and Naomi said in unison. "Married?" Nicole repeated weakly.

"Yes, married. I love Helen, and she - she loves me, and we wedded." Chris stopped. Helen had closed her eyes, looking pained. "My apologies, Helen, I should have told you," he said to her quietly. "I-I never expected - I hope you can forgive me." Chris was feeling extremely uncomfortable.

Helen's expression didn't waver. "I think we will be using separate apartments for a while," she replied finally. Her voice was strained. Squaring her shoulders, she turned to her two guests.

"Please, ladies, follow me, so that I can see that you are both made comfortable for your - visit." Helen picked up her skirts and walked out of the workroom with quiet dignity, Naomi following her. Helen didn't see the pain in Chris's eyes. Nicole hesitated, looked at Chris, and then followed the other two women.

Chris sagged against the worktable, his eyes burning with tears. He wasn't sure if they were from anger or fear. He looked at Michael, not expecting sympathy from him as Helen's kinsman. Michael's expression was not angry. "How do you feel about that woman?" he asked Chris.

Chris knew his reply was important to his relationship with the priest so he chose his words with care. "I have a few fond memories of our relationship, but I have a lot of painful ones as well. I loved her once, but since I met Helen, I have had thoughts for no other woman."

Michael nodded. "Helen is as unpleasantly surprised as yourself, but I think she will get over it in time. 'Tis unfortunate that she has been hurt by men in the past, for 'tis certain that she is thinking of those hurts. You are going to need a lot of patience."

"Yes, but she is worth it, Michael." Chris spoke in a whisper, but there was no hesitation this time. This was not lost on Michael. The priest had experienced his own disconcerting physical reaction to the arrival of Nicole Carpenter, which he had no idea how to handle.

The next morning, Helen remained seated after Robert and Allyson's images had disappeared from the mirror. She and Chris were both shocked beyond speech. The arrival of their unexpected guests was bad enough without the added stress of this news.

For the first time since her marriage to Chris, Helen had spent the night alone. They had not made love every night, but she had enjoyed sharing the bed with him, especially waking up each morning in his arms. To her disgust, she had cried herself to sleep the night before, feeling cold and alone. She was angry with Chris and herself. Helen hated the part of herself that wanted to go into his arms and forgive him, no questions asked. She needed his strength now, physical and emotional, but she had too much pride to ask for it.

Chris slept little the night before. He was reasonably sure he hadn't done anything wrong, unless not telling Helen everything about his previous life had been a mistake. The last thing he had expected was anyone from his past joining him in Myrridia, and after her breakup with him, Nicole was at the bottom of the list. He'd willingly give his right arm or anything else to ease the hurt and betrayal Helen now felt. In his own day, he'd start by sending her flowers or chocolate, but those methods of apology wouldn't be in vogue for some time yet. He knew Michael was right - Helen needed time to sort out her feelings. He would give her as much as she needed.

He had been deeply hurt when Nicole had broken off their engagement, impatient with him. He knew medical residencies were difficult, and not just for the residents. He had wanted her to pursue her own career with the intention of joining her, wherever she had settled into work, and finding a job in the same city. She had been deaf to his reasons. A week after their breakup, he had tried to call her, but she had left Syracuse without a forwarding address. He had tried her parents, and though her mother was sympathetic, she told Chris that Nicole wanted a clean break. He had moved to Portland, Maine, throwing himself into his work to avoid any close relationships with women for the next few years.

A year ago, he'd answered a curious job advertisement and ended up in Myrridia. Helen had an immediate, physical impact on him, and his emotions soon caught up with his hormones. He barely thought about Nicole since he'd been in Myrridia…couldn't remember what she even looked like.

He now held a hand out to Helen. She accepted the assistance in standing but didn't look at him. He wanted to put his arms around her, tell her he was sorry, but thought better of it. He needed to have a long talk with Nicole, but he wanted an impartial third party present, someone whose word Helen would accept, like Elijah.

Helen left the workroom, and Chris followed her to the study. In spite of the personal strain between them, they had work to do. Helen sat at the desk, deep in thought for a few moments. She finally made eye contact with Chris.

"How do you feel about Reginald and Eleanor coming with us to Rhennsbury?" she asked, her tone all business. At Chris's blank expression, she added, "For the coronation."

"Oh." Chris thought about it. "I suppose it is something they would always remember, but would they be in any danger while we are there?"

"I do not know. Reginald more than Eleanor, perhaps, as the duchy's heir. We need to decide since we will need to leave at first light tomorrow. We should attempt to travel faster and lighter than last time." She picked up a piece of parchment and pretended to scan it. "At least most of your clothes and gear are packed, as you expected to go to Rhennsbury at any time, to advise Reginald on his war plans. You can help with the children's things."

"Of course."

Helen let out a breath. "Unfortunately, the children and our guests will slow our travel." Her gaze turned challenging. "I have no intention of leaving those two women in Saelym with no supervision."

"Oh, I agree, Helen. Though it could lengthen their stay here."

"Or shorten it," Helen countered. "Edward Fitzroy opened that window before - he may be able to do it again." Changing the subject, she asked, "Why did you not tell me you loved another before you came to Saelym?"

Chris blinked. "I-I did not think it was impor -" He stopped speaking as Helen glowered at him. "I no longer love her; it is over between us!" He met her angry expression, his own sad. "I am sorry, Helen. Of course it is important. I should have told you. But honestly, I never expected Nicole of all people to follow me here."

Helen's voice was quiet, but her eyes flashed. "So you fall in and out of love, then?"

Chris wanted to weep with frustration, but kept his voice even. Losing his temper wouldn't help his cause right now. "No, Helen. It took me a long time to get over Nicole. She broke off the engagement. She was impatient, and I wanted to wait." He wanted to ask Helen if that sounded like his behavior with her, but he didn't dare. Her expression hadn't softened.

"Did you share your bed with her?" Helen now asked.

Chris's heart sank. Telling himself again that honesty was best in the long run, he whispered, "Yes." His eyes met Helen's evenly. "We were going to marry one day. Helen, I am truly sorry. I realize I have hurt you, badly, but I am unsure what to do to make it right between us. I should have told you more about myself, my previous life. I hope you can believe me, trust me again, in time."

"Mayhap some of the fault is mine," Helen admitted. "I have been ill-treated by men for most of my life. I know you are not Christian - not at all! - but I -" Helen stopped and shook her head, refusing to give in.

"The fault is not yours, Helen. If men were brighter, more decent, they would be - women." Chris gave her a tentative smile. Helen didn't return the smile, but her expression softened slightly.

"Back to business. If Elijah has not returned by tonight, we will have to leave him a message explaining everything. Summon a page, please."

Chris stepped out of the study and called out. Within moments, a young boy in Saelym livery appeared and bowed. Chris preceded the lad into the study.

"Two errands, please, young man," Helen said. "First, if Matthew is in the castle, tell him his presence is requested as soon as he is able. If he is not here, 'twill have to wait. Second, bring our two guests here. Have you got that?"

"Aye, my lady," the page said, then he scurried out of the study.

Helen had seen to Nicole and Naomi's needs when she led them to their guestroom the night before. She offered to have a light meal sent up and told the two women to make themselves comfortable. She had shown them nothing but courtesy.

After Helen left them, Naomi sank onto a stool and said, "Whew! I think Mama or that Martinez woman might have said something to you. I'm sure Mama must have known that Chris and this duchess were at least fond of each other. Married!" She frowned. "Though I think Chris is going to get the worst of it."

Nicole stared around the room for a few seconds before replying. She was trying to keep her own emotions under control. She'd felt it had been so important to talk to Chris again. She took in the fact that there was minimal furniture in the room, all of it functional. She walked over to the room's single window and stared out at the dark sky. She felt the beginnings of tears behind her eyes and blinked furiously. Once she'd succeeded in pushing the tears back, she turned to face Naomi. "I would have stayed behind if I'd known Chris had fallen in love with someone, let alone married her. You've got to believe that."

Naomi's expression was compassionate.

"I don't have any intention of breaking them up. I just hope I get a chance to talk to her. And to Chris. I'm sorry we told that Martinez woman we'd expect to be here for a month," she sighed.

"You can always hang out with 'Lijah and me," Naomi offered. Nicole smiled at her gratefully. Naomi stood and joined Nicole, putting a hand on her shoulder. "Look, Nicole, *I* believe you. I'll make sure Elijah believes you, too. We'll try to figure out how to get you home sooner."

"Thanks, Naomi."

They ate most of the meal that was delivered to their room some time later. A maidservant knocked, proceeding to carry in a wooden platter with cold fowl, cheese, and brown bread. There had been a single small pewter plate, two linen napkins, and a knife for slicing the bread and spreading fresh butter. The maid had returned a few minutes later with a decanter of wine and two goblets. The women began by nibbling at the food, then devouring it as their appetites took over. Naomi sighed with contentment. "I guess we won't starve," she said.

Nicole chuckled. When they'd finished eating, Nicole placed all of the used items on the tray and left it on a small table next to the room's door.

"Now what?" she murmured. "Time to think about sleep?"

"Guess so," Naomi replied, as each woman eyed the single bed warily. It was about the same size as a modern-day double bed. Naomi had done some research for the trip and mentioned that the mattress, even in a noble household, could be infested with anything. Nicole made a face before she pulled the furs down and checked the linens.

"I can't tell if we have company or not," she said. "And how do we -?"

Naomi grinned and held up a ceramic pot. "Chamber pot," she said.

Nicole grimaced before smiling. "One thing's for sure," she said. "We'll appreciate all those modern conveniences when we get home."

Naomi laughed her agreement. As they finished their preparations for bed, both women stripped down to their underwear. Nicole placed her glasses on the table next to the bed before blowing out the candle. She hoped Helen would give her a chance to apologize for barging in on them. Her heart was heavy as she lay back in the bed a few inches from Naomi. She also wanted to learn more about the young, good-looking priest who'd been present in the workroom. He'd barely registered on her at the time, but as she'd followed Helen to the guest chamber, his presence intruded on her thoughts.

The two women slept fitfully, due in part to being in a strange place and in a tense situation. Not long after dawn they gave up and donned their clothes from the day before - jeans and a long-sleeved linen blouse for Naomi and rayon skirt and cotton sweater for Nicole. The same maid who'd brought their supper rapped on the door some time later, and, when allowed in, exchanged their tray from the evening before with a breakfast tray and curtseyed before leaving. Naomi didn't think she imagined the speculative look thrown her way; she suspected it was due to her trousers. As the two women ate the eggs, bacon, and fresh bread, they debated waiting for a summons or going exploring.

A knock on the door startled them. Naomi opened it. Outside was a boy who looked about nine years old wearing a green tunic with a silver eagle on its front. "My ladies, you are summoned to the study by their Graces. Follow me, please."

Naomi stifled a giggle, afraid of insulting the boy's dignity. Nicole arched an eyebrow at her before telling him they were right behind him. Her lips twitched.

Matthew, Saelym Castle's steward, was already in the study, standing with his back to the room's window when the page delivered the two women. The boy closed the door behind them. Chris stood and indicated the two chairs facing the desk. They sat, giving Helen their attention.

"Ladies, there has been a change in plans," Helen began. Naomi was about to speak, but Helen asked her to wait. "Chris and I have been summoned to the capital, Rhennsbury. You will be traveling with us. The journey is going to be more arduous than the norm, but I assure you 'tis only because the situation is urgent. The king has been slain and..." At this, Matthew inhaled sharply and crossed himself. "...we must help his son."

Nicole and Naomi were stunned. "If it's easier for you, we can stay here..." Nicole said.

Helen's brows lowered in a frown. "No, 'twill be best for you to come. There is a man in Rhennsbury who could help you return home more quickly," she said.

Nicole took a deep breath as she stood and held out a hand to Helen. "That's fine by me, your ladyship," she said. Helen stared at the hand for a moment, touched it briefly and inclined her head. Nicole returned to her chair, feeling deflated.

Naomi wasn't intimidated. "I want to see Elijah before I go anywhere," she said, crossing her arms and setting her jaw.

"Elijah will catch up to us if he is not here by tonight," Chris assured her. "Trust me, he will not be able to stay away, between you being here and the events in the capital."

Naomi wasn't completely reassured but nodded her acceptance. If he didn't catch up to them in a few days, she'd leave the group and head back to the castle. She wasn't going to be pushed around by a duchess, not where her family was concerned. She'd take on a queen, too, if necessary.

Helen stood. "Well, ladies, on a practical note, we will have to see about getting you each another set of clothes. Nicole, your skirt will not work for riding, and Naomi, your - trousers - are unseemly. For that matter, do either of you ride?"

"No," they replied. Naomi raised an eyebrow, letting the other comment pass for the time being.

"Then you are going to have to learn," Helen said tartly. Then to Chris, "Find Abigail and let her know of our travel plans. She will know what my needs are. And do not forget your formal clothes and coronet. You will need them." Helen swept out, the other women on her heels. Nicole pointedly looked away from Chris.

Matthew gave Chris a reassuring look. "The duchy will be fine in your absence, your Grace," he said, the emotional nuances in the room passing him by.

"Of course, Matthew," Chris replied automatically, as he held the door open and followed the steward out. He ascended the stairs to the next floor and rapped quietly on the schoolroom's door. Reginald was halfway to the door when Chris opened it and stepped into the bright chamber.

"Father?" Reginald was surprised. His father almost never set foot in the schoolroom.

Chris nodded to Reginald then turned to the tutor. "Master Nigel, a matter of urgency has come up in Rhennsbury. Lessons will be put on hold for a couple of months."

"Your Grace," the man began. Chris held up a hand before crouching to be at Reginald's eye level. Eleanor had joined them by this time.

"Children, you are coming with your mother and me to the capital. The king has died, and you are to accompany us to Prince Robert's coronation."

Reginald let out a whoop at the news. He didn't understand the full import, only that he had a reprieve from the schoolroom. He also remembered Robert from the previous summer and was excited at the prospect of seeing him again. Eleanor took hold of one of Chris's hands.

"The k-king is dead, Father?" she asked. "What will happen to Prince Robert? What is a corn - cori -?" She gave up.

Chris gave her a hug. "Prince Robert's father is dead, Ellie," he explained patiently. "Prince Robert has to become king in his place - the ceremony is called a coronation."

"Oh." She leaned her head against him. "Will we get to see him again?"

"Of course." He straightened and held out his other hand to Reginald. "Now we need to see about getting your things ready to travel. It is going to take at least a fortnight to get there."

Eleanor's eyes widened. "A fortnight?"

Reginald led the way out of the chamber. "Plus a fortnight back, and however long we are in Rhennsbury. No lessons for over a month!" Chris smiled. Just so Reginald had his priorities straight.

Elijah Holmes and his traveling companion, a healer-monk named Brother Peter, arrived in Saelym late that afternoon. Elijah wasn't sure which news upset him the most: Reginald Claybourne's death, getting right back on the road, Nicole, or Naomi. He thought it was mostly Naomi, though traveling was a close second. He was tired from the trip to visit another, elderly monk, who'd taught him a few more things about how his Healing Talent worked.

He had hugged his sister fiercely then admonished her for coming. She countered by asking him what he was doing traveling with a monk. When he had explained about his healing ability, she had started laughing but stopped abruptly when she saw the hurt in his eyes and apologized.

Elijah finished his minimal packing - most of his essential belongings had gone with him to the monastery. Before retiring for the night, he rapped on Chris's door. He wasn't surprised to find Chris alone, though it made him unhappy.

"You want to talk about Nicole?" he asked, watching his friend's face.

"There is nothing to talk about, 'Lijah," Chris replied, gesturing Elijah to a chair. "Helen is furious with me, Nicole is hurt, and I have to be patient." Chris's frustrations rose to the surface. He bit back a profanity. "My fear is that Nicole came here to try to renew our relationship and take me home," he added finally.

"How do you feel about that?" Elijah had sat but he still observed his friend.

Chris ran a hand through his blond hair. "How do I feel about that?" he echoed. He laughed hollowly. "I feel exactly nothing about it, pal, except that if she ruins what Helen and I have, I will have -"

"No you won't," Elijah said, chuckling. "You're too nice. Not like Naomi and me." Chris was about to retort, but Elijah continued. "Of course you want to. You're only human, and until you'd met Helen you'd been celibate too long."

"What does that have to do with anything?" Chris demanded, close to losing his temper, though most of his anger was due to frustration with the strain between him and Helen rather than annoyance at Elijah.

Elijah shook his head. "Maybe nothing. Then again, maybe something." He shrugged. "What was your first thought when you saw Nicole?"

Chris recalled the night before. "Disbelief, followed by - nothing," Chris said, surprising himself. "There is no pain anymore. Seeing her no longer hurts."

"That's what I wanted to know. I'm glad for you. I'm surprised my mother didn't tell her about you and Helen, unless she was testing you and Nicole. She didn't know you and Helen had married. Knowing Mama, she hoped you'd realize you were still in love with Nicole and we'd all come home." Elijah smiled wryly. "Helen will come around - right now she's jealous that you had serious feelings for another attractive woman. Who, I might add, is about the same age as Helen but looks a few years younger."

"What? Helen jealous? That is just silly," Chris began to protest. He stopped, thinking suddenly about Helen's insecurity about her body and her so-called advanced age. Maybe his friend was on to something. It was Helen's maturity as well as her physical charms that had attracted him. Elijah mistook his silence for being finished.

"Why not? It's not like you're deformed." He raised an eyebrow. "At least not where it shows." He grinned momentarily. "The worst thing she can say about you, until last night, is that you look too much like Christian. She's very much in love with you. I think she's insecure, and considering how men have screwed her, can you blame her?"

"Okay, you may have a point. I do not care what her reasons are, though. I just know she is worth waiting for, no matter how long it takes. I love her, plain and simple."

Elijah smiled. "So show her and tell her now and then. Of course, Godiva chocolates wouldn't hurt." Chris rolled his eyes. Elijah raised a finger and waggled it at his friend. "And don't spend any time alone with Nicole."

Chris shook his head. "I already figured out that much on my own, Ann Landers. Will you talk to her though? Find out exactly why she came here?"

"Naturally. 'Inquiring minds want to know.' I'll be my usual subtle self." Elijah ducked out of the room before Chris could throw something at him. Instead, Chris smiled good-naturedly and wished his friend a good night.

Helen had been unable to find a riding skirt long enough to fit Naomi. Naomi's solution was to wear her jeans. Helen was unhappy with the suggestion, since it smacked of sinfulness, but because of the urgency of the situation, she agreed to it. Naomi agreed to wear a man's tunic and surcoat with the jeans. She'd worry about dresses when they reached their destination. In the meantime, her jeans would have to do. No tailor or seamstress could get a riding habit made in time. Nicole borrowed one of Helen's since the two women were of a similar size, despite Helen's fears otherwise.

As Helen prepared for sleep that evening, her thoughts returned to her and Chris's wedding night. She had gone to her apartment after the quiet ceremony in the castle chapel, to remove her formal clothes. She'd then donned shift and dressing gown and crossed the corridor to Chris's chambers.

Chris had taken her into his arms, lifting her off the floor and carrying her into the bedroom. As he returned her to her feet, he began stroking her hair, which hung down loosely past her waist. "I knew your hair would be glorious," he'd murmured, then bent down to inhale her signature scent of lavender. He unbelted her dressing gown, letting it drop to the floor. His smile was almost shy. "Thank goodness this is not the first time for either of us."

"You have not saved yourself for me?" Helen teased, in part to cover her own nervousness. She glanced at the bed she'd shared with Christian from time to time, still worried that Chris would find her body old and unattractive.

Chris started to reply, then recognized her tone. He watched her climb into the bed and pull the covers up to her chin. He began to remove his trousers, though it took longer than usual because his fingers had begun to shake. His body was ready to make love to Helen, but he was still anxious, unsure of his ability to please her, given her poor treatment by Christian. Chris eased onto the bed next to Helen, sliding under the bedclothes, and put his arms around her, kissing her deeply. He wasn't going to force her to show her naked body to him until she was comfortable with the idea, but he could tell by holding her through his lightweight tunic and her thin shift that there was nothing wrong with it.

Helen returned Chris's kiss, relaxing a little when he didn't insist on lighting several candles and asking her to show herself to him. She was self-conscious of the fact that she'd borne two children, and her body was no longer as thin and firm as it had been when she'd married Christian, even though she knew it had

had an effect on Chris for several months now. She held his body close to her own, enjoying the slow pace Chris set. He was proving already to be a more considerate partner than Christian ever could have been.

Despite his body's intentions, Chris wasn't about to rush things. Helen was the most important person in his life, and having had some sexual experience, he knew that women often enjoyed foreplay as much as, or more than, the sex act itself. He also had no idea what kind of lovemaking, if the term even applied, had occurred between Helen and Christian. She never talked about it, and Chris knew better than to ask.

"You are so beautiful," Chris murmured between kisses. He bared Helen's left shoulder and began kissing her there. Helen stiffened slightly at the unaccustomed words and action. She stared at him.

He felt her reaction and backed off slightly. "What?" he asked, feeling tense himself.

She touched his cheek, brushing her fingertips along the line of his jaw. Chris's loins reacted instantly at the gentle touch, but he fought his hormones. He didn't think she was ready yet.

"You truly think this old body is beautiful?" she whispered, unable to hide her disbelief.

Instead of replying right away, Chris took her firmly in his arms and kissed her lips again. He then brushed his lips across her throat before kissing her nose and smiling. "Helen, you are not old, and neither is your body. Remember that I am older than you," Chris assured her. "Though there is a maturity about your beauty that attracts me as much as anything else." As he cupped his hand over one of her covered breasts, her nipple hardened in response. He kissed her again. "I love your fullness - all your body has done is softened into womanhood. You have had children, and I can think of no better reason for changes to a woman's body than that."

He kissed her shoulder again. Her eyes followed his movements. He met her gaze and smiled before kissing her eyes, then her nose again. "I love your hazel eyes, your nose, your lovely face." He shifted so he could pull her toward him and inhaled her hair's delicate fragrance again. "I never thought the smell of lavender could be so arousing," he said, a hint of laughter in his voice. "Helen, I love everything about you. Yes, I wish we could have children together, but if you are infertile, there is so much more to you than that." He kissed her again, then ran his finger along her cheek. "I can hardly believe this is real."

Helen kissed him with sudden ardor, finally trusting his words and actions. Christian had never talked on the rare occasions she'd shared his bed. When their lips parted, she shivered, and again his loins reacted. Still not wanting to rush her, Chris suppressed a moan. To his surprise, she eased out of his arms and lowered the bedcovers, looking at his bare legs for the first time. She ran her fingers along one, traveling up his thigh, and smiled at him. Chris had to bite his lip, before taking her in his arms again. He was incapable of holding back any longer.

He continued to hold her in his arms when they were finished. Helen rested her head against his chest; he couldn't remember the last time he was this comfortable. She said quietly, "Do you wish me to stay?"

Chris nearly sat up. "What! Of course I want you to stay! Sleeping together is, well, almost better than sex!" He tightened his arms around her for a moment, and then relaxed them. "That is, unless you wish to leave." He sounded like a forlorn little boy.

Helen smiled. She reached down to adjust her shift and paused. "You have a scar," she said. "Christian had many, but not here."

Chris glanced down. "It is a scar from an appendectomy. I had to have surgery once, when I was in the Navy." He reddened in embarrassment as she touched it gently, her expression concerned, before she snuggled next to him again.

Helen felt contentment. She'd endured conjugal relations with Christian out of duty, but she'd never enjoyed them. It surprised her to feel such a strong physical attraction to Chris, given his outer resemblance to Christian. She felt comfortable with him, a feeling to which she was unused. She had known in her head for some time that he loved her; he'd proven it by choosing to remain with her instead of returning to his home or even asking her to accompany him there. After this sharing of their bodies, she opened her heart to him. She sighed and held one of his hands to her breast, then lifted it to her lips and kissed it.

Chris stroked her hair with his other hand, enjoying the intimacy. He could think of few things better than sleeping and waking up with a woman he loved. "Thank you," he said.

"For what?" Helen asked, curious.

"For staying." Chris turned her to face him. "I would not have forced you to stay. I love you more than anything, and I can think of no place I would rather be right now than here, with you, like this." He kissed the top of her head.

Helen smiled as she studied his face, taking in his features, his blond hair, his green eyes. "No man has ever said such a thing to me. I love you, too." She kissed him.

As Helen now reached the end of the memories, she felt the trail of tears down both cheeks. She loved Chris with heart and soul, and missed the closeness they'd shared since Easter.

The next morning dawned clear and warm. Elijah had offered to remain in Saelym with Nicole and his sister, but as appealing as his idea was, Chris and Helen felt Elijah's usefulness in Rhennsbury outweighed leaving him behind. Besides, there was the possibility that Edward could help the two women return home.

As the traveling party was making final preparations, Helen gave Naomi and Nicole each a sharp knife. "For eating and self-defense," she explained quietly. The two women nodded their understanding; some things were the same as at home.

Helen chose their mounts carefully. As both women were novices, she had to compromise between speed and gentleness. Naomi showed no fear of the animal and required only a boost from her brother to mount. She grasped the reins in one hand and patted the mare's mane with the other one.

Nicole was nervous. She hoped for a sidesaddle, but Helen told her such a thing did not exist.

"It's like getting on a man's bike, Nicole," Elijah told her, cupping his hands and giving her a boost as well.

"A bike, my as-" Nicole stopped, embarrassed. "I've never ridden a bike with a mind of its own." She bit her lip as the animal picked up her tension and danced about for several moments. She dug her knees in a little, terrified she would fall out of the saddle, and forgot to take the reins a groom held out to her. "Don't these things come with seat belts?" she asked plaintively.

"You will be fine," Michael said from her other side, with an encouraging smile. "I can lead her for a while so you can get a feel for riding." He took the reins from the groom.

Nicole gave him a grateful look and started to relax a little. To her astonishment, the mare quieted too. Chris paused before helping Helen mount. They were both surprised at Michael's behavior - he was usually more reserved. Chris assisted Helen into her saddle and then mounted his own animal. She thanked him, raising an eyebrow at her cousin. Michael had insisted on traveling to Rhennsbury. He'd met Robert during the prince's stay in Saelym the previous summer and fall and wanted to attend the coronation. Besides, he'd be able to assist Helen Magically if needed. She agreed, but she told him to avoid Edward Fitzroy. Michael had unintentionally worked an illegal spell in Edward's presence not long after his ordination as a priest, and Edward had seen to it that Michael would never rise in the Church's ranks. Michael agreed that he needed to stay clear of the bishop.

Once the party had left the town behind, Naomi proved a capable novice horsewoman. After Nicole got somewhat comfortable with her mount, Helen set everyone at a steady canter. The journey from Saelym Town to Rhennsbury ordinarily took about a fortnight in decent weather, but Helen hoped to knock a day or two off. With spring having arrived and barring a major downpour, the weather was in her favor.

By midday, Eleanor insisted on riding with Chris, rather than with her governess. She felt safer. She had complained at first when Helen had told her she couldn't bring her kitten, but brightened when her mother told her she'd be apt to meet new cats at the royal castle. She slept every few hours within the folds of Chris's cloak, and he was happy to have her company.

Reginald rode next to Helen on a small mare. He did his best to keep up with the adults, but nodded off in the saddle occasionally, and Helen had to take the reins.

The party spent their first night at an inn. Elijah, who was sharing a small room with Michael, told the priest he was going to spend some time with his sister and Nicole. Michael debated joining them, but decided to let them speak privately. He hoped that Elijah could help mend things between Helen and Chris. He knew Helen respected Elijah's opinion on many types of matters.

Elijah rapped on the door of the room Naomi and Nicole shared. Naomi opened it, her expression wary until she saw it was her brother. "You should bolt it," Elijah drawled, gesturing toward the door. "We need to talk." As Nicole moved to leave the room, he added, "All of us." She looked away from him but sat on a stool. Naomi pulled up a stool near her and sat.

"About what?" Naomi demanded.

"About what we're doing here," Nicole replied before Elijah could.

"Exactly," he confirmed. "What were you thinking?" His eyes narrowed as Naomi raised her chin in defiance. "Or were you thinking?"

"I came here to see you again," Naomi said defensively. "Not that you seem to appreciate that fact. Mama said you and Chris had good reasons for staying in this backwater, but she misses you. So do I, though I'm not sure why I bother. Why did you stay? This healing stuff?"

"Mostly. Naomi, I miss everyone, too. I haven't completely ruled out coming home. I hold my breath every month when Michael opens that 'window' with Angelita, knowing one time he or she's going to fail, and I'll be here forever. I can think of worse fates, but I don't have the same emotional reasons to stay here that Chris does." He smiled. "You may have noticed that he's got it bad for Helen, and he's crazy about her kids."

Elijah turned to Nicole. "Okay. It's your turn. I'm guessing you crossed space and time to try to get back with a man *you* broke up with."

Nicole looked away. "Guilty. Look, Elijah, maybe you won't believe this, but if I'd known Chris was in love with Helen, married to her, I wouldn't have come. I said as much to your mother and that Angelita woman." She paused, taking a deep breath. "Frankly, I'm ticked off at both of them. They might have warned me, and I would have backed off."

Elijah raised an eyebrow, nodding once. "You've got a point. I said the same thing to Chris. But neither of them knew that he and Helen had married. Michael was going to pass that information over the other night. And, like I told Chris, my mother probably hoped he would ditch Helen and come home with you, and I'd follow him."

Nicole nodded. "Fair enough. I admit that breaking off our engagement was the stupidest thing I've ever done. I had second thoughts, and now it's too late." She stared at him. "I really do wish I could fix things for Chris and Helen. If that means going home when we get to Renn - oh, wherever - then I will. But I don't think it's that simple."

"You'd be right," Elijah agreed. "It's never that simple where people's feelings are concerned. I'll accept your words as honest, until you prove otherwise. Fair?" Naomi was about to interject something when Nicole shook her head and spoke to Elijah.

"Yeah, fair. Tell Chris I'm sorry. Oh, tell Lady Helen, too. I never realized medieval women were so - capable."

"You should have spent more time studying history than science or computers," Elijah pointed out with a smile. "Then you could get lousy jobs, like Naomi, who studied English."

"I just got my library science degree at NC Central this past December, I'll have you know," Naomi said smugly. She changed the subject. "So what's all this 'healing' stuff about, anyway? You mean Mama was right about 'voodoo' talents in her family?"

"Apparently," Elijah replied. He finally sat on the bed. "I don't know how much you remember about why Chris came here,

Naomi, but it was to prevent an assassination attempt on Christian Lattimore, Helen's first husband, and a dead ringer, if you'll pardon the expression, for Chris." He looked thoughtful. "Though the two men are - were - nothing alike on the inside."

"So, what, Elijah? Chris failed and the assassination happened. I mean, Christian is dead, right?" Nicole asked.

"No."

"Huh?"

"Christian was dead when Chris and I got here." Elijah had their full attention. "He was murdered over a private matter, which I am not at liberty to discuss. Anyway, the so-called assassination attempt played out at Christmas, and Chris got badly injured." Naomi's eyes widened; Nicole covered her mouth with one hand.

"He was shot in the shoulder - a crossbow bolt. It was actually intended for Prince Robert Claybourne. Bishop Edward Fitzroy got the story half-assed from the beginning." Elijah shook his head. "Fortunately, the bolt went through muscle tissue and missed Chris's lung." He took a steadying breath. "I was trying to keep him alive long enough to stitch him up. This talent took over. He has no scar, no stitches. It's like the injury never happened, but, trust me, it did."

"And now, this Prince Robert's father was just killed?" Nicole asked. She shuddered. "I think this place is way too exciting for me. I'll be glad to go home once we get where we're going."

"Yeah, King Reginald is Robert's father."

"Could it be the same person, then, who tried to kill the prince?" Naomi asked.

"I don't know," Elijah said. "That's what Helen, Chris and I hope to help Robert find out." He chuckled at a memory. "Poor kid - I thought he was the one who killed Christian. He admitted to hating the man but denied killing him."

Naomi changed the subject back to his talent. "So this monk, Brother Peter, is teaching you how to use your healing 'gift'?" she asked. "It seems like you already know how it works."

"It's more complicated than that. It was a lucky accident, brought on by stress. Now I have to learn how to control it." He grinned. "I'm becoming adept at the art of self-hypnosis."

"That doesn't surprise me. You've always been able to put me to sleep," Naomi quipped.

"Younger siblings." Elijah rolled his eyes. "As usual, you prove your ignorance. May I continue?"

"Please," Nicole said. "This is all alien to me, but fascinating. Ignore her."

"Don't worry, I will." Elijah assumed a professorial expression.

Naomi rolled her eyes.

"My Talent is a special Magical gift, at least here in Myrridia, or so I'm told. Magic operates on two levels. There are things you can do, alone, as long as you're in trance or otherwise mentally focused. Then there is high ritual, the really spooky stuff, where a practitioner works with at least one other person." He paused. "If I relax my mind, I could determine your moods by the way the air 'feels' around you."

Naomi looked skeptical.

Nicole raised a curious eyebrow. "Can you really?" she asked.

Naomi crossed her arms. *I dare you*, her expression said.

Elijah smile faded as he stared at the fire burning in the room's fireplace. Brother Peter's first lesson had been to teach Elijah to discover his own mental triggers toward relaxation. Elijah had since learned to summon a sphere of light; it provided practical assistance if he were to attempt any healing in darkness. He debated summoning one now; he suspected it would freak out his companions. He glanced at his sister and fought a smile.

Elijah took a deep, focusing breath. He raised his right hand to shoulder level and exhaled, concentrating on light. "Luminatus," he murmured. He was dimly aware of someone taking in a sharp breath as a small sphere of golden light appeared in his hand. He lowered his arm, and the light remained hovering in the air. He took a few more quiet breaths before turning to face the women. Naomi was simple - skepticism and attempted denial despite the sphere of light she could see. Nicole was harder to read, but Elijah got a sense of nervousness in general and disbelief warring with awe.

Elijah took another deep breath, and as he exhaled, he felt the room return to normal. He made a slight gesture with his hand and the light winked out. He looked at the two women.

"So?" Naomi asked, recovering.

"Not that I need any help in your case, little sister," Elijah said. "You're a skeptic, and you don't want to believe in Magic, the same feelings I had until a few months ago. Nicole, you're more difficult. Nerves, a lack of belief, yet fascination, too."

"Close enough," Nicole admitted. "You sure surprised me with that light. You really did that?"

"Uh-huh. Actually, that was a relatively easy thing to do Magically."

"Easy, he says," Nicole muttered to herself.

"So, it's all hypnosis and meditation?" Naomi asked, still only half convinced.

"No, that's how you prepare," Elijah corrected. "I don't know where the healing itself comes from, or any other Magical gifts. I guess it's in my mind, but I always feel a warmth through my hands. I have absolutely no scientific explanation for it. Heck, some days I still don't believe I can do these things." He chuckled. "On a grander Magical scale, people like Helen and Edward Fitzroy leave me in the dust. I wouldn't tick her off if I were you."

"Oh, great," Nicole moaned.

"He's teasing us, Nicole," Naomi said, scowling at her brother. "Helen's more civilized than that. She's a woman, remember? Not an unenlightened ape like Elijah."

"Unenlightened?" Elijah repeated with a snort. "Wait until you meet the noble barbarians in Rhennsbury," he warned.

The weather cooperated for most of the journey. The sun shone most days, though there were a few thunderstorms. A long, steady rain developed when they were a couple of days outside of

Rhennsbury. The horses stopped when the rains fell in sheets obscuring visibility, refusing to budge until the storms passed.

Nicole still wasn't comfortable controlling her horse, and the mare sensed it. Unlike the other horses, the mare began making its way through the mud with difficulty. Nicole took her left hand off the reins to wipe her forehead in another vain attempt to get the water out of her eyes. Her eyeglasses were tucked into a pocket of her riding habit, but it didn't matter, she couldn't see a thing anyway. She didn't realize that her horse was the only one moving, so she didn't call out. She gave the mare its lead.

By the time the rain slowed to where Nicole could put her glasses on, the horse had wandered deep into a forest. Nicole wrung out part of her cloak and used it to dry her face. The sun came out, but she noticed it was low in the sky, shining through the trees. It dawned on her that no one was nearby, and neither was the road. She looked at the trees again; they seemed thicker than they had a second ago. "Hello?" she called, her voice cracking. "Anybody?" Her voice was louder the second time. She strained to hear a reply but heard only water dripping from the trees. She was lost. Night was coming and she was alone.

Oh, God! Now what? And where am I? Where was an interstate highway with exit signs, warm motels, and restaurants when she needed one? She tugged on the reins and was surprised when the horse obeyed and stopped walking. Nicole slid out of the saddle and looked about her immediate surroundings. The horse was following a trail barely wide enough to accommodate the animal. Nicole shivered in her wet clothes and debated turning around, continuing on, or staying where she was.

She heard a rustling noise in the trees. Her head turned in the direction from which it seemed to come. Her mind conjured up images of raccoons, foxes and wolves. Stifling a scream and galvanized by her fear, Nicole was able to get back into the saddle before her imagination made it to bears. She decided to keep moving. *The forest has to come to an end sometime*, she told herself. She started to cry.

* * *

No one noticed Nicole's absence until the rain slowed to the point where the horses were ready to move again. Naomi noticed first - Nicole had been traveling just ahead of her. As her horse began to walk, she tugged on the reins.

"Elijah, Nicole's not here." She had turned in her saddle to speak to her brother.

"What? Darn it. Wait here." Elijah spurred his mount and trotted to join Helen and Chris, near the head of the party.

"Helen, Chris, we have a problem," he called as he reined in next to them. "Nicole's gone missing."

"What?" Chris asked.

"By our Lady," Helen snapped. "We do not have time to go searching for her." She looked around them. "She could be anywhere."

"You cannot mean to abandon her, Helen," Chris protested, knowing he was on shaky ground. "She could get killed!"

"Surely she has enough sense not to go wandering off in a storm, in a strange place," Helen retorted. "We cannot spare the time. Unless my lord wishes to go look for her himself." Her tone was deadly quiet.

Chris was angry, too. As he tensed, Eleanor squirmed in the saddle to look at him. Seeing his expression, she started to cry.

"Please do not argue with Mother. I hate it when you fight. You scare me!"

Chris made an effort to relax. "I am sorry, Ellie," he murmured. "I will not fight with your mother, I promise." She sniffled and huddled up against him.

Elijah stepped in before Chris could say anything else to Helen, especially something he might later regret. "Nicole's still an unsure horsewoman, Helen," he said. "Of course she didn't intend to get lost. Naomi and I should have kept a better eye on her. She may not have realized that the horse had wandered away. Why don't I, or someone, go looking for her and catch up with you in Rhennsbury? You don't want her death on your conscience."

Helen sighed, unable to find fault with Elijah's argument. Chris gave him a grateful look.

"I will search for her, cousin," Michael said. "The rest of you go on. We will meet you in the capital later."

"Michael -" Helen began.

"No, Helen. I will be fine. Go." He tugged on his mount's left rein and turned. He was going into light trance as his horse began trotting away. Helen stared after his retreating back, wondering.

The Saelym party arrived in Rhennsbury two days later, just short of a fortnight. The mood was somber; there had been no word of Nicole or Michael. The strain between Helen and Chris had become evident to all in the last days of the journey.

Chris was frustrated because he felt torn in two directions. He could see Helen's point. Reginald's murder and Robert's troubles were of major importance. But Chris felt as though they had abandoned Nicole. She had no real idea what this world was like, and he was willing to bet she hadn't spent a lot of time studying history. He knew he no longer loved her, but he squirmed in his saddle every time he remembered she was lost.

Helen was relieved that the party had made good time, but her conscience was pricking at her as well. She knew where her duty lay, but the knowledge didn't prevent her from feeling guilty. She continued to hope that Michael had located Nicole, and the pair was not far behind them.

There was a shout from behind Helen and Chris. Chris was starting to turn in his saddle when he felt something strike him between his shoulder blades.

"Murderer!"

"Traitor!"

He started to make out the words, then realized someone was throwing rotten vegetables at him. "What the -?" he began, when Helen spurred her mount to speed up, despite the crowd of people in the street. Most of the folk scattered as her horse quickened its gait. Chris followed suit. The remainder of the traveling party followed their lead, staying at a canter until they were crossing the drawbridge to Rhennsbury Castle.

Chris slid out of his saddle, helping Helen to dismount next. He was still rattled by what had happened in the city.

"The city folk seem to feel that Christian is somehow to blame for Reginald's death," Helen told him. "Perhaps it is rumors of a change in their friendship. Were you hurt?"

Chris shrugged. "No. I might bruise, but I am fine. Do you want to go straight to Robert and Allyson?"

"Aye. Comfort will need to wait." Helen watched as Naomi dismounted without assistance. Several of the grooms looked on in admiration. Helen allowed herself a slight smile as Elijah came up behind his sister, touched her lightly on the shoulder, then scowled at the grooms. The men pretended to occupy themselves.

Chris held out his elbow to Helen. She placed one hand in it, lifting her skirts with the other. "Let us go," she said.

Chapter Four

Edward arrived at Rhennsbury Castle near midmorning the day after Reginald's murder. He was determined to get a few things straight with Robert before their relationship deteriorated further. Robert might now be the king, but he needed to learn his limitations, especially with regard to the Church. Edward strode to the Great Hall and rapped firmly at the door to the royal study. He was shocked to hear Allyson's voice call "Enter."

He stalked into the chamber and stopped a few feet shy of the desk. He stood still and glowered at her, his arms folded across his chest. She was seated at the desk. It was his opinion that she had no business there. "Where is your brother?" he demanded. "And what are you doing in here?"

Allyson stood and held out her hand, ignoring both questions.

Edward ignored her gesture. "Well?" he added.

"Be rude, then," Allyson said, sitting and feigning calm. "Robert is sleeping, and you are not going to disturb him. He went to bed less than two hours ago. You of all people should know what kind of night he had."

Edward snorted as he took a seat in one of two wooden chairs opposite her. Allyson arched an eyebrow. "Oh, aye, he spent a good part of the night worried about his humiliation. Never mind the fact that his father, the king, was murdered in cold blood." He leaned forward, his elbows on the desk and his face inches from hers. "Your brother prevented me from learning as much as possible about Reginald's death."

Allyson met and held his gaze. "And how much more would you have learned from the woman?" she countered. "Not that I expect you to care that sifting through her memories carelessly could have cost her her sanity."

"She was a whore!" Edward snapped.

Allyson's eyes darkened. "You will refrain from using that kind of language in here," she said icily. "Vivian may have been a prostitute by profession, but you cannot know for certes that it was by her own choice. Robert did the only humane thing under the circumstances. As his uncle and a churchman, you should be glad that he was able to show that degree of restraint. 'Tis expected of those of royal blood."

"Restraint? Is that what thwarting those with more experience is called?" Edward retorted. "Thank you for the lecture, young woman."

Allyson's eyes narrowed. "You are out of line, sir. Did you come here to talk in a civilized manner, or do you wish to be kicked out of the castle onto your ecclesiastical bottom?"

Edward paled with fury. "You are the one out of line, Your Highness," he said, his voice as cold as his eyes.

Allyson's heart skipped a beat, but she kept her features even. If Robert could stand up to him, so could she. She stared at Edward until he sat back, his expression still thunderous. Deliberately she waited several more heartbeats before speaking again. "Robert and Father had a poor relationship at best, Edward. How would you feel if your father had died in such a way? I feel humiliated, but at least I was here in the castle, not in the brothel. Though I shall still receive pitying looks from Rhennsbury's residents." She paused intentionally. "Besides, Robert oversaw Vivian's execution this morning."

"She is dead, then." Edward's anger deepened at a lost opportunity to gain additional knowledge from the woman.

"Oh, yes. Anything else?" Allyson picked up several letters and began placing them in separate piles. It was a dismissal.

Edward remained seated.

After several moments of silence, Allyson looked up. "Yes?"

"You have no business here, going through the king's correspondence," Edward stated. Allyson sat back and crossed her arms. "Really? May I point out that I have more royal blood in my veins than you do?" Allyson's expression was challenging. She was surprised by her audacity, but she successfully kept her nervousness hidden.

Edward recoiled as though slapped. Apparently he was going to get as little respect from Allyson as her brother gave him.

"Robert and I have already contacted Lady Helen and Lord Chris in Saelym and asked them to come," Allyson continued. She bit back her smile as Edward paled.

His expression swiftly changed from shock to anger. "So Robert told you about the substitution?" he demanded.

Allyson shrugged; to her mind it hardly mattered. "No. Duchess Helen told me."

"How dare -?" Edward stopped himself. He added Helen to the list of persons with whom he was furious. He narrowed his eyes as he stood. "This is not yet finished," he said, his tone deadly quiet.

Allyson let out a breath as the study door closed behind him. She freely admitted that her uncle terrified her, and she had no doubts that he spoke truly.

Robert had finally gone to bed after speaking with Chris and Helen. He'd slept fitfully for a few hours, rising around midday. Paul looked at him with concern, but Robert gave his squire a slight smile and shake of the head. His father was dead, murdered in the most embarrassing way Robert could imagine, and now he had to notify Myrridia's leading nobles of Reginald's passing. He picked up the book he'd been holding when his father arrived at his chambers the night before, tucked it into his tunic, and made his way to the nearest stairwell.

Robert descended to the Great Hall, where two liveried guards saluted him. He crossed the large room and let himself into the study.

Guilty, Allyson looked up from the desk, where she'd been organizing the correspondence. She stood quickly. "I am sorry, brother. I thought I would begin sorting things while you rested."

Robert waved her back into the chair. He sank into the one Edward had sat in earlier. "It can wait a little." He smiled ruefully. "I have been trained for this since I left the nursery. So why do I not feel ready?"

Allyson's smile was genuine. "You prove your readiness by understanding the gravity of the position, not just the power and prestige. Only a power-hungry man or a mad one would embrace the position eagerly. You recognize your duty and you accept it, but you do not have to welcome it." Her smile faded. "Besides, Father's death was sudden and violent." She paused. "Do you want to talk any more about it? I know you and he were not close. He and I were no closer."

Robert shook his head. "Another time, maybe, but my thanks for the offer. I think it is more imperative to get the news out about his death and prepare for -" He stopped speaking suddenly and crossed himself. "For the coronation," he concluded, his blue eyes widening at the prospect.

Allyson thought quickly. "Father got through his coronation. I have never heard any rumors that he disgraced himself, so you will be fine."

"If you say so," Robert said, looking doubtful. "There is something else we need to talk about," he went on.

Allyson glanced at him sharply. He'd sounded hesitant, which was unusual. He withdrew the book from his tunic and placed it on the desk before her. "I think this is yours," he said quietly.

Allyson looked from the book to her brother's face. It was a journal she had begun and titled "Allyson's Book of Secrets." His expression was troubled but not angry. "You opened it and saw the title page," she stated.

"Aye." He looked guilty. "I did not mean to invade your privacy, Ally, but I had not seen the book before. I did not think it was mine, and I wanted to return it to its owner. And I was curious." He looked at his hands.

"Jesu," Allyson swore. "I hid the book in your room after you had gone to Saelym. Mother and I had words about my Magical studies, and she became suspicious about my knowledge. I was afraid she would find it in the library, but hoped she would not search your chambers. I meant to retrieve it, once Mother departed for the convent, but I had no idea how to bring up the subject with you." His head had come up, and he'd watched her face throughout the recitation. "Do you think I am a heretic?" she asked.

"What? Of course not," Robert replied. He glanced at the book. "Why, are there heretical things in there?"

"I suppose that depends on your definition of heresy," she countered. "You did not look through it?"

Robert smiled and shook his head. "Just the first page. Then Father came to my room uninvited last evening, with plans to entertain me." His eyes clouded with the memories from the night before, and he was quiet for several moments before resuming his train of thought. "I think my definition of heresy is a far cry from Edward Fitzroy's. Allyson, I-I think it is not my business what kind of Magic you practice, though I hope you would give me some warning if - if -" he faltered.

"If I sold my soul to the Devil?" she asked.

Robert swallowed hard and fought the urge to cross himself. "Nay," he said. "I - It is just that…oh, I do not care what you do personally, but there are political…complications that could… arise."

Allyson laughed. Robert blinked in surprise. "Robert, I have no intention of practicing Dark Magic. I have just had thoughts about changing some rituals slightly from their - approved -

formulae." She motioned toward the book. "That is what I have written down in there. I have not tried to use any of them."

Robert looked relieved.

"Yet."

He took a few deep breaths. "I - Just be careful. I may not be able to protect you from the Church."

"Aye." Allyson's expression turned as troubled as her brother's. After several moments of thought, she cocked her head. She tapped the book. "This reminds me. I happened to glance through a book you had on your shelf when I hid this one. How and when did you learn how to read Arabic?"

Robert sat back in the chair, startled. "I –" he began. He stared at his hands for a few moments, as though they had an answer for him. He raised his head again, to meet his sister's curious gaze without flinching. "A little over a year ago, I met a monk, in the city. Paul was with me – I was trying to escape Father's wrath. I cannot even remember what our disagreement was about." His eyes focused beyond his sister momentarily. "Paul was looking at a display of daggers while I checked over some scrolls and books. I picked up the book you must have seen on my shelf –" Allyson nodded as he glanced at her "- and was looking at it, curious. This monk, Brother John, just appeared at my side and offered to teach me some of the language." Robert shrugged. "So once a week for a few months, I met Brother John at The King's Arms.

"He told me such tales of lands far away, Ally. I may never travel to them, but if I learned naught else from this man, he assured me that there are many ways to worship God. He also said that the differences often led to bloodshed." He smiled slightly. "I guess I would not think you a heretic, just because you want to change what Edward and men of his ilk consider correct ritual."

Allyson returned the smile. "I think I feel a little better. How interesting, though. I admit, I cannot even imagine such places. Do you suppose I could learn some of the language?"

"Why not?"

* * *

Robert had to consciously restrain himself when the castle herald announced the arrival of the Duke and Duchess of Saelym nearly a fortnight later. He wanted to greet them in the courtyard, but forced himself to remain in the study. His public relationship with Christian wouldn't survive a friendly welcome.

He had been miserable during the intervening days. The circumstances surrounding Reginald's death had made the rounds of the castle grapevine, and the servants' reactions were mixed. Most of them, passing Robert in a corridor or serving him a meal, gave him sympathetic or pitying looks. He tried to keep his features impassive, nodding to indicate he'd seen them, but the stress was taking its toll on him.

A couple of his father's Councilors had already arrived in Rhennsbury, though they were surprised to hear of Reginald's death. They'd been answering the summons Reginald had sent out a few days prior to his death and had missed Robert's message. One, James McDermott, the Earl of Kilhenry and a man whom Robert respected, had gone to aid Edward Fitzroy with plans for the coronation. Robert was willing to wait until midsummer, but Edward, and then James, argued for an earlier date. They agreed upon the first of June. Robert told them to do what they felt was best. Edward reminded him that he could ignore everything else, but he did need to be available for fittings. Robert looked blank at first, then he sighed.

James felt sympathy toward the young man, and assured him, "We will see that you are bothered as little as possible, Highness. But, I suggest you do not grow any taller in the meantime." It had taken Robert a few moments to realize what James had said, but he'd managed a smile.

Allyson came into the royal study not long after the herald made his announcement. "What is taking them so long to get here?" she fussed.

"Calm yourself, Allyson. I am as impatient as you, or more so, but the city is crowded. There is a major event coming up in a couple of weeks," Robert said with a touch of sarcasm to hide his trepidation.

Allyson frowned at him. "I am so glad to see Your Majesty so serene. I am excited to see them!" She flounced into a chair.

"Then go greet them in the courtyard." Robert smiled as his sister flung herself out of the chair with as little dignity as she'd sat in it. She was out of the door moments later. He wished he could have followed her.

Allyson reached the doorway as Helen and Chris mounted the stone steps. Still without her royal dignity, she threw herself into Helen's arms, just shy of knocking the older woman over. Chris steadied them both before remembering to bow.

Allyson told him to straighten up, hugging him as well. Sobering suddenly, she looked from one to the other. "What is going on?" she asked as she sensed the strain between them.

"Nothing we cannot work out between ourselves, my dear," Helen replied. "Let us greet your brother." She motioned for Allyson to lead them.

Robert stood as the three entered the study. He kissed Helen's hand as she curtseyed, and shook Chris's hand after he bowed. "Please, forget the formalities. I want to enjoy some friendly faces." Robert gestured toward the chairs, and the two women sat.

Chris studied Robert for several seconds, noting the youth looked nearly haggard, showing signs of strain. "If you need to talk, you know where to find me," he said quietly. Robert nodded, smiling his appreciation. Chris walked over to the room's narrow window. "I understand a little of your pain, Robert. I lost my parents suddenly, violently," he said, following a hunch.

"Yes. I remember you said something about that before Christmas. You said it still hurt a lot, and you were upset with Father, about always being in his cups." Robert glanced down at the desk. "I feel guilty about Father. He and I were not close. I do not think he liked me. I always disappointed him." He took a deep breath. "I-I know I did not like him!" Robert sank back in the chair.

Chris stepped over to him. "What happened to your father was not your fault, Robert," he said, lifting Robert's chin and looking him in the eye. Having been raised a Catholic, Chris understood guilt, though he sometimes had trouble dealing with it himself. He thought briefly about the current situation with Nicole, opting to push it from his mind. Robert needed his support right now; there was nothing he could do for his former fiancée. "I daresay he brought it on himself, to a degree."

Robert stared at him, shocked. Chris continued, "I know we're supposed to speak well of the dead." Chris crossed himself and Robert followed suit. "If he were slain by a political enemy, it could be retaliation for something he had done years ago. I apologize, but it is likely enough."

Robert nodded. "I am so angry with him." He stood face to face with Chris. "I mean, he let himself get murdered in a whorehouse!" He looked down, ashamed of the outburst.

"Robert, there is no crime in being mad at him," Chris said, giving the youth a quick hug. Robert's head shot up, unaccustomed to the physical contact, but he didn't tense. "His death is disgraceful - to him, to you, to the kingdom. There is no shame to you for getting furious. I would be angry too, if it were my father."

Robert stepped back, staring at Chris for several moments, sensing nothing but sincerity. He turned to face Helen and Allyson. "I am sorry, ladies. Lady Helen, it is good to see you, regardless of the circumstances. Welcome to Rhennsbury." He smiled.

As Chris and Helen walked to their guest chamber after meeting with Allyson and Robert, Helen thanked Chris for handling Robert.

Chris smiled and shrugged. "To tell the truth, I was improvising - making it up - as I went along. How many people get to see his private self?"

Helen now smiled. "A short list, indeed. You are in a select group." She counted on her fingers as she listed names, "Allyson, myself, you and his squire."

"God, the poor kid. And now he is responsible for the whole country. I sold my father's farm after he and Mom died. I was sixteen and nowhere near ready to take it over." Chris shook his head. "Whatever I can do to help him, I will."

Helen sobered. "Find the man who killed Reginald. The killing may not stop with him. Robert could be next."

"Of course, but especially in light of the attempt against him at Christmas. If I have to, I will throw myself between Robert and - whoever - and fight them, to the death," Chris promised.

"Let us hope it does not come to that," Helen said. "Last December was harrowing enough." Smiling again for a moment, she added, "Besides, your swordsmanship is not exactly - skilled."

Chris grimaced but he had to agree.

When they arrived at their door, Helen asked Chris to go to Elijah's chamber for a while. Before he could protest, she added, "'Tis so Naomi and I can bathe."

"No problem." Chris kissed her hand lightly before departing.

Helen stared after him for several heartbeats then looked at her hand. "By our Lady, I have to get this situation worked out, and soon. Lives could depend on it," she muttered. Entering the chamber, she called for Abigail to request hot bath water from the castle kitchen, and afterward, to fetch Naomi.

Chris was surprised to receive a summons to the royal study a short while later. He knocked and went into the chamber as Robert called for his entry. Chris stopped as he recognized Edward, and his expression turned wary. He inclined his head to Robert before greeting the bishop. "Edward," he said, coolly polite.

"Doctor. Good to see you again," Edward lied.

Robert gestured Chris to the remaining chair. "Please sit, Chris. Edward has pestered me since Father's death regarding what to do about the situation in Saelym. I told him it could wait until you arrived." Robert kept his voice even, but Chris detected a hint of mirth in his eyes.

Chris eased into the indicated chair. "Naturally," he said.

Edward turned to Robert. "You should expose him as an impostor," he stated. Chris laughed. Robert raised an eyebrow as Edward turned in his chair. "You find this amusing, Doctor?" he asked.

"Uh-huh. Correct me if I am wrong, Edward, but I believe my presence here was your idea?"

Robert's lips twitched. Edward glowered at the pair of them.

"Why should I expose him, Edward?" Robert asked.

"Because it is the truth," Edward smiled smugly. "You never liked Christian Lattimore. Many will gossip if you change that relationship now."

Chris shook his head, "Not hardly. It will be a credit to Robert's maturity that he can put aside his personal differences with the Duke of Saelym. Besides, I got the impression earlier today that some of the city's residents think that Christian and Reginald had a falling out." He shared with them that vegetables had been thrown at him as well as accusations of treason and murder.

Robert's eyes widened in disbelief. "I have not heard any rumors of such. Jesu. Were you hurt?"

"No." Chris shifted in his chair and gave Robert his full attention. His change in posture wasn't wasted on Edward. "Robert, I do not care what you want to do about me. You are the king, in name anyway, and you need to do whatever is best for Saelym and Myrridia. If that means I have to keep playing at duke, then I will do it. If I had my way, I would go home and take Helen and her children with me, but that is not feasible. Then you would have no one to be duke, and I am sure that would turn into a political disaster." He paused for a moment. "I can swear an oath to you, right now, if you want."

Robert shook his head. "An oath is not necessary. But 'tis better to keep you in Saelym, as duke, than to open the duchy to attempted usurpation. I am sure that is why Father kept quiet about the substitution." He glanced at Edward, who sulked in his chair. "What about the possibility of Chris turning the duchy over to Reginald Lattimore when the boy reaches the legal age of sixteen?"

Edward was silent. Robert turned back to Chris, who shrugged. "Whatever. It is your decision, and I will abide by it."

Edward knew he'd lost the argument. "No good will come of this," he muttered and moved to depart the study.

"Maybe you should have thought of that before you opened that window last year," Chris retorted.

"Remember your place, peasant!" Edward snapped as he stalked out of the chamber.

Robert paled with anger at the insult. Chris sat still for several seconds. After he recovered his aplomb, he grinned at Robert. "Our prelate gets testy when things do not go his way, yes?"

Robert snorted, his anger abating somewhat. "You should have seen him when Father was murdered. He was furious with me, and part of me wanted just to give in to him, but I could not. I think I was more afraid of doing that than fighting him." He paused. "You know, you do not owe any loyalty to me or Myrridia, Chris."

"Yes I do," Chris said without hesitation. His eyes clouded. "I made a promise to your mother, and personally, I like you. If the latter includes loyalty to your political self, so be it."

"Are you still unwilling to share why Mother ordered Christian's death?" Robert asked.

Chris forced himself to meet the prince's eyes. "Sorry, Robert, but it really is not my place."

Robert inclined his head in respect, though he was still curious. "I shall continue to think about it, though. The only thing that makes sense is that Christian tried to hurt Allyson-" He broke off as Chris was unable to keep from tensing. "What did he do? Please, Chris."

Chris bit off a profanity. "You really do not want to know, Robert."

"I believe you are right, but perhaps I need to know, so I can understand."

Chris stood and paced nervously for several minutes, then stopped and stared out of the window. He didn't want to damage his relationship with Robert, but whether he told Robert the truth or not, the young man was going to get hurt. He kept his back to Robert as he spoke. "You remember telling me that you thought Christian was going to assault you on the way to Saelym last year?" he asked quietly.

He didn't hear Robert nod. Robert cleared his throat. "Yes, sir."

"He tried to do the same thing to Allyson, not long after Edward traveled to my world." Chris heard Robert inhale sharply. "Her maid told your mother's maid, and Margaret asked the sergeant, Jack, to do the deed. Christian had also abused the woman Jack married last year, so he had his own personal reasons." Chris stopped speaking, afraid to turn around and face his young friend. He let the silence build.

"How could he?" Robert asked finally, his voice small. Chris turned quickly and joined him now. He put an arm around Robert's shoulders, and the prince sagged against him. "I would have killed him myself had I known," he added in a whisper.

"Which is why Allyson did not tell you or Margaret. She swore her maid to secrecy. God, the poor girl - she needed women around her, to help her through the trauma. But, no, she had to keep it to herself, until Helen and I got here last December. Then she must have wanted to die of fright, until she found out who I was." He squeezed Robert's shoulder, then stepped back. "I am truly sorry - I hoped never to tell you. You have enough to worry about."

Robert didn't trust his voice yet. He'd suspected Christian of such a deed, but hearing the idea confirmed was much worse. He put his head on the desktop. Chris returned to his chair and waited for Robert's emotions to quiet. Robert eventually raised his head.

"I knew there was evil in the world, but this is - I mean, I thought it possible, but to hear it spoken as true - is - is shocking beyond words." He spoke quietly, but Chris sensed there was a lot of turmoil beneath the words. "Did he honestly think he could get away with committing treason on that scale?" He stared past Chris. "Do I even need to ask? He threatened me as well."

Robert stood and moved to the window, staring out. "I do not feel very well," he admitted. "Christian tried to assault Allyson and hurt or frighten me, then someone tried to kill me last year. Now, Father is murdered." He turned to Chris, his eyes pleading. "Am I next? I am legally old enough to be king, but I had not planned on all of this - this - Chris, I do not know what to do!" He turned back to the window, ashamed of his outburst.

Chris wished he had answers. "Robert, I have no idea either. I have already promised Helen that I will do whatever I must to protect you, though we had best hope that there is no sword-fighting." Robert faced him and smiled fleetingly. "I hate to make you feel worse, but Elijah and I asked Helen the same thing about Allyson, about Christian acting in such a way. She said it was Allyson's word against Christian's." He paused and forced himself to look Robert in the eye. The prince had tensed, expecting more, and worse, to come. "Helen asked us which one we thought your father would believe."

Robert took a step back, shocked. "I am sorry, kid." Chris swore mentally. Robert was too young to be dealing with all of this. The prince had too much on his plate as it was. He saw Robert's eyes turn cold and resisted the urge to squirm. He didn't think the young man fell into the category of leader who blamed the messenger.

"Edward wonders why I feel so little loss at Father's death and why I would rather have you for an advisor than th-that -" Robert paused to get his anger under control. "I-I think I need to go outside for a while." He moved past Chris. "Would you come with me to the courtyard?"

"If you want me," Chris said.

"I have few enough friends, Chris, though you still number among them." Robert managed a ragged smile. "Though it will look questionable for us to be seen together." He sighed. "Folk might as well get used to it."

While Chris was talking with Robert, Allyson rapped on Helen's door and smiled at Abigail when the maid opened it. "Is Lady Helen available?" she asked.

Abigail curtseyed. "If you do not mind biding a while as she finishes up in the bath, Your Highness," she replied. The princess nodded and perched on a stool in the sitting room to wait for the duchess.

Helen entered a few moments later, her hair still wet from the bath. She inclined her head, asking Allyson if she wanted some wine.

Allyson rested a hand on Helen's arm. "Nay, Helen. I apologize for interrupting you, but you need to talk about whatever problems you and Chris are having." As Helen began to protest, Allyson went on. "Nay, you have helped Robert and myself enough, especially when I needed someone to talk to about what Christian tried to do to me last year. Now it is my turn to listen."

Helen studied the princess for several heartbeats. "Aye, Highness, you are a woman grown now." She sat on a stool near Allyson and stared at her lap. "What has your mother told you about men?"

Allyson raised an eyebrow. "Nothing very good," she said. "What has Chris done to you, Helen?"

"Chris has not -" Helen began, but her voice broke. Her shoulders began to shake. Nonplussed, Allyson stood and pulled Helen up with her. She put her arms around Helen, holding her tightly until the emotion passed.

"Do I need to punish him for something?" Allyson demanded.

Helen shook her head, wiping her eyes on her sleeve. Taking a linen handkerchief from her pocket, she blew her nose. "Nay, there is no point. 'Tis not his fault that he has a past life. I knew that when I married him."

"Married him?" Allyson asked, shocked. "Y-you really -?"

Helen looked into Allyson's eyes. "He insisted on it, actually. Oh, Allyson, we had a wonderful few weeks before, before - everything fell to pieces. First Elijah's sister and Chris's former betrothed, then the news about -"

"Chris's what! Helen, what are you talking about?"

Now Helen gestured Allyson back to her seat. "'Tis what started our troubles. Michael and I had maintained contact with a Magical practitioner in Chris's world, in case Elijah decided to return home."

"He is not leaving Myrridia, is he?" Allyson interrupted. Helen looked at her, distracted momentarily.

"Nay, not as of now. But the last time we spoke with Angelita, she passed a message over that said Naomi Holmes and Nicole Carpenter wished to come here for a visit, or some such. I asked Chris who they were. Of course, Naomi is Elijah's kin. I admit that Chris was speechless with shock at mention of the other name - he insisted he had no idea why she would want to come here. It turns out that she was hoping to take him back to their world."

Allyson crossed herself. "Surely not, Helen. He-he loves you. He does love you, does he not?" Her eyes narrowed in suspicion.

Helen stared past the princess. "I am no longer sure," she whispered. "Nicole is probably the same age as me, but she looks so much younger, closer to your age. And her body is small and firm, not sagging like my own. Why should he wish to stay with me, when he could be with her?"

Allyson stood as her temper flared. "He professed love for you, for one thing! And he married you!" She took several deep breaths. "God, but men are impossible! Helen, if we did not need them for producing children, why else would we put up with them?" She took a good look at Helen's distraught face and calmed immediately. "Oh, Helen, I am sorry." She went over to Helen and squeezed her arm. "There is naught the matter with your looks. Chris would be a fool to give you up, if he has any kind of deep feeling for you." She attempted a shaky smile. "I should hope for so much with Prince Wilhelm of Esterlyn, if that wedding is even still to take place."

Helen shook her head. "King Wilhelm may insist on another postponement after Reginald's murder. Allyson, Prince Will is a fine young man according to my brother. I know you have never met him, but you could do much worse. Consider the King of Wyckendom's eldest son, Nicholas. I have heard that he is a cold man - I fear there will be war with Wyckendom in a few years, should his father pass on."

Allyson's expression saddened. "Peace never lasts for long, does it? Father was going to make war on Wyckendom this year. With his death, that will not happen, but Robert may have to defend Myrridia against the same kingdom. The only thing that changes is the timing. Mother had the right idea, entering a convent. All I am good for is being a political pawn."

"As opposed to being the heir to the throne?" Helen countered. "You were born first, my dear. As a boy, you would have inherited Myrridia, and all Robert would have had to do was be waiting in the wings for something untold to happen to you. He would have likely been forbidden to marry, unless he left the kingdom to make his own way far from here. Or entered the Church. Younger princes all too often feel useless, and yet kings always insist on having at least two or three sons."

"I wonder how Mother managed to avoid producing more?" Allyson asked. "Perhaps because she lost a number of them before our births?"

"Aye, in part. Also, your mother was at least as strong-willed, and dare I say obstinate, as your father. He would yell and rant, while she would ignore him."

"Father was not the only one she ignored," Allyson put in, then covered her mouth. "I did not intend to say that out loud. Oh, Helen, you must think I am an ungrateful, spoiled -"

Helen laughed softly. "My dear, I think no such thing. I admire and respect your mother, but I have never made the mistake of thinking her a warm, nurturing woman. She was as much a man as your father, and I believe he learned that and was unable to deal with it. It made her that much better a queen. But a mother - I doubt it."

Allyson gave a genuine smile this time. "The only mother I can remember is my nursemaid from early childhood. Once I left the nursery to take up needle craft and other ladylike pursuits, I had no mother. Oh, there was the woman I called 'Mother,' but that was more often 'my lady' or 'Majesty.'" She giggled. "'Tis typical of a noble household."

"Aye," Helen agreed.

So why are you so much more likable?"

"What?" Helen asked, surprised.

"You are a duchess, probably the only ranking duchess in Myrridia, since the Duke of Latham is a widower. Yet you are not aloof like Mother - Helen, you are the truest friend I have, a-a sister."

"Margaret and I are different people, Allyson. I cannot say why she is the way she is. Remember, too, that I was fortunate to see much less of my first husband than she did with your father. If I had to put up with Christian's constant presence, I daresay I would have become quite the shrew."

"But, Helen, in that case, Chris would not have fallen in love with you." Allyson frowned in frustration. "By our Lady, men never make life simple."

"'Tis one of life's fundamental truths, my dear," Helen said, smiling in agreement.

Robert paced in the courtyard for a long time after speaking with Chris. He wanted to talk to his sister about what had happened, to let her know that he knew about it, but also respected her right to privacy. Despite his own experience, he could still hardly credit that the Duke of Saelym, his father's sworn vassal, would have the temerity to attempt such a deed. Physically assault the princess? Robert could think of few things more treasonous. He finally returned to the royal study, slipping into the chamber quietly.

Allyson stood at the window, staring out, but turned and faced him. "Are you busy?" she asked. "I needed to talk to you about something."

Robert tensed immediately at the sight of her. "What?" he asked warily, trying to school his features into neutrality.

"'Tis about Chris and Helen," Allyson replied. "What is the matter?"

"I – 'tis nothing. What about Chris and Helen? Is something wrong with them?"

"Yes," Allyson said, a trace of impatience creeping into her tone. "I fear that Chris will leave her."

Robert didn't hide his surprise. "He will not leave her," he said, not having to feign confidence in the words. "He loves her. He is more apt to try to take her back to his own world."

"What?" Allyson shook her head. "Have you not noticed the strain between them?"

Robert thought back to their arrival. There had been something odd in their behavior. "'Twill pass, I am sure. I am also certain it is not our affair. Or has Lady Helen spoken to you of the matter?"

"Yes," Allyson said. "I sensed a strain between them and went to talk to her. She did not *want* to tell me, but she needed to talk to someone." She stood and frowned. "They cannot both be right!"

"True," Robert agreed. "I suppose all we can do is wait and see, and give them both our support. 'Tis the least we can do for them."

Still troubled, Allyson nodded. She moved toward the room's door, and Robert stepped aside for her. She looked him over from head to toe. "You need sleep."

"I need more than sleep," Robert retorted. "A trip away from Rhennsbury would not hurt," he muttered.

Allyson opened the door and paused on the chamber's threshold. "Is that why you are so upset?" she asked. Robert forced himself to meet her eyes - he'd pushed aside his original emotional turmoil after their conversation.

"That and everything else happening," he replied.

"'Tis the truth." Allyson said with a sigh as she exited. Robert let out a long breath. Maybe he'd broach the other subject with her later. Then again, maybe he wouldn't.

* * *

Naomi felt like a new person after her bath. She was used to taking a shower daily, and she'd just gone two weeks without bathing. She decided she'd had enough of this world - it was time to get back to indoor plumbing. Abigail had asked among the castle servants and obtained a cream-colored linen shift and pale yellow dress for Naomi, and a pair of deerskin boots. Shift and dress fell to mid-calf, but Naomi wasn't nearly as worried about it as Helen and her maid. In her opinion, the slightly shorter skirt would make it easier for her to deal with obnoxious men, by freeing her to kick them where it would do the most damage. When she shared her reasoning with Helen, the duchess mulled it over for a moment, and agreed with her.

Naomi joined Elijah in his chamber for a while, and they did some catching up. She filled him in on how their mother was doing and the latest news about their other siblings. He told her about some of his experiences in Saelym and Rhennsbury, and the lack of prejudice he'd encountered. She followed him down to the Great Hall early in the evening for supper, stopping just inside the chamber to stare. She'd never seen anything like it. The room was huge and already crowded with people. Naomi noted a number of well-dressed people, whom she assumed to be members of the nobility. The servants were scurrying about, trying to stay out of the way of their social betters as they finished preparations for the meal. All of the tablecloths were of royal blue, with gold trim along the edges. She glanced toward the rafters and saw a number of banners. Elijah followed her gaze and pointed to a green and black one with a silver eagle. "Saelym," then he pointed to a gold griffin on royal blue. "That's the royal device. You learn much about heraldry?"

Naomi shushed him instead of replying. She let him lead her into the room, since she had no idea where they were going. They were not dining at the high table, but Elijah promised to introduce her to Robert and Allyson after they finished eating. "I'm sure

Robert wants to meet you; every other male in this place is drooling," he said sourly.

"Yeah, and they would be flirting outright if you had said I was your sister and not your wife!" Naomi retorted. "I don't need your help with men, Elijah. I'm all grown up now in case you hadn't noticed."

"That's precisely the problem," Elijah pointed out.

Naomi disregarded him and smiled at the man sitting across the table as she took her own seat. The man glanced at Elijah, who glowered, then returned the smile, though it was closer to a leer.

Naomi rolled her eyes and said, "Men."

Elijah chuckled.

As promised, Elijah took Naomi to the high table, reminding her on the way to curtsey. Naomi hissed back that she wouldn't forget, and dropped to one knee as though she'd been doing it for years. She ignored her screaming leg muscles. Robert kissed her hand as she straightened. He seemed taken aback at her height as it matched his own. Naomi thought she saw a relieved expression on Allyson's face when Elijah introduced her as his sister and made a mental note to ask him about the princess later.

A churchman was looking at her. She nudged Elijah. "Who's he?" she whispered.

"Bishop Edward Fitzroy. Do you want to meet him?" Elijah asked, his eyes twinkling. "If not, I don't mind snubbing him."

"Sure, I'll meet him."

"Okay, you asked for it."

Edward inclined his head as Elijah made the introduction. He debated holding out his ring but put the idea aside as an unnecessary complication. "Have you come to Myrridia to take your man home?" he asked. Did he dare get his hopes up?

Naomi snorted. "Elijah is my brother, sir, and he is more stubborn than a mule. I wanted to see him one more time."

"Angelita Martinez, the Boston practitioner, aided you then?" Edward raised an eyebrow in surprise, though his hopes sank after hearing her words.

"Yes, though she was none too happy about it," Naomi replied. Elijah took her lightly by the elbow and steered her toward the exit. She glared at him.

Far from intimidated, Elijah said, "You need to be careful how much you tell him. He is not a nice guy."

"You keep saying how awful he is. Why?" Naomi asked.

Elijah looked to the ceiling before answering. "Edward is a micromanaging control freak who encouraged his half-brother, the late king, to make war often, so he, Edward, could do as he pleased in the Church without interference. You know our country's separation of Church and State? There's no such animal here."

Naomi got his point. She just didn't understand why her brother wanted to stay here. A Magical gift wouldn't be enough for her. Women didn't have true equality back home; she had no intention of remaining in a place where things were more uneven.

For the first time in nearly two weeks, Robert wasn't dreading going to bed. He hadn't slept well since his father's murder. He'd been having troubling dreams, usually ending with a vision of his father's bloody, naked body, causing him to wake up in a cold sweat.

Now that two of the people he trusted most had arrived, he didn't fear the visions recurring. He smiled at Paul as his squire turned the bed down. Robert was still sleeping in the same apartment. He didn't think he was ready to move into the king's chambers yet. He wouldn't even consider the change until after the coronation, and wasn't sure he'd be ready then. Thanking Paul he climbed into the bed and pulled the blankets up to his chin. He was asleep by the time his head hit the cushions.

Allyson was thoughtful as she prepared for sleep that evening. She was worried about the strain between Helen and Chris and fearful Chris might leave, despite her brother's assurances otherwise. She was convinced Helen would be devastated should that happen. Allyson had been pleasantly surprised when Chris helped her brother upon his arrival. She had given her brother all the support she could, but she was also affected by their father's murder. And Robert could use the masculine support.

She knew Robert would need as many good men around him as he could get. She wondered if her brother would have the authority to re-form his Council and decided to look through some old law and history books over the next couple of days. She smiled to herself at the thought such a shakeup would cause.

She said a quiet prayer, requesting that Helen and Chris be able to work through their difficulty, then blew out the candle on her bedside table. She, too, fell asleep quickly.

As Chris and Helen prepared to retire, Chris asked her if she wanted him to make other sleeping arrangements. She declined, saying it would cause too many tongues to wag. "But I am not ready to resume relations yet," she concluded, tensing.

"I am not Christian," Chris said, recognizing her reaction as an old habit. "If a lady says 'no,' even if she is your wife, 'no' means 'no.' I wish it were - oh, never mind. We can sleep back-to-back if you prefer."

Helen looked relieved, and then took one of Chris's hands in both of her own. "I am sorry. I-I am just not sure of - myself, you. Thank you for your patience," she said.

"It is no matter, Helen. I love you, and you are worth waiting for," Chris said.

As they settled into the bed, Helen said in a quiet voice, "Hold me, please. I am frightened." Sensing her fear was for more than the two of them, Chris complied, trying to give her some of his own physical strength. He was worried about Allyson and Robert himself.

Nicole had spent a miserable night in the saddle. She couldn't think of any alternatives. She was used to a suburban lifestyle and couldn't remember going camping, even in childhood. Every time she heard something move in the nearby brush, her head turned around and she tried vainly - without her glasses - to see what, if anything was in the trees. An owl began to hoot some time after dark. After the bird quieted, Nicole heard more rustling noises, then a loud squeaking. She grimaced as she imagined the large predatory bird enjoying its meal. She tried to huddle further into her cloak.

Not long after daylight, she stopped her horse near a stream and dismounted. She relieved herself some distance from the water, then washed her face and rubbed a couple of fingers across her teeth. She wanted a hot bath, with scented bath oil and a glass - make that a bottle - of wine, after a full-body massage. She noted with dismay that the day had dawned foggy, and the mist showed no signs of burning off quickly.

After drying her face and hands on her cloak, Nicole took the reins and began leading the horse at a walk. She decided to follow the stream. At least she'd have water to drink. Her stomach growled quietly, and she remembered she hadn't eaten anything since breakfast the day before. She had some emergency food rations in the saddlebag, including dried, salted meat, but she opted to wait a while before eating. She was hoping to catch up with the others even though she had no idea in which direction she, or they, were traveling.

There was a rustling noise to her right. She turned to stare, but she was unable to see beyond the nearest trees. She was thoroughly frustrated since her hearing was now making up for her poor vision, and it only fueled her imagination. She told herself it was a bird, or some other harmless animal. She gulped, took a firmer grip on the reins, and continued walking.

When she imagined the sun was overhead, she stopped. Her mare stopped as well and began placidly cropping grass from the forest's floor. Nicole found the meat and chewed on a piece of it, trying to find a logical way out of her situation. She couldn't think of a better plan, so after her horse had a long drink from the stream, they continued as before.

As night began to fall, the horse stopped walking. She was ready for sleep even if Nicole wasn't. Nicole tried to cajole the mare, but the horse was stubborn. Nicole gave in. She sat on the ground with her back up against a large tree. She searched her pockets for the knife Helen had given her and clutched it in both hands. She didn't expect to sleep that night.

For a while she sat awake, listening to the sounds around her. *I should have stayed home*, she thought, feeling thoroughly miserable. *Coming here was one of your dumber ideas, Nicole. Chris doesn't care about you anymore.* "And why should he?" she whispered. "You dumped him, and he found someone else." When an animal called to its mate, her horse pricked up its ears and looked about. Nicole tightened her grip on her knife. *God, I hope there aren't any snakes around here. Nicole, stop scaring yourself.*

Cecelia Falkes woke suddenly some time before dawn. She held her breath, remaining immobile on her pallet, listening for sounds outside her tent. She'd been living alone in the forest clearing for nearly a month and was grateful for the arrival of spring; she needed fewer fur coverings for warmth. She wanted the relative proximity the clearing had to Rhennsbury and planned to enter the city within the next several days. She had no fears about being alone since she was protected by her powerful Magical abilities.

Calling on those abilities now, Cecelia slipped into trance with the ease of long habit. Her mind shifted forward and out of her body. She left the tent and began searching in the surrounding wood. As she made out Nicole's sleeping form against a tree, Cecelia's body relaxed. She knew what had wakened her - a visitor.

Her eyes snapped open as her mind reunited with her body. Who was the woman and why was she traveling alone? Cecelia rose from the pallet and stretched, catlike. She would find out soon enough.

Despite her fears, Nicole fell asleep. She woke up, startled by the sound of a human voice. It took another couple of seconds for her to realize the voice was female.

"Are you lost?" the voice repeated.

"I - Yes," Nicole stammered, getting tangled in her skirts as she tried to stand. She should have thought to wear jeans instead of a long skirt. She hadn't thought far enough ahead to realize she'd have to ride a horse if she went anywhere in this world. The woman now offered her a steadying hand. "Thanks." Nicole noticed that at least the sun was shining.

"I am Cecelia, and I live nearby. That is a fine-looking mare. Is she yours?" the woman asked.

Nicole looked the woman up and down. She was a couple of inches or so taller than Nicole and had long, heavy blue-black hair, hanging in a braid over her right shoulder, and blue eyes. Her dress was of linen, dyed a deep indigo hue and fashioned into a simple style, and her full-length cloak was black. Her face was tanned from spending many hours outside. Nicole tried to guess her age and failed. "Hello, Cecelia. I'm Nicole. I am - a foreigner. The horse belongs to Chris - the Duke of, oh, drat it, Lattimore." Nicole was aggravated with her poor memory and unmanageable skirts, so she missed the momentary narrowing of Cecelia's eyes.

Cecelia held her anger in check, asking with genuine curiosity, "What is that thing - you wear on your face?"

Nicole was confused until she remembered she still had her eyeglasses on. She removed them and handed them to Cecelia, who looked them over thoroughly. "They are called spectacles, and they help me see. I'm nearsighted - shortsighted."

Cecelia raised an eyebrow, and then she held them before her own eyes, peering through the lenses. "Are you blind, then? They make my eyesight worse." She smiled as she handed them back to Nicole.

"I can see without them, but the vision isn't clear, especially in the distance. Even your face was blurred just now."

"Ah." Cecelia nodded her understanding. "Nicole, would you like to accompany me to my camp? 'Tis not far and I daresay you are hungry." Nicole's stomach growled its agreement. Nicole gave an apologetic smile.

"Please."

Cecelia took the horse's reins to lead the mare. Nicole fell in step just behind her. Cecelia was glad Nicole couldn't see her face. She was trying to figure out how to take advantage of this accidental, but fortuitous, encounter.

It hadn't taken Michael long to find the path Nicole's mare had taken. At first, he'd slowly followed it. He couldn't make the speed he would have liked while in trance, but he was worried about losing the trail. Once the path narrowed to a deer-sized track, he returned to full awareness and had no trouble following the mare's droppings. He traveled steadily the second night, dozing in the saddle occasionally.

He was about an hour behind Nicole when he reached the place where she had spent the same night. Michael was surprised to discover two sets of footprints leading away. He was relieved that Nicole had found aid and decided to follow the trail on foot.

Cecelia tried to keep her voice neutral but interested as she attempted to glean information from Nicole during their walk to her campsite. She was aware of the events in Rhennsbury, but had heard little gossip affecting other parts of the kingdom.

"Are you a friend of the Duke or Duchess of Saelym?" she asked.

Nicole hesitated before answering. The duke had to be Chris, but she couldn't tell this woman she had been engaged to him. "I've known the duke for several years," she said finally. "I suppose you could call us friends."

Cecelia was skeptical of her answer. Friends? "Were you traveling to Rhennsbury?" she inquired with deceptive casualness.

Nicole wondered if the king's death were common knowledge. She figured it would be sooner or later.

"Yes. The duke and duchess are on their way to aid the prince, since his father has been murdered." Nicole was unsure if she had everyone's names straight, so she omitted them.

Cecelia looked thoughtful, but she did not seem surprised by the news of the king's death. "Odd. I had the impression that

Prince Robert despised Christian Lattimore. I imagine loyalty to the crown would outweigh personal considerations."

Nicole shrugged. "It's all new to me. Cecelia, I am traveling to Rhenns - whatever - so that hopefully I can get home sooner. I don't have any burning desire to stay here a minute longer than I have to." Nicole almost succeeded in keeping the bitterness out of her voice.

Cecelia noticed it and raised an eyebrow, then clasped Nicole's hand in feigned sympathy. "A love affair gone sour?" she asked.

Nicole stopped walking. It wasn't strictly true, but close enough. She withdrew from Cecelia's grasp, then buried her face in both hands. Cecelia waited patiently for the emotion to pass.

"I-I apologize, Cecelia. I loved him once, and he loves another now. I have been lost and scared, a-and I guess it's all caught up with me."

"You are safe now, Nicole," Cecelia lied. "We are nearly at our destination."

Nicole stopped in her tracks when they arrived at Cecelia's campsite. It was in a clearing in the woods. There were the remains of a campfire, with a supply of fresh kindling to light a fire later in the day. The tent was made of heavy fabric and looked sturdy as well as nearly weatherproof, despite the evidence of mending. A well-tended mare was tethered a couple of yards from the tent, cropping grass contentedly. A pair of pots and a few wooden spoons were on the ground near the campfire.

Cecelia held the tent flap open for Nicole to enter. Nicole held up her skirts as she crouched slightly to step into it. Cecelia pointed to a footstool, then poured an amber-colored liquid from a clay jar into two pewter cups. She emptied the contents of a linen packet into one of the cups. "'Tis mead, Nicole, with a few of my own herbs. It will relax you a little." Nicole glanced around the tent's interior as she accepted a cup from Cecelia. There was a narrow sleeping pallet up against one cloth side in addition to a pair of footstools. There was also a small table, where Cecelia returned the clay jar.

Nicole took a few deep breaths then began sipping the liquid. It was sweet, but not overly so. Cecelia raised her cup.

"A toast to better days, Nicole," she said, smiling.

"Better days for us all," Nicole agreed, taking a larger swallow of the liquid after holding the cup out to touch Cecelia's. "Thank you, Cecelia. Is this how you make a living - selling herbs and mead and such?"

Cecelia shook her head. "Actually, I am a trained herbalist, or apothecary, and an experienced midwife. I also have a few - Magical talents." Her smile hardened, and her eyes began to glitter. "And you, Nicole, are going to be a tremendous help to me."

"Me?" Nicole wasn't sure she'd heard Cecelia correctly. Her thoughts were getting muddled. She couldn't seem to focus on anything.

"Yes. Rest well, Nicole dear. I will deal with you anon. As soon as I deal with whoever is following you." Cecelia helped Nicole to the pallet, easing her down. In moments, Nicole was asleep. Cecelia went outside to wait.

She didn't have to wait long. Michael entered the clearing and stopped, taking in the tent, the two horses tethered nearby, and the banked fire. Cecelia stood still.

"Good morning, Father. Are you lost, or in need of other assistance?" Her tone was pleasant; she was curious to learn his identity. She had sensed his Magical ability before he reached the clearing.

"Good morning, mistress. I am Father Michael. I am part of a traveling party from Saelym, headed toward Rhennsbury. One member of our party is missing, and I hope you have discovered more than her mount." He gestured toward the horses.

Cecelia raised an eyebrow. "The duke sends his priest to recover his paramour?"

Michael flushed. "Paramour? I do not understand. I am in search of a friend." He winced at the lameness of his reply.

Cecelia laughed. "Is that how his Grace refers to his female conquests these days? The man's boorishness knows no limits.

Aye, Nicole is here. She is sleeping. You are the duchess's cousin?"

"Aye," Michael replied warily.

"Excellent." Cecelia raised her arms dramatically. Michael's horse sensed the gathering of Magical energies and backed away. Michael also felt the change in the air and stepped back, raising one arm in a defensive posture before slipping into trance. His heart pounded as a strong fear surfaced. He knew his Magical limitations.

Cecelia's blue eyes glinted as she smiled. She focused her hatred of Christian Lattimore before her as she lowered her arms. The air before her thickened and darkened. A burst of blue-white lightning shot from the disturbed air and struck Michael. He fell to his knees, his Magical defenses overwhelmed by the strength of her attack. His mind barely had time to appreciate the swiftness with which Cecelia had summoned such a degree of Power; her abilities rivaled or surpassed those of Edward Fitzroy.

He continued to defend himself to the limit of his abilities, but it wasn't long before her powerful mind broke through to his. Instinctively, he withdrew to his own inner core, in a desperate hope she couldn't, or wouldn't, follow him. As his consciousness faded, his last thought was a prayer for Nicole's safety.

Cecelia was disappointed with the ease of her victory. The priest did not have the level of talent his cousin, Helen Lattimore, reputedly did. She was surprised at the strength of his feelings for Nicole, and she hoped Nicole, at the least, was fond of him. This chance encounter was shaping up to be a boon to her plans.

She crouched beside where Michael had fallen. She touched his forehead, then altered his conscious memory of their encounter. She replaced it with an innocuous greeting and fainting spell due to fatigue or hunger. The true events she hid behind a Magical wall strong enough to withstand Michael's subconscious probing, but not so strong as to prevent Edward Fitzroy, or another powerful practitioner, from getting past it. She wanted the Saelym party and other nobility in Rhennsbury to know the degree of Power they were facing.

She reentered the tent and studied Nicole's sleeping form. She debated between planting an unconscious trigger in Nicole's mind to attack Christian Lattimore the next time he smiled at his current ladylove, whoever that was, and making Nicole aware of what Cecelia required, using Michael's life or sanity as the price of failure. She decided on the latter.

Cecelia roused Nicole, who blinked and stared at her surroundings without recognition for a moment. "We need to talk. Come with me," Cecelia ordered. Her false friendliness of earlier was gone.

Bewildered and still drowsy, Nicole followed Cecelia out of the tent. Seeing Michael lying prone on the ground nearby, Nicole ran over and knelt beside him. Her wits returned, and she turned and looked at Cecelia, her eyes narrowing. "What have you done to him?"

Cecelia smiled. "Nothing compared to what I will do if you do not obey me, Nicole." She folded her arms across her chest.

Nicole paled, but her expression was angry. "Oh?"

"I want the Duke of Saelym dead, and you are going to kill him for me, whether you wish to or not."

"Excuse me? Kill him yourself." Nicole was shaking but kept bravado in her voice.

"Nay, I have more important matters to which to attend," Cecelia replied coldly. "The king should have executed the duke in December for his failure to save Prince Robert's life, but the idiot had to do the impossible and save the prince's life instead. He will die this time, and you will be the agent of his death."

"No."

"You prefer the good Father to die a painful death now, or go mad and live out his years? I assure you I can do either one."

"You're despicable, Cecelia. You're asking me to choose between two innocent lives -" Nicole continued to argue, surprised at her audacity.

"Christian Lattimore is no innocent!" Cecelia spat before reining in her emotions. Her body shook with rage.

"Christian - oh, for God's sake!" Nicole knew she was in trouble. Christian was dead, and she couldn't kill Chris. Cecelia didn't realize the duke had been slain, but her hatred for the man was obvious. But, she, Nicole, couldn't be responsible for bringing harm to Father Michael. He'd been the nicest to her since her arrival, with the exception of Naomi and Elijah. Besides, she was becoming increasingly fond of him as he'd helped her improve her riding skills along the journey.

"All right, Cecelia. I will try to kill the duke. You don't exactly leave me a lot of choice in the matter." She mentally apologized to Chris. She figured he would have no trouble defending himself from her. Physically, she was no match for him.

Cecelia was suspicious of Nicole's sudden surrender and changed her mind. "Trying is not enough. Must I do this the hard way?" She walked over to Nicole and slapped her across the face. Unprepared, Nicole recoiled. Cecelia gripped Nicole's shoulders, thrusting her mind forward. Cecelia's progress slowed due to surprise. Nicole had latent Magical ability but seemed unaware of the fact.

Cecelia smiled again, but there was nothing pleasant in the expression. It was inevitable that Helen Lattimore would discover Nicole's talents, and when Helen found them, Christian would be attacked within moments.

Nicole was struggling, appalled by the violation of her privacy. Cecelia forced Nicole into trance, providing a double benefit. Nicole became still, and Cecelia was able to set up her sequence of planned events. Cecelia took her time; she wanted no mistake. She was pleased to note that Nicole had sufficient Magical power to cause a hemorrhage within the duke's brain, which, if it didn't kill him, would render him harmless. The beauty of her plan was in placing the blame squarely on Helen and Nicole. Pleased, she withdrew from Nicole's mind, blocking the memory of their discussion as she exited. Cecelia debated searching through Nicole's memories of her love affair with Christian but decided she really didn't want to know the lurid details.

Looking dazed, Nicole turned to Cecelia. "What has happened to Father Michael?"

"I think he may have passed out from hunger," was Cecelia's smooth reply. "Let us get him to the tent, and then give him some wine."

When Michael regained consciousness, Nicole was seated on a stool next to his pallet. Her face was pinched with pain and worry. Michael started to sit up, moaning as a painful throbbing passed through his skull. He sank back down.

"Father Michael, are you hurt?" Nicole asked, taking one of his hands in hers and rubbing it.

Michael tried to recall what had happened. He remembered a short encounter with a dark-haired woman, but something about it didn't ring true. Realizing he had found Nicole, he shook his head.

"A headache, Lady Nicole. Are you hurt?"

"No, but I've got a blasted migraine," Nicole replied. She released his hand, stood and fetched him a cup of wine. "The woman who owns this tent, Cecelia, said you slid out of the saddle in a faint - hunger or something."

Michael sipped the wine and frowned, causing the pain to intensify. He winced. "I do not think that is so, but we need to get back on the Rhennsbury road and catch up with the others. I will remember what happened at some point. What was it you said you had - your what?"

Nicole smiled. "A migraine. It's a severe kind of headache. I get them sometimes, if I'm tense about something or I eat something I shouldn't. I'm sure it will go away as soon as we meet the others. Are you able to ride?"

Cecelia entered the tent as Nicole finished speaking. "It is late in the afternoon. I recommend that you wait until morning to resume traveling. I can set you on a trail that will lead you to Rhennsbury. I trust you will join me for a light supper?" Her tone was nothing but pleasant, and her smile was genuine.

Nicole and Michael left Cecelia's campsite not long after dawn the next morning. Cecelia helped them prepare the horses and gave them some additional provisions. She led Nicole's mare to a narrow path, then handed the other woman the reins. "God speed to you both," she said with false sincerity.

"Thank you for your hospitality, Cecelia," Nicole said. Michael bowed in the saddle, silent. He had slept little the night before. He was certain his memories had been altered, but he was unable to sense any foreign tampering. The latter thought terrified him.

He and Nicole were silent throughout the morning. Michael was wrapped up in his thoughts, and Nicole's migraine had intensified. They stopped at midday to eat and rest, and to allow the horses to eat and drink.

"Shouldn't we be out of the woods by now?" Nicole asked.

"Aye, unless Cecelia has steered us falsely," Michael replied. "Or we have taken a wrong turn. There has been no one to ask for direction, so I suppose we should stay on this path unless we come to one that is wider or more traveled."

At sunset, Michael asked Nicole if she were ready to stop.

"I think I'll rest better once we're out of these woods. They're creeping me out!" Nicole replied.

A couple of hours later they left the forest. The stars appeared overhead suddenly, and then they could see a crescent moon to their left. Michael stopped his horse and dismounted, then aided Nicole in alighting. She murmured her thanks.

She took several steps to work off some of her stiffness. "Do we just sleep in the open?" she asked, suddenly feeling shy.

"Aye. We can rest together or apart, however you are comfortable."

"I-I'd rather sleep with you - I'm still pretty scared." Nicole hugged herself, feeling a sudden chill breeze and shivering. Michael went over to her and offered her his cloak. She wrapped it around her shoulders, willing her body to warm. "You must think I'm a wimp."

Michael chuckled. "I have no idea what a wimp is."

"Thank you for coming after me," Nicole said quietly. "I feel so stupid, getting lost like that. And you got hurt - I feel like it's my fault!"

Michael tensed at her words. He turned her to face him. "How could my fainting be your fault?" he asked.

"I don't know!" Nicole wailed. "I wish I could get rid of this blasted headache - then I could think straight!" She pulled away from him. "I want a Kleenex."

Michael looked puzzled. "A clean ex? Ex what?"

Nicole didn't know whether to laugh or cry. She took a couple of deep breaths instead. "A Kleenex is a dispos - small piece of - cloth you blow your nose into."

"I think many ladies carry linen ones. We can ask Helen later. Speaking of Helen, I think she can help you with your headache. I apologize, Nicole. I would give you some relief myself, but my head is out of sorts, too."

"Well, you're patient to put up with my whining. Let's try to get some sleep, so maybe things will look better in the morning." She eased to the ground and Michael joined her. He was about to turn his back, to preserve her privacy, but she shifted closer to him. "Will you hold me?" she whispered.

Michael was unprepared for the heat that spread throughout his body at her words. His instinctive response was denial, but he realized she was more frightened than she admitted. He cautiously put his arms around her, and Nicole moved her body up against his, her face resting on his shoulder.

"Thank you," she murmured, unaware of his discomfort. She'd forgotten he was a priest.

Michael felt his face flush as he remembered his vows. He'd never experienced this degree of intimacy with a woman, and he had no idea what to do when his loins responded to Nicole's nearness. He was spared total humiliation by the fact that Nicole was already asleep. It was some time before Michael drifted into sleep, unsure if he were grateful for the distraction from his other problems.

Chapter Five

Edward Fitzroy might be considered by many to be the most powerful man in Myrridia, but Anselm DeLacey, the Duke of Latham, was the most respected. He was in his fifties, with a full head of white hair and steely gray eyes. His eyes lost their glint if he was in a good mood. He seldom achieved one if the subjects of Rhennsbury and Reginald Claybourne came up.

He had been the Duke of Latham since his uncle's untimely death in battle during one of Reginald's father's campaigns, a failed invasion of a neighboring kingdom, Esterlyn. Anselm's uncle, cousins and father were all slain in the decisive battle that put a temporary end to Cedric Claybourne's plans of conquest. He had been ten years old at the time, too young to be conscripted into the army, or he might have been another casualty.

A neighboring nobleman had administered the duchy, nearly running it into the ground, until Anselm reached the legal age of sixteen. The man had taxed the duchy's inhabitants to near starvation in an effort to swell his own estate's coffers. When

Anselm had protested this fact to Cedric at the time of his legal swearing in, he had received little sympathy and no recompense. He had agreed to serve on the Royal Council a few years later, but only in an attempt to change the way things were being done. He didn't have much success. When Reginald inherited the throne, Anselm had had enough of the Claybournes, and refused to continue to serve.

Since then, he spent most of his time within Latham's borders, traveling on occasion for a wedding or a christening, but he had not set foot inside Rhennsbury's walls. After he reached the age of fifty, he spoke honestly to Latham's noble visitors, and he'd heard through gossip that Reginald often accused him of speaking treason. However, he never followed through on his threats of execution, concerned that his own loss of popularity would be permanent.

Now, for the first time in over twenty years, Latham's standard, a silver fox on a scarlet background, was sighted approaching the capital. The day was cloudy and dry, with a warm breeze. Anselm had never met Robert or Allyson Claybourne, though he had admired their mother, Margaret. He had heard much about the prince and princess from visitors, and he'd been impressed with what he'd heard.

Anselm tried to keep his features impassive as his party rode through the city's streets, but he was dismayed at the degree of deterioration. Some buildings were on the verge of collapse, and he was certain that several of the alleyways leading off the main street led to gambling dens, houses of prostitution, and God knew what other manner of illegal establishments. He sighed behind his neatly trimmed mustache and beard. If he were as impressed with his new king as he hoped to be, he'd wind up staying to help clean up the city.

His son rode up next to him. "Father, 'tis the most disgraceful sight I have ever seen," he commented.

"Aye, Lucas. Rhennsbury did not look like this when I was last here, but it has been many years. Let us be optimistic about her future." Anselm nodded and waved to several citizens; some appeared old enough to remember him.

When the herald announced the arrival of the Duke of Latham and his party, Robert was in his study, meeting with Chris, Edward and James McDermott. James had stopped in his tracks at seeing Chris in the study, talking quietly with Robert.

"What is this jackass doing in here, Your Highness?" James exclaimed. Ordinarily he kept his emotions in check, but after the two men's last encounter at Christmastime, he had as much of the Duke of Saelym as he could take. "You do not intend to accept his counsel, Sire?" he asked in a quieter tone.

"Have a seat, James," Robert replied evenly. "You deserve an explanation." Realizing that Robert was about to tell James the truth about Chris's identity, Chris and Edward exchanged questioning looks. Ever since Chris had decided to remain in Myrridia, the relationship between him and Edward had been strained, but both men felt uneasy now. Chris stood and offered his chair to James, who took it reluctantly.

"I do not understand, Your Highness," he said.

"You will in a moment," Robert assured him. "This man is not Christian Lattimore." James stood and was about to say something when Robert waved him back into the chair. Chris raised an eyebrow in Robert's direction, but Robert just nodded and motioned for Chris to take over.

Chris took a deep breath and crossed his fingers behind his back. "My name is Christopher McCabe, sir, and I am a doctor from a - a very far away place. Edward asked me to stand in for Christian because of the unfortunate resemblance I have to the man, and to prevent him from being murdered last Christmas. Edward had gotten wind of the plan, though he got a few of the details wrong."

At this, Edward scowled. Robert's expression remained steady.

Chris continued, "Being ignorant of what kind of man the duke was, I agreed to stand in for him. But, someone else murdered Christian months before the Christmas attack." Chris paused for breath, ignoring Edward's flashing eyes. James was staring at Chris, openmouthed.

"Can I tell you something I have wanted to say to you since that horrible Council meeting last December?" Chris went on.

James closed his mouth, then nodded, unsure.

"I was appalled at what Reginald was planning. I-I wanted no part of it! Voting for war was the worst thing I have ever had to do." He glanced at Edward, who glowered. "Please say nothing, Edward, you know how I feel about it."

James stood and walked over to Chris, then circled him, looking him over completely. Robert had sat back in his chair to let Chris do the talking, but he smiled when Chris finished.

"By the saints, I have a hard time crediting this story," James finally said. "But there is something about you that is different."

"Try looking at his teeth," Robert offered with a trace of laughter in his voice. Edward shot him a look but had to agree.

Rolling his eyes, Chris bared his teeth for James, who grinned. "Ah, yes. You cannot be Lattimore. Well, then, a pleasure to meet you, your Grace. I assume you are staying here in Myrridia, taking over for the late, but far from lamented, duke?" James asked him.

"Yes, despite good advice to the contrary," Edward put in.

Chris retorted, "I have my reasons, Edward, most of which are none of your concern."

"As a churchman, they are my concern," Edward insisted.

"Maybe, but, and correct me if I'm wrong, gentlemen," Chris said to Robert and James, "I do not believe that Saelym is part of Belgravia's diocese."

"Fortunately for you," Edward muttered.

James held out his right hand to Chris. "I look forward to working *with* you in the future.

"Likewise, sir."

Robert now spoke after the herald announced the arrival of the Latham party. "I need some advice, sirs. I-I have never met the Duke of Latham. Do you think I should greet him in the courtyard, or make him come to me?" He was confused, and a little alarmed, at meeting the man.

James was the first to reply. "I suggest you greet him in the courtyard, Sire. One, it would be courtesy, and, two, it would show that you respect his age and reputation. Three, your father would have made him come to the study." The last was spoken with a smile, which Robert returned.

"The courtyard it is. Thank you."

Helen was with Robert in the courtyard when the Latham party arrived. She suggested to Chris that he wait until later to meet the duke, reminding him that Anselm would not be predisposed to think highly of him. Chris had told her, chuckling, that Robert had already informed James McDermott that he was not Lattimore, but that he could wait. Helen was thoughtful; she hoped that Robert knew what he was doing. She promised Chris that she would see that he met Anselm later that day, in the castle's library.

Anselm allowed a groom to help him dismount. He waited for his son, daughter, their spouses and children to join him, then went to greet his new king. He bowed respectfully, giving Helen a genuine smile and kissing her hand. "A pleasure to see you again, your Grace. It has been too long."

Helen curtseyed. "I agree. May I present you to Prince Robert Claybourne, your Grace?"

Anselm scrutinized Robert, making no attempt to disguise the fact that he was doing it. When he finished, he smiled again. "A definite pleasure, Your Highness. I am optimistic about Myrridia's future. I apologize for my rudeness, but I am an old man, and I do not cater to popular opinion any longer."

He felt tense while the duke looked him over, wondering how much of his father showed on the outside. He still wasn't sure how much of what he had heard about this man was truth and how much legend. Hearing Anselm's words, Robert relaxed slightly, "I am pleased to meet you, your Grace, and welcome back to Rhennsbury. I look forward to receiving your counsel in the future. I think I will need it," he concluded in a quiet voice.

"I am at your service, Sire." Anselm introduced his family. After the formalities were complete, he turned to Helen once more and asked, "I assume your esteemed husband is here, my lady?"

"Actually, Anselm, I need to talk to you about him. If you have some time available after you have refreshed yourself?" Helen smiled but offered no other explanation.

Anselm was curious, but he remembered enjoying verbally sparring with her at their one previous meeting, at his daughter's wedding five years ago. "After supper, Helen. The choice of venue is yours."

"I was thinking of the library."

"An odd choice, but if Christian can find it, I will see you both there." His eyes twinkled. Helen smiled more broadly this time. Anselm turned back to Robert. "I will see you at supper, Your Highness," he said, bowing again.

One man watched the party from Latham as it passed by him on Rhennsbury's main street. He was standing near a jewelry vendor's stall, out of the way of foot and horse traffic. He stared after the group, looking thoughtful. He nodded to the jeweler out of courtesy, and began walking briskly in the opposite direction from that of the Latham party. He retrieved his horse from the run-down inn where he and the animal had spent the previous night, both sleeping in the stables. Considering the lack of wealth and social position of many of the inn's patrons, he felt he was better off. There had been fleas in the hay, but he'd slept in worse places. The man rode out through the city gates as another noble party arrived. He took advantage of the temporary chaos to pass by unchallenged. Turning off the road after a few miles, and following a little-used dirt path leading south of the city, he gave the horse its lead. He was in no hurry to reach his destination as his news was far from urgent.

Three hours later, horse and rider approached a clearing in the forest. The small campsite had been set up several weeks prior. A much-mended tent was raised a few yards from the fire pit, and a dark-haired woman now came out of the tent, having heard, and sensed, their approach. She wore a smile, but it was not intended for the rider. He dismounted.

"You have news, brother?" Cecelia asked.

"Aye. The Duke of Latham has arrived in Rhennsbury this morning, and the Duke and Duchess of Saelym arrived two days ago. As I left Rhennsbury, the Duke of Castrella was entering the city."

Cecelia nodded. "I do not care about Castrella, yet. I was uncertain if Latham would come. Perhaps Robert Claybourne is not the man his father was. That could affect our plans." Her voice was controlled, but her brother, Sebastian, could sense the turmoil of emotions under the words. The wrongs committed by Reginald Claybourne and Christian Lattimore went back many years.

Sebastian's eyes darkened. "Prince Robert is nothing like his father, Cecelia. I told you that last year." He thought back to the attempt on Robert's life at Christmas, remembering that Gerard, the man who'd shot the crossbow bolt at the prince, had planned to shoot the Duke of Saelym. He and Cecelia got into a serious argument after the fact. He'd accused her of changing their plan, and she'd admitted it, pretending to repent and agree with her brother.

"So you say," she allowed, crossing her arms. Her attitude was one of disbelief.

Sebastian fought his temper. "Do you still plan to slay him, then?" he asked. "Prince Robert has no major Magical ability, and his swordsmanship is lacking. Lattimore despaired of making a competent swordsman out of him."

"That could have changed since last year," Cecelia countered. "'Tis of little account at the moment." Her smile was smug. "We will not assume anything. I am pleased to tell you that I may have solved our difficulties with Lattimore."

When Sebastian registered surprise, she told him of her encounter with Nicole and Michael. "I sent them toward Rhennsbury on a less than direct path," she concluded with a smile.

Sebastian nodded during the recitation but snorted after Cecelia finished. "'Tis only one thing I find hard to credit - Lattimore in love with a woman. Otherwise, 'twould seem to be a fortuitous meeting, though you need to be careful."

"I agree with what you say about Lattimore. For certes, his feelings are a temporary lust, but all I care about is exploiting the situation. Have no fear, I will take care of myself," she assured him.

"We may have an alternate plan as well," Sebastian said. "I have put the rumor mill to good use. In the taverns, I have said to any that will listen that Lattimore and the king had been on bad terms, and perhaps it was the duke who ordered his death. The duke left quickly enough for Saelym after Christmas, which was much remarked upon as being unprecedented. My words have not fallen on deaf ears, and I believe the city's lord mayor may be seeking audience with Prince Robert in the next day or so. The prince was never a friend to the man, so he may not hesitate at having him executed."

"Excellent work, but be careful. I trust you do not repeat the same rumors at the same establishments?"

"Nay, sister. If I return to a particular tavern, I sit and observe, speaking only if I am spoken to," Sebastian said.

"Good. Keep it up. I am looking forward to meeting with Robert Claybourne once and for all. I do have a message for you to deliver to him." Cecelia reached into her threadbare purse and handed Sebastian a small piece of parchment. It had no signature but it was clearly a death threat. "I will sign the next one with our family's crest. I want no doubts in the end as to who rid Myrridia of the cursed Claybournes."

Sebastian stared at the paper for a moment before studying his sister. Her expression was defiant. "Do you even listen when I tell you the prince is different?" he asked.

Cecelia shrugged. "I want him on the defensive, when I accuse him of the crimes his father and Lattimore committed." Lowering her eyes, she continued, "I swear, brother, that I shall not kill him if he will return the earldom to us."

Sebastian possessed no Magical gifts with which to sense her lie. He remounted slowly, following Cecelia's command to return to Rhennsbury and observe events. As Cecelia watched her brother's departure, her expression was thoughtful. She feared his constant, lengthy absences allowed him too much time to think on his own. He should never have admonished her in regard to Nicole and Michael. She had also hoped to sway him in regard to Robert Claybourne. She recalled his time serving in Rhennsbury Castle as a man-at-arms. He now insisted the prince had shown him nothing but respect, and it was a matter of honor to her brother to spare the young man's life.

When they'd argued violently after the Christmas attack, she'd felt no threat. Sebastian couldn't hurt her. Cecelia smiled. Men always thought the sword or some other weapon would solve their problems. Magic was more dependable. She and Sebastian no longer shared the same ultimate goal, and she was sure he would rebel if he knew of her other plans. She would need to use firmer measures to keep Sebastian in line.

Michael and Nicole resumed traveling not long after daybreak. Both had slept fitfully, bothered by dreams that disappeared when they woke. Michael was relieved to note that his physical reaction to Nicole had dissipated during the night. After they'd been riding for about an hour, they could see Rhennsbury's walls in the distance. Nicole stopped her horse for a few minutes, to take in the view. The closest she'd seen to a medieval town was a reenactment program on the History Channel.

It was midmorning by the time they arrived at Rhennsbury's southern gate. They'd seen no sign of the Saelym party. Michael pointed out the castle beyond the city. Nicole told him she hoped to get a better look at it later. He promised to give her a tour of the city and castle, once they both felt better.

They were detained at the gate as the sentries were being cautious. They knew to expect many more strangers in the city than usual, but they were taking their time letting common folk through. Nicole bit her lip in frustration. Michael was getting angry. There was a shout from inside the city.

"Father Michael Pembroke?"

Michael strained to see who had spoken his name. "Ambrose?"

Father Ambrose, Edward Fitzroy's secretary, joined Michael and Nicole. He got into a heated discussion with the guards. After he threatened to return with the bishop, the guards allowed Nicole and Michael into the city.

Michael dismounted and the two men embraced briefly. Michael introduced Nicole as a guest in Saelym. Ambrose bowed slightly to her.

"Why did you come to Rhennsbury, Michael? Edward will not be pleased to see you," Ambrose said.

"Aye, but I did not come here to see his Excellency. I am here for the coronation. Lady Nicole got lost on the road, and I was the best man to be spared for the search." Michael took the reins of both horses, walking with Ambrose along Rhennsbury's crowded main street. Nicole half-listened to their conversation, taking in the sights, sounds and smells. She thought the city stank. She tried not to stare as people made their way past them going in the opposite direction, but she wanted to see the clothing and headgear. The children were dressed in clothing similar to the adults. She almost fell out of her saddle when an angry voice spoke just behind her.

"Father, do I employ you to consort with heretics? And what are *you* doing in Rhennsbury?" Ambrose and Michael stopped walking and tensed as they recognized Edward's voice. Ambrose recovered first.

"Excellency, they were detained at the gate, and I happened to be there. I was returning to your residence." Ambrose stopped speaking before he started to stammer.

"I was attempting to rejoin the party from Saelym, Excellency," Michael began.

"They arrived two days ago," Edward pointed out. "Why were you not with them?"

"That is my fault, sir," Nicole spoke up. "I got lost and -"

"And who are you?" Edward kept his voice down with an effort, recognizing her accent.

"Nicole Carpenter, an old friend of Chris -"

"Good God, woman, be careful!" Edward interrupted. "Refer to him by his title in public. Are you ignorant?"

The pain in Nicole's head flared, and she lost her temper. "Pardon me, Exemplary," she retorted, pretty certain she didn't have the correct title and not caring. "Do we have your divine permission to continue onward to the castle?"

Ambrose and Michael winced. Edward paled with anger. Calming himself, he faced the two priests. He appraised Michael. Frowning, he exclaimed, "What has happened?" His tone turned to concern.

"Excellency?" Michael was taken aback by his superior's change in manner.

Edward held out his right hand. Michael backed away a step. "I am not going to hurt you, Father. But I believe your mind has been tampered with."

"I would far rather discuss it with Helen, sir," Michael pleaded, ready to faint with fright.

"No. Come with me. You, as well," he said to Nicole. Ambrose gave Michael an apologetic look.

The foursome soon arrived at Edward's residence. Edward directed Michael and Nicole to his private study and told them to relax, then left.

Nicole stared out the window, not seeing the flowers blooming in the garden. "Are you okay?" she asked Michael. She wasn't happy with their detour, preferring, like Michael, to rejoin the others.

"Only if 'O-K' means scared to death," he replied. He paced until Edward returned, with Ambrose at his heels.

"Sit down, Father." Edward turned to Nicole. "You may stay, if you promise not to interrupt."

Nicole nodded, and stood next to Michael. She took his left hand in both of hers, trying to give him a reassuring smile. "I won't let him hurt you," she promised.

Michael gave her a slight smile. "Thank you, but you cannot stop him." He turned to Edward, holding out his right hand and taking a deep, steadying breath. He focused his gaze on the crucifix hanging on the opposite wall and eased himself into trance.

As Michael's breathing became more rhythmic, Edward began to relax his own mind. He had grasped Michael's hand in one of his and now gently touched Michael's forehead with the fingers of his free hand. Michael shuddered once, but he was now in a deeper trance.

Edward eased his mind into Michael's and immediately detected the wall blocking the young priest's memories. He tried to bring it down himself, but failed. Opening his eyes, he nodded to Ambrose. Ambrose joined him, laying his hands on Edward's shoulders. He consciously relaxed, letting his own energy flow into Edward.

When Edward recognized the Magical signature, he resigned himself to failure. Unlike his attempts with the assassin's mind the previous Christmas though, this time the wall yielded to the two men's combined strength. The success did little to ease Edward's mind.

Edward restored Michael's memory of Cecelia's attack, though he dulled its intensity. The amount of Power the woman had at her command, and the lack of effort she'd put into the attack, surprised him. After he and Ambrose returned to normal consciousness, Edward roused Michael. As Michael struggled to assimilate his new memories, Edward looked at Nicole thoughtfully.

"Who is this woman?" he asked her.

"Woman? You mean Cecelia? The woman in the woods? What's she done to Michael?" Nicole asked.

Edward ignored her questions. "Yes, Cecelia."

Nicole was about to answer when Michael gave a cry and buried his face in his hands. After several moments he looked up and met Edward's gaze. "What has she done?" he whispered.

"The message was for me. You were a pawn. I suspect she used you to demonstrate her abilities and that the same has been done with your companion." Nicole and Michael looked at each other. Nicole gulped. "Her message is clear. She is a formidable talent and will stop at nothing. She ordered Robert's death at Christmas. I have to wonder if she is somehow involved in Reginald's death, though as yet there is no evidence of Magic in it. Mistress Carpenter, I suggest that you seek out Helen Lattimore at once. I have not the energy to discover what this woman may have done to you. Princess Allyson can assist her if necessary."

Edward forced himself to see Michael and Nicole out. Michael was unsteady on his feet, and Nicole assisted him. Two of Edward's grooms helped the pair mount, and Edward directed one of them to escort Michael and Nicole to the castle. He handed his ring to the man. "Use this to get them through the gate."

The man bowed. "Yes, Excellency."

Nicole was exhausted by the time she and Michael reached Rhennsbury Castle. She was worried sick about Michael - he'd not spoken a word during the short journey - and her headache had worsened. She slid out of her saddle and hurried over to help Michael down. Nicole informed a castle servant that they were with the Saelym party. The maid curtseyed and headed into the castle.

Nicole supported Michael, talking to him quietly. She wasn't sure if he could understand her, but she hoped her chattering would distract him. It felt like an hour, but before long, Chris, Helen and Elijah arrived in the courtyard. Elijah gently picked up Michael, carrying him like a baby.

Helen was upset at the sight of her cousin but managed to sense Nicole's pain as well. "Chris, help her to our chambers. I will join you as soon as Michael is comfortable."

Chris nodded and put an arm around Nicole's shoulders. He led her up the stairs and into the castle. Nicole didn't even notice his touch. When they arrived at the appointed room, Abigail dropped her embroidery at their entrance and led Nicole to a chair. Chris asked the maid to keep an eye on Nicole while he went to request bath water. Abigail inclined her head as she removed Nicole's cloak.

After requesting bath water from the kitchen, Chris knocked on Elijah's door. Elijah was settling Michael into the bed as Chris entered. Michael was protesting feebly that he was fine, just tired. Helen was skeptical.

Exasperated, Michael said, "Helen, you have to help Nicole. Her memories have been altered, and Edward -"

"What about you, Michael?" Helen interrupted.

Michael shook his head. "It can wait. A strong practitioner named Cecelia attacked me. Edward had the decency to mute the memory somewhat. This woman had put up a wall that I could not detect. I knew something was wrong, but I was unable to discover what. I think Nicole's headache will worsen until you help her. Please, cousin."

Chris absently listened to Michael as his physician's eye took in the priest's overall condition. The younger man looked fatigued, and Chris couldn't recall seeing the lines of worry around his mouth and eyes before. "Rest and the quiet company of his friends is what Michael needs, Helen." Chris's tone was hesitant; as a doctor he was on firm ground, but right now he didn't want to come across as critical of her.

"He is family, Christopher," Helen began, turning her frustration on him. She shook with anger.

Chris went to her and put his arms around her, welcome or not. She tensed at first, but finally relaxed against his touch. Chris stroked her hair, quietly intoning, "Yes, family. I am worried about him, too. I-I feel like he is my cousin. I want to help him - I admit I have no idea what all these Magical attacks and altered memories are about, but they scare the daylights out of me."

Helen turned to face him and didn't pull away. "'Tis very serious. I know he will recover in body. You are right to be scared. I would never, as a practitioner, attack someone with

Magic. I would defend myself if I had to, or the people I care about. Nor would I ever alter a person's memories unless it is by his or her request. So far, I have had no one ask. Thank you for your concern about Michael. He is important to me." Helen's voice had softened. Chris lifted her chin and kissed her lightly.

"Which makes him important to me," Chris murmured after their lips parted.

Helen turned to Elijah. "You will stay with him?"

"Of course. If one of you doesn't mind, send Naomi in here. She can help, and I can order her about." Elijah smiled, though his eyes remained serious.

"Done."

"Edward said you may want Princess Allyson's assistance with Nicole, Helen," Michael put in. "Take care of her, please. She has no idea what has been done to her." Michael lay back, exhausted. He motioned to Elijah. "I am in capable hands."

Helen nodded. To Chris, she said, "See if you can locate a page and send a message requesting Allyson's presence. Then join me next door."

A few minutes later, Helen aided Abigail in stripping off Nicole's garments. Abigail assisted Nicole into the round wooden tub. Nicole sighed as she relaxed a little in the hot, lavender-scented water. Abigail offered to wash her hair. After a moment's thought, Nicole accepted. Like Naomi, she was used to taking daily showers. She now couldn't remember how many days she'd been in Myrridia; she had to be filthy.

Helen waited while Nicole bathed. She observed the other woman's pallor and the dark circles around her eyes. Helen also noticed the pain reflected in Nicole's eyes and pursed lips. She went into an adjoining room, returning with a decanter and a linen packet. She poured some of the wine into a goblet, then measured out a little of the packet's contents. She handed the goblet to Nicole, which Nicole took reluctantly.

"What is in this besides the wine?" Nicole asked. "I mean - I'm sorry - but Cecelia put something in her mead that made me pass out."

Helen frowned. "I have added naught but feverfew to perhaps ease some of your headache. I assure you I would not put anything in there to cause you harm, regardless of our personal differences." She paused. "Though Michael is convinced your pain is Magical in origin."

Nicole met her gaze and nodded. "Lady Helen, I believe you." She stifled a sigh. "I wish all of my headaches were magical." She managed a wan smile before taking a few sips of the wine.

Helen helped Nicole stand when she had finished soaking in the tub. Nicole's knees almost gave out, but Helen kept her steady. Abigail wrapped a large towel around her. Helen got a spare shift and assisted Nicole in donning it. There was a quiet knock at the door.

Abigail opened it.

Chris stood outside the doorway, looking sheepish. "Is it safe to come in?"

Abigail pulled the door wide. "Aye, my lord."

"Were you successful?" Helen asked.

"Yes. We should get a reply before too long."

Helen led Nicole to the bed. Nicole started to protest, but Helen was insistent. "You will be exhausted by the time we are finished," Helen assured her.

"What are you planning to do?" Nicole asked, starting to feel like a cornered animal. She remembered Michael's fear of Edward's help, and just watching the interaction had scared her.

"I need to see if your mind has been tampered with. If it has been, and I am able to, I will restore your memory." Helen kept her tone calm.

"Will it hurt?" Nicole whispered.

"It might," Helen said, with a look of sincere apology.

There was another rap at the door. Chris answered it, bowed, and led Allyson in.

She was blunt. "What do you need, Helen?"

"A possible Magical tampering, my dear. Are you able to assist?"

"I suppose - of course. Whatever you need." Allyson's tone sounded more confident than she felt.

"Good." Helen took the remark as it was spoken and returned her attention to Nicole. "Have you ever been in trance?"

"No."

Helen debated forming a protective Circle for her Working and decided to take no chances. She asked Abigail to keep visitors away as the servant collected candles and Helen's altar cloth. Once the makeshift altar was set up on a trunk, Abigail stood by the room's door.

"What about me?" Chris asked.

Helen told him to sit behind Nicole. At his hesitation, she added dryly, "Believe me, I would as soon have another, but the fewer folk involved in this, the better."

Chris settled himself behind Nicole, trying to shift her as little as possible. Nicole tensed, but her discomfort was due to anticipation of what was about to happen rather than Chris's proximity. His arms around her did little to make her feel comfortable or safe.

Allyson began walking in a clockwise circle. Helen stood in front of the altar, facing toward the east, and began a ritual invocation to the four Archangelic guardians. "Before me Raphael, guide us to answers, Behind me Gabriel, travel with us to gain knowledge, To my right Michael, protect us from harm, To my left Uriel, teach us the way."

Allyson joined her as she finished walking. "Protected by those on High, we beseech thee, O Lord God, in this endeavor. For Thine is the Kingdom, and the Power, and the Glory, forever and ever. Amen." Chris knew it wouldn't help anyone Magically, but he added his own "amen" to that of the women.

By the time the glowing Circle was complete, Nicole found herself relaxing. She felt safe all of a sudden. Allyson called forth a small sphere of golden light and left it hovering in the air near the bed.

Helen moved from the altar to the bed. Quietly, she said, "Nicole, I want you to focus on the glowing sphere. You can see it and naught else. You can feel your eyes getting heavy, but you will still see the light when you close your eyes. How do you feel?"

"Tired." Nicole closed her eyes obediently and took several deep breaths. She felt herself relax slightly and was surprised to note that she could still "see" the light.

"Continue to relax, seeing only the light." Helen took one of Nicole's hands in hers. She caught Allyson's gaze and nodded for the princess to join her. Allyson put her hands on Helen's shoulders and began to put herself into trance. When Helen was satisfied that both women were sufficiently relaxed, she gave Chris a small smile then began her own mental focusing.

When she was ready, Helen probed gently at Nicole's mind. To her surprise, she met resistance. Nicole had abilities! Helen tensed and pulled back, noting a momentary tightening of Allyson's hands on her. When she had relaxed again, she made another attempt, with a little more force. Now Nicole tensed, but Helen was past the barrier.

She sensed the Magical wall that had been erected, but she did not recognize the spell with which it had been done. She tried a simple counter-spell to no effect. She gathered energy from Allyson and used a stronger counter. The wall flickered but held firm. Nicole squirmed and Chris had to tighten his arms around her. He wasn't sure if he heard her whimper.

Helen mentally prepared for a third and final try. Apologizing to Nicole and Allyson, she used the strongest spell she could legally perform and succeeded in bringing down the wall. Nicole cried out, and then fainted. Chris stared at Helen with growing alarm, but she could no longer see him.

Helen was frantically trying to back out of Nicole's mind. She was aghast at what she had discovered behind the wall and knew she had to return to herself as soon as possible. Chris was in danger, and she feared she was too late.

Allyson had let go of Helen and begun a spell to aid Chris as Helen broke off contact. Helen's eyes flew open, expecting to find

Chris in an unconscious heap. He was staring at her and Allyson, his alarm far from abated.

"Is she -?" Chris began.

"Are you -?" Helen started. "What has happened, then?" She took several deep breaths, as Chris reassured himself that Nicole's pulse was strong and steady. Allyson stopped her summoning and stared at Chris, surprised but relieved.

Once Helen regained control, she helped Chris settle Nicole on the bed. Nicole was starting to regain consciousness. She moaned, then put a hand to her head.

"What the -? My headache, it's - oh, my God - Chris!" Her voice had risen to a scream, when she realized Chris was looking at her with calm concern.

He glanced at Helen. "I give up. What should have happened to me? I apologize, but I cannot please any -" He stopped, the gravity of the situation overcoming his lame attempt at humor.

"The woman who caused all this, Cecelia, placed a trigger for Nicole - who has Magical gifts, by the way - to kill you with a brain hemorrhage. My restoring her memory was the catalyst. Are you certain you are fine?"

Chris had paled. "I-I think so. If my brain had started to bleed, I would be out by now, surely. So what went wrong?"

Nicole had recovered her wits by this time. "I have a theory. Cecelia wants 'Christian' dead, not you. She doesn't know about you. I'm sorry, Helen, but how long has your husband been dead?"

Helen half-smiled, "My former husband has been dead for almost a year, so I doubt he noticed this last attack overmuch."

"It would not have slowed him at all even if he were alive, Helen. He never used his brain." Allyson's voice held an undertone of bitterness. She had not recovered completely from Christian's attempted assault on her over a year ago.

"You make a good point, my dear." Helen held out an arm and Allyson joined her, the two women embracing. "Let us disperse the Circle, so we can rest. I will send for your maid since you can hardly be seen alone in Chris's company." Chris grimaced but had to agree. Nicole gave them all a questioning look but didn't ask.

"You will want your bed back, Lady Helen," she did say, sitting up.

Helen pushed her down. To Chris's astonishment she said, "We can share it for a while. You need rest, too. Then we need to discuss your Talents."

"My what?"

Chapter Six

Chris didn't leave the chamber until he was certain that Helen was sleeping comfortably with Nicole. Abigail assured him that she would see that the two women were not disturbed. Before falling asleep, Helen had reminded him of their appointment with Anselm DeLacey after supper.

Chris decided to attend supper for Robert's sake. Robert was grateful. He'd been disturbed when he received word at the last moment that his sister was unwell. He didn't feel any better with Helen's sudden absence. Chris was able to tell the prince what had transpired. Robert expressed concern for Father Michael and Nicole, and Chris promised to pass along his good wishes.

Robert pointed out the Duke of Latham to Chris, though Chris would have recognized the man anyway. DeLacey glanced in their direction several times during the meal, raising his left eyebrow quizzically. He raised a goblet to salute Robert when the young man stood to depart.

Chris waited for Anselm just outside the doors to the Great Hall. Once the Duke of Latham joined him, the two men walked to the library in silence. Anselm walked without aid, but Chris noticed he favored his left leg slightly. Chris got a fire blazing as Anselm settled into the room's most comfortable chair. He wondered if Lattimore would have said something about it. His predecessor wouldn't have deigned to meet with the man and have a civilized conversation.

Anselm used the time Chris was occupied to study the younger man. He was surprised to see the Duke of Saelym light his own fire rather than summon a servant. He was still amazed at the degree of closeness he'd observed between Lattimore and Robert Claybourne during the meal. The man didn't seem to match his reputation. Anselm was fairly certain he'd seen signs of intelligence and humor, rather than debauchery.

When the fire satisfied Chris, he straightened and joined DeLacey, pouring wine into two goblets. It gave him a chance to look over the older man. Anselm reminded Chris of one of his medical school professors. That man had often interjected his opinions into his lectures, including his politics. Chris had gotten to know him outside of class and found the man as intelligent as he seemed, but also highly approachable. He now hoped for the same with Anselm DeLacey.

Chris couldn't tell Anselm's exact age, but he knew the man had to be at least in his fifties. He carried himself like a much younger man, belying the white hair and lines on his face. Chris was fairly certain some of the lines around Anselm's eyes were due to laughter. Anselm was wearing a simple crimson wool surcoat, and his wool cloak was clasped with a brooch depicting a silver fox. His whole ensemble suggested simple elegance.

Anselm broke the silence as Chris sat in another chair. "How is your lady wife? She was not at supper, so I hope all is well?" He was genuinely concerned.

Chris nodded. "Yes, sir, Helen is fine. She had a - busier - afternoon than expected. She is resting."

Anselm's eyebrow shot up. It took conscious effort for him to lower it, but by that time his eyes were twinkling. "You, sir, are not Christian Lattimore. I suspected as much during the meal, but you have done naught but prove it since we entered the library."

Chris crossed his fingers and plunged in. "You are correct, sir. My acting ability has suffered without Reginald around to prompt me to play the jackass. It is a very long story, involving Edward Fitzroy -"

"Pardon me, but you need say no more," Anselm interrupted. "However, if you are not Lattimore, then where is he?"

"He is dead."

Anselm blinked in surprise.

"He was murdered last summer. I stood in for him last Christmas, and an unrelated assassination attempt against Prince Robert failed. It is all very complicated, but Robert would probably be dead if Christian had been present instead of me." Chris looked defiant.

Anselm smiled. "Your presence could prove fortunate for everyone, then. I assume you are not from these parts." Chris nodded. "And yet, you stayed here. The duchess, perhaps? She does not appeal to the majority of men, but if I were twenty years younger..." He trailed off, smiling.

Chris blushed, also smiling. "You are perceptive, sir. I love her very much."

"Naturally. You *are* an intelligent man." Anselm leaned back into his chair. "So, what should I call you in private?"

"Chris, or Christopher."

"Well, Christopher, tell me what you know about Reginald's death," Anselm said, his head now cocked forward in a listening posture.

Chris filled the older man in on the details of Reginald's murder. Anselm gave a long, low whistle when the tale was complete. "Do you know anything about the man who stabbed him?"

"Only that he was dressed in dark clothing, and likely not a priest," Chris replied. "Edward has speculated that Reginald's death is related to the failed attempt against Robert."

"Aye, an idiot could see that connection if the motivation were political. Though it would have to be domestic as well. Hmm. No, that is not right. Reginald and Robert have no enemies in common that I can think of." He paused and smiled. "Wait, an idiot did see a possible connection. I must congratulate him."

Chris smiled at Anselm's irreverence. He knew Edward was no idiot. Anselm continued. "The act was planned, the prostitute was involved, willing or no. And to leave Reginald in such a humiliating position, I think this man must have a sense of humor. Frankly, I loathed Reginald Claybourne, but it was a personal dislike as well as political. I would have killed him in haste, without forethought, and I would not have tried to murder his son. At least not until I had met him."

Chris thought about Anselm's reasoning and appreciated the man's candor. Anselm concluded, "I feel sorriest for the prince. He has to bear the brunt of the humiliation, though he will not see pity from me."

"Yes, sir. Can you think of anyone with a deep-seated reason for killing Reginald?" Chris smacked the chair arm suddenly. "God, I am clueless sometimes," he said in exasperation. "There could be a woman involved. Her name is - drat it - Cecelia."

"Cecelia? The name is vaguely familiar, but I will never remember the connection tonight. I think we should meet again on the morrow, Helen as well. I will send for you, or you send for me."

The two men shook hands after standing. Chris felt no surprise at the firmness of Anselm's grip.

Chris stopped at Elijah's room before retiring to his own chamber. Naomi let him in, letting herself out. "God, he's a tyrant," she muttered.

Elijah smiled at Chris. "She's just mad because I took charge before she got a chance. How're Nicole and Helen?"

"They were sleeping a couple of hours ago. Man, it gets weirder and weirder." Chris told Elijah what happened with Nicole and Helen. Elijah's expression didn't waver until he heard about the brain hemorrhage.

"Are you sure your head's okay?" he asked, concerned.

"I am fine," Chris asserted. "If she had hurt me, I *know* I would have passed out by now, or had some memory blackouts, or something."

"Humor me." Elijah fetched one of the burning candles and held it so the flame was before Chris's eyes. Their pupils contracted. "Good. Now roll your eyes around. In every direction, not just upward! Smartass." He put the candle back. "Okay, you seem fine, but I'm keeping an eye on you."

Chris rolled his eyes again. "Well, Naomi will thank me for getting you off *her* back." He sighed in mock disgust then sobered. "How is Michael?"

"Sleeping. He had a nightmare earlier and woke himself up. He needs rest, time - honestly, I'm out of my depth. I'm sorry Brother Peter didn't come. I could use his advice since Michael's problem is of a Magical nature. This mind-altering stuff is alarming."

"You think? It terrifies me. It makes me think about all that chemical warfare, mind control conspiracies, brainwashing - you know, the things our government swore they would never do?"

"Uh-huh. 'The Manchurian Candidate' for instance? Hi, Michael. How are you?" Michael had moaned in his sleep and now woke. Shifting his weight to sit, his head started to hurt again. He gave the two men a weak smile.

"I have felt better, thanks. I just had the most incredible -" he stopped, blushing. He had Chris and Elijah's full attention. "Lady Nicole distracts me," he added lamely.

Elijah cracked up. Chris grinned. "So, that is how you say it in Myrridia." Michael looked confused. "Sorry, Michael. I know priests are men, and I have problems with that celibacy requirement myself -"

"Not that he hasn't spent the past few years living like a monk," Elijah interjected. It was Chris's turn to redden. "Until he met your cousin, anyway," Elijah finished.

"You were not exactly chasing every skirt you saw, Elijah," Chris retorted.

"You don't know what I did when I was on call overnight," Elijah said archly.

"Well, the nights we were both on call, we met in the cafeteria, for coffee, not cigarettes," Chris pointed out. Elijah shrugged. Michael looked more confused. "I am sorry, Michael. Did you need to talk about something? Nicole?"

"I - No, not really. I mean - oh, I do not know what I mean!" Michael leaned back against the cushions, his eyes closed, his pain and fatigue obvious.

"I'm sorry, too," Elijah added belatedly.

"No apologies needed. I appreciate the distraction. It is just - Nicole, she confuses me. I have never experienced this sort of feeling for a woman before. I care for Helen, of course, but Nicole - my own body betrays me." Michael paused for breath, embarrassed.

Chris and Elijah exchanged a look.

"You don't think -" Elijah began.

"Why not?" Chris turned to Michael. "Have you ever - known - a woman, in the Biblical sense?"

Elijah stifled laughter. "What my esteemed colleague is trying to ask, Michael, is have you ever had sex?"

"I - No." Michael avoided their gazes. "Why?"

"Your body is telling your brain it wants to have sex with Nicole," Chris explained.

Michael paled. "But lust is a sin."

Elijah spoke. "Yeah, maybe. Sex is a normal thing, Michael. Your body's pointing out an attractive woman, literally. It's up to you to ignore it, or act on it."

"Are you trying to help him or hurt him?" Chris interrupted.

"I-I guess I have to ignore it. I cannot act on it. I would have to obtain dispensation - oh, never mind. And, I would not like to insult her," Michael added quickly.

"I doubt she'd be insulted," Elijah muttered in Chris's ear. "How do you feel about it?"

"I have absolutely no opinion on Nicole's sex life," he retorted. "It does not concern me in the least. We should help him get back to sleep."

"Just checking."

Chris rolled his eyes again.

Helen woke while Chris was in the library with Anselm. She shifted slightly in the bed, to see if Nicole were still sleeping.

Abigail came over. "Do you need anything, mistress?"

Helen requested her dressing gown, easing herself off the bed. She asked Abigail if food had been sent up. Abigail pointed to the table, on which sat a platter of fruit, cheese, bread and cold meat.

Nicole woke a short time later. She sat up with a start, raising her hands to her temples. "My headache -" she began, as a look of horror crossed her face remembering her encounter with Cecelia.

Helen hurried to the bed. She sat and took one of Nicole's hands, holding it firmly in both of her own. "Nicole, take a deep breath. She is not here. She cannot hurt you."

Nicole complied, taking several deep breaths. She finally withdrew her hand from Helen's. "It's all real, though. What happened, I mean."

"Aye."

"It's so unbelievable. Me, with magical talents. I'm a scientist - a computer geek." Nicole tried to smile. "How did she know?"

"She may not have known at first. She certainly took advantage of you once she found out, though," Helen said. "I wish I could have softened the memory for you, but I was too exhausted by the time I got her bloody wall down, and I was worried about what she had intended for Chris."

"I sensed your fatigue, I think. Before all of the memories overwhelmed me." Nicole shuddered. "I don't like anybody's

122

mind, or memories, being tampered with. I want to go home." The last was said on a pleading note.

Helen looked thoughtful. "I suppose we can talk to Edward tomorrow. He should be able to get you where you belong. Are you so eager to go because of what happened, or to get away from Chris and me?" The words were out before she could stop them. Helen immediately regretted them. "I am sorry. That was rude of me."

"No, it wasn't," Nicole said. "The ex-girlfriend showing up at the wife's house - or castle - uninvited, now that's rude. You're right, though. I think I've done enough harm to you and Chris."

"Why did you come looking for him?" Helen decided to take advantage of Nicole's willingness to talk about the subject.

Nicole was willing - it kept her from dwelling on Cecelia. Although she was still worried sick about Michael. "I was hoping he still had feelings for me. I know I could have fallen in love with him again." She met Helen's gaze and smiled. "I doubt he's even thought of me since he saw you. I don't think he ever did anything spontaneous with me."

The relationship was too complicated for Helen to understand. "So, why did you part?" she asked.

"That's easy. I was too impatient to wait for him. He's several years older than me, and I-I guess I wasn't mature enough. I broke off our engagement and moved away. I didn't contact him at all. I dated several men, but they were losers - no good."

"I recognize the type," Helen said dryly.

Nicole glanced at her and smiled. "A couple of months ago, I decided to look him up again," she continued. "If he had married, I wasn't going to contact him. We did have something special once. If he'd been willing, I'd hoped we could start again." Nicole's voice had softened. She stared unwaveringly at Helen. "He loves you - he married you. I have no desire to come between you. I am so sorry to have barged in on you both - I wouldn't have come if I'd known..." She trailed off as Helen remained quiet, looking at her.

Helen finally asked, "Do you love him?" She took one of Nicole's hands.

"As a friend or a brother, Helen, not as a wife." Nicole knew the words were true as she spoke them without thought. Helen let go, nodding.

"You were listening on more than one level." It was a statement.

"Aye. You are not angry?"

"No. I sensed something that - felt? - like you. I want you to know the truth. I could have protested, yes?"

"Of course."

Nicole relaxed a little. "That Cecelia woman in my head -" She shivered. "You, I don't mind. I don't get that." She lay back against the cushions for a moment, then sat forward again, tensing. "Do you want your bed back?"

Helen smiled. "I am fine. Stay there until you feel strong enough to get up. Nicole, you are not afraid of contact between our minds because you know I intend you no harm. Nor harm to anyone else."

Nicole nodded and let her mind wander. It occurred to her how unpretentious this Magic was, and how real. There was no showmanship or melodramatic spell casting. She didn't think Helen or Cecelia had used any props, just the power of their minds. She looked at Helen with a new respect. "I am amazed with the simplicity of this Magic, Lady Helen. Even more than the fact that I apparently have these - Talents."

Helen laughed. "Oh, 'tis not simple. I have had many years of practice so it looks that way."

Nicole smiled. "That doesn't surprise me - it's often true of experienced pros - practitioners. What I can do with a computer at home passes for magic with most lay persons. It's because they don't understand how the computer - a machine - works. It seems reasonable that the same would be true of Magic."

"Exactly, I think," Helen agreed.

Nicole was thoughtful for a moment. "If I'd brought a computer with me -" She broke off with a chuckle. "It would have lasted a few hours on just a battery. Never mind."

Helen had no idea what Nicole was saying. She changed the topic. "Of course, if you wanted to pursue training in the Magical arts, you would need to stay in Myrridia. And that would mean that you, Chris and I would have to get past our current situation."

"Agreed. I'm not sure if I want to stay, though. I mean, I know I came here looking for Chris, and at first I didn't even believe what Naomi's mother told me had happened to him and Elijah. I guess I planned that if Chris wanted to - you know - that we'd have gone back home together. I have a life waiting for me. I never in my wildest dreams expected to end up dealing with duchesses and bishops and royalty! Not to mention people getting murdered. I'm just an average person."

At Helen's questioning look, Nicole tried to explain. "I'm an ordinary citizen with an ordinary life - I don't have a high social or political position in the world. I have a job, and I'm trying to further my education. If I'd been born here, I would probably be working on a farm or in town or in a castle as a seamstress or some other horrid, boring job!"

"Yes, but you would have had no access to education in that case, so would you know what you were missing?" Helen asked.

"Point taken. Like you, I am a woman of my time. From my perspective, I don't know how you stand it," Nicole said.

"The greatest good and the greatest ill that my father did for me was to have me educated. It was necessary for me to make a better marriage, to be a competent mistress of a noble household. It also made me aware of the limitations on women, regardless of their social station. I would personally like to see more status for women, in general, though no progress will be made as long as people like Reginald Claybourne and Edward Fitzroy are in power," Helen explained.

Nicole could sense Helen's frustration. "You've given this a great deal of thought."

Helen nodded.

"What would you do - if you could?"

Helen looked down at her hands for a few moments, debating. "This is in the strictest confidence, Nicole. You must not tell anyone, unless you return to your own world, in which case you can tell anyone you like. I have not even discussed this with Chris, though I plan to ere long."

Nicole perceived the change in Helen's tone and appreciated the solemnity of what she was about to hear. "I understand, Helen. No one in Myrridia will hear anything from me. I swear it."

"Fine. Has Elijah told you anything about Edward and the Church's regulation of Magical practice?"

Nicole was surprised by the change in topic. "No, I don't think so. He's said some disparaging things about Edward as a person, like how ambitious he is." She paused. "You mean the *Church* is in charge of *Magic*?" There was incredulity in her tone.

"Oh, yes. Only officially sanctioned rituals and spells may be performed. Anyone who tries to amend or improve an existing form can be arrested if they are caught. This is true even if they are trying to improve the safety of the practitioner in the ritual. The penalties range from excommunication, to banishment, to death." Nicole was shocked at first, but then got angry.

"Wait just a minute. This sounds like what some corporations do in my time. A large, impersonal committee decides what kind of working conditions people are subjected to. If someone complains because several people have gotten maimed or killed because of a faulty piece of machinery, that person is punished, and nothing gets done to improve the conditions for the rest of the workers. Is that the kind of thing you're talking about?" Nicole was breathing hard.

"That sounds about right," Helen said, dismayed by what Nicole had just said. "To continue what I was saying, there is a group of Magical practitioners that is working outside the Church, hoping to break her stranglehold over Magic. Michael and I are part of this group." Helen met Nicole's gaze evenly, knowing she had entrusted her safety to this woman.

"You are renegades, then," Nicole said, nodding. "Your secret is safe with me, Helen. I don't think I'm in Edward's social circle, if you know what I mean."

Helen now nodded.

"I'm a libertarian at heart."

At Helen's blank look, Nicole smiled. "It doesn't matter. Let's just say I don't believe in state-sponsored religion, state-sponsored execution, or church-sponsored government. And, I believe in the rights of everyone, not just the rich and powerful, or worse, rich and famous. I've struggled to get where I am, and as a woman, it wasn't easy, but at least I am able to be independent. Knowing about this situation in Myrridia has almost convinced me to stay and help you with your work, but I can't make such an important decision without more thought."

"You are independent?" Helen focused on the single word.

"Oh, yes. After I left Chris, I didn't find any other men to my liking. So, with no conscious intentions of it, I made a life for myself. I'm not even sure why I decided to look him up again, except that I wanted a close relationship with someone, and he'd been the best I had met..." Nicole trailed off.

Helen looked down again. She could understand Nicole's last statement; Chris was the best man she had met. She admitted to herself that she missed the closeness they had shared since Christmas, when they'd declared their true feelings for one another, until the arrival of Nicole and Naomi.

There was a quiet rap at the door, and Chris let himself into the chamber. Helen and Nicole turned to look at him.

"How are you?" he asked.

"I am rested, Chris, and Nicole is recovering well. Make yourself comfortable. The three of us need to talk. I apologize for not taking care of this problem sooner." Helen looked away from him and missed the expression of hope that flared suddenly in his eyes.

"No apologies, Helen. It was a shock for you, and I should have told you more of my past." Before sitting, Chris took one of her hands and kissed it. "Besides, how many men can you trust?" He smiled.

"There is you, and you are debatable, my one brother and Michael. And Elijah, of course, with whom you always know where you stand." She smiled. She and Chris both knew subtlety wasn't Elijah's forte.

Nicole watched the two of them interacting and sighed. Even as a scientist, she suspected love was the strongest physical force on the planet, and these two had a bad case of it, maybe terminal. "Can I interrupt?" she asked. Chris and Helen looked at her. "It's obvious to me that the two of you have eyes only for each other. Yes, I'm jealous, but I'm jealous of that something between you, not either one of you in particular. I can say from experience, Helen, that you have one of the good ones, and - as if you don't already know! - there ain't many of them. I had my chance and I blew it. But if I hadn't, we all wouldn't be here right now. You'd be a widow with an underage son as duke, and what else would be different? Chris and I would maybe be making wedding plans finally, but he and I wouldn't be here. That's for sure. So go ahead and blame me for what's happening, but blame me for sending Chris to you, too!" She crossed her arms and lay back against the cushions, smiling smugly. "Feel free to thank me at your leisure."

Helen laughed out loud. Chris had reddened a little, but he now smiled at Helen. "Thank you, Nicole, for a breath of fresh air. I think Helen's the reason I came to Myrridia in the first place; I just had no way of knowing it. I thought I was trying to keep her husband alive, silly me. I never intended to fall for her - it just happened."

Helen took his hand. "I never intended to fall in love with him, either. When he first arrived in Saelym, I was furious with Edward and him for Edward's mad masquerade. Like I did not have enough to do with administering the duchy, now I had to train a strange man to pretend to be my husband. And there was the fact that my husband was now dead. I found myself growing fond of Chris, and then he was nearly killed. I admitted to myself and to him that I loved him, and then you showed up from his past. I think I was less than rational, and I apologize. I just felt the familiar betrayal I had experienced so often."

"I am sorry, Helen," Chris said. "You are the most important person in the world to me. No offense, Nicole. When you left me, I was hurt. Then I got confused and tried to look you up, but you had already left town. I wondered for a long time if I had done something really stupid and let the best woman I had met up until then get away. I threw myself into my work and ended up frustrated with the way the corporations were running the medical system. Edward's offer seemed like a good idea, crazy, but good."

"There is that word again - corpor - corporation. Is this some new evil I am fortunate to be ignorant of?" Helen asked.

Chris laughed. "You do not want any part of them, Helen. Science has all but conquered the devil, but he has been replaced by corporations." He looked at Nicole for support.

"Yes."

Nicole looked from Chris to Helen. "I think you two are going to be fine, especially as a team. And I really think Edward is going to be sorry he ever invited you here, Chris."

Helen chuckled. "Oh, he already is, Nicole. Edward was livid when he was unable to convince Chris to return home. I am sure he has considered Chris partly at fault for Reginald's death." Chris and Nicole both looked surprised. "Christian would have remained in Rhennsbury after Christmas, and Reginald may not have gone to that brothel," she explained.

Nicole shrugged. "So Edward's no genius. He should be playing Chris's strengths instead of looking for another Christian."

Helen shook her head. "No, Nicole. Chris does not fit into his power plays. Edward is going to be the next Archbishop of Rhennsbury and therefore head of Myrridia's Church." She crossed herself before continuing. "The current archbishop is in poor health, so it is just a matter of time. With Reginald and Christian often making war, Edward could pursue his own plans with relatively little interference. Now Reginald and Christian are gone, and to understate, Robert is not the man his father was, for which all of Myrridia should be grateful. The problem will be, when Edward is archbishop, who will have the power to stop him?"

Helen then explained to Chris about the underground group of Magicians. He was surprised and relieved. "I am glad to hear about these people, Helen, and it is no shock to me to know that you and Michael are involved. There is hope for the future then, from both a Church and Crown perspective. Let me know if you ever need my assistance."

"Thank you. What I will need from you in the future is your ability to run the duchy in my absence." She put a hand up to stop his interrupting her. "No, I do not plan to abandon the duchy, but sooner or later Edward is going to discover that I am involved, and I may have to go into hiding. I will still be in contact with you, but you will have to be able to convince Edward otherwise. And, I will need you to take care of Reginald and Eleanor."

Chris nodded. He was genuinely fond of the two children, and he would do anything to protect either one of them. He hadn't considered the idea of losing Helen in any way, temporarily or permanently, and he felt unsettled at even the thought of it. He would do whatever was needed. "You know you can count on me," he said quietly.

"Thank you again. I-I suppose this makes us even." Helen attempted a small smile. "We have each kept something important about ourselves from the other."

Chapter Seven

Though the next morning dawned cloudy, Elijah asked his sister and Nicole if they wanted to go and play tourist in the city. He had already checked on Michael, and the priest said he felt much better. His eyes were clear of pain and fatigue.

Naomi was enthusiastic, and Nicole, after being reassured that Michael was fine, said she could use the diversion. Helen loaned her a dress and suggested Elijah check with a couple of the seamstresses in town, to see if they had anything that could be altered quickly for Naomi or Nicole. He agreed and thanked her for the idea. Once they reached the city, all three received curious looks - Elijah and Naomi because of their skin and height, Nicole because of her eyeglasses. Elijah assumed most of these people must be visitors to the city. The natives had long since gotten past their first shock at seeing the unusually tall, brown-skinned man. A few of them nodded to him or doffed their hats, to Naomi's amusement.

Elijah took them first to Rhennsbury Cathedral, where both women spent a good part of the morning admiring the workmanship inside and out. Naomi spent a few minutes standing in the nave's central aisle, sensing an air of reverence in the building. Nicole walked along one side, studying each of the windows, taking in the stained-glass artwork. She recognized a few scenes from the New Testament, but if some of the pictures depicted saints, she had no idea who they were. She touched a couple of them, marveling at the brilliance of the colors, then sat in a pew for several minutes, attempting to relax her mind. She closed her eyes and visualized the work that had to go into constructing such a building, and without the benefit of 21st-century building methods. She ruined the moment when she decided technology was most likely the main explanation for why modern construction could be notoriously unreliable. Before catching up with Elijah and Naomi, she lit a candle and said a quick prayer for Michael's mental health.

Elijah initially left the women to their explorations and checked with a deacon to see if the archbishop, Francis McHenry, were receiving visitors without an appointment. The man went to inquire, and when he returned, he told Elijah to come along. Elijah collected the two women, then knocked on the study door.

Francis greeted them all warmly, then apologized for not rising. "My physician informs me that my health is good for a man of my age. Alas, that is not the same thing as good." He smiled and held out his right hand. It trembled slightly; Nicole suspected it was some degenerative illness secondary to old age. She wondered if he were as old as he looked, estimating his age at around seventy.

Elijah shook the offered hand, wishing him a good day. Uncertain, Naomi and Nicole curtseyed, then shook his hand as well.

Francis chuckled. "More of yours, Sir Holmes?"

Elijah smiled and turned to Nicole. "You're not Catholic, are you?"

"No, Episcopalian." She paused, then grinned. "Catholicism light." Elijah laughed. He turned back to the archbishop who was gazing at him with bemusement.

"Yes, Excellency. My sister belongs to the same - sect - as myself, though Nicole is closer to your own. They're here in Myrridia for a short time."

"Enjoy your stay, ladies. Thank you for stopping by." It was a dismissal. As Elijah was closing the door, he swore he heard the archbishop mutter, "Interesting."

After breakfast that same morning, Reginald Lattimore clamored to see Robert. He and Eleanor had had some interaction with the prince the previous summer when Robert had accompanied Christian to the duchy. Robert had spent a number of weeks teaching the two children when the regular tutor had resigned abruptly. Eleanor smiled and shrugged her shoulders when Helen asked her if she wanted to come along.

Chris sent a page to inquire if Robert were busy and to explain their request. Robert's reply said to come by whenever it was convenient. Reginald grabbed Chris's hand and began tugging him toward the door almost before the page had exited. Chris looked at Helen.

"Why not get it over with?" she asked, her eyes twinkling.

Chris removed Reginald's hand for a moment and picked up Eleanor. He held his hand back out to Reginald and said, "Walk, do not run. Please be on your best behavior and remember to call Prince Robert 'Your Highness.'" Reginald impatiently agreed and swung the chamber door open with his free hand.

Chris let Helen walk a few steps ahead. When they reached the Great Hall, Reginald was not intimidated by the size of it, despite the fact that the room looked larger since it was empty, with the tables pushed up against the walls. Eleanor's eyes widened and she hid her face in Chris's shoulder. They crossed the room's expanse and Helen knocked on the door of the royal study.

"Enter," Robert called.

Reginald let go of Chris, pushed the door open, and walked in first. Robert stood as he recognized his guests and stepped away from the desk. Reginald stood still and bowed, then lowered his head, suddenly shy. Robert grinned. "Reginald?" The boy's head came up. "How are the Latin and arithmetic coming?"

Reginald stared at the floor and scuffed one foot. "I would rather not say, sir," he mumbled. Robert exchanged a meaningful glance with Chris and Helen, then straightened his features before speaking to Reginald again.

"Arithmetic still gives me problems, Reginald, and now I have to keep Rhennsbury's accounts straight." Reginald glanced up, suspicious, then saw that Robert was serious.

"I guess I have to study more, then," the boy said, looking glum.

Eleanor squirmed in Chris's arms. He put her down, and she gave a dignified curtsey before stepping up to Robert. He crouched down to her level and kissed her hand.

"Good morning, my lady," he said with a smile.

"Good morning, Your Highness. Do you have any kittens I can play with?" Eleanor's face was all seriousness.

"Kittens?" Robert was taken aback.

"Eleanor had to leave her cat in Saelym, Highness," Helen explained, her lips twitching. "I told her there would be cats here in Rhennsbury."

"Ah." Robert thought a moment. "We can go check in the kitchen and stables if you wish," he said to Eleanor.

She nodded. "You are still very good-looking, sir, almost as handsome as Father."

Helen had to stifle her laughter. She was unsure which man reddened more. She also knew Eleanor would never have said it about Christian and that thought saddened her momentarily. "It would appear, Sire, that the marriage proposals have started already." By the time the words were out, she was chuckling.

Robert grinned, appreciating the jest. "You are the prettiest one so far, Lady Eleanor, but I fear I am a trifle old for you."

"I do not wish to marry you, sir. I want to see the cats." Eleanor crossed her arms. "Mother said I could play with the cats here."

Reginald's expression had gone from glum to condescending. "That is not the proper way to speak to a king, Ellie," he said smugly.

Eleanor squealed and ran to Chris, holding her arms out for him to pick her up. "Is he going to put me in the dungeon?" she wailed.

Chris was now the one trying desperately to keep a straight face for his adopted daughter. He looked at Robert. "Sire?"

Robert stifled a chuckle, remembering that the girl had been skittish around him when she'd first met him in Saelym. He debated teasing her, but decided against it. He joined Chris and held out a hand to her.

Eleanor tried to pull Chris's cloak around her. "Save me, Father," she whispered.

"Prince Robert is not going to hurt you," Chris tried to reassure her.

Reginald looked from his father to Robert. "Are you sure, Father?" Chris gave him a stern look and the boy looked abashed. Eleanor asked Chris if they could leave now.

"Lady Eleanor?" Robert asked quietly. "Do you not want to meet the cats?"

Eleanor peeked at him and realized he didn't look angry. "Yes, please." Chris put her down, and she held her hand out to Robert. He waved the others out of the study and promised to return Eleanor to their apartment once he'd introduced her to a few of the stable cats.

After leaving the cathedral Elijah made an effort to stay on Rhennsbury's main streets. Most of the buildings were two stories in height, with shops downstairs and living quarters above. Occasionally they would pass a structure that appeared purely residential. Nicole pointed to one, saying it was Edward's. Elijah scrutinized it, filing the information away for future reference.

Some buildings were made of wood, others of stone, and many were in need of repair. Elijah told his companions that Saelym Town was more prosperous and better maintained. He checked with an outdoor vendor to find a nearby seamstress's shop and led the women there. "So you can find something to wear besides borrowed clothing," he explained. "Chris and I took the trouble to get something appropriate to wear *before* coming here." Naomi ignored the criticism while Nicole admitted he had a point.

The seamstress, a woman named Enid, solved the challenge of Naomi's height by suggesting she add a border at the bottom of an existing pale green dress to lengthen it. She showed them several samples, and Naomi agreed to one of them. "I can have the dress ready by mid afternoon tomorrow, my lord," Enid assured Elijah. Nicole picked out a subdued gray-blue dress in a simple style.

"Nicely inconspicuous," she said as they exited.

Passing by one alleyway, the three noticed shouting and hoots of enthusiasm. They stopped walking and looked down the narrow lane. Naomi was the first to realize that several of the establishments were brothels. She nudged her brother. "The world's oldest profession." Elijah narrowed his eyes, then realized what a stout, well-dressed woman was saying.

"Good Lord," he said. "It's the medieval equivalent of talk shows." He pointed. "That must be where the king was murdered, and the commoners are having a field day."

Naomi started to chuckle, then sobered. "Imagine the reporters descending like vultures in our day. They'd be parked here and at the castle gates." She shivered.

Nicole tugged on Elijah's arm. "Can we go somewhere else? I-I'm a little nervous." Elijah put a reassuring arm around her and took his sister's elbow with his other hand.

At midday, they entered an inn called The King's Arms, which appeared to be doing a bustling business. The common room was crowded, but Elijah found enough space at one table for the three of them. One man offered his lap to Naomi. She sat between her brother and Nicole, who was being looked over by a stout man with bad teeth, worse breath, and several years' accumulation of dirt. He offered to buy her meal. Nicole declined and turned sideways to face her companions.

"He certainly makes the losers I've dated look better," she remarked. "Or at least smell better. Ugh." She made a face.

"Welcome to the other ninety-plus percent," Elijah said with a smile. "A select few are born into the aristocracy, some go into the Church, and the masses try to keep from starving." Sobering, he added, "It's not really that different from home. Most of the money and power is in the hands of a select few, and they're the ones who make the rules."

Naomi snorted. "So how much progress have we really made, then? We have more toys and conveniences, more ways to spend the money we don't have."

"More things to distract us from what's important," Nicole put in.

Elijah agreed with them. "Yeah. Chris and I decided there were a lot of things we had no trouble living without, but I still miss hot showers on demand and toilets. I guess you get used to what you have and work with it. I don't remember feeling poor while we were growing up, though now I know we were." He changed tack. "I may still end up coming home."

Naomi took it as an opening to bring up Allyson. "Unless you get a better offer from the princess?" she asked. Nicole stared at her.

"What!" she exclaimed. "Princess?"

Elijah felt his face get warm. He didn't answer his sister right away. "What makes you think she's even interested?" he finally countered.

"Her look of relief when you introduced me as your sister," Naomi replied smugly. "You *do* have the hots for her, don't you?"

"I - No." Naomi looked skeptical, Nicole, amused. "I'm attracted to her, but it's something beyond physical. She and I would make a great team trying to thwart Edward Fitzroy."

"Why do you dislike him so much?" Nicole asked. "Not that I'm a fan of his. He's certainly demanding and cranky enough."

"Because he doesn't care about people unless they're useful to him." Elijah's tone was more vehement than he'd intended, and both women backed off slightly.

"And he can get away with it because he's so high up in the Church," Nicole surmised.

"Bingo."

After returning Eleanor as promised, Robert was summoned to his chambers, to be measured again for his coronation garments. The tailor assured him he would have some of the pieces ready for a first fitting in a couple of days.

A page rapped at the door and entered. He ran up to Robert and handed him a folded piece of parchment. "For you, Sire," the boy said, sketching a bow as he slid to a halt.

Robert frowned. This was highly irregular. "Where is the messenger?"

The page bobbed his head. "He said he had other urgent messages to deliver, sir."

Robert dismissed tailor and page then sat on a stool, reading the message. Paul had entered the room from the bedchamber at hearing the noise. He looked at Robert with concern as the prince paled. Robert shook his head, stood, and headed for the sitting room's door. "Later," was all he said. Paul fought his instinctive urge to follow Robert.

As he reached the stairwell, Robert paused long enough to speak to two castle guards at their posts. "Chase down the page who was just here, and - and try to find this messenger," Robert ordered. The two men bowed and hurried down the stairs. Robert shouted for another page as he strode into the Great Hall on the way to the royal study. He collapsed into a chair, closing his eyes. When a page entered, he directed the boy to summon Allyson, the Lattimores, and to request Edward Fitzroy's presence.

Anselm DeLacey had requested Chris and Helen meet him in the library late that morning. He greeted them both warmly, telling Helen he was pleased to see her looking well. When she looked at

Chris in confusion, Chris and Anselm gave her a brief synopsis of their talk the previous evening. Helen had been so fatigued the night before, once Nicole had retired, Chris had forgotten to tell her about it.

Anselm said he had given the name of Cecelia a good deal of thought after leaving Chris, but he hadn't remembered anything of note until that morning. He began searching through some of the books. "There was a Cecelia something associated with Reginald's last foray into Wyckendom, I am certain of it. Would you happen to recall the surname of the Earl of Tippensdown?" he asked Helen.

Helen thought about it. "Falcon? No, but something similar."

"Aye." He snapped his fingers. "Cecelia Falkes. And here is the volume I had despaired of finding." Anselm handed Helen a leather-bound book. "I know your eyes are better than mine. If you can, read through this today, and we can meet again tonight. If you have no other plans, that is."

"None as of yet," Helen replied. "If that should change, we will let you know at supper."

A page stepped into the library. "Your Graces, the prince wants to see you immediately!"

Anselm said, "You two go ahead. I will catch up."

Allyson arrived at the study first. "What is it?" she asked after catching her breath. There were lines of tension around Robert's mouth, and she thought he looked pale.

"As soon as the others get here, I will tell you," Robert replied in a strained voice.

Allyson paced impatiently until Chris and Helen arrived shortly thereafter. "Anselm will be here soon, Highness," Helen said.

Robert waited a little longer for Edward, then plunged ahead. Edward could catch up.

"I have just received a death threat," Robert said, handing the parchment to Chris. Allyson stared at her brother, openmouthed. Helen gave the younger woman's shoulder a squeeze, then held her hand out to Chris.

"May I?" she asked.

Chris handed her the message as Robert whispered, "Please."

Helen went into light trance, tracing the fingers of one hand across the page. She now paled. "'Tis Cecelia." Chris steadied her as he immediately thought of what had happened to Michael and Nicole; her words alarmed him.

Edward knocked and let himself into the room, an apology on his lips. He stopped, staring at the four of them. "What has happened?" he demanded.

Helen handed him the parchment wordlessly. He read through it, then looked at Robert. His nephew nodded before dropping his gaze. Edward now repeated Helen's actions, also recognizing the Magical Signature.

"The same practitioner who attacked Father Michael and ordered the assassination attempt on you last year, Your Highness," Edward stated.

Robert closed his eyes and clasped his hands together, leaning his elbows on the desk. When he opened his eyes, he stared at each of the others in turn. "This much we do know," he began, counting points on one hand. "This Cecelia wants me dead. Does this have anything to do with Father's death? I find her timing suspicious. Who the devil is she?" He paused. "Is there any way to stop her? I-I am a little nervous." He attempted a smile to accompany the understatement.

Chris smiled slightly. "You are not alone in this, kid. I should know better than anyone." Chris told them what Cecelia had tried to do to him through Nicole and Helen. "Christian has some serious enemies, but are they the same enemies as Reginald's?" He scowled. "It does not make me think highly of her if she is threatening you. *You* haven't done anything to anyone yet - you have had no chance, not that you would." He glanced at Helen, his eyebrow raised in a question. She nodded once.

"Anselm DeLacey has mentioned the name Cecelia Falkes of Tippensdown, an earldom in-"

"Wyckendom," Helen added smoothly.

"Yeah, there." Chris shot her a look of thanks. "Suppose this Cecelia is the same person *and* a gifted Magical practitioner." He had Robert's full attention.

"Tippensdown," Robert said thoughtfully.

"Your father and Christian acquired the earldom several years ago," Edward said impatiently, glowering at Chris. "What does that old battle have to do with anything?"

"Reginald and Christian might have made the tactical mistake of leaving behind a survivor, who could be looking for revenge. It at least makes a little sense for why Robert is being included," Chris retorted. "Look, I am no military genius -"

"Then stay out of it!" Edward snapped.

Robert silenced him with an angry look. "What I meant to say," Chris said, pausing to look at Robert and keeping his tone even with an effort, "is that maybe this Cecelia *thinks* she is in the right, though I do not think anyone here would argue that her methods are."

"Are you mad, Christopher?" Edward demanded.

"I want to suggest the possibility that diplomacy could work," Chris concluded, ignoring the bishop.

"Diplomacy?" Robert was confused but intrigued.

"At home, one of our recent leaders made apologies to different groups for - historical mistakes."

"You think I should *apologize?*" Robert was stunned. "Kings do not apologize, Chris, not according to anything I have learned."

"They most certainly do not!" Edward exploded. "Keep your modern nonsense to yourself, Doctor, or go home. Apology implies weakness."

Chris didn't back down. Though surprised by the suggestion, Helen came to his defense. "'Tis unexpected enough that it might work," she pointed out.

No one had noticed Anselm's entrance during Edward's tirade. He now spoke in agreement with Helen's words. "Why not, if all else fails?"

"It sets a precedent, you -" Edward stopped before he uttered the insult.

"Robert would not be apologizing for his own actions, only those of the preceding administration. A man's word is his bond. It may only cost him some money or land," Anselm said.

"You find that acceptable, your Grace?" Edward's voice was deadly quiet.

"Preferable to the cost of His Highness's life, *Excellency*," Anselm replied, not intimidated by Edward's tone.

Robert cleared his throat. "Land is not a problem, but the treasury is - is nearly empty." Edward turned on him.

"You would apologize and then just hand over land, land that your father and his loyal men fought and died to obtain?"

Robert flushed with anger. "'Twas the infantry who paid the price, Edward. They did not all choose to fight. I seldom agreed with what Father and Christian did. I am willing to do whatever I have to now. I have to agree with the Duke of Latham - Myrridia needs me alive if she is to have any hope of stability in the near future." He sagged in the chair, drained.

"I will help you, and Helen, if you need Magical defense," Allyson stated. Helen agreed. "What about you, Edward?"

"Of course."

"Whatever I can do with a sword," Chris offered, "though you know how little that is."

Robert smiled weakly. "Is Elijah any better?"

Chris looked sheepish. The ladies laughed. Anselm said dryly, "He is not Christian Lattimore."

Elijah, Naomi and Nicole were returning to the castle late in the afternoon, when two men-at-arms wearing royal badges ran past. Elijah turned and looked after them. "I wonder -" he began.

A black-clad man emerged from a crowded storefront and made to pass the three of them, but bumped into Naomi unintentionally. She stumbled but recovered.

"Sorry," was the terse remark.

"You have a way with women," Naomi called to his back. The man stopped and turned around, looking at all three. He smiled and walked back to them.

"My apologies, my lady. I could buy you a drink, if that would be acceptable recompense for the insult?" he asked.

Naomi was taking in his features, the unruly coal-black hair, deep blue eyes, neatly trimmed mustache and beard. He was even a couple of inches taller than she was. There was a small scar an inch from his left eye.

"Where and when?" Naomi said, before Elijah could step in. Nicole's lips twitched as she fought a smile.

"How about The King's Arms, this evening, after sundown? I can meet you there." His voice was deep, and Naomi found the accent sexy all of a sudden.

"I will see you then, sir," she said. The man saluted the three of them, then turned and strode briskly on his way.

"Naomi, are you crazy?" It took all of Elijah's control not to shout. "He could be a cutthroat, or a rapist, or -"

"I don't think so -"

"You don't even know his name!" Elijah went on.

"He didn't speak like a low-life, Elijah. 'Acceptable recompense?' And, I will remind you, brother, that I am a consenting adult, and I don't need to report in to you." Naomi crossed her arms and thrust out her jaw.

Elijah fought his temper. "Naomi, in case you've forgotten, you aren't in twenty-first century Durham, which is *safe* compared to this town. Women have no rights here, remember? Of course, if you want me to fight a duel to the death after this idiot rapes you, go ahead." He sighed. "I've got half a mind to take you both to Edward right now -"

"Which puts you half a mind ahead of most men," Naomi put in.

"What did *I* do?" Nicole asked no one in particular.

They finished the walk to the castle in silence.

Sebastian had no idea who the exotic dark-skinned woman was, though he knew the tall, dark man with her was Lattimore's associate. He guessed the pair must be relations or a married couple, though after the woman's prompt acceptance of his offer she likely wasn't his spouse. He had not intended to utter anything other than an apology, but her beauty had overwhelmed him. The dark skin, the darker eyes, the high cheekbones, and he sensed the spirit and intelligence behind those eyes.

Part of him hoped she did not keep the appointment. His sister would be displeased as soon as she learned of the incident. He would be reporting to her tomorrow, hopefully with news of a mayoral visit to the castle. He hoped to be passing on good news about Lattimore.

Several parties of nobles had arrived in Rhennsbury by nightfall, including more of Reginald's Council members. Robert decided not to publicize the death threat, at least for the moment. There were still several days until the coronation, and he hoped to resolve his father's murder before then.

A deputy mayor had come to the castle that afternoon to see about the possibility of a royal audience for his superior. The castle steward checked with Robert, and an appointment was scheduled for midmorning of the following day.

When Elijah and his companions arrived at the castle, he walked the two women all the way to their room. Then he crossed the corridor and rapped on the McCabes' door. When Abigail let him in, he asked her if Chris or Helen were in. She nodded, gesturing.

Helen was sitting at the dressing table, staring into space, lost in thought. There was a small book lying open in front of her. Chris was pacing back and forth on the far side of the bed. Both now looked at Elijah.

"Yes?" Helen asked.

"Sorry to interrupt, but, as I suspected, Naomi is going to be a nuisance before she goes home!" Elijah let out the frustration he'd suppressed during the walk back to the castle.

"What has she done?" Chris asked, omitting the "now."

"She's made a *date* with some guy who bumped into her in the street," Elijah said.

"What?" Chris and Helen exclaimed in unison.

144

"Yeah. No name, no idea who he is. No badge of nobility, though he did have a sword." Elijah sat on the bed. "I don't know if I'm more worried or angry."

"I hate to make you feel worse, Elijah," Helen said, "but he could be a mercenary soldier, looking for work."

Elijah moaned. "Maybe I'll just kill her."

"We'll send one of our men-at-arms with her," Helen offered. "Since escorting us here, they have had little enough to do. If she refuses, then she does not go."

"Thanks, Helen, but you have no idea how stubborn she can be."

"I think I might." Helen smiled.

"So, what are you doing?" Elijah changed the subject.

"Trying to learn something from history," Chris replied. He pointed to the book in front of Helen. "Helen has been sharing with me some unfortunate recent history. Correct me if any of this is wrong, Helen. Five, no, almost six, years ago, Reginald planned to start annexing his western neighbor, the kingdom of Wyckendom. He wanted to continue with that this year." Elijah nodded. "Well, when he and Christian invaded this particular earldom, Tippensdown, they - they massacred the earl and the members of his family that were there, just slew them all, including the women and children."

Elijah whistled. "So not good. What does this - massacre - have to do with what's happening now?"

"One or more of the family survived, since they were absent from the earldom at the time. He, she, or they could be looking for vengeance," Chris explained.

"One daughter, Cecelia, was in the royal capital, Laurconsburg, at the time of the attack, but she disappeared about a year later. There is no other information about her, except that she was a student of Magic," Helen added.

"There is also a younger son unaccounted for," Chris took over again. "His whereabouts at the time were unknown, and whether he is dead or alive is impossible to confirm. It is possible the two of them could have gotten together and planned to avenge their family."

"Are there descriptions of either of them?" Elijah asked.

"No," Helen replied, "not here, anyway. We are going to speak with Anselm DeLacey, the Duke of Latham, later this evening. He may remember more about the family, since Tippensdown borders his duchy. If not, then we go further back and look at other battles." She paused, frowning. "Frankly, I think this is the relevant battle - we *know* Nicole and Michael's attacker is named Cecelia, *and* she has sent Robert a death threat. How many women named Cecelia, with confirmed Magical ability, can be going about Myrridia unchecked?"

Chris and Elijah exchanged glances. They didn't believe in coincidence either.

Allyson spent the afternoon in the castle library. She began by pulling the tapestry aside from the room's wide window, and glancing down into the castle courtyard. The increased light made the room less dim. She summoned a sphere of light and left it hovering near one of the shelves, then pulled a chair before the shelf and started working from the top down. She sneezed several times from inhaling disturbed dust, but her search panned out on the third shelf she tried.

Allyson was carefully reading a scroll that looked at least a century old. The parchment had turned brown at the edges and was brittle to the touch. She happened on a reference to the Royal Council. During the ninth century, one of her ancestors had dissolved the Council upon ascending the throne.

If her memory were to be trusted, he was not one of the better Claybournes, but she was only interested in the precedent. If he could do it, so could Robert. When the Council had been re-formed two centuries ago, the same clerical members remained, but they'd always been Church appointees rather than royal ones. Robert had the chance to acquire a majority of sane men on his Council.

She rolled up the scroll carefully and carried it to her chambers. One of these days, she was going to reorganize the library. Neither

her father nor her grandfather had been interested in scholarly pursuits. As the sister of the king, she'd have little enough to do, until she inevitably had to get married. In the meantime, the more useful she made herself around the castle, the longer she could postpone her nuptials.

After his audience with the others, Robert retired to his chambers to try to still his churning thoughts. He already had numerous worries, and the death threat only added to his burden. He shared the threat with Paul, then said he was withdrawing to his bedroom for a while. Paul was about to follow him, but Robert's expression stopped him in his tracks. The squire busied himself in the dressing room instead, taking inventory of Robert's meager wardrobe.

Robert joined him there a short while later, his expression apologetic. He glanced around the room and smiled sadly. "'Tis a poor wardrobe for a king, yes?" he asked.

"'Poor' is too kind a word, Highness," Paul replied. "You need more than coronation garments."

"Aye, but the treasury cannot afford it right now," Robert said. "I cannot figure how Father was going to finance this war and make wedding arrangements for Allyson. The Crown is close to bankruptcy."

"Should you be telling me this?" Paul asked.

Robert shook his head. "I doubt it. I can hardly admit it to Fa - my - Councilors, though." He sighed. "I shall have to borrow money to get through the summer. That should make the moneylenders happy." His shoulders sagged. "Assuming I live long enough to become king in truth."

Paul crossed the few feet separating them and grasped Robert firmly by the shoulders. "Highness, I think little of someone who refuses to sign his or her name to a death threat."

Robert stepped away, tensing. "It is not the death threat itself, Paul. Cecelia did not have to sign her name - Edward and Helen confirmed her identity. She is the woman who ordered my death last year, and if she should threaten me with Magic, how can I defend myself?" He turned his back to Paul. "'Tis very embarrassing," he concluded in a whisper.

Paul wanted to offer comfort but thought better of it. His relationship with the prince was closer than that of servant and lord, but it wasn't intimate. "'Tis little help, Highness, but you are surrounded by those willing to help you."

Robert faced him again, his eyes flashing. "Aye, and I am grateful, believe me. But it is so - so frustrating!" He took several deep breaths to calm himself. "I should be able to defend myself. I do not like this feeling of helplessness - I have no control over what may or may not happen in the next few weeks." He withdrew to the sitting room and sank into a chair.

Paul joined him after a few minutes. "Is there aught I can do to help?" he asked.

"Nay," was the quiet reply. Robert glanced up at him and attempted a smile. "Which is worse, Paul? To have to be defended from a Magical attack by a pair of women, or to be the worst-dressed king in recent history?"

"Do you really want my opinion?" Paul asked.

"Go on."

"Neither is so awful. Not having the sense to realize your limitations would be worse." Robert glanced at the squire sharply. Paul continued. "'Tis not your fault you have little Magical ability, nor is it your fault that your father died suddenly and left the treasury in such a poor state. You will do whatever is necessary to keep Myrridia from becoming ripe for invasion. Once your coronation is past, you will have little cause to parade through the streets of Rhennsbury, at least until you marry. Aye, the citizens prefer their kings handsome and well dressed, but you manage the former well enough, and you cut a finer figure than your father did when he -" Paul cut off abruptly, remembering his place.

Robert wasn't letting him off the hook. "When he went into the city along with Christian Lattimore on their numerous visits to Rhennsbury's brothels and the pair of them looked like illiterate louts?" Paul's face turned crimson.

"That was not exactly how I was going to say it," he defended himself.

Robert bit his lip, but he wasn't angry. "Paul, Father seldom took pains with his appearance unless he had an important foreign dignitary present, or it was a holiday Mass or something. I have no plans to wear fine, expensive clothes all of the time, but I will not walk about the castle clad in stained, ill-fitting garments, either." He stared past Paul. "'Handsome,' am I?" he asked, biting off a snort.

Paul shrugged. "Ask the maids and the noblewomen."

Robert flushed as he recalled his time in the brothel with Mary. Paul's expression turned questioning, but the prince withdrew to the bedroom, muttering something about having to prepare for supper. Paul didn't point out that Robert had no preparations to make.

Supper was not as noisy as had been the norm when Reginald was alive. A few eyebrows were raised when James McDermott greeted Chris cordially. There were quiet mutterings at several tables.

Robert had toasted the company at the start of the meal, thanking them for responding to his father's summons so promptly. He then thanked them for their support and promised, with a smile that didn't reach his eyes, to call on them for assistance. He announced there would be a Council meeting as soon as all of the members were in Rhennsbury. He felt drained as he finished speaking, exhorting the company to enjoy the meal. He didn't like being the center of so much attention but told himself to get used to it.

Allyson spoke to Robert quietly about what she had found in the library. He thanked her for looking; he hadn't the time. He started to think about changes he could make in the Council's composition. He asked Allyson if she would consider serving, at least until he got married.

Allyson was surprised by the offer. "I-I do not know," she stammered at first. At his look of disappointment, she said firmly, "Of course, but *only* until you marry. Speaking of marriage..."

"Never fear. I have more important things to worry about than Father's marriage plans for you. They may have died with him - I will look into it right after the coronation. I can promise you that you will have final say in any other offers."

"Thank you."

At a lower table, Nicole asked Elijah if there were someplace she could go walk, out in the air. "I think it's the smells, or the fires, but I feel hot and a little nauseous. I don't have to go alone," she added quickly, remembering their foray into the city that afternoon.

Michael said from her other side, "There is the courtyard, or if you want to get away from four walls, there are the castle's ramparts, though it will be windier there."

Nicole nodded, then looked at Elijah again. "Yeah, go ahead. It's not you I'm worried about," he said with a smile.

Michael helped her stand, then escorted her out of the Great Hall. "It can get too crowded, as well," he said sympathetically, "and that is only going to get worse as Robert's coronation nears."

They walked along the corridor and climbed the stairs in the nearest stairwell. Nicole held onto his arm with one hand and held her skirt in the other. She didn't know how the other women managed, unless they were just used to it. Helen seemed to glide along rather than walk. Maybe it took years of practice. Not for the first time, Nicole wished she'd gotten laser surgery for her vision.

The effort paid off when they stepped through a door into the open air. "Ooh," Nicole breathed, seeing torch- and firelight from the city below. "It's beautiful, and the moon - it's huge! So are the stars!" She took several deep breaths, exhaling each slowly. "Thank you," she added quietly. A breeze ruffled through her bangs, and she turned her face into it for a moment. It smelled like - fresh air.

Michael smiled. "I like the solitude sometimes. Usually only the guards make their rounds, otherwise you are alone. You can come up here any time." He saluted as one sentry passed, carrying a spear. The sentry nodded, and Nicole ducked her head to him.

"I think it would be easy to fall in love in a place like this," Nicole said. "Where I come from, we have romanticized historical eras, like this one, leaving out the poverty, disease, war. All people remember is the pageantry, the clothes, the art and literature that have survived. I-it seems to mean more taking it all as a whole, even if it's sometimes a little overpowering. Does that sound silly?"

"Not at all. I would not mind visiting your world sometime, just to experience it, but I think I would want someone to guide me. I fear the consequences otherwise." There was laughter in his voice.

"I wouldn't have had the courage to come here like Chris did, not knowing anyone. Part of me is surprised that I'm here at all. And after finding that Chris and Helen had, well, you know, I feel stupid besides."

"I think you have more courage than you think, Nicole," Michael said quietly. "And you are not stupid. You had no idea."

Nicole smiled. "You're sweet to say so, Michael." The priest was grateful for the darkness as he felt his face turn warm. It was his turn to face into the breeze, in an effort to cool himself. The attempt was wasted, as Nicole leaned into him, continuing to stare at the city below. He put an arm around her shoulder awkwardly and decided that regardless of the peril to his soul, he would enjoy the limited time he had with her. He could always confess his lustful thoughts to another priest or Saelym's bishop. Later.

As Robert was leaving the Great Hall after supper, Edward caught up with him. "Is there somewhere we can talk, Highness?" he asked.

Robert nodded, then led Edward in silence to the deserted courtyard. A few torches flickered in embrasures set in the castle's walls. Robert walked along one of the cobblestone paths before stopping near a rose bush. He inhaled the aroma of the blooms for a moment before he turned to face Edward. "So?"

"It is about what you said earlier, about the treasury being empty. Is that true?" Edward asked.

"Aye. Rhennsbury is on the verge of collapse, and there is no money for repairs. Father was planning a major, long-term military campaign, though I have no idea how he planned to finance it. I do not even know the best way to pay for the coronation." Robert was unable to keep the frustration out of his voice.

"Do not worry about the coronation. The city merchants will be happy enough to extend credit," Edward assured him. "And I am certain Reginald had intended to levy a tax to pay for his campaign."

Robert's eyes flashed with anger. "Oh, aye, that will help! Where would he have gotten the tax money? You cannot get blood from a turnip!"

"From the nobility, of course, Highness -" Edward began in a consoling tone.

Robert's expression didn't change. "And exactly where would *they* have gotten the money?" His voice was dangerously quiet. "From their farmers and others ill able to pay," he answered his own question. He debated telling Edward he had no intention of going ahead with his father's plans for conquest, but he decided it could wait until the upcoming Council meeting. "All Father was worried about was conquering these two kingdoms and uniting them with Myrridia under his rule, regardless of anyone else's opinions in the matter. Nor did he care about how his own lands were doing." He swore.

"Rhennsbury's merchants will do well with the coronation, Robert, and with all of the visitors to the city." Edward tried a different approach, but Robert had an answer for him.

"And precisely how many of those visitors will be coming for return visits, with the city as it is now? It is humiliating - for Myrridia, for me..." Robert trailed off, losing his train of thought, and sat down hard on the nearby stone bench. In his emotional turmoil, the pain didn't register.

"None will notice, High-" Edward began again.

Robert snorted. "Oh, yes, they will. Rest assured, many people will notice and spread the word. 'Twill take a miracle to get through these next weeks without at least some laughing behind their hands." He looked up at the night sky. "I will get through it, but it will take a while to forgive Father for doing this to Myrridia. The treasury will be built up again, Uncle, but not at the expense of the people. Change is coming. Good night." Robert stood and walked back to the castle.

Edward remained where he was for several heartbeats. Change was what he feared the most. He'd been able to maintain a certain balance over the past several years, and that balance was now in peril. He swore under his breath. He did not care for his nephew's assertiveness.

Helen and Chris left the Great Hall with Anselm. He led them to his guest chamber, where he shooed his family members to other rooms, threatening them with a history lesson if they remained. His four-year-old granddaughter asked if she could stay.

"Of course, my dear, if you do not think you will be bored," Anselm replied in a softer voice than usual.

"You are not boring, Grandpapa," she said as he lifted her into his lap. He had sat in the room's single chair, motioning Chris and Helen to stools. Chris added a log to the fire before sitting.

"So, what did you discover?" Anselm asked, as his granddaughter settled back against him.

"As many questions as answers," Helen replied.

Anselm nodded. "I have thought of little else today, and I have remembered a great deal of what happened at the time. The battle at Tippensdown nearly six years ago is perhaps one of Myrridia's worst moments in history. Reginald was so bloody determined to unite Myrridia with Wyckendom, and Esterlyn to our east for that matter, regardless of the cost to all. You read about the earl's family." He paused. Helen and Chris nodded.

"Cecelia Falkes was not killed with her family because she was at the royal Court in Laurconsburg, already a stellar student of Magic at age sixteen. Many in Wyckendom expected her to become one of the most powerful Magician's in their history, in part since she was a younger daughter and would not be forced to marry before developing her Talents to the fullest," Anselm explained.

"Like Margaret Claybourne married Reginald and had to put her Talents aside," Chris put in.

"Aye, exactly. Margaret Dupre, as she was born, showed a lot of promise before her marriage to Reginald, though I do not think she would have been in the same league as Cecelia. According to the rumors at the time, Cecelia would be as powerful as Edward, or yourself, Helen. Some said even stronger." Anselm smiled at her.

Helen returned the smile, then said, "She sent the message to Robert today, and also hired the man who tried to kill Robert last Christmas. Edward was unable to glean any information from that man's memories because his mind was protected by a spell Edward could not break."

"Interesting," Anselm said, hearing this news for the first time. "That must have put our esteemed bishop in a foul mood for weeks. Or is he still angry about it?"

Helen suppressed a chuckle. "Oh, after that message today, his anger and frustration are back to the fore."

Anselm looked thoughtful. "This news does raise the possibility that Reginald's death and the attempt against Robert a few months ago are related as I suggested yesterday. But there is no woman involved in Reginald's death, is there?"

"A prostitute," Helen replied, "but she was hanged the next morning. Would you know anything about a brother of Cecelia's surviving?"

"This is all rumor, Helen, but this is what I have heard. There was a younger son about a year or two older than Cecelia who may not have been killed during the massacre." Anselm didn't hesitate to use the word 'massacre' - his granddaughter had fallen asleep. "He may have been spying for his king in either Myrridia or Esterlyn at the time. His name was Sebastian, I believe. He has not been heard from since, though it is probable that he returned to

Wyckendom, learned of his family's fate, and went into hiding, with or without Cecelia."

"So both of them would have plenty of reasons to want Reginald and Christian dead," Chris noted. Anselm agreed. "But would they want Robert dead as well? Or do they consider him guilty by reason of being a Claybourne? And what about Allyson? Can she inherit the throne?"

"Aye," Helen replied. "She could be in mortal danger as well. She is an untried though potentially quite powerful Magical practitioner in her own right, but she is not trained to be a match for this Cecelia, not yet anyway. What about Sebastian's military prowess?" She directed the last at Anselm.

"Again rumors, but I believe he was an expert swordsman and accomplished archer. He would need to be very competent in the event he got himself into trouble. Should he be exposed as a spy, he might need to make a hasty exit and take a few men out in the process. I would assume he could defend himself well." Anselm absently stroked his granddaughter's hair, not disturbing her.

"We have a lot of trouble, then," Chris said. "I am nowhere near the swordsman Christian was, so who does that leave to defend Robert? Magically he is much better protected, but what if - if it is indeed Cecelia Falkes - she wants to go one-on-one?"

"I would like to think they are both reasonable human beings, if they could be made to see past their own hurt. That is the stumbling block to what you suggested earlier, Christopher, using diplomacy. Neither one may be able to forgive Robert for what his father did."

"What if Saelym offered reparations?" Chris asked, glancing at Helen. She looked surprised, then thoughtful.

"It could be done, I suppose. Saelym is in good financial shape at the moment, though a couple of bad harvests could change that. If it became the deciding factor, then I would be behind you on it, Chris. Right now, Myrridia needs Robert and Allyson, and anything that avoids more bloodshed is a good thing to me. Unlike Edward, I do not see diplomacy as a sign of weakness but of strength."

"Thank God for women," Chris said with feeling. "If women were in charge, things would be a whole lot better." He grimaced. "Well, except maybe women like this Cecelia, anyway."

Helen smiled. "So, who is in charge of the earldom now?"

Anselm looked surprised. "I do not know," he said finally. "Perhaps we should speak to Robert."

"Now?" Chris asked.

"Why not?"

Anselm carried his granddaughter into a bedroom and handed her to his daughter. The three then walked companionably to Robert's apartment. Paul opened the door at their knock, and his eyes widened in surprise. He turned into the room, holding the door open a crack. "My lord, 'tis the Duke of Latham and Duke and Duchess of Saelym."

"Show them in, Paul," Robert called from the bedchamber. He was entering the sitting room as they filed in. He was still dressed and motioned them to seats. He perched on his writing table and gave them his attention. "I assume you have thought of something important," he said.

"Aye, Highness," Anselm replied. "We would not disturb your privacy this late were it otherwise. Have you thought more about the earldom of Tippensdown?"

"I have thought of little else," Robert replied. "What of it?"

"Who is in charge of it now?" Helen asked.

Robert frowned, then turned and picked up several parchments lying on the writing table. He smiled guiltily. "I went through a lot of Father's old correspondence and brought it here." He looked through the papers. "As far as I can tell, Father left a garrison there, but he has not named anyone earl." He was thoughtful for several moments. "'Tis not like Father. I can only guess he had no trustworthy candidates in mind, unless after he annexed the entire kingdom of Wyckendom, he had planned to award the various titles to those men who proved bravest on the battlefield." Disgust had crept into his tone by the time he had finished speaking.

Anselm nodded. "I am surprised at Reginald's lapse as well." His eyes twinkled momentarily. "Reginald Claybourne was no

156

genius in most subjects, but strategy was his one gift." He paused, then asked Robert evenly, "Whom would you name to the post?"

Robert blinked in surprise. "I had not even thought about it, but I guess I have to." He grinned suddenly, looking his age. "My first choice would be Elijah Holmes."

Chris fought his smile; Elijah would kill him. Helen had no hesitations. "Elijah is a splendid choice, Robert, but there is one small difficulty." Robert's face fell. "Elijah wants no part of any title, as I recall."

"Aye, you are right. I will have to work on him - I mean - think on it." Chris raised his eyebrow at the verbal lapse.

Chapter Eight

Naomi had agreed to being escorted by a single man-at-arms to the tavern where she was to meet her "date." The soldier, John, said he would give her some privacy once they arrived at The King's Arms, but he would keep an eye on how things developed. If the man seemed trustworthy, he would leave the rest to Naomi's judgment. Elijah was still unhappy about the excursion, and Helen had tried to talk her out of it, but Naomi tried to assure them that she would be fine.

Naomi and John arrived at the tavern, and she looked around the common room for the man she'd met earlier. He was sitting at a table in a corner of the room, away from the fire, but he stood when he saw Naomi enter. Naomi wiped her suddenly sweaty palms on her dress as she joined him at the table. She got straight to the point.

"My name is Naomi, and you are?" she asked.

"I am Sebastian. I am pleased to meet you properly, Lady Naomi," he replied, assisting her to sit.

"I'm not a lady, Sebastian. I don't have a title. I'm from - well, a long way from here," Naomi stated, chuckling at the understatement.

"I am not from Myrridia, either," Sebastian said.

"Oh?"

"I was born in Wyckendom, a kingdom about a fortnight's journey from here," he explained, not giving any more detail. A surly young woman came over to the table and asked Sebastian if he were ready to eat or drink now. She scowled at Naomi. Sebastian asked Naomi if she wished to dine, or just have some ale. She told him she'd already eaten. The young woman left to fetch two tankards of ale, her expression unwavering.

Naomi asked Sebastian about the weather and what to expect for the summer months to make small talk until the woman returned with their drinks. The young woman set the tankards down forcefully, spilling some of the contents onto the tabletop. She slopped the liquid around the tabletop with a dirty rag, making the mess worse, and left abruptly.

"No tip for her," Naomi said lightly.

"Excuse me?" Sebastian asked.

"Where I come from, we leave extra money if we eat away from home and the service is good. That money is called a tip." Naomi looked thoughtful. "Although if the service industry is as wonderful a place to work as in my time, I can hardly blame her."

Sebastian detected the sarcasm in her words and became even more interested in knowing this woman better.

"We can go explore the city if you would rather not stay here," he offered, then added, "There are a few places that are safe after dark."

Naomi raised an eyebrow. "I'm sure there are, but are *you* safe after dark?"

Sebastian met her gaze. "That depends on what you mean by 'safe.' You intrigue me, with your dark skin, your beauty, and your obvious intelligence." He smiled.

Naomi smiled back. "Well, at least you're honest." Deepening her voice, she said, "'Honey, I could look into your eyes forever, but I'd really like to get you out of those clothes and admire your eyes while we're having sex.'"

Sebastian laughed outright. "You are truly like no other woman I have known."

"That doesn't surprise me." She shrugged. "You saw my brother earlier. He'd kill you if you tried to charm me out of my clothes."

"Who invited him this evening?" Sebastian countered.

"I didn't." She paused. "Admit it, though, you'd like to charm me out of my clothes."

"'Twould be up to you. It was not my intention when I asked you for a drink, though the idea excites me." As much as he'd like to distract himself with Naomi's charms, he didn't dare, at least not until his business in Rhennsbury was concluded. He had no idea where Naomi's loyalties lay at this point, but if her brother were on good terms with Lattimore, the possibility of a relationship of any kind with her was unlikely.

After they finished their drinks, Naomi and Sebastian left the tavern. John discreetly trailed them along the street at a fair distance. Sebastian quickly realized they were being followed and mentioned the fact to Naomi. She turned and smiled at John before winking. "He's my escort - Duchess Helen insisted."

"You and your brother have friends in high places, 'twould seem," Sebastian said lightly, though he tensed on the inside.

"I'm only in Myrridia for a short time, Sebastian. I'll be going home by the end of the month, or right after the coronation. I wasn't upset about that before this evening. But now you have done a very bad thing," she admonished him.

"Oh? Do I pique your interest, my lady?" he teased.

"Something like that. I would like to get to know you better." Naomi was enjoying the game now.

Sebastian turned to her and placed one hand under her chin. She was nearly as tall as he was. He tilted her face up slightly and bent down the inch or so to meet her lips with his own. He kissed her slowly, and her arms reached behind him and stroked his back. He put both arms around her firmly, kissing her a second time.

160

When their lips parted again, Naomi whispered, "Good thing Mama doesn't mind white men. I'm not complaining about your technique, Sebastian, but why did you have to do that?"

Sebastian paused before replying. "I thought you should make an informed decision before leaving." He released her, then held out his arm for her to take. They walked together along the dark street, heading toward the city gate that opened on the short road leading to the castle. He made sure that his sword was visible to the few folk out on the street, to deter mischief. The silence between them was a comfortable one. Sebastian escorted Naomi to the castle's main gate, then kissed her again.

"I am not what you think, Naomi," he said in parting. "You would do better to go home and get away from the things yet to befall Rhennsbury." He turned quickly and headed back into the city, though it took a conscious effort for him not to turn around and look back at her.

He castigated himself as he hurried along the city's main street back to his accommodation. Cecelia would be furious when she found out about his assignation. What had possessed him to say that to Naomi? At the least, he'd nearly betrayed himself, never mind his sister.

He shook his head to clear it. He'd been physically attracted to women before, but he'd never acted on the feelings while involved on an assignment, unless the actions would have *aided* the assignment. Such an opportunity occasionally arose.

A sharp pain struck his left temple, and he stumbled and almost fell before regaining his balance. He crouched, assuming a defensive posture, and looked around. There was no one on the street. His face drained of color as he realized the brief attack must have been Magical. But who? Cecelia? The spasm passed, and Sebastian increased his pace back to the inn.

Naomi stared after Sebastian's back long after he disappeared into the night. She wondered if she had just received information, or a warning. She shivered, suddenly feeling cold. John joined her and walked with her into the castle's entry yard.

A few minutes later, Naomi let herself into the room she shared with Nicole. "Boy, is he ever hot!" she exclaimed. "He reminds me of Alan Rickman in the Robin Hood movie. Sex on two legs."

Nicole smiled, still thinking about her evening with Father Michael under the stars. "Stop it before I start drooling. You don't have a problem with that - chocolate/vanilla barrier?"

"Do you have a problem with Denzel?" Naomi countered. Nicole's smile widened, and she conceded the point. Naomi continued, "I don't have any problems where sexy men are concerned." She sobered suddenly. "It's complicated, though. He said something - I probably ought to talk to Chris and Helen." She went to the door.

"Wait for me," Nicole called, scrambling after her.

Naomi was across the hall when Nicole rejoined her. Naomi rapped firmly. A muffled curse was heard from inside the room. After several seconds, Chris flung the door open, his hair rumpled, his expression murderous. His under-tunic was hanging outside his trousers.

"What!"

"Oops. Did I interrupt something?" Naomi asked innocently.

"No," Helen said dryly from the bedchamber, putting her dressing gown on over her shift and entering the sitting room.

Naomi didn't try to hide her astonishment. "Have you two made up?"

"We were trying to when some fool knocked on the door," Chris said with exaggerated patience. "Was there something *important* you wanted to see us about?"

Naomi had momentarily forgotten, but recovered. "Yes. It's about my date. He said something that was vague, but, oh, I don't know." She frowned in frustration. "Maybe I'm just reading too much into it."

"What?" the other three exclaimed together.

"Well, he didn't say anything specific, but he suggested I go home before anything else bad happens in Rhennsbury, like he knew something." She paused and smiled. "Shame if he does - he's a gorgeous SOB."

"Naomi!" Chris said in exasperation.

She shrugged.

"Did he give you a name?" Helen asked.

"He said his name was Sebastian," Naomi replied. "He didn't give a sur -"

"*Sebastian?*" Chris and Helen exchanged glances.

"What?" Naomi now demanded.

Chris raised an eyebrow at Helen. She shrugged. "They will find out soon enough," she said.

"'Sebastian' is the name of Cecelia's *brother*," Chris said quietly. Naomi looked confused. Nicole sagged against the bed.

"Cecelia's the one who hurt Michael and me," she whispered. Naomi looked sick. Helen helped the taller woman to a chair.

"I hate to make things worse, but you should see Edward in the morning. He has had a glimpse of the man who slew Reginald, and you should describe this man to him. Chris and I will go with you," Helen said.

"Of course."

"Yes, Father?" Edward asked his assistant the next morning. He was working on some paperwork for the archbishop.

"The Lattimores are here, Excellency. They are requesting an audience as soon as possible. The duchess says it concerns the king's death," Ambrose replied.

Edward stood. "Send them in at once!"

Ambrose bowed and scurried out. Edward was still standing when Chris and Helen entered, followed by Elijah Holmes and his sister. Chris and Helen dutifully kissed the proffered ring; Elijah and Naomi ignored it. Edward frowned.

"Well, what is this about Reginald's murder?" Edward asked impatiently. He motioned the women to sit before resuming his own seat. Chris and Elijah assumed protective positions behind Helen and Naomi, respectively.

"Naomi had an assignation last evening with a man who may know something, or even be involved," Helen replied evenly.

"What?" Edward exclaimed, standing again. He narrowed his eyes at Naomi. "Describe the man," he ordered curtly.

"Your courtesy leaves a lot to be desired," Naomi said, folding her arms across her chest and looking obstinate. Edward slammed his hand down on the desk. The others jumped.

"I did not get to where I am today by being nice," he said quietly. His smile was unpleasant.

"Really?" Naomi asked sarcastically. "Sebastian, my date, is tall, taller than me by a little. He has dark hair and deep blue eyes, with a well-kept mustache and beard. Oh, yeah, and he's white." She kept her features impassive.

Elijah laughed. Helen and Chris choked to stifle their own laughter. Edward glowered. "The last will prove most helpful indeed." His sarcasm matched hers. "I would like to 'see' his image, as you saw him."

Naomi looked alarmed. "What, with Magic?"

"I think not," Elijah said vehemently. "You aren't getting into her head. Helen can do it."

"No, Elijah," Helen said, "I have not seen the man. Why else come to Edward? He will not hurt Naomi - I will not let him." She gazed at Edward as though daring him to contradict her.

"No one is going to get hurt," Edward said testily. "Mistress Holmes?"

"Yes, sir?" Her tone was uncharacteristically subdued.

Edward walked over to where she sat, holding his hand out to her. She took it with hesitation. "I am not going to hurt you, you have my word. My word is still worth something here."

Naomi nodded, swallowing hard. "Will I feel anything?"

Edward glanced at Elijah. "Only if you share some of his gifts."

Naomi took a deep breath. "Okay. Go ahead."

Edward moved behind her, letting go of her hand and resting his hands on her shoulders. "Think of something calming," Edward directed in a quieter voice. Naomi complied and relaxed a little. "Mistress Holmes, now please envision this Sebastian and think of naught else." Edward gave her a few moments, then he slipped into trance. Sebastian's image was at the forefront of Naomi's mind. Edward spent a short time memorizing the man's features, then withdrew back to himself.

Elijah had moved next to him.

"I'm fine, 'Lijah," Naomi said, rolling her shoulders. "I didn't feel anything."

Edward returned to his chair. "He could be the same man, though I cannot be certain. Mistress Holmes, you got a much clearer image of him, but you were not drugged and bleeding." His voice had hardened by the time he finished speaking.

"Do you need to share that experience with someone, Edward?" Helen asked. As a Magical practitioner she was genuinely concerned. "Reginald was your half-brother, so you are hardly objective."

"Thank you, Helen. Perhaps after these people are brought to justice. Why do you suspect this Sebastian?"

"Because he told me to leave town before anything else happens," Naomi replied.

Edward nodded. "He could be involved then. Who is he?"

"Does the surname Falkes mean anything to you?" Helen asked him. Chris looked at her in surprise, but she shook her head to keep him quiet.

"Falkes?" Edward was about to reply in the negative when a memory came to mind. "Are you referring to the earldom of Tippensdown, in Wyckendom, *again*?" He paused. "I thought they were all dead."

"You mean murdered? Guess again." Chris couldn't help himself.

"'Twas a campaign," Edward began automatically.

"You do not slaughter women and children 'on campaign,' Edward. At least not if you pretend to be civilized. I keep forgetting who it is we are talking about." Chris crossed himself, for the slain family, not their killers.

"Cecelia Falkes was at Court, as a student of Magic. She showed great promise. She had a brother Sebastian who may have been away spying at the time of the massacre," Helen added. She took a deep breath before continuing. "It might be possible to avoid more bloodshed, if they are willing to give Robert the benefit of the doubt and he has the courage to buck tradition."

Edward's eyes flashed angrily. "I care as little for the suggestion now as when Christopher broached it yesterday." He paused, choosing his next words carefully. "You are suggesting that Robert ignore the law in regard to regicide," he countered. "He will never get that suggestion past the Council, never mind the people."

"I would not be so certain of that, Edward," Helen said with a smile. "Robert may be Reginald's son, but he is not Reginald. You had noticed that?" Her tone was all innocence, and Edward didn't like the tone or her words.

Robert was pacing in the study when a castle page announced that the Lord Mayor of Rhennsbury had arrived. He told the page to send the Mayor straight in.

The Mayor, Henry Black, entered the room and bowed. He was a short, stout man, about forty years old, with graying brown hair, brown eyes, and a neatly trimmed mustache and beard. He was also the head of Rhennsbury's wealthiest goldsmith family. He was dressed in his robes of office, with a symbolic key to the city hanging from his belt. His robes looked new and fit him well. Robert indicated a chair and Henry sat.

"I trust the day finds you in good health, Your Highness," he greeted Robert.

"Aye, well enough. And you as well." Henry nodded. "How may I help you this morning?" Robert did not see the need to put off business with multiple pleasantries.

Henry crossed one leg over the other, assuming a position of relaxation, but Robert sensed it was a pose.

"It concerns the Duke of Saelym, my lord," Henry said. "There are some ugly rumors in the city, and I feel duty-bound to inform you."

Robert tensed. "What sort of rumors?"

"Many citizens feel that the duke is behind the death of your father, may he rest in peace," Henry went on, crossing himself. Robert was about to follow suit, but stopped. "Ever since Christmastide, the two men have lacked the close friendship they had before."

"I am not going to speculate on the relationship between the two men at this time, sir," Robert began, stalling to find words that would be neutral. He could hardly expect the entire city to believe that he was now on good terms with the duke, even though it was true. "I do not believe that the duke would ever consider committing treason, even if he and Father were estranged." He managed not to choke on the words, remembering Christian's attempted assault on his sister. The duke hadn't even been estranged from his father when that episode had happened.

"I am only passing along what I hear, Sire. Many are calling for the duke's immediate execution." Henry shifted in his seat. Robert almost stood up at these words, but managed to remain seated through an effort of will.

"And what proof do these people offer of his guilt, sir?" The need for courtesy was beginning to grate on Robert's nerves. The last thing he needed right now was to have to protect Chris as well as himself. His concentration was already being spread thin. He briefly wondered how one man was supposed to maintain control of everything all of the time. He wanted to know how his father had done it, having spent so much of his time in his cups.

Henry shrugged. "They do not offer proof, except that he arrived in Rhennsbury so quickly after the king's murder, Sire. He must have known the king was dead, else why come?"

Robert relaxed slightly, though his expression remained solemn. "The Duke of Saelym, like many others, was summoned to Rhennsbury by my father."

"Yes, Sire, but those summonses left Rhennsbury only a couple of days before his death," Henry countered.

Jesu! Robert thought. This situation was demanding delicate political maneuvering, and he lacked the necessary experience. He didn't need the city's residents clamoring for Chris's head. He steepled his fingers, leaning his forearms on the desktop.

"I assure you, my Lord Mayor, we are investigating my father's death, and we shall check into every possibility. I do want to thank you for bringing this matter to my attention. It will be looked into." Robert stood, effectively ending the conversation. If the Mayor had wanted a commitment, he would have to leave disappointed. Chris McCabe was one of the few people that Robert could trust at this point. Henry Black rose as well, his face impassive.

"Thank you, Sire, for hearing me out. It must be a difficult time for you and the princess. The citizens' thoughts and prayers are with your family." The words sounded rehearsed.

"Then, please, my lord, thank them for us both," Robert replied as he escorted Henry to the door.

Robert returned to his pacing. After a short while he summoned a page to fetch Chris, Helen and Elijah to the study. When the trio arrived, he asked them to sit, but remained standing himself. He tried to smile, but gave up when the attempt failed.

"Things are getting worse, I fear. The Lord Mayor of Rhennsbury was just here, and he informed me that the people of the city are clamoring for Christian's head. They think that Christian had Father murdered, and now they want him executed for treason. The whole thing is absurd, of course - if Christian were alive, he and Father would be on good terms, and - and -" Robert gestured helplessly, running out of steam. Changing his approach, he continued, "It took all of my political training to get the man out of here without promising anything." He finally managed a rueful smile.

"By our Lady!" Helen exclaimed, exasperated.

"If you don't mind my pointing this out, Your Highness, how are you going to explain to your Council, never mind the people of the city, your own 'reconciliation' with the duke?" Elijah asked. "You may as well get used to having to defend that maneuver."

"And, what exactly does this mean for me?" Chris asked. "I mean, should I avoid going into the streets any time soon, or what?"

Robert scowled, but his anger and frustration weren't directed toward the people in the room. "Well, Sir Elijah, I will answer your question first; I think it is the more complicated. I intend to change the composition of the Council when it meets in a couple of days, and when the new members are sitting at the table, I have thought about telling them the truth about Chris."

"Can you do that with the Council, Robert?" Helen asked. "And I will caution you not to tell the truth about Chris to them all."

"I can change the Council, Lady Helen. Allyson found a predecessor who did the same thing when he ascended the throne. I want to hear your reasons for not informing the others of Chris's identity." Robert leaned back against the wall.

"Some may accept the information, Highness, but others will say Chris has no right to the title of Duke of Saelym and clamor for young Reginald to be named duke immediately. Then they will jump in and ask to be regents for the duchy. You cannot hope to rid the Council of all bad elements. I do not think telling James McDermott will be a problem, and I know Anselm DeLacey will not, but if you feel you must tell others, do it individually. You are the king, and you can keep Chris on the Council with no explanation or simply state that you feel 'Christian' has changed his ways. Such has been remarked upon in Saelym."

Robert nodded. "You make several good points, my lady. I need you and Chris in Saelym, so I do not dare take the chance that he could not retain the title. Or, even worse, I may not be able to keep him from losing his head. Thank you - this does change things."

Robert turned to Chris, looking apologetic. "I think the best course for your safety is to put you under house arrest. I think you should stay away from the city, and you will have to be accompanied by one or two guards whenever you leave your chambers. I-I am sorry."

Chris was stunned. "That sounds like an admission of guilt! And how can I help find Cecelia and Sebastian if I am unable to go anywhere?"

Helen winked at Elijah. "I think we could find a few ways to pass the time in our chambers," she said to Chris with a smile.

Chris frowned. "As wonderful as your suggestion is - and I can think of no better way to spend my time - you will be out protecting Robert, while I - oh, bloody -! Can anyone come up with another way?" he pleaded.

"If I can think of one, Chris, you will be the first to know. I would far rather inconvenience you now, than have someone murder you in the streets. I need you too much!" Robert looked as miserable as Chris felt.

"Okay, but I do not have to like it."

Elijah tried to help. "Look on the bright side, pal. You go around scowling at everyone, they'll assume you're Christian," he said blandly.

Chris glared at Elijah. "Next time you want to be helpful, stop."

Helen changed the subject. "How do you plan to change the Council, Robert?"

Robert gave her a grateful smile. "Add the Duke of Latham and my sister. Allyson said she would serve until I marry."

Chris forgot his frustration. "A woman, Robert? You are quite a radical."

"I am proud of you," Helen added.

Robert flushed. "You would have been my first choice, Lady Helen, but with 'Christian' already there, I did not think I could get away with both of you."

Chris snorted. "So, replace me with Helen. She would be better anyway."

Helen shook her head. "Thank you both, but with my obligations to Edward, I cannot. Though, if Chris were unable to attend for some reason, I could serve in his stead."

Robert turned to Elijah. "I need to ask you a favor." He sounded hesitant. Elijah tensed.

"Yes, Sire?"

"If an odd number of men left the Council in disgust after these changes, would you be willing to serve?" Robert stared at the floor, unsure if Elijah would get angry or start laughing at him.

"I-I guess I'm flattered, but I don't know if I can commit to it." Elijah seemed more flustered than mad. "I mean, I'm not even sure if I'm staying in Myrridia forever." Robert had now met his gaze and nodded.

"I could accept it as a temporary arrangement," Robert said.

"My common sense is telling me to head for the hills, but if you need an even number, I'll do it. Your mother wanted to give me a title, but I was able to talk her out of it. I should've known my luck couldn't last forever." Elijah held out his hand to Robert, who shook it firmly.

"Thank you."

Late that morning, Sebastian waited in the middle of a long line of petitioners waiting to speak with the Mayor. He made occasional conversation with those near him in line. He had no intention of actually speaking with the man; he hoped to hear what had happened during the Mayor's audience with Robert Claybourne. His patience was rewarded.

Henry Black entered the waiting area. He had returned straight from his meeting. He frowned and motioned for his deputies to join him. He spoke in a normal voice, reporting what had transpired, and Sebastian learned that Lattimore would keep his head for the nonce. It was a minor setback.

Sebastian had no qualms about taking on the duke in a sword fight. He preferred to publicly challenge the duke to a duel, to avenge the deaths of his family members. Sebastian was surprised that Robert had refrained from ordering a quick execution, but he admired the young man's ability to put his personal feelings aside and wait for clear evidence of guilt. Sebastian felt renewed stirrings of doubt regarding his sister. He had no argument with a young man who had been a child at the time of their family members' deaths, especially since he'd already interacted with

Robert while employed at Rhennsbury Castle and knew him to be fair-minded.

Sebastian did not have to worry about making an inconspicuous exit. Henry Black informed the waiting petitioners that he would not hear any cases until mid-afternoon. He told everyone to come back later; he would see them in whatever order they arrived at that time. Many complained, having waited for a good part of the morning. Sebastian slipped out unnoticed.

He collected his horse and rode out to report to Cecelia. She sensed her brother's approach and met him outside the tent. "Is Lattimore dead?" she asked. Her eyes flashed with strong emotion. She knew about his assignation with Naomi.

Sebastian ignored her expression. "Nay. He is not to be executed immediately, nor has he taken to his bed due to poor health. I told you that young Claybourne has more intelligence and self-control than his sire, and he will not execute the man without evidence of his guilt." Sebastian paused. "A pity," he added.

"This prince would be hard pressed to have less intellect than his father," Cecelia remarked bitterly. "I should like to meet him face-to-face, but I doubt he would grant us immunity."

"We can petition for it anyway," Sebastian pointed out.

Ignoring her brother, Cecelia pursued her own line of thought. "Could we get into the castle without permission?"

Sebastian looked insulted. "You forget with whom you are dealing. I could get us in there, but are you so keen to play the role of scullery maid?"

Cecelia laughed. "I have done worse things out of need, though I admit I have never taken orders well. Why not? 'Tis better than sleeping outside every night. I would like to observe Robert and his sister before we continue with our plans. If he is intelligent and far-sighted - well, but I do not see how more death can be avoided. We have murdered a king, and the penalty for that is death."

"Could you allow Robert to live? I had no idea you had a soft, sentimental side," Sebastian said.

Cecelia snorted. "It is not sentimentality. Reginald Claybourne deserved to die, worse than he did. If Robert can meet my demands, then I will let him live," she lied. "Not so with Lattimore."

Sebastian nodded, accepting her words. "I shall avenge our family on him. 'Twas he who slew our mother after raping her and our sisters."

Cecelia's eyes went cold. "Aye. I went by the castle a few weeks after the massacre, long before I met up with you. I was dressed as a nun. Using prayer as a pretext, I 'saw' what had happened to our family. Claybourne and Lattimore were the worst, though there were two barons whom I would gladly send to Hell also. Reginald Claybourne has paid for his crimes; Lattimore will have his turn. As far as Robert Claybourne goes, we shall have to see what happens."

She preceded Sebastian into the tent and began packing her few essential household items. She hung her herb bag on her belt, as well as a small purse. Sebastian lifted the packed saddlebags, went outside, and saddled up Cecelia's mount before arranging the packed bags on the saddle. They would leave the tent and furniture behind, for the time being. Cecelia set a spell of protection around the clearing. It would deter would-be thieves. Sebastian helped Cecelia onto her horse before mounting his own, then they began their trek to Rhennsbury.

Chapter Nine

Baron Nigel Jennings of Thorburg, a Royal Councilor supportive of Reginald Claybourne's war plans, had the ill fortune to be in the common room of his favorite Rhennsbury tavern, the Bronze Unicorn, when Cecelia and Sebastian arrived that evening.

Cecelia had been in a foul mood since Sebastian told her of his rendezvous with Naomi. She called him every epithet she could think up, then invented a few. She admonished herself for allowing him so much freedom. How dare he? And with the sister of Lattimore's dark-skinned associate. Cecelia had to make a conscious effort to refrain from killing her brother in a fit of temper. She'd sensed that something was occurring the previous evening and sent her brother a Magical warning.

It had been easy to manipulate him at first. He'd burned as much for revenge as she had, when they'd crossed paths two years ago, and she'd taken quick advantage. She'd not seen him since a number of years before the massacre, and hadn't been certain he was even still alive. Since Sebastian lacked her Magical gifts, she had unobtrusively gained control of part of his mind, gradually leading his thinking to agree with hers. Unfortunately, total control could not be maintained when they were separated, and now Sebastian had begun to reassert his own, more fair-minded, opinions. She would have to tread warily around him, especially regarding the prince, though she could express her anger about his meeting with Naomi. She thanked the saints that she'd not informed him of all of her plans. Unaware of Cecelia's thoughts and manipulations, Sebastian remembered Naomi's face and the shape of her body and let his sister's insults go right past him.

Sebastian entered the inn alone first, to see about a room vacancy. The inn looked disreputable enough that he didn't think it would be a problem. In the common room there was a heavy haze of smoke from the large hearth, where the carcasses of several rabbits were being cooked. The room also smelled of sweat, ale, and old urine. After bargaining for a few moments, Sebastian paid for three nights. The innkeeper inclined his head, thanking "milord." Sebastian scowled and went back out to collect his sister and their belongings.

After making certain the horses were comfortably stabled, Sebastian joined Cecelia in the common room. The ferret-faced Jennings was trying to strike up a conversation with her. Sebastian sat next to Cecelia, laying his hand casually on his sword's hilt. Jennings ignored him. He'd had a few tankards of ale and was spoiling for a good fight, preferably in a bed with a hot-tempered woman.

Cecelia smiled and put her hand on top of Sebastian's. "Leave us be, brother. My lord has made me a very generous offer. Come upstairs after midnight." She held back from enforcing her words with Magic.

Sebastian tried to keep his features even, but his stomach was churning. He recognized the baron by his device, a silver boar, and wondered why the nobleman was staying in such a low-class establishment. He could surely afford better, unless he was looking for trouble. Sebastian hoped Cecelia knew what she was doing. He stood as they did, then didn't sit again until they'd disappeared upstairs.

"I am not going to like this," he muttered. The innkeeper gave him a sympathetic look and a brimming tankard. He then pointed out a raucous game of dice in a dim corner. Sebastian nodded. Maybe he could pick up some coin; the evening might not be a total loss.

Nigel was panting by the time he and Cecelia reached her chamber. She smiled. He took it as encouragement and began unlacing his trousers. Cecelia unlaced the throat of her bodice, and Nigel pressed a hand to her breast.

"Are you man enough, my lord?" she purred, then kicked him swiftly in the crotch. She was still wearing her riding boots. Nigel fell backward, involuntarily crying out, then covering himself.

Cecelia crouched down next to him, touching her fingertips to his temples. He scurried backward until his back struck the room's wall.

"Wh-who are you?" he whimpered, his courage gone.

"Cecelia Falkes, of the earldom of Tippensdown in Wyckendom. Think back about six years, Baron Jennings." Her voice began as sweet innocence, but was cold as ice when she finished. Like Sebastian she had recognized his device as soon as she saw him sitting at one of the inn's long tables. He'd aged a little since the massacre at Tippensdown, but he was unmistakably one of the men who'd raped her older sister, after the Duke of Saelym had finished with her. She burned for revenge.

"Nooo -" Nigel began. Cecelia easily overwhelmed the weak-minded baron. She was able to exert her own will over his with a simple spell she improvised. He would live out his days in insanity. She smiled as another idea occurred to her. She concentrated on setting a single trigger, which would set a certain series of events in motion if the right precipitating action occurred. Lattimore would pay, and so would his traitorous wife.

Cecelia's eyes darkened at the thought of Helen Lattimore. She knew the woman by the duchess's reputation as a Magical practitioner. How could Helen serve the Church, and men, with no complaint? Cecelia had no regard for the Church's strictures against certain Magical formulae; she freely broke the law as it suited her purposes. Men ran the Church. She only kept Sebastian around because he proved useful on occasion, and he kept her informed of events.

She stood and left Nigel in the room's corner. She straightened her skirts absently, crossed the room, and sat at the table to wait for the inevitable scene with her brother. She had to figure out how to regain control of him; she didn't want to kill him.

Chris was still in a bad mood as he and Helen prepared for bed that evening. After supper they'd gone to the library and had looked through another book on history, but they'd discovered nothing new. Two royal guards had remained outside the library, and even though the door had been closed, Chris still knew they were there. Two different men were now stationed outside the guest chamber.

Helen took his hand in sympathy. "'Tis only temporary, until Christian's name can be cleared. When it comes to your safety, I agree with Robert."

"Intellectually I know it is for the best, Helen," Chris said. "I guess I just cannot stand what it implies, not to mention the lack of privacy!"

"Well, I hope to distract you since we now *do* have some privacy." Helen discarded her dressing gown, then she nervously removed her shift. "You say you want to see me without -"

Chris stared at her for several seconds, openmouthed. He collected himself with a start, then handed her the shift. "There is no need, not like this," he said softly. "Though you have distracted me. God, you are beautiful." He didn't see anything wrong with her body and told her so.

Helen blushed, then pulled Chris's face to hers, kissing him with passion. It was the best compliment she'd ever received. After their lips parted, Chris removed all of his own garments.

Helen smiled. "Come to bed, my lord." Chris needed no further encouragement.

Sebastian let himself warily into the bedchamber a little after midnight. He had picked up a few copper coins during the dice game. He'd refrained from cheating, though, hoping to remain inconspicuous.

Cecelia was seated at the room's table, sipping ale. Sebastian looked at her before gazing carefully around the room. He became aware of the soft, high-pitched keening at the same time he saw a dark bundle in a corner.

"What have you done?" he whispered.

"Nothing less than he deserved," Cecelia replied defiantly.

Sebastian turned on her. "You cannot just eliminate every one of Reginald Claybourne's favorites as the fancy strikes you! I *thought* we were working together. After the priest and woman, now this - what are you doing? Why did you not kill him?"

Cecelia remained calm. "I am simply taking advantage of the opportunities that present themselves," she lied. "I plan to see that this vermin is sent to Edward Fitzroy so he and Robert Claybourne are reminded of the Power they are up against. I am sure the bishop will do the appropriate thing." She added with a sly smile, "Besides, the baron may yet aid me."

Sebastian looked to the ceiling for guidance but found none. Her words chilled him to the bone. "Would you tell me these things before you act on them?" he pleaded. "I do not want to see you executed. The prostitute could turn me in, but I would swear I acted alone. The Magician who 'hired' Gerard last Christmas was someone I employed." He took a deep breath. "I am willing to be executed for all of it. I no longer fear death. Agreed?"

"Yes, Sebastian. You have made your point. My behavior will be exemplary from here on out." Sebastian didn't trust what he heard underneath the agreeable words and now wondered if any of the words she spoke were true.

* * *

Edward woke to a frantic knocking at his bedroom door before dawn. He rose and yanked the door open, glaring at his assistant. Ambrose didn't cower or apologize.

"Excellency, to your study. The Baron of Thorburg is here, delivered by a pair of mercenaries. He is mad!"

"What!" Edward quickly donned his cassock, then followed his assistant. In spite of Ambrose's words, Edward was shocked at the sight of Nigel Jennings.

The ferret-faced baron was now slack-jawed, with a hunted look in his eyes. His thin hair was in disarray, and he kept tugging at his left earlobe like he was trying to hear something.

Edward crossed himself. "Summon a protective Circle, Father," he ordered, going over to the stricken baron.

"What? You do not mean to learn the spell?" Ambrose was horrified. "Excellency?" he added belatedly.

Edward met his assistant's concerned gaze. "I have to. I need all of the information I can get about this enemy." His tone softened slightly. "I am uneasy as well, Ambrose, that is why I want protection. I will ask you to pray throughout."

"Yes, sir, of course." Ambrose began the familiar ritual. Edward knelt next to Nigel and touched him on the arm. He wanted to ascertain if the man were hurt physically. Nigel flinched and tried to back away. Edward took a deep breath, touching Nigel's carotid pulse, willing the man to sleep. In a moment, Nigel's eyes closed, though his body shook as though with the palsy.

"The Circle is ready, Excellency."

"Thank you, Father. If you see me in distress, intervene immediately," Edward directed.

"Yes, sir."

The part of Edward's position that he despised was identifying illegal spells. He especially hated those spells for which there was no reversal. Placing his fingers on Nigel's forehead, he eased his mind forward.

He was surrounded by chaos. It took him several moments and sheer will to orient himself. He "saw" no evidence of Nigel's memories. Where was the spell, the Signature? Edward was panting with exertion. He finally withdrew to himself, defeated. He raised his gaze to see his worry reflected in his assistant's face.

"I could find no trace of the spell." His shoulders slumped.

Ambrose had no misconceptions about his and Edward's respective levels of ability. "'Tis impossible."

"Apparently not." Edward held out a hand and Ambrose helped him stand. The priest led him to a chair into which he sank gratefully. Ambrose then dispersed the Circle.

"What happens to him?" Ambrose pointed to Nigel.

"He is going to Robert's Council meeting in a few hours. After that - I do not know."

The previous evening, Robert had announced a Council meeting for midday. All of his father's Councilors had arrived in Rhennsbury. He also sent word for his sister, Elijah and Anselm to be present.

Chris and Helen discussed the meeting when they wakened in the morning. Chris felt that since the majority of his interactions with Robert since their arrival had been private, he needed to behave like Christian during the meeting, to keep the other Councilors from becoming suspicious of his masquerade. Helen reluctantly agreed. Chris stared out the window. "Besides, there is Robert's credibility with these men, too." He suppressed a sigh as he turned to face her. Her expression was compassionate.

She joined him and touched her hand lightly to his cheek. "No matter. Will you let him know beforehand?"

Chris took her hand and kissed it before replying. "I will try to get a message to him. If not, he is going to have to hide his surprise. I am assuming he can still do that well."

"Aye."

"But," Chris continued. "I will vote my conscience if there are not enough votes in Robert's favor to at least give him a tie. Those other jackasses can think what they like. At least James and Anselm will not be surprised." He smiled slightly. "There is one advantage to having the final vote."

Robert slept fitfully, anticipating the objections likely to surface at the meeting. It would be his first real test as king. He spent part of the morning with the tailor, but recalled nothing of the session. He was able to briefly escape to the courtyard, pacing in an effort to quiet his mind. Unfortunately, it caused him to miss Chris's message, which a lazy page left in the royal study rather than delivering in person. At midday, Robert squared his shoulders and strode to the meeting room.

Chris's guards were standing outside the Council room's door. Both bowed to Robert, and one opened the door for him. Robert saluted them. Several conversations stilled at his entrance. He noted with satisfaction that there were two additional chairs. Helen was standing behind Chris. Everyone except Edward and Nigel Jennings was present.

Suddenly self-conscious, Robert kept his gaze forward until he got to the head of the table. He crossed himself before sitting in his father's chair. He now met the gaze of each person in turn.

All heads turned when Edward came in, supporting Nigel. Robert stood. Edward took in the faces in the room. He said to Robert, "Another message from Cecelia, Highness."

Robert paled, gripping the edge of the table to steady himself. Helen and Allyson exchanged glances. Helen went over to Edward and Nigel.

"Is there aught -?"

"Nay." Edward pitched his voice so it carried around the room. "There is no evidence of the spell worked. I attempted to discover it this morning – 'tis the reason for my tardiness." That was as close to an apology as Edward would go.

Several men crossed themselves. Edward continued, "This is the baron's last Council meeting. The spell cannot be reversed. You will have to appoint someone to replace him, Highness." He addressed the last to Robert.

Robert was still trying to regain his calm. He finally sat. "Yes. The Duke of Latham." His voice had steadied by the time he finished speaking. Anselm bowed, then sat in an empty chair.

Helen told Edward she would watch over Nigel while Edward attended to the meeting. "Why are you here?" he asked her in a whisper. She raised a finger to her lips and nodded toward Robert.

"My lords, Christian Lattimore is currently under house arrest due to suspicious circumstances surrounding my father's death. It is up to you gentlemen as to whether he sits in on this meeting, or the duchess in his stead." Robert kept his voice even. Chris glared at him, only part of his anger feigned. Edward's eyebrows shot up in surprise.

Fergus MacTavish, the fiery Earl of Tavendish stood. His eyes flashed. He was a firm supporter of Reginald and Christian. "Your pardon, Highness, but his Grace is the least likely person to have murdered your father. I do not care what may or may not have happened between Reginald and him last year."

Archbishop Francis McHenry nodded. "I have never agreed with the man, Sire, but I see no reason to bar him from Council. House arrest is a good decision considering the mood of many in Rhennsbury."

Robert looked around the table. He saw no objections. Edward got over his surprise and relaxed slightly.

Roger Fitzgibbon, the Duke of Castrella and a war supporter, spoke. "Why are these two present, my lord?" He pointed to Allyson and Elijah.

"Allyson is to serve on this Council." Muttering began. Robert held up a hand. "Hers is a temporary appointment, until I marry." He smiled slightly into the silence. "There are no marriage plans, yet."

"That will make for an odd number, Highness," Edward pointed out as he noted Robert's proposed change.

"Aye. Sir Holmes has agreed to serve, to make the number even, unless one of you wishes to resign." Robert looked around the table again. Most of the men exchanged looks. Chris stared ahead, not meeting anyone's gaze.

Fitzgibbon stood. "I will resign," he announced, looking at Hugh Thurstyn, Castrella's bishop and close colleague of Edward, who nodded. "We do not need foreigners on this Council." Elijah ignored the insult and let out a relieved breath.

Owain Griffyth, the dark-haired Baron of Morwaith, and another man who favored war, decided to try one last argument. "Can you do this, Sire, change the Council?" he asked.

"Yes, We can," Robert replied, using the royal pronoun for the first time. It was wasted on no one. His stomach turned over, but his voice remained steady. Chris was still frowning, but inside he was impressed with the teen's political skills.

Edward could sense the balance of power shifting, and there was nothing he could do about it. Well, almost nothing. "I do not recall a precedent, Sire," he said quietly, from Robert's right.

"There is precedent," Robert stated, then recounted a few of the details Allyson had uncovered. He concluded by thanking Fitzgibbon for his many years of loyal service to Reginald. Roger sketched a stiff bow, then left the chamber quietly. He knew he could keep up with Council matters via Hugh Thurstyn and Fergus MacTavish, whose earldom shared a border with Castrella.

Elijah stepped up to the table and asked to be excused. Robert nodded and thanked him. He winked surreptitiously, to let Elijah know he still hoped Elijah would be on the Council one day. Elijah leaned over to wish Chris luck, then left, shaking his head but smiling.

Robert motioned Allyson to Fitzgibbon's empty chair, next to Chris. Since he had to remain in character, Chris ignored her, but he sent her a mental apology. She studiously avoided looking at him, then glanced casually at the others sitting at the table. She inclined her head to the archbishop, then gave her attention to her brother.

Robert moved on to the next order of business. "You are all aware that Father had intended to continue his invasion of Wyckendom this summer. Those plans are no longer under consideration, due to the circumstances. I feel that the time and energy can be better spent repairing buildings in need of it and taking care of other issues closer to home. What Myrridia needs most is stability. Any comments?"

Edward was continuing to write down Robert's announcements. "What would you have the men do who have already gathered to make war, Sire?" He kept his tone neutral and didn't look up from his writing.

"How many would complain about the opportunity to return to their farms and manors?" Robert countered.

Abbot Ranulf Tamblyn of Holy Grove Monastery, a man who sided with the archbishop, agreed quietly from the opposite end of the table. "I do not doubt that Myrridia will be at war with someone in the future, but let us all hope for several more years of peace and prosperity," he said.

Robert knew he was walking a fine line. He didn't want to pursue his father's intended plans, but he didn't want to come across as critical of his father, either. He knew he wasn't prepared to lead an army into war, especially a war in which he did not believe.

He moved to his next subject with reluctance. "A couple of days ago I received a message," he began, handing the parchment to Chris to begin passing around the table. "The threat is direct enough; someone wants me dead." Several of the men around the table began muttering again. Robert continued, "Does anyone here have any knowledge to share about Father's murder? Edward Fitzroy was able to get an unclear glimpse of the man responsible, but this man may not be acting alone. This note is from a woman named Cecelia, a formidable Magical practitioner, and the person who ordered the attempt against my life last Christmas."

A couple of men exchanged looks, but none spoke. Anselm DeLacey stood. "May I, Sire?" Robert inclined his head.

"There are two people who would bear a serious grievance against your father, yourself and Duke Lattimore." Anselm refrained from crossing himself. "I suggest that everyone here," he paused as he met each person's eyes evenly, "recall the invasion of the earldom of Tippensdown, in Wyckendom, six years ago. The earl and his family were slaughtered, except for two of his children, who were not present at the time and cannot be confirmed as dead now." Anselm paused as the others digested his words. Then he played his trump.

"Should this pair be the guilty party, they may be civilized enough to accept the return of the earldom and leave Myrridia in peace. This restraint may be more than anyone can reasonably expect, though. I for one know what your father would have done in the circumstances." For several heartbeats, there was silence at the table.

"He would have executed them." Chris was the first to speak, and his tone was flat. He didn't approve of what Reginald would have done, but he hoped a few of the men took his words as being critical of Robert. A couple of men nodded.

"What are you suggesting to our young king, DeLacey?" Fergus asked. "He should just hand over the earldom and thank this pair for murdering his father, Myrridia's king?" There were snorts and mutterings around the table, with an occasional thoughtful word.

"The earl puts words in my mouth," Anselm said. "Will more killing put an end to this situation?"

"Forgiveness and no punishment implies weakness, you old -" Edward had stood. "Do you want Myrridia's enemies to think her king is weak? I was under the impression that age brought wisdom!"

A few cheered Edward; the majority did not. Francis McHenry stood with assistance from James McDermott and Ranulf Tamblyn. "Fitzroy, sit down." Though his voice trembled, the authority behind his words was heard by all. "Forgiveness is good enough for God, so why not men? Yes, murdering a king is wrong. So is slaughtering an entire family, including women and children. I believe there were one or two infants." Allyson closed her eyes in an effort to blink back tears. "It takes more strength to forgive one's enemies than execute them. I support the duke's suggestion. I will even go so far as to suggest, Your Majesty, that you put the word out through the city that you wish to speak with these people, granting them immunity to do so. It is time to stop this cycle of death." The archbishop sat down, exhausted.

Robert was stunned by the archbishop's words and didn't try to hide it. It was one thing for Chris to make such a suggestion - he was from a faraway place and time and freely admitted his differences. "Would my lords and lady like to put the Duke and Archbishop's suggestion to a vote?" Robert's voice was quiet. "I will abide by the vote's outcome."

"'Tis a mistake. I am against it." Edward, as always, had the first vote. There were two abstentions, from Oswald Pierce, the Earl of Logrenham, and Geoffrey Renburg, the Duke of Grovesden. Both men had disagreed with Reginald's war plans during the Council meeting held at Christmas, and now told Robert they felt this idea sounded good, but they weren't certain one way or the other. James McDermott didn't hesitate in voting favorably; he understood the toll fighting took. All of his sons were dead from previous battling.

Chris had kept a mental count of the votes. His negative vote would leave Robert a tie. He was almost relieved. Since Robert needed him in Saelym, he ignored his conscience. He wasn't surprised at the instant nausea he felt, though. Robert didn't outwardly react to his vote. Chris was impressed. He looked at Robert with defiance; Robert kept his gaze forward.

Edward finished tallying the votes and turned to Robert. "Two abstentions, five against, and five in favor. A tie, Sire. You will need to cast the deciding vote," he said neutrally.

Robert sat back for several moments, then took a deep breath. His next words could cost him control of the Council. "My lords, my lady, We feel that the effort should be made to reason with this pair. It remains to be seen if these two, if they are indeed the last of this family, can be persuaded to end the killing. If not, We shall have no choice but to defend Ourselves, in whatever way necessary, Magical or otherwise. Everyone knows my limitations in that regard. If it comes to a sword fight, I shall defend myself." He met the eyes of each person at the table. "Or should someone else stand in as champion?"

"Lattimore, of course," MacTavish said quickly. "He is Myrridia's finest swordsman. And Fitzroy, if Magic is involved."

Robert's scowl was unfeigned. He didn't want "Christian" defending him, and he didn't want Chris put into a dangerous situation he couldn't handle. For that matter, he really didn't want Edward as a defender either. Chris sat back and glowered, his arms crossed.

"Why should I?" he countered in a near growl. Allyson shifted away from him slightly. Edward fought a smirk but mentally conceded Chris still had acting ability.

"I will do whatever is needed," Edward put in equably, though inwardly he had his doubts of his capability to fight this practitioner.

Allyson stood and frowned at the pair of them. "*I* shall stand with my brother," she stated. "Should he need to defend himself, then these people will not stop with him. Do any of you object?"

Some muttering occurred and Robert shot her a sharp look, but there were no vocal objections. Edward inclined his head in Allyson's direction but didn't show his relief. Besides, she had a point. Robert fought his disgust at Edward; though he didn't want to be beholden to his uncle, he didn't appreciate the bishop's cavalier acceptance of Allyson's offer. She was untried under dangerous Magical conditions. And Cecelia was well beyond dangerous.

"I can defend myself in a sword fight," Robert said through gritted teeth.

Chris snorted. "If your opponent were a girl," he put in. Several men guffawed. Allyson turned and slapped him, forgetting for a moment that he wasn't Christian. She felt remorse a moment later, but an apology would have to wait. Chris didn't seem put out by it.

Robert nodded to himself. "If that is the way you feel about me, how do you explain your action of saving my life during last year's hunt, your Grace?" he shot back. "I am sure several men at this table would like to know." Chris shrugged as Owain and Fergus tried to catch his eye. "You are impertinent, sir. I could order you under full arrest and have you escorted from this chamber to the dungeon. Folk in Rhennsbury are asking, nay demanding, your execution. 'Tis naught but my restraint that keeps your neck out of a noose. Remember that."

Chris raised a calm eyebrow, then glanced around the table. "So much for gratitude. If you have no need of my talents, I will not insult your pride, Highness. Defend yourself. It is only Myrridia that hangs in the balance."

Robert bit back a profanity as he stood. If he hadn't known it was Chris, he would have sworn it was Christian speaking. "If there is naught else?" he asked. When no one replied, he continued, "Thank you all. This meeting is adjourned."

After shooting Chris an unreadable look, he joined Helen and Nigel. "What happens to him, now?" he asked quietly, his eyes showing his fear of her reply.

Helen shook her head. "If he cannot be restored to sanity, he is doomed to live out his days like this, or we must...." She couldn't finish her reply.

Robert closed his eyes, crossing himself. Allyson and Chris joined him after all but Edward and the Archbishop had left the Council room. Allyson had murmured her apology for the slap. Chris shrugged it off. He told her he'd earned it, or worse, after that meeting. He in turn quietly apologized to Robert, who waved his words aside. Allyson looked at Helen. "May I try?"

"No," Helen said.

"Absolutely not," Edward agreed.

Allyson turned and glared at Edward. "I was not asking you, Excellency," she said.

"What makes you think you can succeed where Edward has failed, Highness?" Francis McHenry had paused in exiting the room upon hearing her words.

"The person who did this is a woman, and so am I," Allyson replied.

"Then Helen and I will summon protection. But let me warn you - think about this carefully. You are not fully trained, and we may not be able to come to your aid should you need it."

Allyson swallowed.

Robert looked alarmed. "Ally-" he began.

Allyson squared her shoulders and looked her brother in the eye. "If I am no match for her, best to find out now, rather than when your life is on the line."

Robert opened his mouth to speak, but he could think of no argument. Finally he said, "Be careful."

"I will."

Francis led the small group to the castle's chapel. Helen gave Allyson what instruction she could. Chris helped Edward bring Nigel, his guards behind him. Robert brought up the rear. He and Chris would wait outside the Circle, giving the others moral support. Robert took advantage of the chance to thank Chris for his acting after admitting his initial surprise at Chris's vote. Chris smiled.

"Just so you know I meant none of what I said. I would gladly defend you, but preferably as myself."

"Aye." Robert turned and gave the others his attention.

Edward walked the Circle's boundary as Francis stood before the altar and began an invocation, surreptitiously leaning against the altar for support. "Before me Raphael, lead thy servants to knowledge, Behind me Gabriel, go with thy handmaiden, On my right Michael, protect us from evil, On my left Uriel, teach thy handmaiden." Edward, Allyson and Helen joined Francis in finishing the prayer. "We beseech Thee, O Lord God, to aid us in this endeavor. For Thine is the Kingdom, and the Power, and the Glory forever and ever. Amen."

Helen gave Allyson a few last-minute words of encouragement before easing Nigel into sleep. Allyson knelt beside Nigel's prone body. She took in his unkempt state before touching his forehead lightly. She unconsciously moved a lock of his hair back from his forehead. She closed her eyes and slipped into trance.

She visualized an image of Cecelia from her Working with Helen a couple of days ago. Then she slipped into Nigel's lost mind. She was momentarily overwhelmed by the chaos she encountered, but she kept her consciousness focused on the image of Cecelia. Instead of trying to fight the spell to discover its identity, she tried to relive the attack as it happened. She had to withdraw several times as the Power of the spell nearly overwhelmed her own sanity, until she recognized the anger behind Cecelia's Magic. It was the rage and strength behind the spell, rather than the spell's complexity, which had destroyed Nigel's mind. Allyson went deeper into trance in an effort to move beyond the raw emotions and daunting level of Power. She realized the anger was a potential weakness in the woman, though she didn't know how to combat the anger to weaken the spell enough to restore Nigel's sanity.

Allyson's increased level of concentration allowed her to pass beyond the feelings surrounding the spell to the spell itself. She marveled at its simplicity and lost all awareness of time passing as she memorized it.

Helen, Edward and Francis watched her, concerned. Each wanted to add their strength to hers, but she didn't request aid. Helen's heart went out to the younger woman when her features contorted with pain and horror.

Allyson finally sat back on her heels, panting for breath. "Parchment," she whispered. Edward handed her his pen, ink and paper from the Council meeting. Allyson wrote silently, the scratching of the pen the only sound. Her expression of horror faded as she finished writing. She handed the parchment wordlessly to Francis.

"I wish I could forget this spell, but until I face Cecelia, I need to know what I am up against," she said quietly. "I did learn something more important than her spell - she is angry and careless with her powers. She has great ability, but the spell is simple enough." She paused, frowning. "I think there may have been more tampering, but I lacked the strength to discover it."

Edward and Francis stared at the young woman still kneeling on the floor. She seemed unaware that she had just, unaided, accomplished a deed thought impossible. Helen, also surprised, went on and dispersed the Circle.

Chris went to Helen, Robert to his sister. "Is she all right?" Chris whispered.

"Aye, just exhausted. She may prove to be Myrridia's greatest practitioner. She just eclipsed Edward's abilities," Helen replied. Her brow knit. "Perhaps she used an unorthodox method. If so, she will need to tread carefully around Edward."

Robert knelt next to Allyson. She was crying quietly. "What? Are you -?" He put an arm around her.

Allyson turned and buried her face in Robert's shoulder. When her crying abated, she met his gaze. "There is naught to do for him. He was not a good man, but he does not deserve this!" She hid her face again. Robert held her, looking up at the two Churchmen.

"What do we do for him, Excellencies?"

Edward opened his mouth, but Francis began speaking first. "He can go to Holy Grove Monastery. The monks will care for him. He would not be the first of lost mind. Someone with healing abilities may be able to give him some comfort."

Robert nodded. "The Crown will pay for his keep. His son will need to take his place as baron."

Francis smiled his approval. "As you command, Sire."

After Robert saw that Allyson was conducted to her apartment to rest, he went to the courtyard. He sat on one of the stone benches and pondered the meeting and its aftermath. Edward joined him soon after.

"I hate to intrude, Robert," he said. Robert looked up at his uncle.

"You are upset by the talk during the meeting. Sit down." Robert shifted a little and motioned Edward next to him. "I know he was my father and your brother. Of course I am angry and upset with these people. I am not certain I can forgive them on a personal level, at least not soon."

"Then why are you even considering doing this?" Edward asked. He was angrier after hearing Robert's words.

"Because it is not just about me, or you, or any one person. I am the king now - well, almost - and I have to do what is best for Myrridia. Father may have been killed because of something he did; I have to accept that, though I do not have to like it. Father was the law; he was not above it. I want things to be different, better. Can you not understand that?"

Edward sighed. "You are going to be a formidable leader, Robert. You already know how to argue a point and read a man's character. Of course, part of my feeling is personal, but I still do not think this is the best course. All I can do is advise you. But a few words of caution - do not try to change too many things too quickly. That will lead to internal rebellion."

Robert nodded. "Aye. The last thing Myrridia needs right now is war, internal or otherwise." He met Edward's eyes.

"I will support you, but I still do not like it," Edward told him.

"Thank you. We all have to do things we would rather not. I know I cannot afford you for an enemy. I would far rather count you an ally." Robert held out his hand. Edward grasped it and shook it firmly. Edward stood and walked to the castle.

"I hope you remember that, Robert," he said aloud. Robert's head shot up, his expression disbelieving for a moment before becoming thoughtful. How ambitious was his uncle? He tensed as he heard footsteps approaching a few moments later along the cobbled walk. Seeing it was Chris, he relaxed. Chris arched an eyebrow, glancing back the way he'd come.

"Something on your mind?" he asked.

Robert frowned and started to shake his head. His shoulders sagged. "'Tis Edward - something he just said to me."

Chris nodded. "You want to talk about it?"

"Not really." Robert suppressed a sigh. He gave Chris a summary of the conversation, ending with Edward's parting shot.

Chris whistled. "Not that he is ambitious or anything." He shrugged. "That is not news, you know. Though I am surprised he let it slip. I guess it is a warning, and it is up to you to ignore it or not. Any thoughts?"

Robert stood and paced for several moments. "Thoughts? I have too many thoughts as it is!" He took a deep breath. "How did Father keep everything going along? He always drank to excess, at least when he was here in Rhennsbury. 'Tis all I can do to get through one day at a time. And I am sober! What with Father's murder, the coronation, death threats *and* an empty treasury, I am at the end of my rope."

"Steady there, lad," Chris said, joining him and grasping his shoulders firmly. He didn't dare give Robert any more support than that, as servants could be passing by the courtyard at any time. Robert immediately stiffened, due to his tumultuous emotions; he was used to the physical contact, at least with Chris. He pulled away, turning his back on his friend. He stared up at the courtyard's wall, willing his body and mind to calm.

Chris nodded to himself. "You know where you can find me," he said quietly. "I will be waiting."

Robert turned, his expression pleading. "No, wait, please. I need to talk to someone, and there are just so few people I can confide in. I just - I need a few moments, 'tis all."

Chris nodded, his brows lowered in concern. It wasn't like Robert to admit he needed anything. He feared the young man was closer to a breakdown than he'd be willing to acknowledge. Inspiration came to him. "I can go see about horses. Have you been out of the castle since - ?" He mentally swore at himself. Robert shook his head.

"Paul and I will join you in the stables shortly." He managed a wan smile. "You have the escort nearby as well." Chris grimaced, saluted, then turned back to the castle.

Helen stayed with Allyson after Robert left. She sensed the younger woman was exhausted but needed to talk about her experience. Allyson sat heavily in the chair in her sitting room, waving aside Diana's offer of assistance. The princess closed her eyes for several moments, leaning her head back against the chair. When she opened her eyes again, she met Helen's concerned gaze and gestured to a nearby footstool.

Helen sat. "Do you want to discuss what just happened with Nigel Jennings?" she asked.

Allyson shuddered at the memory. "Yes and no." She stared off into space, trying to gather her thoughts. "The thing that surprised me most was how simple the spell was, once I was able to focus on it alone. I think I could have reversed it, had it not had the backing of her full Power and anger." She looked straight at Helen. "Her Power frightens me. I have only worked with Edward once, one-on-one, and she is as powerful as he is, perhaps more so. But her strong emotions add to her Power. Edward is much calmer Magically." She allowed herself a slight smile. "He loses his temper, but he never puts his temper into his Workings."

Helen nodded. "Aye, I see a difference there. Why do you think you succeeded where Edward failed?" As Allyson hesitated to answer, Helen added, "I have no intention of sharing the information with anyone, my dear, least of all the bishop."

"Thank you, Helen." Allyson stared off again. "I think Edward failed because he is so rigid in following formulae strictly. I kept an open mind, focusing on the image I had of Cecelia from when we helped Nicole. I tried to approach the spell directly at first, as I have been taught, but when that did not work, I tried several other avenues. I had to work past Cecelia's emotions - Mother of God, she is so full of hate! - and then her Power. I had to go deeper into trance than I have ever gone. I am scared to death to face her. Oh, Helen, what am I to do? Robert needs me, but, but -" Allyson buried her face, her shoulders shaking.

Helen rose and went over to her, putting an arm around Allyson's shoulders. "Let it out now, my dear." She stayed with the younger woman until the emotion passed. Allyson finally looked up, her eyes still bright, but she managed a shaky smile. "You know Robert can ask Edward, or myself. You need not face her."

Allyson shook her head. "That is just it, Helen. I have to be the one to face her, or Robert. Her hatred of Father and Christian came through her destruction of Nigel's mind. I never realized the mind was so fragile, at least in one so weak as the baron. It was as though she was playing with him, like a cat plays with a mouse. I know she could not defeat me so easily, nor could she destroy Robert's sanity so quickly, but her callousness is terrible. She will not stop until Robert and I are both dead, or have fled Myrridia."

She brought up her chin, her expression becoming determined. "Myrridia needs Robert, and I will not sit back and watch her slaughter him Magically."

"Aye, Allyson. But there is no shame for you to fear her at the same time. I think 'tis time you got some rest. If you wish, I will help you sleep." Allyson nodded, allowing Helen to help her rise and lead her to the bedchamber.

After seeing to Allyson's needs, Helen went to the guest chamber belonging to the Jennings. She thought Lady Gwendolyn, Nigel's wife, might take the news better from a woman. Gwendolyn's maid told Helen her mistress was in the solarium, stitching, and Helen asked the woman to fetch her.

Helen didn't have to wait long. Gwendolyn arrived with her daughter-in-law. Helen had taken the liberty of pouring wine into two goblets, and now offered them to the other women.

"What is it, Helen?" Gwendolyn asked. She'd been concerned by the summons - it wasn't like Helen - and her concern deepened when she saw Helen's face.

"'Tis about Nigel, Gwen," Helen said softly. "I thought you might prefer privacy."

Gwendolyn sat. "Nigel is a twit. What has happened to him?"

Helen was unable to think of an easy way to break the news. "One of the people who may be responsible for Reginald's death has attacked Nigel with Magic. He is mad, Gwen."

The words took several moments to sink in. "Mad? Nigel? Is there aught to be done for him?" Gwendolyn's words were rushed. Her daughter-in-law, Catherine, had paled.

Helen went over to Gwendolyn and took one of her hands. "No, Gwen, there is naught to be done. Allyson was able to identify the spell after Edward failed. The archbishop has offered the hospitality of Holy Grove Monastery to Nigel. The decision is yours, and your son's."

Gwendolyn inclined her head, tears running down both cheeks. "I did not love him, but he did not deserve -" Her voice broke.

Catherine went over to her mother-in-law, putting an arm around Gwendolyn's heaving shoulders. "Easy, my lady. Let me send for Richard." She called the serving maid over and bade her find him.

"Do you want to lie down?" Helen asked Gwendolyn, who shook her head.

Helen and Catherine gave Gwendolyn what comfort they could until her son, Richard, arrived. Catherine gave him the news about his father. He stared at Helen in stunned disbelief. "Is naught to be done?" he asked angrily, turning on her. "What good is Magical ability if it cannot undo its own evil?"

Catherine motioned Helen toward the door, apologizing to her quietly as she let Helen out. "He is much like his father," she confided.

Helen inclined her head, accepting the apology. "Let me know if Gwen needs anything."

"Aye, thank you."

Sebastian spent the day in the city, looking into the possibility of getting Cecelia and himself ensconced in the castle and thinking about what his sister had done to Nigel Jennings. His emotions were in turmoil.

He made inquiries at the castle's main gate about temporary employment. He guessed that with many members of the nobility staying at the castle, there would be a need for more help. He would avoid getting Cecelia a job as a serving maid or some other menial position, to save her the humiliation of a public beating if she forgot to show sufficient respect to her so-called betters. He tried to ignore the voice of his conscience telling him that perhaps she would deserve it.

He had to be careful around the castle, though. Even though he now had mixed feelings about his plans with Cecelia, it would not help if Naomi or others who might recognize him were to see him. He'd been clean-shaven during his tenure at the castle, but some of the residents, like the guard sergeant, Ian, were sharp-eyed. He had since castigated himself several times for keeping the appointment with Naomi as well as saying what he had. He hadn't been able to stop himself, and that thought scared him. He was usually in tight control of himself - his gestures and his words. That control had saved him several times in the past, when he'd been spying for the king of Wyckendom. Normally when he felt an attraction for a woman, he used it to help his assignments; he couldn't figure out what was different about Naomi.

As he was leaving the castle gates, he saw a priest with the young woman who had accompanied Naomi and her brother in the city when he'd met them. He decided to melt into a group of travelers and follow the pair into the city.

He wondered what the priest was doing in the company of a woman, alone. It was his own worldly guess that the man had inappropriate thoughts of the woman, and perhaps they were going to a safe place for an assignation. He had no idea who either party was, unless they were the pair that Cecelia had encountered several days prior, but he hoped to learn something useful. He followed them as they walked through the crowded streets, with their heads together occasionally in conversation. Now and then the priest would point out something to his companion, though they did no shopping with any of the street vendors. They did go into a seamstress's shop for a few minutes and emerged with a wrapped package. Sebastian wished he could get closer to overhear their words, but there were too many people about and it was possible the woman would recognize him if he got too close.

Nicole had asked Michael if they could walk somewhere, while Chris, Elijah and Helen were at the Council meeting. She felt claustrophobic within the castle; she found the thick stone walls oppressive. He said he would be glad to show her some more sights in the city, since he wouldn't have to worry about running into Edward Fitzroy, who was also at the meeting. He sensed her discomfort while indoors and was sympathetic. He told her how he felt closed in by the rules of the Church at times.

The two were oblivious to Sebastian. Michael was glad to spend the time with Nicole since he had no idea how much longer she would remain in Myrridia. Nicole needed time and fresh air to consider what she wanted to do. Even with the loud noise and strong smells of the city, she felt more comfortable than when she was inside the castle. Elijah had given her a few coins, and they stopped to pick up the altered dress for Naomi. Once they were walking along the city's high street again, they resumed their conversation.

Nicole now told Michael that Helen had determined that she had "Magical abilities," and that she, Nicole, was unsure what to do with the knowledge. "I don't know that I want to stay here. I think I would miss so many things. I would have to work for someone in the Church, wouldn't I?" she asked Michael. "Plus I'm not sure I could get used to living in some of these buildings. I never thought I was claustrophobic before."

Michael debated telling her about his unapproved work. Apologizing to Helen, he said aloud, "You would not have to work for the Church, necessarily. There would be other options."

"You mean the renegades?" Nicole asked. "Helen told me about it. She said that you were one of them, or I wouldn't even bring it up, since she asked me not to."

"Aye. Some, myself included, would be willing to teach you how to use your Talents," he offered.

"I still don't know. Although I can't seem to stop thinking about it!" She smiled despite her frustration. "I have problems with the long skirts. I'm afraid I'll just shoot off at the mouth and get myself thrown in prison or something. This place takes a lot of getting used to." *Shut up, Nicole, you're whining!* she thought.

Michael smiled as he pointed out the Mayor's residence to her.

Robert and Paul joined Chris in the courtyard as promised. Their mounts were already saddled, and Robert spoke to his animal quietly for a few seconds before mounting easily. He led the others through the portcullis, then immediately guided the horse off the cobbled road leading into the city. What with the mood of the citizens, there was no point in putting Chris in needless danger, especially since the man was trying to help him.

The party was silent as they rode past nearby farmland. The only sounds were the jingle of harness and the occasional snort of a horse. Robert eased out a breath, consciously relaxing himself. His horse sensed the change and nickered softly. He waited until they had ridden a few miles and were close to the forest before pulling his horse to a stop and dismounting. He tethered the animal to a nearby tree, then joined the two men-at-arms.

"The duke and I need to speak privately for a while," he said. Paul raised an eyebrow then smiled. He and Chris's escort moved away, to stand guard while out of earshot.

Chris had dismounted and walked a short way into the trees. He turned as he heard Robert approach and gestured to a nearby oak. Robert nodded, then eased to the ground, pulling his knees up and hugging them. He leaned his chin on his knees. Chris sat a couple of feet away, facing him.

"So, you have all the answers for me?" Robert asked with feigned lightness.

"Sure, and pigs can fly," Chris replied. "If you want a 'quick fix,' I am not your man. However, as a physician, I felt it would be good for you to get away from the castle for a while. Will it solve all of your problems? Not hardly." He leaned forward. "Even if it did, there will be new problems tomorrow, or next week, or whenever."

Robert watched him. "You only tell me what I already know." He stared past Chris for a moment. "I told Allyson, the day after Father's death, I have spent most of my life training for this responsibility, so why do I feel so overwhelmed by it?" He stretched his legs out before him. "And Edward is not helping."

Chris snorted. "Edward helps Edward. End of story." He grasped one of Robert's hands and squeezed for a moment. "Unlike him, you do not exist in a vacuum." At Robert's puzzled look, Chris stopped. "Okay. You know that you are part of the world, specifically Myrridia. Some people would say that you, as king anyway, are a physical symbol of the kingdom. Whatever. My point is that you know that things you do, decisions you make, will have consequences, sometimes widespread. And you care about those consequences. Unlike Edward, who only sees how things affect him, and the things he cares about. Which I think is only the Church. And unlike your father, who could not see past his own nose most of the time. Am I right so far?"

Robert smiled briefly. "Aye. But there is more than that." He forced himself to meet Chris's eyes, where he saw only compassion. "I feel torn in so many directions - I have felt that way since - since Father died. First, I had to stand up to Edward, to protect a woman's sanity in the brothel, then I had to watch her put to death, for aiding the man who killed Father."

Chris nodded. "How do you feel about execution as a punishment?"

Robert glanced at him in surprise. "Is there another option in your world?"

"Sure. Lifetime imprisonment. With a chance at parole for good behavior. We have the death penalty, too, but there has been a lot of controversy over it as a punishment in a modern so-called civilized world. It is sobering to be a citizen in a country that puts criminals to death, when the only other nations that do it as well are all - have repressive regimes. Do you follow?"

Robert shook his head. "I am not certain. Perhaps I would if I understood more of the types of - regimes? - your world has. I cannot quite grasp the idea of lifelong imprisonment, and there is no way to provide for such here. I feel 'tis a serious thing to order another human being to be put to death - and not a decision I feel I could make lightly. Should such a day come, I think I would no longer be able to look at my image in a looking-glass."

"Robert, you are a serious young man. Some days you are probably too serious. Young men your age, in my world, are on the cusp of becoming adults, at least physically, and many of them are years short of full emotional maturity. Nicole had a theory once, that it took men two hundred years to mature." Chris chuckled momentarily. "I will spare you the details - it involved a fictional character who had assumed a - physical - state that allowed unlimited longevity of life, without physical aging, near immortality. Anyway, this character had lived about two hundred years and was finally showing some signs of impending adulthood.

I find your maturity nothing short of amazing sometimes. Then I remember you are a product of your world."

Robert mulled the story over. "Two hundred years. It might have taken Father that long. But he only got about forty." He ran a hand through his hair. "Then I have my guilt about Father, and our lack of a relationship. Now I have death threats from a woman I have never met because I was too young to have been involved in the warring that killed her family, but she does not care. And should I get beyond that threat, I shall inherit a kingdom without a treasury."

"You will get past the immediate threat, kid," Chris stated. "I have faith in the people around you, except for my own ability with a sword. But, you are in luck - 'Christian' wouldn't have defended you in public, anyway."

Robert managed a smile. "At least not until last Christmas. I believe that had tongues wagging throughout the city for a good month." He sobered. "I guess I feel as though my life is out of my control. 'Tis new for me - my life has never been my own, truly, but I had made my peace with my future position. Father's death was sudden, and I just cannot seem to get anything to go right."

"Give it time," Chris said. "Edward is the control freak, not you. I understand where you are coming from, though, at least to a degree. Sometimes life throws too many things our way at one time. We have a saying, though - 'if it don't kill you, it just makes you stronger.'" He blinked at the phrasing. It sounded strange to him.

Robert rolled his eyes. "So much for your modern wisdom. I guess that some things really do not change that much."

"Uh-huh. Human nature would be one of them. Look, you are going to get through this. It might not look good right now, but let me repeat. You are not alone. Helen and I are available, as well as your sister." He chuckled. "If you need distraction, I heartily suggest you spend some time with Nicole or Naomi. Naomi is - how can I put this? She has no filter - she just says whatever is on her mind, heedless of the consequences. With Nicole, all you have to do is ask her opinion on something, and I promise you will get more than you bargained for."

Robert laughed. "Great. My conversational skills with women are poor enough as it is." He stood and held out a hand to help Chris rise. "Thank you for talking. It has helped, a little. Though I think a storm might be approaching. It may be best to head back to the castle now."

Chris glanced toward the west, where the sky was darkening with heavy gray clouds. "I am right behind you."

Robert took Chris's advice that evening and invited Nicole and Naomi to dine at the high table. Elijah stared at Naomi, amazed, when she dropped the bomb as they were about to enter the Great Hall. "So when was the last time you got to dine with royalty?" she concluded.

Elijah cracked his knuckles idly. "Probably not long after I saved Chris's life last year," he drawled. "It managed to make me popular with Robert *and* his father for a few minutes. Enjoy. Oh, and you can bet he has a good reason for wanting your presence. It's not just a free invite." He nodded to the two men on guard duty as they entered the Hall.

Naomi sniffed. "You're just jealous because you won't be eating with your princess."

Nicole looked from brother to sister. "I still have to learn about this 'princess' stuff. Are you both in love or something?"

Elijah gave her a push. "Don't keep the king waiting." Nicole let out a squeak, then lifted her skirts slightly to follow Naomi to the high table.

"I hope I'm dressed well enough for it," she muttered under her breath. When she arrived at the table, she pushed her glasses up her nose. She realized belatedly that she had no idea which person at the table *was* the prince. She was saved humiliation by Allyson, who remembered her from the other afternoon. Nicole eased into the empty seat next to the princess.

"Welcome, Lady Nicole," Allyson said. "Have you been presented to my brother yet?"

"Unh-uh. And neither has Naomi, I'm willing to bet," Nicole said.

Allyson smiled. "Actually, Elijah presented her the first evening they arrived from Saelym. 'Twas while you were still lost. I believe she also had a few words with Bishop Fitzroy."

Nicole mulled the information over. "I wonder if she was as intimidated as I was." She shook her head. "Probably not. I don't think anything fazes - bothers - her."

Allyson chuckled. "Methinks you could be right."

Robert joined them at the table. He held out his hand to Nicole. "I am Robert Claybourne. You are Nicole Carpenter?"

Nicole started to stand, so she could attempt to curtsey in the tight space. Allyson gently pushed her back down. "No ceremony tonight," she whispered. "He did not mention his title."

Nicole flushed, then held her hand out to Robert. To her surprise, he lifted it to his lips before releasing it. Now she was more flustered. "I - Yes, I'm Nicole. I'm pleased to make your acquaintance. You and your sister are the only royalty I'm likely to meet. Am I babbling?"

Allyson smiled. "Yes, but never mind. 'Twill help put my brother at ease. I cannot recall a time he willingly surrounded himself with so many women."

To her and Nicole's astonishment, Robert turned crimson at the remark. To cover it, he lifted his goblet and saluted the company, then turned to face them again. "'Twas not so long ago, Ally, though not willingly," he murmured. "In the brothel. I would as soon forget it."

Allyson's expression turned wicked. "And just what happened that night, to embarrass you so much. And do not put me off with tales about Father's humiliating death. There is more to it."

"Nothing I wish to discuss in public," Robert said in a tone of quiet warning. Allyson subsided, but her eyes continued to dance. Naomi leaned forward, having taken the seat on Nicole's other side.

"So, do you need advice about women, Your Highness?" she asked innocently.

Allyson had lifted her goblet to take a sip of wine and put it down before she spilled it. She started to laugh, then covered it with a feigned choking fit. Robert wasn't fooled, but helpfully hit her once across the back, perhaps a bit harder than was necessary.

He smiled and met Naomi's gaze evenly. "And what wisdom can you share about women, Lady Naomi?" he asked.

"We're smarter than men," she replied tartly. She gestured toward the room. "And we have better table manners. You may not have noticed this, but these men are pigs. Well, with a few exceptions of course."

"Naturally," Robert agreed. "But women are smarter? I thought 'twas just the women in my family. And Duchess Helen."

Nicole realized he was feeding Naomi as much rope as she wanted. "Actually, Your Highness, women are smarter in many ways. Though curbing our tongues isn't always one of them." She shot Naomi a Look.

"This evening I was hoping for honesty," Robert countered. "And I was told by a mutual friend that I could expect it from the two of you."

Naomi narrowed her eyes. "Would it be a light-skinned or dark-skinned friend?" she asked.

Robert noted that the minstrels had begun to increase the tempo of the music. "An answer for a dance," he replied.

Nicole gulped. "I don't think so. I don't know any of your steps."

Naomi stood. "I'm game. I'll even lead." Allyson laughed.

Robert had started to stand, then stopped suddenly. Chris had warned him. "'Twould set tongues wagging, I fear," he said as he gained his feet. "I would be glad to teach you the steps, though."

"Okay. One condition." She grinned at Robert's cautious nod. "We dance right in front of 'Lijah."

"Naturally."

Nicole and Allyson watched the pair walk to the center of the Hall, where the floor had been cleared. "She's as tall as he is," Nicole pointed out.

"And much more forward," Allyson added. "I think she is much like Elijah - you always know where you stand. How about you?"

"Me?" Nicole shrugged. "I have a habit of trying to fade into the woodwork. I don't have any desire to be the center of attention." She cocked her head at Allyson. "Can I be frank?"

"Of course."

"I don't know how you and your brother stand it. I mean, you must have to live your lives in a fishbowl."

"Fishbowl?" Allyson pondered the concept for a moment. "Like a fish living in clear glass, so that all can see its every movement?" Nicole nodded. "Hmm, I suppose that is true to a point. More so for Robert than me - I am only a daughter after all."

"Stupid world," Nicole muttered. "Not that it's all that much better where I come from."

Allyson took a sip of wine. "I was prepared to dislike you," she noted. "Helen is a close friend of mine."

Nicole pondered the information. "I guess I can see that. I'm also sure that you can understand the concept of me looking for an intelligent, sensitive man. Although I might have found another one." She gazed around the Hall, hoping for a glimpse of Michael's cassock. "God, but I've got some serious thinking to do."

"Oh?" Allyson was curious.

"You remember - my so-called Magical Talents?" Nicole suppressed a sigh. "I'm a computer nerd - I've never believed in Magic, in any way, shape or form. Reproducible results, that's my motto."

Allyson considered the phrase. "But, we obtain 'reproducible results' with Magic," she said. "'Tis the point of repeating certain rituals."

Nicole looked at her. "Really. I guess I *do* need to look into this more."

* * *

It took Naomi only a few minutes to catch on to the steps of the pavane. "This is a lot more dignified than the dancing I'm used to," she told Robert. "Of course, hip hop would probably shock you speechless."

"Hip hop?" Robert repeated carefully. "You are not talking about rabbit steps, I take it?"

Naomi missed a step and trod on Robert's foot as she started laughing. "Sorry," she said. *"Rabbits?"* She giggled a little longer but managed to get her rhythm back. "No, I don't mean rabbits. Not hardly." She lifted an eyebrow. "So, was it Chris's idea or 'Lijah's?"

"Chris's."

Naomi nodded then glanced around them. "Robert, is it my imagination or is everyone looking at us?"

Robert smiled. "Of course. They will be speculating whether or not you have shared my bed as the reason for your sudden royal favor."

Naomi's brows lowered. "Did you know that when you asked me to dance?"

"Nay, I had forgotten. Would you rather sit again?"

"Unh-uh. Let 'em talk. I've probably got a questionable reputation anyway, or will by the time I go home." She waved at Elijah as they passed his table. His expression was amused, as was Michael's.

"Older siblings," she muttered.

"Pardon?"

"Older brothers, or sisters," Naomi repeated. "Is your sister in love with Elijah?"

Robert stopped dancing, and managed to keep Naomi from falling at the sudden cessation of movement. "What!" He thought back to when Elijah and Allyson had first met. She'd been taken with him, but she'd never confided anything further after that. "My apologies, Lady Naomi. Are you all right?"

"Better than you, I expect," she replied. "'Lijah denies being in love with her, but she's a big part of why he's still here in Myrridia."

"I shall have to talk to her about it sometime." Robert began leading her back toward the high table. Chris had been right; talking with Nicole and Naomi *had* been enlightening, though maybe not how his friend had intended.

Chapter Ten

The next morning dawned clear and mild, with the promise of summer in the air. Robert was closeted in his study with Chris, James and Anselm. He was trying to compose the proper words to coax Cecelia Falkes and her brother to the castle. He was the first to admit he dreaded a personal encounter with the pair. He kept reminding himself that he had to do it, but the words did little to relieve him.

They all looked up when the herald's trumpet sounded. "Who could -?" Robert began, but stopped as the herald made his announcement.

"Princess Juliana DiStephane of Esterlyn!"

"Who invited...?" Robert stood too quickly, knocking over the jar of ink and muttering an oath. "Do I look presentable? Why did someone not warn me?" His royal blue tunic was clean but far from new. He hoped Paul's mending wasn't too obvious. His boots were scuffed, but it was too late to change.

"Your Grace?" he said to Anselm. "Do you mind accompanying me to greet our royal guest?" He hoped the others couldn't hear his panic.

"Of course, Highness. At my speed, you will have a chance to rehearse your greeting," he said smoothly, winking at Chris and James. He stood and followed Robert.

Chris turned to James. "Does she need an invitation?"

"No. If memory serves, Juliana is the younger daughter of King Wilhelm. He is sending her as a courtesy, and to observe firsthand what kind of man Robert is. He must have heard the news of Reginald's death via mirror - probably from a churchman. I would be surprised to see a member of Wyckendom's royal family come, considering Reginald's plans."

Chris nodded. "I need to learn more international politics, not that I have mastered all of the domestic situations."

James laughed. "'Twould take a lifetime of study. Let us retire to the library in case Robert's latest guest wishes to come here first." Chris gathered up the message Robert had been composing and followed James.

Princess Juliana DiStephane, at sixteen, was less than impressed with what she saw of Rhennsbury as she and her escort rode through the city. Parts of the city were in need of repairs, and fairly soon if the buildings were to be saved. She shook her head in disgust. Her home, the royal seat of Lynxhall, was well maintained.

The party had spent the previous night at an inn a few miles outside the city so they could arrive at Rhennsbury Castle early in the morning, relatively fresh. Juliana was wearing her better riding habit. The outer dress was of muted gold linen, which went well with her honey-colored hair and hazel eyes. Her hair was braided and partially covered with an ivory veil, and a gold coronet helped to hold hair and head covering in place. Her cloak was light brown, and she had pushed it back on her shoulders in the warm sun.

She waited for a castle groom to help her dismount, then she glanced coolly toward the stone stairs leading to the castle's main entrance. She knew the herald had made his announcement, and she had no intention of entering the castle alone. A member of her escort moved to her side.

"Is there aught I can do, Princess?" he asked.

"Not yet, Marc. Let us give our hosts a few more moments, then I will get obnoxious." She smiled.

"Aye." The man bowed and stepped back.

Robert came through the door, Anselm right behind him. He paused for a few moments at the top of the stairs, searching for his guest. He met her even gaze, and he couldn't help staring. She took his breath away.

Anselm cleared his throat, and Robert returned to earth. He descended the stairs quickly, avoiding tripping and falling by pure luck. He came over to Juliana and bowed, kissing the hand she had extended. She curtseyed as he straightened.

"Welcome to Rhennsbury, Your Highness," Robert said, then smiled ruefully. "I regret to say she does not look her best," he added.

"I am relieved that you realize it, Prince Robert," Juliana said, keeping her tone polite. "I thank you for the welcome." She held out her hand again, and Robert belatedly offered his arm. Blushing slightly, he escorted her up the stairs, where Anselm repeated the welcome.

"Would you prefer to go right to your guest room, Your Highness?" Anselm asked.

"That can wait, sir. I bear tidings from my father." Juliana smiled, aware of the fact that Robert was nervous.

Robert wasn't nervous - he was terrified. Besides being beautiful, this princess didn't even look as though she'd been on the road for weeks. She exuded an air of self-assurance, and he got the distinct impression she didn't like him at all.

He escorted her to the study, with Anselm behind them. He left the door open and motioned Juliana to a chair. He was grateful that Chris and James had gone.

Juliana sat gracefully in the indicated chair and looked around the room before speaking, glancing at the hunting tapestries and map of Myrridia on the walls and noting a lack of clutter on the desk. "My father, King Wilhelm, sends condolences on the death of your father and wishes you a long and happy reign." She knew the words sounded rehearsed; she'd been practicing them since leaving Esterlyn. She wouldn't admit it, but she was nervous about being in the presence of the Claybournes. Their warmongering reputation intimidated her. She had been sent from Esterlyn because her elder brother was too ill and her younger brother too young; her sister had refused to come.

Robert acknowledged the greeting, thanking her. She didn't register her surprise at the small courtesy. Juliana continued. "I also have a written missive from him, my lord, in one of my saddlebags. My father regrets to inform Your Highness that the marriage contract negotiated between Princess Allyson and Prince Wilhelm is cancelled, due to the disgraceful circumstances surrounding Reginald's death and his plans to invade Wyckendom." Juliana had turned pink at the severe lapse in diplomacy, but her father's written words were harsher.

Anselm inhaled sharply. Robert flushed to the roots of his hair. He thought he'd been tense before. He was speechless, and his sympathies were with his neighbor. When he had recovered enough to speak calmly, he said, "No blame to the messenger. I will send a polite reply to your father when you return home. The plans for war have been called off, and the wedding cancellation was likely unavoidable under the circumstances."

For the first time since setting eyes on Rhennsbury, Juliana was impressed. Like her siblings, she had grown up hearing horror stories about the war-crazed Claybournes, and their latest scion had been provoked yet avoided speaking in anger. She and Robert both knew he had been insulted. She raised her opinion of him a notch.

Juliana was unsure what to make of his appearance. His clothes were clean enough, but they were far from new. She wondered if Reginald had not extended much of an allowance or if

Robert was conscious of money. She would have loved to ask the state of the treasury, though she knew she would not get an answer, nor deserve one.

She decided he was good-looking, with his dark hair and blue eyes. He had clear skin and even teeth, and he showed no signs of dissolution. She guessed every woman in the three kingdoms and beyond would be looking to marry him by summer's end.

In turn, Robert couldn't help being impressed with Juliana. In addition to her physical charms, he sensed an impressive intellect, and a wit to match. He wasn't sure if they were allies or enemies, considering his family's past actions. He stood and held out a hand to help her rise.

"I will show you to your quarters now, if you are ready," he said. "Feel free to send your father's message along as soon as you wish." Juliana placed her hand in his elbow and allowed him to escort her.

After delivering his guest to appropriate accommodations, Robert went out on the castle ramparts for some fresh air. He took several deep gulps, willing himself to calm down. She was the most beautiful woman he'd ever seen, and he wasn't sure what to make of his reaction to her.

Nicole knocked timidly on the McCabes' door that morning. Abigail opened the door and motioned her in.

"Is Helen here?" Nicole asked.

"Aye." Helen entered the room from the adjoining one. She took in Nicole's pallor and thought she sensed pain in the other woman.

"Is your head bothering you again?" she asked, motioning Nicole to a chair.

Nicole declined the seat. "No, much more mundane. It - it's my monthly -"

"Of course. Follow me," Helen directed, returning to the other room. Nicole obeyed. It was a dressing room and also used for storage. Helen opened a cupboard and withdrew several strips of linen. "Do you need something for the pain?" Helen asked.

"I - How did you know I was in pain?" Nicole asked as she took the offered linen, her expression puzzled.

"The same lines around your mouth as the other day, when you had the severe headache. I can prepare an herbal mixture for you, or ease the discomfort with Magic. Whichever you prefer."

"Magic? Herbs?"

"Raspberry leaf and a few others. It is good for many women's difficulties. Is your pain always so severe?" Helen was curious.

Nicole nodded. "Ever since I was twelve. Sometimes I'd miss school because the pain was so bad. At least I would if I was lucky enough to wake up with it. It was a little better when I took birth control pills for a while, but I didn't like -"

"Did you say 'birth control pills'?" Helen was incredulous.

Nicole smiled. "We have made a little progress. Condoms, too. They're, uh, elastic sheaths for men to put on their -" Nicole flushed, unsure of Helen's reaction.

Helen burst out laughing. When her laughter passed, she said, "Sheaths for their members? Mother of God, do men actually agree to this? And what about the Church?"

Nicole chuckled. "The Church is in denial, naturally." Helen snorted. "Men agree to use condoms because it can keep them from getting certain diseases. Some men claim they like sex better with a condom. Chris never - oh, God, I'm sorry!"

Helen grinned wickedly at Nicole's look of dismay. "Do not worry yourself. Though I do think I will ask him if he brought any of these 'condoms' to Myrridia. Do you think he will blush?" Helen's expression was now conspiratorial.

Nicole laughed. "You can count on it."

"Birth control," Helen mused to herself. "The idea."

Helen showed Nicole how to use the linen strips, then heated wine before adding the raspberry leaf and other herbs. Deciding distraction would help, she asked Nicole, "Have you thought about staying here?"

Nicole sighed. "I haven't *stopped* thinking about it. I always think about Michael, and not in an appropriate way."

Helen raised an eyebrow. "You have carnal thoughts about my cousin?"

Nicole chuckled. "Okay, carnal is a good word. But he's a priest, so I have a problem."

"Not necessarily," Helen replied with a smile. At Nicole's blank look, she continued, "Michael's vow of celibacy was optional. I am sure that if he has similar feelings toward you, then Saelym's bishop would be willing to work with him."

"Optional? I thought -" Nicole shook her head. "I guess it would help if I were the same kind of Christian as you guys."

"Can I give you some advice?" Helen asked. Nicole nodded warily. "If you decide to remain in Myrridia, and if you and Michael have feelings for one another, act on them sooner rather than later. The archbishop may need to be consulted, and Edward Fitzroy, who will be our next archbishop, would be less inclined to aid Michael due to personal animosity."

Nicole looked at Helen with new respect. "You are so incredible. You - you're encouraging me to - pursue - your cousin, and I'm your husband's ex-girlfriend!"

"Well, should you remain here, I would far rather you 'pursued' my cousin than my husband," Helen said dryly. "Personally, I bear you no ill, and as a practitioner, I would like you to learn about your abilities. I think you would bring a unique viewpoint to the practice of Magic. Especially with your sigh-en - I do not know the word."

"Scientific training?" Nicole suggested.

"Aye."

"Lord knows I've had the scientific method drummed into me. I'll give it some more thought, and I'll let you know. But I don't think it'll be objective logic that's the deciding factor."

"It was not so for Chris, either."

On his return to the Great Hall, Robert passed by the library and recognized Chris's guards. He knocked and entered the room. Chris and James looked at him, both noticing Robert's high color.

"Have you taken care of your royal guest?" James asked.

Robert turned redder. Chris and James exchanged knowing looks, but took pity on the young man and refrained from teasing him. Robert told them about his conversation with Juliana. "Are all princesses beautiful?" he asked as he concluded.

"Aye, Robert, 'tis the law," James said, smiling. "Consider your sister."

Robert sighed. "I think she hates me. Or worse, feels sorry for me."

Chris shook his head. "Maybe she is being cautious. She does not know you any more than you know her - she only knows what she has heard about your family." Robert grimaced. "If she has any intelligence - and she is a woman, so it is very likely - she will be impressed that you did not throw her out of the castle on her, oh, never mind. Especially when you consider your father's reputation."

"I agree," James added. "Do you want to get back to this summons for Cecelia and Sebastian?"

"I suppose so. How will we find them?"

"Elijah will want my head on a platter, but send Naomi with an escort. There are two guards just outside -" Chris suggested helpfully.

"Never mind them," Robert said. "Elijah can go with her as well. Nice try, though."

Chris shrugged modestly.

Sometime later Elijah kept his swearing silent as he accompanied Naomi and two royal men-at-arms through Rhennsbury's streets. The sergeant, Ian, had tried to make conversation with him at the start of their errand, but all Elijah wanted to do was get it done.

"God, you're a pain," he said to Naomi for the fourth time.

"Change the record," Naomi retorted, then smiled at the other two men.

"There he is. Sebastian!" She shouted the name.

Sebastian turned slowly, his hand on his sword hilt. He lowered the hand to his side as he took in Naomi, her tall brother, and the two soldiers from the castle. He bowed to her, keeping his features even with an effort.

"A pleasure to see you again, my lady." He ignored the three men except to note Ian's surprised recognition, but was pleased to see the brother's frown deepen as he kissed Naomi's hand. "How may I assist you?"

Naomi handed him a sealed parchment. "A message from Prince Robert Claybourne. He expects to see you and your sister Cecelia first thing tomorrow morning. He guarantees your safe passage." She dropped her voice to a whisper. "If I were you, I'd leave town."

"As His Highness wills. Cecelia and I will come." Sebastian saluted the foursome, then turned and walked off. He was soon out of sight, lost in the crowds of people.

"You're incorrigible," Elijah snapped.

"He's not evil," Naomi shot back.

"And when did you get your degree in psychology?" Elijah asked smugly. Naomi glowered at him.

"I don't need one, Mr. High and Mighty Doctor," she retorted. She turned to the two guards. "Back to the castle, sirs?"

Ian chuckled. "After you, my lady." He leaned toward Elijah. "He is an honorable man, Sir Holmes, if 'tis any comfort to you."

Elijah's scowl deepened. "It's not, but thanks for trying." His eyebrows shot up. "You know him?"

"Aye, although he used the name Simon when I knew him, and he did not have the mustache and beard. He worked at the castle, and he was always respectful, even polite, to the prince. I cannot imagine his trying to -" Ian's eyes widened. "He hated the former king, though, now that I think on it, and admitted that he was a lord's son. Tippensdown."

"Swell," Elijah muttered as they made their way to the castle.

After making certain he wasn't followed, Sebastian slowed his pace as he returned to the Bronze Unicorn after the encounter with Naomi. After taking the stairs two at a time, he rapped once at the chamber door then slipped in. Cecelia was sitting at the table, staring at a lit candle. She raised a hand in greeting, but it was several moments before she turned to face him.

"You may want to bathe. We have been summoned to Rhennsbury Castle." Sebastian dropped the rolled parchment on the table in front of her. Raising an eyebrow, she broke the griffin seal and read through the message.

"But I have nothing to wear worthy of royalty," she murmured.

"Then I suggest you check the city. You do not want to shame the family name." Sebastian rolled his eyes; he had no intention of dressing for the occasion.

Cecelia stood and went over to the still-packed saddlebags. She opened one and pulled out an indigo velvet gown, shimmering with silver threads. "I regret I have no coronet, but I will do my best. Do you think this dress will do? Making it kept me occupied this winter."

"You always planned to meet him."

"Aye, but not so soon. I will need another if we require a second meeting. 'Twill be difficult to make an entire dress in a few days, but not impossible, at least if there is fabric to be had."

Juliana sat on Robert's right at the high table that evening. He had met her as she approached the doors to the Great Hall and escorted her to the table. He apologized for the lack of a feast but gave no reason. Juliana smiled to herself, wondering if it were due to lack of money.

She had dressed in her second-best gown, reserving her finest for the coronation. This one was dark yellow silk, with a pale off-white shift underneath, showing at sleeves and throat. She wore the same veil and coronet as earlier. Most male heads in the Hall turned and stared as she and Robert walked the length of the room.

Robert had taken pains with his own appearance, even taking the time for a hot bath. He was wearing his newest tunic. Earlier he had begged Paul to work a miracle on his boots. The squire had succeeded - the boots looked almost new.

Robert had sent a message to the McCabes, asking Helen to sit on Juliana's other side. He hoped that Helen, as a woman, would be better able to keep a conversation going than he would, considering the evening before with Naomi and Nicole.

Helen and Chris were already at the high table when Robert and Juliana arrived. Helen curtseyed deeply to the younger woman, murmuring a greeting, and then Chris bowed and kissed her hand. Juliana raised an eyebrow for a moment; she'd expected a leer from the Duke of Saelym. This man hadn't even glanced at her bosom. She surreptitiously checked to make sure it was still there.

Helen was happy to spend a good part of the meal talking to Juliana. Helen had been born in Esterlyn and lived there until marrying Christian and moving to Saelym. She asked Juliana how her brother's earldom fared.

Juliana finally remembered being introduced to Helen once at Court, when Helen was fourteen and Juliana had been a small child. She then happily spent most of the meal chatting about her home. Helen was pleased to catch up on the gossip and do Robert the favor at the same time. She suspected he was nervous in the young woman's presence and preoccupied with his upcoming meeting with Cecelia and Sebastian.

After supper, Allyson climbed the stairs in one of the castle's towers and went out on the ramparts. She was surprised to find Elijah and Naomi, arguing.

"I-I am sorry. I did not mean to interrupt -" she began.

Naomi said, "Don't worry, Your Highness, I'm tired of listening to him. I've been looking for an excuse to leave - you've done me a favor. Thanks." Naomi lifted her skirts and stalked to the stairs.

"We're not finished!" Elijah called.

Naomi raised the middle finger of one hand to him for reply and kept walking. Elijah swore, then apologized to Allyson. She smiled.

"Is Naomi younger than you?" she asked.

"Yes. Why?"

"Then, I think I can understand some of your frustrations. Do you ever wonder if she will fully grow up?"

"Ever? More like every minute since she came to Myrridia," Elijah said.

"Oh. Robert is not that bad."

Elijah laughed. "You mean he still acts immature? I thought he was older than Chris, who's over thirty, you know."

Allyson's eyes widened in surprise. "I did not. I thought he was Christian's age. He looks young for his years." She put a hand on Elijah's arm. "Do you want to walk to the next tower? It -" She stopped as she sensed the energy that flowed between the two of them.

Elijah stepped back a pace. "You felt it, too." She nodded, looking at him in confusion.

"I have never had that happen before. I have had contact with Helen and Edward, and others, in my studying, but - what do you think it means?"

Elijah looked away. "I hoped it meant I was going insane, but we can't both be crazy. Or maybe it's some strange manifestation of love. But, I can look at you, and you're beautiful, but you don't have the - usual effect." He looked back at her.

Allyson's gaze dropped for a moment, and she smiled. "So it would seem. I have had that effect on men. Perhaps we are to be partners in Magic, then. You can heal; I can do other things. More than I thought, if yesterday means anything. Do you think I could avoid marriage and practice Magic instead?"

Elijah held out a hand to her. She took it. They both relaxed once the electricity passed. "I think you should do what you love, or love what you do. Helen told Chris and me what happened, and I'm with Helen - I'd hate to see that much Talent wasted." He dropped his voice to a conspiratorial whisper. "Get your brother married with two or three kids and you're off the hook."

Allyson laughed. "What about this foreign princess? He seems taken with her."

"She's very beautiful. I'm glad Robert had the sense to notice. She looks smart, too."

Allyson giggled. "Do you think she is a good breeder? Fertile?"

It took Elijah a second to realize what she meant. It was his turn to laugh. "Now, if I could just work out the problems with *my* sibling. She's in lust with the enemy."

"Say it is not so." Allyson had sobered.

Elijah sighed. "I wish."

At sunup the next morning, Sebastian went down to the inn's common room to request some breakfast be sent upstairs. With the offer of an extra copper coin, the innkeeper was happy to oblige.

It was still early when Sebastian and Cecelia made their way toward Rhennsbury Castle on foot. She wore a full-length black cloak over her dress to hide the fineness of the garment. Sebastian was wearing his usual black, relieved only by a silver brooch at his throat and the hilt of his sword on his left hip. He carried the parchment guaranteeing their safe passage.

Despite the safety, he felt nervousness grip him as they passed through the castle gates. It was one thing to make anonymous inquiries; it was something else to arrive as himself, at the home of his former enemy. He glanced at Cecelia, but her expression was blank. The guards at the gate let the pair pass through without question after glancing at the parchment's seal.

A small man of middle years, with thinning gray hair, greeted them as they approached the castle's stairs. "Lady Cecelia? Lord Sebastian?" he asked as he bowed out of courtesy. At Cecelia's cold nod, he continued, "I am Samuel, Rhennsbury Castle's steward. Please follow me; the prince awaits you."

Sebastian smiled to himself for a moment. Robert was of legal age to use the title of "king." Sebastian was not surprised that the young man had enough respect for the seriousness of the title to put off using it until it was official.

Against all advice, Robert waited for Cecelia and Sebastian in the courtyard with only Anselm, Helen and two royal guards in attendance. Allyson had asked to come, to get an impression of

Cecelia. Robert had countered with not wanting Cecelia to be able to take Allyson's measure. Helen offered to provide Magical support, and Robert accepted. He declined Chris's presence in the fear that Cecelia would realize Chris wasn't Lattimore, or worse, that she would think he was.

Robert now paced nervously as Anselm sat on a bench, with Helen standing next to him. Robert was wearing his prince's coronet this morning, though it threatened to slide off with his constant movement. He also wore his father's ring on his right middle finger, but he had to keep his fingers clenched to keep it from slipping off. He stopped pacing as he heard footsteps approaching on one of the cobbled paths. Anselm stood and joined him; Helen remained where she was.

Cecelia had let her cloak fall open, revealing the high quality of her gown. She also had a blue-silver aura shimmering around her head and shoulders in lieu of coronet or veil. Her blue eyes flashed fire. Sebastian was a calm contrast, his eyes reflecting merely curiosity.

Robert had enough Magical gifts to see Cecelia's aura, and he mentally conceded her ability to effect a dramatic entrance. His eyes widened after a moment as he recognized Sebastian. Sebastian raised an eyebrow in response but said nothing. Robert returned his attention to Cecelia for a moment. Her anger had not faded.

Sebastian bowed politely. Robert inclined his head, then frowned with impatience, as he had to grab his coronet before it fell off. Cecelia remained stiffly upright.

"Thank you for coming," Robert said, ignoring Cecelia's lack of courtesy. "Would either of you care to sit?" He motioned to a nearby stone bench.

"No, princeling," Cecelia spat. "We have nothing to say to the Claybournes except to issue a challenge. Name the time and place."

Even Sebastian was taken aback by Cecelia's rudeness. It took all of his self-control to keep his features impassive. He hoped Robert would still state his reasons for summoning them.

Robert had taken a step back as though he'd been slapped. He glanced at Sebastian a moment, a question in his eyes. He realized that Cecelia's words were as much a surprise to her brother as to the rest of them. He began to feel that Edward had been right all along, and that there was no place here for diplomacy. Anselm stepped forward.

"I think the *king* deserves an apology, my *lady*," he said. "He could have called for your arrest, given you a swift mock-trial, and had you executed by sundown." The firmness of his voice belied his age.

"On what charges, my *lord?*" Cecelia countered.

Anselm motioned toward Sebastian. "Regicide. For yourself, a graver offense - illegal Magical practice."

Cecelia laughed. "You have no proof," she mocked.

Robert had recovered himself. "Thank you, your Grace," he said quietly to Anselm. Turning to Cecelia and Sebastian, he continued, "My intent had been to offer you the return of the Earldom of Tippensdown, with the only stipulation that you sign a five-year peace treaty with Myrridia. That offer is no longer available. As you are a woman, if not a lady, Cecelia, you may name the time and place. We accept your challenge." Robert's voice sounded calmer and more confident than he felt.

Sebastian swore under his breath at Robert's words. He had no quarrel with the youth, and the prince's offer of Tippensdown would have been more than fair. Sebastian wondered if his councilors had agreed to it. He glanced sharply at Cecelia. If this was his sister's idea of exemplary behavior, he didn't want to see good, let alone poor.

"The day after tomorrow at midday, in the City Square," Cecelia said smoothly.

Anselm spoke. "Too public, and that day is market day. Name another place."

"Nay, it must be public. The more so, the better. Unless Your Highness is afraid." She smiled menacingly and flared her aura.

Anselm turned to Robert. "The security will be impossible. Inside a building, at least."

Undaunted, Robert shook his head. "That would mean castle or cathedral. I will not shed blood in the cathedral, and I do not think this pair will return to the castle willingly."

Sebastian shook his head. "You are right, Your Majesty." Cecelia's head shot around to glare at her brother's use of the regal title. Even Robert looked surprised for a heartbeat.

Sebastian ignored his sister. "How about the following day, or one that is not a market day? And what about a weapons' practice field?" he suggested.

Robert nodded. "Excellent idea. 'Twill be safer for any people who come to watch. I do not want innocent bystanders to be hurt."

"Aye, my lord. We have no quarrel with the folk of Rhennsbury." Sebastian turned to depart.

Cecelia crossed her arms. "Which day?" she asked through gritted teeth.

"Today is Wednesday. Friday is a market day. Let us meet Saturday at midday, at the archery field on the eastern side of the city. If that is agreeable?" Robert spoke the last out of courtesy.

"It will have to be," Cecelia replied rudely, turning her back and stalking toward the castle. Sebastian bowed, then followed his sister at a sedate pace.

Robert let out his breath and collapsed onto a bench. He crossed himself. "God, I am terrified."

Helen touched him lightly on the shoulder. "She is not invincible. She is quick to lose her temper. I fear more for anyone facing Sebastian. He seems very competent and even-tempered, a fair match for Christian. I think you and Allyson can defeat Cecelia, though 'twill not be easy."

"You would be correct, Lady Helen," Robert said. "Sebastian worked at the castle last year, though he used the name Simon then. I rather liked him." He stared toward the castle wall, trying to still his thoughts.

Anselm agreed. "Why do I not have my son, Lucas, spar with Chris? He is reasonably good with a sword and may be able to increase Chris's faith in his abilities." He paused, thoughtful, and turned to Robert. "You might consider contacting Sebastian privately, to reason with him. He may be willing to leave Myrridia forever if given the opportunity. I get the impression he is a man of honor."

"He is," Robert asserted. "That is why I am so -" He shook his head. "Damnation."

Helen nodded. "Let us go inside and speak with Chris and Allyson."

Neither Sebastian nor Cecelia spoke until they left the castle. Cecelia turned on her brother first.

"How dare you?" she demanded, hands on hips.

"He would have given us back the earldom, no questions asked, requesting only five years of peace in exchange." Sebastian was just as angry as his sister was.

"Out of cowardice," she said with scorn.

"Nay, out of a sense of fair play. A lack of which you seem to share with his father and Lattimore."

Cecelia took a step back. The words stung more than if he had struck her. "You bastard! I have a mind to -"

"I do not fear your Magic. Do your worst." Sebastian folded his arms and turned his back on her.

"That dark-skinned tramp has turned your brain," Cecelia said.

Sebastian whirled to face her again. "She has naught to do with this. We could have finished everything just now, but you had to be unforgivably rude!" He strode a few paces away from her. He feared striking her in his rage. "What game are you playing?" he asked once he got his anger in check.

"He is a Claybourne. He deserves to die. And Lattimore as well, though he should be dead or incapacitated by now." Her eyes narrowed. "Have you lost the will to shed his blood? Will you betray me or are you still with me on Saturday? I begin to doubt your loyalty to our family's memory," she said.

Sebastian stared at her. His eyes went cold. "I still hope to avenge our family on Lattimore, but that is a private matter. I never intended to shed Robert Claybourne's blood. He was naught but fair to me while I worked in the castle. *You* said you would consider sparing him before, despite trying to kill him last year. Now you say he deserves to die. Make up your mind."

Cecelia looked at him evenly.

He frowned as he felt a sharp pain in his right temple. "Go ahead, use your Magic. After Saturday, I hope never to see you again. Your ambition is worse than that of many men. Let us return to the inn." Sebastian kept his features neutral as the pair walked through the crowded city.

"I have used Magic on you before, brother, to bend you toward my will. I shall do so again if you cross me." Sebastian schooled his features; his sister's words rocked him to his core.

Many of the citizens of Rhennsbury were still clamoring for the Duke of Saelym's head. The people of his capital had not loved Reginald Claybourne, but they had respected him. The common folk were both intrigued and repulsed by the lurid details surrounding his death. They now wanted the guilty party punished. Some marched through Rhennsbury's streets, shouting and waving torches or farm implements.

Chris was on the castle ramparts with Elijah during Robert's meeting with Cecelia and Sebastian. He was hoping for a glimpse of the pair. He was worried for Helen's safety as well.

Elijah pointed when a man and a woman departed the castle. "I think that's him. That's his type, anyway," he said sourly.

"If you are that ticked off with Naomi, ask Edward to send her home," Chris suggested.

"You ever try to force a stubborn woman to do something?" Elijah countered.

Chris thought for a few seconds. "Forget I said anything," he said with a chuckle. Sobering, he pointed to a crowd of about thirty men and women approaching the castle from the city. "Can you make out what they are shouting?" The two men listened.

"They want your head, pal," Elijah said. "Or, Christian's anyway."

Chris paled. "God, they do." He looked over to where his guards were conversing, just out of earshot. "Okay, I will put up with it as long as I have to. Let us go see how Robert and Helen are."

Robert was patiently speaking with a blacksmith who was acting as spokesman for the crowd. The steward, Samuel, had offered to disperse the group, but Robert asked for a chance to talk to them first.

"Sire, how did the duke get here so quickly if he did not know the king was dead?"

Robert decided these people deserved the truth. "I wanted the duchess here. She has been a tremendous aid to my sister and me. So we contacted her by mirror. The duke naturally came with her. 'Tis no mystery about it."

The man pondered this information. "You are certain of the duke's innocence?"

"Yes, my good sir. We have discovered the guilty party and are taking as swift action as we may. Hopefully, 'twill just be a few more days." Robert smiled and shook the man's hand.

The blacksmith bowed, tugging at his forelock. "A long and healthy reign, Sire."

"Thank you," Robert said, thinking *I hope so.*

Chris and Elijah met Nicole on their way down. "Is she gone?" Nicole asked nervously.

"Yeah," Elijah said.

A page approached them. "My lords, my lady, your presence is demanded in the Council room immediately."

Nicole blinked. "Me?"

"You are part of this, too, kid," Chris said. "We should not keep Robert waiting."

When the three arrived, Robert, Helen, Anselm, Allyson, and Naomi were already there. "We are waiting for James, Edward, and Father Michael," Robert said. "Please make yourselves comfortable."

Edward was the last to arrive, Ambrose accompanying him. When everyone was seated, Robert filled them all in on the exchange with Cecelia and Sebastian. "I think I am relieved that this will all end in a couple of days. Though I am still worried."

Anselm offered his son's talents to Chris. "I will take what I can get, sir. Thank you," Chris said sincerely. "I have, what, two days to become an expert. No worse than my medical boards."

"That's the spirit," Elijah said, with false heartiness, slapping Chris on the back.

"Elijah, please," Helen said, her face pale. Chris took her hand and leaned over and kissed her lightly.

"Pray for me," he whispered.

"Aye. For us all."

"It may not come to a sword fight," Robert stated. "I cannot be certain, but I do not feel that Sebastian will challenge me for himself. He could still challenge Chris, though that is another matter. It comes down to Cecelia." He looked at his sister. "She is short-tempered, though very powerful. Helen thinks we can defeat her, but it will not be easy. You can back out."

"No. She will try to kill me if I fight her or no. Why put it off? I am a Claybourne, too. And I can utter insults as well as any." Allyson smiled.

"Thanks, I owe you."

"And I know how you can pay me." Allyson's smile broadened. "Get married, have lots of children, so I do not have to."

"If I am still here come Sunday, 'tis a promise," Robert said.

Edward stifled a choke. He thought these youthful high spirits were getting out of hand. "How do you intend to keep away spectators?" he asked in an attempt to get back to the subject at hand. "And what about your personal safety? This challenge is dangerous enough, but so is a public display."

Anselm spoke. "There is no better option. I made the same points, Edward. We must all share information and impressions of this pair, then pray for the right outcome." Anselm turned to James. "Will you help me make arrangements to use the archery field?"

"Aye. And anything else with which you may need assistance, your Grace."

Chris took Reginald to the practice yard at midday. Lucas was already there with his own son, a red-haired lad a year younger than Reginald. The boys had wooden swords and, after a brief introduction, were sparring good-naturedly.

"If only my job were that simple." Chris smiled ruefully.

Lucas nodded. "Aye. First rule is to relax."

Chris snorted. "Exactly the problem. How can I relax when I am uncomfortable with the weapon?"

Lucas was thoughtful. "Have you any imagination?"

"My friends say too much. Why?"

"Imagine I have just said or done something inappropriate in regard to your wife. Use the sword to give me your opinion."

Chris went one better. He imagined Reginald Claybourne putting a hand on Helen, and his reflexes took over. Lucas maintained an effective defense throughout Chris's onslaught. Both men were panting when Chris stopped.

"Not bad for a novice," Lucas observed.

"But not good enough against a master," Chris noted. "I am going to have to use psychology along with the sword."

"What is that?"

"Outthink him."

"Aye. Use any advantage you have. Do you want to have another go?"

"Absolutely."

Chris and Lucas were tired by the time they stopped late in the afternoon. Chris had improved his moves, for the first time successfully combining the actions of his upper and lower limbs. He thanked Lucas and the two agreed to meet again the following afternoon.

Nicole and Michael spent part of the day in the castle's chapel, talking. She knew she needed to decide what to do with her life.

She'd always had a technical bent, since junior high school, but now the lure of the Magical arts was tempting her.

Michael, despite his personal feelings, made every effort to answer her questions about Magic objectively. Finally, she turned to face him, eye to eye.

"Helen told me your vow of celibacy was optional."

Her change of subject caught him off guard. "What does that mean?"

Nicole leaned over in the pew, brushing her lips against his. Michael's instinct was to back away, but he restrained himself.

"Oh, God," he breathed. He then kissed her shyly. "Celibacy was not a problem before I met you," he said, when their lips parted. "I thought it would help me get promoted. Then, I sabotaged my career at the outset. I guess I have not thought about it since. I have not met that many women."

"Michael, I want to learn more about Magic, but I also want to be with you. It was different with Chris - I loved his maturity. I can't stop thinking about you. Would I be a bad person if I caused you to break your vow?"

Michael laughed. "No, Nicole. I think if 'tis consensual, I would be breaking my own vow. I would have to speak with my bishop."

"Do you want me to stay?" Nicole asked.

"More than anything. But, you have to do what is best for yourself. Do you think you can give up so much of your independence? I do not think I am worth that kind of sacrifice, considering I do not even know what kind of a life I could promise you."

"I'll risk it. Is there anything we can do to help defeat Cecelia and Sebastian?"

"Pray. Hard."

Juliana spent the afternoon in the ladies' solarium, chatting with various noblewomen and exchanging stitching advice. Her mind was going numb from boredom until one dowager said,

"There are rumors going about that an evil sorceress murdered the king and plans to seduce and murder Prince Robert."

"Who, pray tell?" a young lady asked.

"I have no idea, but 'tis said she has black hair and the Devil's own eyes. She has made a pact with Lucifer, I am sure."

Juliana excused herself, pleading a need to use the privy. Spying a page in the corridor, she requested escort to the Great Hall. She found the royal study and knocked on the closed door.

"Enter."

Juliana opened the door and went in. Robert was standing with his back to the room's window, his hands clasped behind him. Allyson was seated in the chair behind the desk. Juliana curtseyed to the pair.

"Princess Allyson, a pleasure to see you again, though it seems we are not to be kin by marriage."

Allyson inclined her head, then smiled. "No offense to your brother, Princess, but it is a relief to me. I am not yet ready to wed. Were you looking for one of us?"

"Aye. There is talk that a she-devil is on the verge of corrupting and murdering Your Highness," she said to Robert.

Robert rolled his eyes. "Nay, just my father's past haunting us."

"Do you need Magical advice? I had no idea you had any gifts," Juliana said.

Robert snorted. "My Magical gift is assisting my sister. She has the Talents in the family." Allyson turned pink. Robert continued, "You may as well know - we will be meeting Cecelia and Sebastian Falkes Saturday, to end this business one way or another."

"Falkes? Of Wyckendom?" An expression of concern passed briefly over Juliana's features.

Robert nodded. "What do you know of her?"

"She is rumored to be one of the most powerful Magicians in the surrounding kingdoms. She prefers to aid the oppressed, to avenge her family, at least, there are rumors of such."

Robert belatedly motioned Juliana to a chair. "This is in confidence, Highness," he said. "I personally regret what happened to her family. I cannot change the past, and Allyson and I have to do what is best for Myrridia. Right now, that means stability. And no war."

"You are nothing like your immediate predecessors. I assume you take after your mother. Is it true she retired to a convent this past winter?" Juliana knew Margaret had, but she was hoping to learn why.

Allyson smiled. "She had as much of Father as she could take. She had no qualms since Robert and I were grown. Marry my brother and you can have the whole story."

Robert flushed and glowered at his sister. Juliana returned her smile, saying, "Touché. I deserved that. I shall have to work on my subtlety."

"One question, Juliana. For the next few days, are you friend or foe?"

"Friend, Allyson. At least through the coronation, perhaps through summer." Juliana stood and departed serenely.

"Must you?" Robert hissed. "I *said* I will marry so you do not have to. Is this how you thank me?"

"Calm down. I was hoping to get a reaction out of her. Did you happen to notice that she did not say 'no' or laugh at the suggestion?" Allyson looked at him innocently.

"Oh."

After supper, Chris asked Helen if they could go outside for a while. Since it was a warm evening, they climbed the castle's northeast tower and walked along the ramparts. When they were away from the sentries, Helen stopped walking and turned to face Chris. "What did you want to talk about?" she asked, guessing the reason for his request.

He put an arm around her companionably. "You know me too well. I wanted to get your private impressions of Sebastian, not just his skills with a sword, but how he comes across as a man. Like, does he seem reasonable?"

Helen smiled slightly. "Compared to Cecelia, Edward is reasonable."

Chris chuckled. "I am surprised to hear Edward and reasonable in the same breath, without some contradiction between the two. Really, though, what do you think about him?"

Helen shivered and moved slightly closer to Chris. "I think I have never been more frightened for you. Are you thinking about trying to talk to him, rather than fight him?"

"Yes." Chris took a deep breath. "I realize I should speak to Robert first, but I want to meet with Sebastian privately and offer him recompense. I shall tell him who I am if I have to."

Helen pulled away from him then faced him. "I would rather you did not," she said, her voice strained. "Offer anything from Saelym as an apology, but refrain from going to him alone. He could simply kill you outright, in a fit of anger, thinking you are Christian." She buried her face in his chest.

Chris stroked her hair, then put both arms firmly around her trembling body. He kissed the top of her head. She raised her tear-stained face to meet his gaze. "You must meet him," she whispered, before burying her face again.

Chris held her for a long time. He stared out at the night sky, unseeing, his thoughts on the woman in his arms, his expression a mix of fear and concern.

Before retiring that evening, Robert knocked on the door of his sister's chamber. Diana opened the door, curtseyed, then asked her mistress if she needed anything else for the night.

"No, thank you. Sleep well," Allyson replied. Diana curtseyed again, then retired to her small bedchamber. Allyson looked at her brother. "You want me to observe your meeting with Cecelia and Sebastian," she stated. Robert nodded.

Allyson motioned toward the room's table and two chairs. Robert sat in the one facing the fireplace, resting his forearms on the tabletop. Allyson placed a lit candle on the table and Robert focused his gaze on it. He began to relax, his breathing becoming even.

Allyson stood behind him and placed her hands on his shoulders, soon easing her mind into his. She added his impressions of Cecelia to what she already knew about the woman. She withdrew when she finished, sighing.

"So, Sebastian is Simon. Interesting," Allyson said.

Robert turned to face her. "Aye."

"Cecelia is much worse. I understand her anger at Father and Christian, but she had no right to speak to you that way." Allyson smiled. "At least not until she learned for herself how annoying you can be."

Robert raised an eyebrow. "Annoying? You are the elder, which makes you annoying. I am just a pest."

"Aye, an annoying pest." Her tone was teasing. Robert smiled, chuckling.

Sobering, Allyson continued, "She truly frightens me. I will face her Saturday, but it is a daunting task."

Robert clasped one of her hands. "I can ask Edward instead, you know."

Allyson shook her head, but returned his grip tightly. "Nay, last Christmas Edward could not discover who had tried to kill you. I think it has to be me. Or no one." She closed her eyes, a single tear escaping.

Robert stood and hugged her, refraining from speech. There wasn't a useful thing he could think of to say.

Sebastian remained in the Bronze Unicorn's common room until well past midnight. He had played dice earlier, cheating occasionally, but had spent the last couple of hours sipping ale and feeling morose. Finally he handed the innkeeper two copper coins and headed up the stairs.

Cecelia was standing at the window, staring outside. She didn't turn at her brother's entrance. "I will defeat him, with or without your aid," she said coldly.

Sebastian looked at the ceiling for patience. "He may be willing to give us another chance," he said carefully. "He seems reasonable enough."

Cecelia whirled around to face him, her eyes glittering. "Why should I care if he is reasonable? His father and Lattimore were not reasonable. They cut down our family - your family, for God's sake!" She wiped away a tear impatiently.

"Aye, but do two wrongs make for a right? I detest Reginald and Christian. Hopefully they are both dead by now. But Prince Robert is of a different mold, and I have no quarrel with him." Sebastian knew his words sounded lame, but he no longer cared. "He would have given us back the earldom."

Cecelia's anger flared again. "'Tis not his to return! It is ours; can you not see that? He is no better than the others, just young and untried. He deserves to die." She spat the last.

"And then what? Will you go quietly back to Tippensdown and rule it with a Magical fist? Or do you aspire to loftier heights?" Sebastian feared the answer.

"The earldom will be yours. Why should I not be Queen of Myrridia? Then I shall rid the kingdom of Edward Fitzroy and rule without opposition."

Sebastian crossed himself. He realized his sister was mad with power, and the thought made him nauseous. She had not been that way as a child. He turned on his heel and left the room. As he left the inn, he didn't hear the innkeeper asking if he should have one of his children wait up for Sebastian's return.

Sebastian walked aimlessly throughout the city until the eastern sky began to lighten. His thoughts were of the days when he and Cecelia were growing up, before he'd had to leave Tippensdown. Cecelia had always been full of questions about everything - whether it was asking where the birds went during the winter months, or why only one of her three brothers would inherit the earldom, but none of her sisters. Her curiosity drove their tutors to their limits. Sebastian wondered what had happened to change her so much. Was it simply the violent deaths of their family? She'd been away from the earldom, in Wyckendom's capital city of Laurconsburg, she'd told him when they'd accidentally met some time after the Tippensdown massacre. The expression in her eyes had become hardened. He shook his head. He was still angry about the needless deaths, but all he wanted was some kind of reckoning for them. He'd achieved vengeance with Reginald's murder. Once he knew the Duke of Saelym was also dead, he hoped to be able to put it all behind him, preferably in some land where no one knew him, or else he'd pay the ultimate penalty and find eternal rest.

Sebastian went to the city's north gate and passed through after slipping a copper coin to a sentry. He stared up at the fading stars, looking for answers. He hoped Lattimore was dead, as his sister asserted. The Duchess of Saelym had a reputation for fairness. She had seemed neutral enough in the courtyard with Robert. Sebastian seriously contemplated getting a message to her, and even Robert, to offer to help them capture Cecelia, though he knew of no way to defeat her. He was unhappy with his own thoughts of betrayal. He realized with astonishment that he'd been weeping for some time. It scared him - he hadn't shed a tear in years.

Chapter Eleven

Chris was outside Robert's study not long after breakfast the next morning. When he had awakened, Helen was watching him sleep, her concern of the night before still evident. He hugged her tightly, promising to be careful.

He glanced at his escort, then rapped on the door. At Robert's command to enter, Chris stepped in. Robert looked up from his writing and smiled briefly. He called for Chris's guards to enter as well, then told them they no longer needed to guard the Duke of Saelym. The men bowed as they exited.

"Ah, irony," Chris said, after wishing Robert a good morning. At Robert's questioning look, Chris continued. "If you agree to the proposal I am about to make, you may decide to reinstate them."

Robert raised a wary eyebrow. "You seem very relaxed for a man who could meet a formidable enemy in two days' time," he observed aloud.

"It is a front, I assure you. Inside, I am scared stiff." At a wave from Robert, Chris sat in one of the chairs. "I want to meet privately with Sebastian, today or tomorrow, to make him an offer and an apology." Chris tensed.

"Absolutely not!" Robert exclaimed, standing. "He will kill you," he added, to soften his gut reaction. He met Chris's gaze steadily. "Yesterday Anselm suggested I try to get in touch with him and said he seemed to be a man of honor."

Chris nodded. "So, what are your personal impressions? Does he seem to you to be as unreasonable as his sister?"

"No, but many would be reasonable as compared to her. Even _"

"Edward?" Chris interrupted with a smile.

"Aye." Robert sat again, looking thoughtful. He picked up the quill he'd been using earlier and twirled it through his fingers absently. He looked at Chris. "I knew Sebastian from before I came to Saelym last year. I liked him - he was a member of the castle guard. He always treated me with courteous respect, which I returned. When Gerard tried to kill me before Christmas, I swore I heard Simon's - I mean, Sebastian's - voice raised in anger to the man who had made the shot. Yesterday, I saw serious disappointment in his face when I told him and Cecelia that I had considered returning the earldom to them, but had changed my mind. I think he could be the man who murdered Father, but he could have been retaliating for what Father did to his family. God, I am so confused! I have more sympathy with my father's killer than my father. What kind of a son am I?" Robert's expression was pleading.

"No better or worse than any other, kid," Chris said sincerely. "My father was nothing like yours, but I did not always agree with him." He reached across the desk and took the liberty of grasping one of Robert's hands and giving it a reassuring squeeze. "You have been provoked beyond what most sons have to put up with. Forget about your relationship with your father for a minute. Think like a king. What is the best thing for Myrridia?"

"Peace and stability," Robert replied promptly. His shoulders sagged. "That is the easy part. How does one achieve it, let alone maintain it? If Sebastian killed Myrridia's king, the penalty is death. But if his motive was personal rather than political, does he really deserve to die for it?"

Chris whistled. "Boy, and I thought I had to make serious decisions as a doctor. Okay, are there other options besides execution?" Chris grimaced as he spoke the last word.

"Permanent exile. That is hardly a pleasant choice."

Chris nodded. "Let us face facts. If Cecelia - no - *when* Cecelia is defeated, she will be dead or nearly so. Sebastian will have no family left. He may be happy to leave Myrridia forever. Look, I can talk to him about that option, too."

"Aye. Will you consider an armed escort?" Robert asked.

"Yes, but I do not want one." Robert started to protest. "No, wait, please. I do not think he would meet with me under those circumstances. I know I would not. A single man, maybe."

"You are a brave man, Chris."

"Yeah, right. Although if brave means stupid, you may be onto something."

The castle's herald made an official proclamation to the city that morning. He stood in the city's central square and read the information from a parchment.

"Citizens of Rhennsbury and visitors, Prince Robert Claybourne hereby announces a public confrontation to be held on the eastern archery field Saturday at midday. Cecelia Falkes of the Earldom of Tippensdown accuses the Duke of Saelym and the late King of Myrridia of crimes against her family and calls on Prince Robert to answer for those crimes. She has challenged Prince Robert and Princess Allyson to a Magical Duel."

The herald rolled up the parchment and quietly walked through the gathered populace. Most of the folk wore expressions of stunned disbelief.

* * *

Anselm DeLacey and James McDermott passed through the city later that morning, walking to the Mayor's residence to discuss preparations for the event. The two men were astonished by the reactions to the proclamation.

"I care little for this atmosphere of celebration," James remarked quietly to his companion.

Anselm nodded his agreement. "Mark my words, McDermott, many of the city's merchants will profit in the short term, regardless of the outcome."

"Aye. Although 'tis the outcome that worries me most. You met this woman yesterday. I can understand her loathing of Reginald and Christian. I lost my sons in that debacle. But that hardly gives her the right to condemn Robert."

Anselm was thoughtful. "She is quick to anger, and I think her hatred has set her beyond reason. I suspect she may be a little mad, but then this hurt has had several years to fester. We can only pray for the best, and see that this thing is planned to our advantage." His tone was brisk as he concluded.

"Aye."

A deputy mayor detained the two men briefly, but Henry Black was all apologies as he escorted them to his private study. "I assume you are here to discuss the preparations for two days hence," he stated.

"Aye," Anselm said. "Will it be difficult to prepare the archery practice field in so short a period of time?"

Henry chuckled. "My lords, if there is profit to be had, Rhennsbury's citizens could have it prepared by sunup tomorrow, and still have a full market day."

James was disgusted, but refrained from saying so.

"May we look over the field?" Anselm asked mildly, holding his emotions in check as well.

"By all means, sirs." Henry rose, his guests following suit.

The three men walked purposefully to the practice field. The archery targets had been removed, and seats and vendors' stalls were in various stages of being set up. A wooden dais was under construction to accommodate members of the nobility. A large area was being cleared of debris. One man was offering spaces in the grass to some gullible bystanders for the cost of half a copper coin.

"This field will be ready for His Highness," Henry assured his companions.

"The results of this contest are by no means certain," Anselm said quietly to the Mayor. The man glanced at him sharply before waving the Duke's words away.

Anselm and James walked around the field, speaking with the occasional worker, asking questions or making suggestions. After taking a final look, they headed back to the castle.

Chris took care with his message to Sebastian. Latin had become second nature to him, but he wanted to keep the wording diplomatic yet not weak. Helen helped him with some of the phrasing. A loud knock sounded at the library's door. Helen and Chris looked up, to see Elijah stride in angrily.

"She is not going with you!" He banged his fist down on the desktop. Chris had reflexively lifted his hand from the parchment, and Helen quickly grabbed the ink pot.

"What are you -?" Chris began, as Naomi burst into the room, her expression even more mutinous than her brother's.

"Never mind," Helen finished for him. "If I had to make a guess, Naomi wishes to accompany you should you meet with Sebastian." Chris swore.

"Elijah Holmes, you are not my keeper!" Naomi shouted.

"The hell I'm not," Elijah retorted, his tone quiet but all the more menacing because of it. "You're not going. End of discussion."

"I am going. How else can I ask him to come home with me?" Naomi asked, smugly pleased as all three stared at her.

"What? Are you nuts? Why would -?" Elijah sputtered.

Chris was staring at her openmouthed. He shook his head then said, "You are serious."

"Yes, I'm serious."

"But, he's a killer!" Elijah wasn't giving up.

"An alleged killer," Naomi corrected. "You wouldn't kill someone if they'd killed your entire family?" Naomi crossed her arms. Elijah sagged in defeat. Chris stood and gave Elijah a pat on the back. He'd paled at Naomi's words, being close to the Holmes family, but he couldn't put himself in Elijah's place.

Elijah swore.

"You still cannot come," Chris said. Elijah shot him a grateful look. Naomi's anger returned, this time directed at Chris. She walked over to him, stood with her hands on her hips, just a couple inches shorter than he was. He didn't back down.

"How does your effing Grace plan to stop me?" she asked through gritted teeth.

"I will tell Robert, he will forbid it and send you packing to Edward Fitzroy, who will send you home," Chris replied evenly.

"God, I hate men." Naomi flung herself into Chris's abandoned chair. "You corrupt them early. How do you stand it?" she asked Helen.

"I agree with them in this, Naomi," Helen said mildly. Naomi glared at her. "Why do you think he would even consider going with you?"

Naomi rolled her eyes. "If he *did* kill the king, what options has he got?"

"Death or banishment," Helen replied.

"Exactly. So if he comes with me, nobody here will ever see him again." Naomi leaned back in the chair, her smugness returning.

"I don't care how much logic you use, it's too dangerous. You could get killed," Elijah said.

"I'm about the only person in this town he won't kill," Naomi countered. "So look at me as a bodyguard for Chris. I could at least distract him long enough for Chris to retreat."

Chris snorted. "I think not. I retreat and leave you with him? Elijah will kill me. Thanks, but I will take my chances with Sebastian. Alone."

Elijah smiled his agreement, but didn't speak.

"I'm going, if I have to sneak out now," Naomi vowed.

"You do realize that if she goes to him and something happens to her, I will have to hurt you," Elijah said conversationally to Chris.

Chris nodded. *Like I'm not dreading this encounter enough*, he thought, as Elijah and Naomi left the room separately. He wasn't sure which one of them had won the argument.

After completing his message to Sebastian a short time later and sending it out with Ian, Chris joined Lucas for another sparring session in the practice yard. Today, they'd attracted an audience.

Fergus MacTavish accused 'Christian' of getting soft. Chris did his best to ignore the man's taunting and pay attention to what he was doing. He was relieved to note that he still had his coordination from the day before.

Reginald and Lucas's son, Colin, stopped their own mock-fighting and watched their fathers for a while. After a time, they became bored and Reginald suggested they go to the stables. Colin agreed, and the two boys left the practice area.

A group of armed men were in the castle's entry yard, preparing to depart Rhennsbury Castle for Holy Grove Monastery. They had mounted a docile Nigel Jennings onto a mule with no difficulty. He seemed completely unaware of his surroundings.

Lady Gwendolyn watched with impassive features. She had visited her stricken husband once, but she'd seen no glimmer of recognition in his eyes.

Richard Jennings watched his father, his expression angry. He'd still not forgiven Helen Lattimore or Edward Fitzroy for their inability to help his father. He hated what he saw as the Church's use of Magic to keep the rest of Myrridia's population under Her control. He knew Helen was often Edward's assistant and held her to the same responsibility.

Reginald and Colin stopped on their way to the stables, staring in curiosity at the traveling party. Nigel's head turned slightly as the boys stopped moving, and he stared at them. After a few moments, he recognized Helen's features in the taller boy.

Colin was just saying to Reginald that nothing was happening and it was time to move on to the stables, when Nigel dismounted silently. He stared at Reginald, his eyes unblinking. Reginald stood rooted for several moments, and then he took a step backward, tripping. As he fell, Nigel covered the remaining feet between them and grasped Reginald's arm roughly.

"Father, help -" Reginald cried before Nigel cuffed him on one ear. Nigel removed Reginald's small knife from the boy's belt and held it under his chin. He still hadn't spoken a word.

A sixth sense caused Chris to hear and recognize Reginald's voice. He stopped in mid-move and Lucas barely missed causing him serious injury. He pulled up at the last moment, swearing and grazing Chris's arm.

"What the -?" he began, but Chris was already heading in the direction from which he thought Reginald's cry had come. He stopped in his tracks in the entry yard when he saw Nigel holding the knife to Reginald's throat. Then a paternal instinct took over. He sheathed his weapon.

"Let go of him, Jennings," Chris growled. "If you have a problem with me, you take it up with me."

Nigel moved not a muscle. He acted as though he'd not heard Chris's words, but his head was cocked as though he were listening to something. The knife started to move closer to Reginald.

"No!" Chris shouted and launched himself at the pair. His momentum knocked Nigel off balance, causing him to lose his grip on Reginald. Reginald fell, then rolled away before trying to stand. A pale Colin helped him.

Chris was circling Nigel warily, his sword out again. Nigel stood, staring emptily. He dropped the knife suddenly, as if its touch burned him. Summoning his last ounce of sanity, he raised his gaze to Chris's. "For the love of God, Lattimore, kill me. She is the devil," he choked out before the madness overtook him again. He fell to his knees, his arms outstretched.

"Yes," Chris said quietly. Closing his eyes, he said a quick prayer for Nigel's soul. He opened his eyes and happened to see the two boys looking on in fearful fascination. "Go inside," he ordered.

Helen had entered the entry yard by this time. She'd been in the ladies' solarium with Eleanor when she'd sensed Reginald's cry. She took each of the boys in hand now and held their faces to her skirt. "Do what you must," she said to Chris.

Chris nodded grimly. With his eyes burning, he stabbed Nigel quickly in the chest, surprised and repulsed by the resistance he felt as the weapon progressed through Nigel's body. Chris pulled the sword out and dropped it, then caught Nigel as he fell forward, ignoring the blood coming out of Nigel's wound. As his life ebbed, Nigel's features lost their hunted look and his lips formed a "thank you."

Chris personally didn't care for the man, but he wouldn't wish that kind of mental trauma on anyone. He closed Nigel's eyes and murmured, "Requiescat in pace, Nigel." He raised pained, wet eyes to Helen, who inclined her head.

"He is in a better place," she said.

Chris nodded. "It is still not easy." He'd had to watch patients die, helpless to cure them, but he'd never actively helped one do it.

Gwendolyn came over and stared down at her husband's body. "Thank you, Christian." She began to cry. Richard glared at Chris.

"Your wife is a witch, Lattimore, at Fitzroy's beck and call. Without people like her, the rest of us would not have to suffer like my father did. You should put her away. She has probably tainted your children with her sorcery!" He spat at Helen's feet.

Chris stood after easing Nigel's body to the ground. "You will apologize for the insult you have paid my lady wife. She is no more responsible for the evil act of another than you or I." He softened his voice. "It is difficult to lose a close family member."

"Save your platitudes," Richard snapped.

"Have a care for what you say in public, Baron," Robert said from behind him. He had just exited the castle, having been informed of the events in the entry yard by a page. His face was pale, remembering his own father's recent death. "'Tis a difficult thing to lose a parent like this."

"You hated your father, and all knew it!" Richard turned on him. "Spare me your hypocrisy! Will someone help me get my father away from his enemies?"

Gwendolyn spoke. "Richard, you speak treason. Say no more until your emotion passes."

"Let him speak his mind," Robert said mildly. "I *disliked* my father, Richard. I never wished him dead. It is because of my father that yours is now dead as well. The Crown will pay for his burial. I am sorry." Robert turned and wearily climbed the steps to reenter the castle. Richard stared after his young king, his anger unabated.

Chris kept his own emotions in check until he, Helen and Reginald returned to their chamber. Reginald was still pale and had cried a little. He held Chris's hand tightly.

Chris had had no choice but to clean the sword in the entry yard. A groom had brought him some linen and offered to wipe it down for him, but Chris had declined. He'd felt nauseous when the man then asked if he wanted the blade sharpened.

"May-maybe later," Chris had said.

Chris changed out of his bloodstained surcoat. Reginald now asked if he could stay with his father for a while. Chris nodded and sat heavily in a chair before lifting the boy into his lap. Helen poured Chris a generous serving of wine. When Chris lifted the goblet, his hand was shaking.

"I have never killed anyone before," he whispered. "I have lost patients, but nothing like this." Reaction overwhelmed him.

"Father, I have never seen you cry," Reginald said quietly. He was too surprised to pay attention to what Chris was saying. "You said tears are not manly."

"Sometimes your father can be an idiot," Chris said, smiling for the boy's benefit. He tousled Reginald's hair. "How are you, young man?"

Now that Reginald knew he was safe, he was recovering quickly. "I am fine. I was only scared for a moment. I knew you would save me!" He hugged Chris, then leaned back against him, smiling. He was sleeping before long.

"Amazing," Chris said, shifting slightly to make Reginald more comfortable. Helen took his hand.

"Thank you for rescuing him. Are you all right?"

"No, but I will be. Please tell me I did the right thing."

"You saved Reginald's life. Now I am angrier with Cecelia. It is one thing for her to attack Christian. Reginald is at least as innocent as Robert is. More so. With Nigel, ending his life, you did the only moral thing. If killing bothers you, and I am glad it does, confess it to Michael and do penance," Helen suggested.

"At home, I would be arrested for murder, or at least manslaughter." Chris shivered.

"Are your laws so inflexible?"

Chris nodded. "I think it is to protect the public safety. I could have gone to prison, though maybe not, if the jury looked at extenuating circumstances. But I would still need to go through the motions of a trial." He pulled her close to him with his free arm. "You are right about one thing. I am thoroughly pissed off at Cecelia for threatening an innocent boy. It is no better than Reginald and Christian slaughtering women and children."

Helen paled. "I had not looked at it that way. I think Robert should make that point to her on Saturday, though 'twill only inflame her the more."

Eleanor missed the events in the entry yard. When Helen left the solarium, Eleanor was playing with several other young girls. After a while, she became bored and wandered over to a beautiful young woman who'd been ignoring her embroidery for some time.

"My lady?" Eleanor said shyly, curtseying. "Are you bored?"

Juliana started. She'd been thinking about going out riding. The fresh air would do her good.

"What? Oh, hello," she said to Eleanor. "I was woolgathering. My name is Juliana. You are -?"

"My name is Eleanor. My mother is a duchess. You are very pretty."

Juliana's cheeks turned pink at the unsolicited compliment. She smiled at Eleanor. "The duchess of what?"

"Saelym."

"Would you like to go for a walk, Lady Eleanor? At least I know where to return you when we get back."

Eleanor smiled. "Could we go to the stables?"

"Yes, my thought exactly."

When they arrived at the stables, Juliana took Eleanor to visit her own mare. She held the little girl so she could stroke the horse's mane. The horse whickered quietly and accepted some oats when Eleanor held them out.

"Do you like cats, Lady Juliana?" Eleanor asked. "Prince Robert brought me here yesterday, and I met a beautiful black and white one."

"I had a cat once," Juliana said. "She was a calico." There was a piercing "meow" from behind them. When they turned, they saw a large black-and-white longhaired tomcat looking at them. When he saw he'd gained their attention, he howled again.

"He will fetch things, like a dog," Eleanor said.

"Maybe he thinks he is a dog, although why should he wish to be, when cats are much smarter than dogs?" Juliana asked.

"Maybe he is not a smart cat," Eleanor reasoned with five-year-old logic. She reached into her skirt and withdrew a small woolen ball. She tossed it to the cat, who leaped up and caught it in his teeth. He dropped it and batted it around in the dirt for a while, before finally knocking it at Juliana's feet.

"He wants to play with you," Eleanor told her.

"So 'twould seem," Juliana replied, amused.

They played with the cat until the cat tired of the game and began washing his legs and the base of his tail. Juliana let Eleanor lead the way to her family's guest chamber, then knocked on the door quietly.

Abigail opened the door. "Yes, mistress?" she asked, then looked down and picked up Eleanor. Juliana smiled.

"Is Lady Helen available?"

"Aye." Abigail stepped aside and motioned Juliana in. Juliana took in Helen, Chris and their son. Helen was perched on the arm of a chair, leaning against Chris. Reginald was soundly sleeping. Chris's eyes were closed, but Juliana sensed he was awake. She didn't try to fathom the emotional currents in the room.

Helen stood and curtseyed. Chris opened his eyes at her movement. "My apologies, Your Highness." He glanced to the boy in his lap.

"'Tis no matter. Do not disturb him. I came to return your daughter, who is delightful, and to make certain you are well, Helen. I was concerned when you left the solarium so abruptly."

"'Twas my son, Reginald. The danger is now passed. I will be so glad when Saturday has come and gone, though I fear the outcome," Helen said wearily.

"Cecelia Falkes?" Juliana asked.

"Aye," Helen said, surprised. "How much do you know?"

"Very little, beyond her name and reputation. She is behind Reginald Claybourne's death?"

"'Tis likely." Helen poured wine for them. "This will be public knowledge soon enough." She filled Juliana in on recent events. Juliana paled long before Helen finished her narrative.

"Good God. I could sympathize with her original hurt, but to attack children, blame them for the deeds of -" Juliana stopped suddenly and laughed softly. "Like prejudging someone because of his father's reputation."

"Mayhap. But your father is hardly trying to kill Robert," Helen pointed out. "He wants to know what kind of man his new neighbor is."

"I was thinking of myself, rather than my father, but you are right nevertheless. I must say your husband is a far cry from his own reputation." She turned to Chris. "A reputed warmonger and infant-killer, but at least you care for your own family."

Chris winced, even though he knew the words didn't apply to him. They did apply to his persona, and that made him uncomfortable. Juliana was making him downright nervous. She had an acuity that rivaled Robert's.

"I do not think you are Christian Lattimore," Juliana continued, watching him. "Nay, do not confirm or deny. I should not be privy to such information. Your loyalty is to Myrridia, not Esterlyn. I do promise that I will spend part of my journey home pondering this. I will refrain from mentioning it to anyone, though. You have my word."

"Your word is enough, Princess," Chris said quietly.

Sebastian was pretending to observe the activity at the archery field when Ian delivered the message from Chris. He had been seriously debating turning himself in to Robert and accepting his punishment. The only regret he had was that Christian Lattimore still lived. Sebastian stared at the green eagle seal in disbelief. "Do you need to wait for a reply, Ian?" he asked.

"Aye, Simon." Ian's lips twitched. Sebastian grinned and inclined his head. He asked Ian to accompany him to the cathedral. He'd feel less exposed. He couldn't imagine what the Duke of Saelym wanted of him. He sat in a rear pew, and broke the seal of the message. He read through it carefully, and then he stared at the ceiling, searching for answers that weren't there. His emotions were in turmoil - confusion, anger, relief. Deciding he'd learn more only by meeting with the man, he turned to Ian.

"Yes. Tomorrow. Here in the cathedral at midday."

"Thank you." Ian bowed and left.

Sebastian watched the sergeant's departure. He would arrive well before the appointed time, and if Lattimore had more than one man with him, he'd leave without talking to him. Upon exiting, he lit a candle, saying a prayer for his family. He planned to forget to mention this meeting to his sister.

Cecelia and Sebastian exchanged few words the next morning. Cecelia's expression was sullen, and Sebastian feared he would betray his plans if he fell into idle conversation.

He left their room at midmorning without any explanation. He walked straight to the cathedral and sat in a back pew for a while, lost in thought. Before the appointed time, he went to the upper gallery and settled in to watch the cathedral's entryway.

Shortly before midday, Lattimore came in, accompanied by a single man-at-arms and Naomi. She'd eventually won the argument with her brother, though Elijah had still continued to threaten Chris with bodily harm if anything happened to her. Sebastian swore under his breath but decided to make the best of it. His left hand firmly resting on his sword hilt, he quietly descended and approached the group from the rear.

"Naomi," he called quietly.

Naomi whirled to face him, surprise and pleasure on her face. Chris half-turned, quickly hiding his own astonishment, and immediately handed his sword to the man with him. Sebastian raised an eyebrow, but unfastened his own weapon and gave it to Naomi. He still had a dagger at his belt and another in his right boot.

Chris gestured to a nearby pew, keeping his features neutral. Sebastian nodded and followed him, fighting his instinctive urge to murder his companion. Both men sat. Chris mentally conceded the first victory to Sebastian; he had the feeling the other man had already studied him.

"State your business, Duke," Sebastian said. He saw no need to show this man the courtesy he'd shown Robert, since the man had been nothing short of rude to him when he'd worked at the castle. On a good day.

The antagonism in Sebastian's tone was obvious to Chris. He decided to go in hard and fast. "I want to offer you an apology and recompense for what happened to your family. I know it is not nearly enough -"

Sebastian was stunned and angry. "Not enough by far, Lattimore. What kind of sick jest is this? Are you trying to insult my family?"

"God, no. Not at all." Chris thought furiously. "The last thing I intend is any dishonor to your family. Look, Lord Sebastian, I have something bizarre to share with you, but it is in the strictest confidence." Chris stood and began pacing, not trying to hide his nervousness.

"Why should I care?" Sebastian countered hotly, to cover his growing confusion, especially at the duke's seemingly sincere use of his title.

"For one thing, it explains why I am still standing and talking coherently despite your sister's attempt to kill me," Chris retorted.

Sebastian mulled this over. His curiosity was aroused; the man did seem to be in perfect health. His sister's Magic seldom failed. "Fair enough. I will not share the information."

Chris nodded acceptance. "I am not Lattimore. Christian was murdered last summer at the behest of Margaret Claybourne." Sebastian sucked in his breath. "Edward Fitzroy asked me to stand in for Lattimore because he got wind of your planned assassination attempt. He thought it was directed at the Duke." Chris took the shot, hoping for a reaction. He got one; Sebastian scowled.

"It was supposed to have been directed at the Duke," he stated, but didn't elaborate. He continued to watch Chris, still unconvinced.

"I have opted to stay in Myrridia and do what I can to improve things, which means keeping Robert Claybourne alive."

Sebastian didn't bother to mask his skepticism of the explanation. "You must be Lattimore," he said, staring at Chris to see if there was any evidence of lying.

Chris glanced at Naomi, some distance away. Sebastian followed his gaze, then turned back to Chris. "What does she have to do with it?" he asked.

"You have noticed she speaks with an accent?" Chris asked, in his own American accent. It sounded strange to him now.

Sebastian was getting unnerved. "You are from the same place as she and her brother? But you remain here because you have become loyal to Myrridia, a place that is not your home?"

Chris shook his head. "There is a lot more to it than that. I love Helen Lattimore."

The reply's simplicity wasn't wasted on Sebastian. He was still trying to work out all of the implications of Chris's words.

"Lattimore was murdered last summer," Sebastian repeated. He looked at Chris with a dawning respect. He noticed the intelligence and wit behind his eyes. "You would offer recompense. You are not a woman and child killer then."

"No. Perhaps you would like to hear what Cecelia attempted to do to my son yesterday."

Sebastian doubted it, but he did notice that Chris referred to the boy as his own son. "Go ahead." He steeled himself.

"Nigel Jennings tried to kill him. Fortunately I was able to stop him, and the baron is now out of his misery."

Sebastian crossed himself. "I apologize for the act, sir. My sister had no right to do that."

Chris smiled, relaxing finally. "Thank you, Sebastian, but there is no need for you to apologize. She should do it herself, but I have no intention of holding my breath waiting for it."

Naomi joined them. She'd gotten impatient. "So?" she asked Chris.

Sebastian looked at her. "What?"

"Come with me when I return home," Naomi said.

"What?" Sebastian repeated dumbly.

"Do you want to be executed?" Naomi snapped.

"I do not repent killing Reginald Claybourne. I know the penalty for regicide," Sebastian said.

Chris now spoke. "Robert recognizes the difference between a personal and a political killing. He would accept permanent exile."

Sebastian pondered the information. "Robert is a true nobleman, unlike his sire. Is there a chance he would change his mind about Tippensdown?"

Chris shook his head. "If it were just you and he, I think he would. But because Cecelia will not back down, he does not see where he has a choice in the matter. I am sorry."

Sebastian nodded; it was the answer he had expected. "But you offer recompense from Saelym."

"Yes. Hopefully the idea causes Christian unrest in his grave. Serves him right! I have enough problems with war in general, but I have a real issue with killing women and children. It has gotten so bad at home that those deaths are called 'collateral damage.'"

"Collateral -?" Sebastian crossed himself again. "No offense, Lady Naomi, but why would I wish to go to such a place?"

"To make it better. To keep yourself from getting executed. I don't want to see that happen even if you *did* kill the king. It sounds to me like he had it coming," she asserted.

Chris kept his expression noncommittal. He'd had no love for Reginald Claybourne. "I am prepared to make you this same offer tomorrow, publicly," he said.

Sebastian made a vain attempt to smile. "The least I can do is try to talk Cecelia out of this confrontation. I doubt it, but I will try. If - when - I fail, I will see you tomorrow and will try to act surprised by your offer, or demand restitution myself. I will not tell her about this meeting. She still hopes for 'Christian's' death." He turned to Naomi. "I will let you know what I decide," he promised. She handed him back his sword. He saluted Chris. "Until tomorrow, your Grace." He walked purposefully out of the cathedral.

His use of the honorific surprised Chris. Naomi sank into the pew. "Are you okay?" she asked Chris.

"I think so. You know, we could have probably been friends back home."

Elijah was waiting, his expression a scowl and his hands on his hips, when Chris and Naomi returned to the castle. He finally relaxed when he could see for himself that Naomi was fine. He then asked them if they'd like to share a drink, but Chris declined. He wanted to see Helen.

She was in their chamber pacing. When he entered the room, she hurried over to him. She leaned into him, shedding a few tears of relief. She murmured into his chest, "Did he accept your offer?"

"He will tomorrow, either on the field or privately. He said he will talk to Cecelia, but he does not expect her to change her mind."

Helen stepped back. "She will not. She is too filled with hate. I will be with Allyson later, to give her what advice I can. Thank you for letting me know you are well."

Chris pulled her back against him and kissed her forehead. "I will be with Robert. Whatever moral support I can give him, I will."

That afternoon Michael asked Nicole if she'd like to go into the city, to experience a busy market day. Her first reaction was to decline, but then she changed her mind.

"Why not?"

Eleanor saw them in the courtyard and asked them where they were going. When Michael told her, she asked, "May I come, Cousin Michael?"

"If 'tis all right with your mother," Michael replied with an apologetic look at Nicole. She smiled and shrugged.

Eleanor soon rejoined them, pulling Elijah and Naomi with her. "I saw them in the Great Hall and asked them to come."

"Told us is more like it," Elijah whispered, "but she's hard to deny. You women start young." Naomi smacked him, but Nicole's smile widened.

Eleanor held onto Michael's hand as they walked into the city. It was packed with people. When they finally reached the central square, they couldn't talk without shouting.

Naomi spied a jewelry vendor and began looking over the merchandise with enthusiasm. She poked Elijah in the ribs. "Do you see anything Mama would like?"

Elijah experienced an overwhelming feeling of homesickness. He closed his eyes briefly, recalling his mother's face. He felt greatly torn, until he recalled Brother Peter and Allyson Claybourne. He knew he couldn't return home yet.

Nicole grasped Michael's arm tightly and pointed to their left. "Isn't that - her?" She kept her voice to a whisper, though she wanted to scream. Michael followed her finger and paled.

"Aye." He tightened his grip on Eleanor slightly.

Cecelia was at a cloth seller's stall, looking over several bolts of silk, velvet and brocade. She was almost finished making a new gown for her confrontation with Robert Claybourne, but she allowed herself the luxury of considering another gown to wear after her victory. She could hardly be seen in the same dress if she were being crowned queen.

She sensed eyes on her and turned. Recognizing Nicole and Michael, she smiled. She turned to the vendor, murmured a "thank you" and then walked calmly toward the pair.

Nicole wanted to bolt, but she couldn't abandon young Eleanor. The girl stared at Cecelia with curiosity.

"Who is she?" she asked Michael. "She is very pretty."

"Hello, Cecelia," Nicole said tightly. "You look well."

"I have never been better, Nicole," Cecelia purred. "And how is your love life, with the Duke of Saelym?"

Nicole fought the urge to roll her eyes and surprised herself by remembering the correct honorific. "His Grace is well enough. It would seem you'd have done better to aim for his manhood than his brain. The bleeding seems to have had little effect."

Cecelia frowned before schooling her features into neutrality. "Then I shall see him tomorrow, to watch him die. Who is this young lady with you?" she asked innocently.

"Eleanor McCabe," Michael replied after a split-second's hesitation. "She is being fostered in Saelym, and will join her family as soon as they arrive in Rhennsbury." He promised he'd confess the lie later, but he'd go to Hell before telling Cecelia the truth, especially after what had nearly happened to Reginald. Fortunately, his story had a grain of truth to it, even if it was a small one.

Eleanor had been distracted by some nearby jugglers and missed what Michael had said. Cecelia tried to read the response, but got only confusion for her efforts. She debated pushing harder, but Elijah and Naomi were joining their companions. Cecelia nearly hissed in reflex as she realized who Naomi must be.

"Who's your friend, Nicole?" Elijah asked with feigned innocence. He had an idea because he was suddenly sensing the emotional turmoil around him.

"Cecelia, this is Elijah and Naomi," Nicole said. Cecelia looked Elijah over, openly admiring. Elijah's skin started crawling. Her eyes narrowed when she focused on Naomi. *Bitch,* her expression seemed to say.

"Cecelia, a pleasure," Naomi purred. "Please tell Sebastian I said hello, though I hate to tell him I can't meet with him tonight. Do you mind passing on the message? Thanks, you're a dear."

Elijah fought a choking fit. He was afraid he was going to strangle his sister. Nicole and Michael just stood back and admired her work.

Cecelia was scowling. Without a word, she turned on her heel and stalked off.

"Must you?" Elijah asked Naomi.

"I could take her," Naomi said.

"In a physical fight, maybe, but in a Magical one, you're unarmed," he reminded her.

"Yeah, so where's the victory then?" Naomi countered. "If she's not careful, her face is going to freeze in that expression."

"Really?" Eleanor asked. The jugglers had moved on. Michael suggested they return to the castle. Nicole was the first to agree; her knees felt like water.

Sebastian followed Cecelia to their chamber that evening after supper. He was about to speak when his sister said conversationally, "I met your dark-skinned whore today."

Sebastian paled with anger. "She is no whore," he said in a tight voice. "A lady, perhaps not, but you have no right -"

"Spare me." Cecelia turned her back on her brother and stared out the window at the twilight sky. "I need rest tonight, to aid me tomorrow."

Sebastian dropped onto a stool. "Reconsider," he said.

Cecelia had been focused on relaxing her mind, but she turned quickly, all calm gone. "Reconsider? How dare you?"

Sebastian wondered if he looked as fatigued as he felt. "If you would reconsider, perhaps Robert Claybourne will. You would have the advantage of making the first move, to forego more death or bloodshed. Is that so awful?"

Cecelia crossed the room and slapped him. "Awful? It is unthinkable! Where is your pride? Or have you suddenly turned coward at the prospect of facing Lattimore?" Her smile was brittle.

Sebastian allowed himself a small smile. "Nay, I do not fear Lattimore, or any other champion. I would rather regain the earldom and never set foot in Myrridia again."

"Easy for you. You are a man. You get the title, and what is there for me? Marriage?" Cecelia paced back and forth.

"What about a school of Magic? Outside the Church?" Sebastian suggested.

"You would have me teach, rather than use my Talents. God, you are not a man at all. How did you survive so long as a spy?" Cecelia was trying to goad him into losing his temper.

Sebastian ignored her baiting. "I always recognized when my position became untenable and got out. I have said before that if this Claybourne is willing to compromise, so am I."

"I am not." The words rang with finality.

"You never were," Sebastian said, knowing the words were true as he uttered them.

Cecelia smiled and went back to the window and stared out. When she turned to face him again, her eyes flashed with ire. Sebastian tensed. She crossed the space separating them and shoved him with both arms. He nearly fell off the stool. "Once you were my favorite brother, but I have hated you for years, Sebastian," she said. "You abandoned me!"

Sebastian stood and took a step back, surprised at her strength and shocked by her words. "Abandoned you?" he demanded after taking several deep breaths.

She stared at him with an eyebrow arched in confrontation. "Aye, abandoned."

Sebastian fought his temper. "Father banished me - I abandoned no one in Tippensdown."

"Oh, please. Surely you can invent a more plausible tale than that."

Sebastian grasped her by both shoulders. "Never question my honesty, sister," he said, his voice deadly quiet. He released her and moved away, still staring at her. "Do you remember Isabel Gilbraith, Father's ward?"

"Aye, what of her?" Cecelia countered impatiently. "She was an empty-headed fool."

"She was clever enough. She had been deflowered by one of our grooms and gotten with child. She accused me of assaulting her virtue, partly out of spite that I had spurned her advances. Father took her word over mine, despite my protestations that I had not bedded a woman yet."

Cecelia laughed. "You were fourteen or fifteen. Try another tale."

Sebastian bit back a curse. "I cured myself not long after," he snapped back. "'Twas our eldest brother who got all of the offers from the maids, I might remind you. I refused to marry her, and Father told me never to set foot within Tippensdown again. He would toss in his grave to know that I could inherit the Earldom." He looked at her, and his tone softened slightly. "What happened to you after I left, Cecelia?"

"Like you care!" she retorted, hands on hips.

"I did at one time," he said. "Now, I wonder. Why do you have this need to kill all of the Claybournes?"

"Why should I explain to you? You will never understand." Cecelia stared beyond him, into her past.

The tall, thin girl with dark braids stared defiantly at her mother and fought anger at the older woman's harsh words "You will never amount to anything, Cecelia, never! You are a third daughter. You will either enter a nunnery or marry some provincial knight. Your embroidery is hopeless, your attitude sullen, and your figure impossible. God, 'twould have been better had you died in infancy!"

The girl took a step back. "What about my Magic?" she demanded. She flared her aura around her head.

"Stop that at once, you evil girl!" her mother shrieked, backing off and crossing herself. "I wish to God you had never been born and developed these Talents. I do not know from whence they come!"

Cecelia smiled slyly. "Perhaps Father is not my sire," she suggested. Her mother slapped her.

"How dare you! 'Tis most likely that you bedded a demon to acquire your power."

"I did -"

Her mother slapped her again. "You need to learn to respect your elders and your betters, Cecelia. You show regard for no one, though I blame myself for not separating you from Sebastian when you were children. Running wild with him has ruined you. You will learn the hard way one day, you mark my words."

"You are wrong, Mother, and I only hope you live long enough to see me triumph."

"We are not given so many years, you stupid girl. Accept your fate."

Cecelia had done no such thing. Less than a year later, she fled Tippensdown for the royal Court in Laurconsburg and won over the King's eldest son and heir, Nicholas Severinson. He pleaded her case with his father, and the king agreed to sponsor her Magical studies. Cecelia quickly caught up with and surpassed her fellow students. When she'd lived in Laurconsburg for a few months, Nicholas asked if he could bed her. With visions of a grand title before her, Cecelia agreed and was soon with child.

Nicholas agreed to marry her, but his father forbade the match. The pair bribed a priest a few days' journey from the city to perform a simple ceremony, and Cecelia traveled to a remote convent to have the child and ostensibly further her Magical training at a companion monastery. She left the child, a daughter, in the care of the nuns. When she returned to Laurconsburg, she told Nicholas of the birth. He agreed to allow the child to remain in the convent for the time being. He promised Cecelia that he would make their marriage public after his father's death and continued to spurn all potential wives.

Cecelia bore him another daughter before the Tippensdown massacre. Again, the child was left in obscurity. Cecelia left the capital some time later, confiding to Nicholas that she would avenge her family. Having his own ambitions in regard to Myrridia, Nicholas agreed with her and offered his aid should she need it.

Cecelia returned to the present with a smile at the memory of Nicholas. She'd received a message from him about a year ago, stating that his father's health was deteriorating. She'd sent back a reply telling him of her plans in Myrridia, and her brother's unconscious assistance. Sebastian watched her, his expression wary.

"Try me," he said.

She laughed. "If you only knew, Sebastian," was all she said. She began to take deep, even breaths. She climbed into the bed and soon fell asleep.

Sebastian remained wakeful long past midnight. Before retiring a few hours prior to dawn, he prayed for the right outcome to tomorrow's battle. For the first time he was unsure what that might be.

Robert asked Chris to accompany him after supper. Sensing the young man's disquiet, Chris agreed and told Helen where he was going. She nodded; she had her own plans.

Chris followed Robert to Reginald's old apartment. He glanced at Robert in surprise. "I thought -" he began.

"I wanted us to be alone, and I-I need to get used to this apartment. I am expected to move into it, and soon." Robert opened the door and motioned Chris ahead of him. Chris stopped a few paces into the dim room, trying to remember its layout. He hadn't been in there since Christmas. Robert bumped into him.

"Why did you -? Oh, it is dark." Robert took a deep breath and summoned light. It glowed a soft blue. Chris blinked.

"I did not think you could do Magic," he said.

"This is about my limit," Robert said, a trace of laughter in his voice. "My strongest gift is the ability to read a person's character. As king, I have little need for more."

"For a king, a gift like that is priceless," Chris said. "But showing me your Talents is not the reason we are here."

"No." Robert looked around the room, forcing himself to take in everything. He kept seeing his father's body. He walked to a chair and sagged into it, burying his face in his hands.

Chris's heart went out to the teen. He joined Robert and squeezed his shoulder. Robert allowed himself to relax. After several seconds Chris let go and messed up Robert's hair before pulling up a stool and sitting.

Robert raised his head. "Thanks," he murmured, his eyes bright with unshed tears. "I feel so alone and scared. I know I need to sleep, but all I can think about is Father, and Cecelia. What am I to do?"

"That is easy. Talk about it. Be a normal teen for a while. It is no crime. There will be plenty of time to be a king tomorrow. Look, I can stay as long as you want." Chris was less nervous after his meeting with Sebastian. He had no Magical defense against Cecelia, which just made him feel fatalistic toward facing her. Right now Robert needed him.

A couple of tears slid down Robert's cheeks, which he wiped away impatiently. "What would a normal teen do?" he asked Chris, genuinely curious.

"Well, if you were normal at all, which you are not, your face would have broken out for a start," Chris said with a smile. "Of course, that is usually for the big dance, when you have snagged a date with the most beautiful girl in class. I never had to face a situation like this at your age. I know I would be scared to death, though."

Robert drew in a ragged breath. "What did you do after your parents died?" he asked.

Chris looked pained for a moment. "I alternately cried and ranted. I missed them terribly and thought the whole situation was unfair. I wanted to see the man who had killed them get punished. All he got was his driver's license revoked. I was furious. When I realized nothing was going to happen, I left my home and joined the military." Chris stopped speaking as realization dawned on him.

Robert was watching his face. "What?"

"I guess I have stopped running away from my problems." At Robert's look of confusion, Chris explained. "When Nicole dumped me, I ran away from that, too, and threw myself into my work as a resident. But when Helen and I had difficulties, I stayed with her. And I am sure not leaving you and Allyson in the lurch." He sighed. "I wish I had said good-bye to my parents, though."

"What do you mean? I mean, have they not been - dead - for a while?"

"Yes. But I would visit their graves every couple of years. I did not before I came to Saelym." Chris laughed, but the sound was hollow. "I never thought I would be staying here because Christian would get himself killed. Who knew?" An unnoticed tear slipped down his own cheek. "I still miss them, but I know they are happy for me. They will be glad I have found love and contentment, and a purpose in life. Even if it is taking over the identity of a dead man."

"Is it difficult, becoming another person?"

Chris nodded. "I try to remind myself who I am most days. Today, when I met with Sebastian, I spoke a few words in my native accent, and it sounded strange to me. That scares me. I have become so accustomed to this place. I fear I will lose all of myself sometimes, then I look at Helen, and I no longer care. Until I am alone, or about to fall asleep, and the fear steals over me again." Chris stared at his hands, telling himself they were *his* hands, regardless of the Duke's ring. He looked up again. "Sorry, Robert. I never meant to go off like that."

Robert looked away, wiping his eyes again. "I cannot remember the last time someone shared something so private with me," he whispered. "Loneliness is a high price to pay for power."

"And it is a wise man who realizes it," Chris added quietly. Robert turned quickly to face him again.

"You do not think I am whining?" he asked.

"Lord, no. You could not pay me enough to trade places with you." This time Chris's laugh rang true. "Frankly, this position I have taken has too much power to suit me. If it will make you feel better, share something personal or embarrassing with me. That will make us truly friends."

"Friends?" Robert barely breathed the word. He thought for several moments. "Before Father was killed, I was with one of the prostitutes, talking. Father wanted to make a man out of me. I-I have never bedded a woman." Robert looked down.

"You are how old?" Chris asked quietly.

"Seventeen," Robert said defensively.

"I was twenty-two. You have plenty of time. I sometimes wish I had waited longer, but I was years behind most of my contemporaries. At least, if their stories are to be believed." He snorted. "You will know when you are ready."

Robert flushed. "I was ready when I saw Princess Juliana in the courtyard. The sun was shining, and she looked positively radiant." He frowned. "She does not like me."

"Give her time. Look at Helen and me. She was glaring at me when we met, though I am sure my tongue was hanging out like a love-sick dog."

Robert smiled at the image. "Are we friends now?"

"Oh, yeah. And for a long time to come." Chris stood, holding his hand out to Robert. The young man clasped it, and Chris pulled the teen into a hug. After a moment's hesitation, Robert returned it. "You will be okay, kid," Chris whispered.

"Thanks in great part to you."

Nicole and Naomi looked at their door, startled, when a knock sounded that evening. Nicole had been lost in thought, Naomi, pacing off her nervousness. She wished she could take a jog through the city, but she suspected how well that idea would go over. She opened the door.

"Who is ready for a council of war?" Helen asked pleasantly.

"What? War?" the two women exclaimed as they exchanged bewildered looks.

"For women only, a chance to give Allyson our advice and support. You both qualify."

"I don't have any Magic -" Naomi began.

"It does not matter. As a woman, you can still contribute life experience. I have noticed a natural grace to your movements. Teach Allyson how to move to unnerve Cecelia!"

"Okay." Naomi had brightened.

"And you bring your modern perspective," Helen said to Nicole.

They followed Helen to the library. Allyson was seated in one of the room's chairs, her back to the fire. Her eyes were closed in meditation, though they opened as the three women entered. Juliana was staring out of the room's window. She turned as she sensed their arrival.

Helen made the necessary introductions. She turned to Juliana. "What is your level of Magical training?"

"Close to Allyson's. I am untried under real conditions, but my strength is control," she replied.

"Excellent. I have knowledge of a few forbidden rituals, thanks to my close work with Edward. I will share them with you, Allyson, but that is not to be made public. It is only to show you how to defend against them should Cecelia attempt to use one."

Allyson nodded her understanding. "The less Edward knows, the better for us all. I still think I succeeded where he failed with Nigel Jennings because I approached the problem from several directions."

Helen nodded, her expression thoughtful. "All the more reason to avoid talking to Edward." She paused. "Once you and Cecelia form a Circle - and insist upon it for the safety of spectators! - no one will be able to assist you. Have Robert with you, to draw on his strength, if you are able. Otherwise it will be you and she. Alone."

Allyson paled but nodded solemnly. "I am frightened," she said, burying her face in her hands. Helen was about to go over to her, when Nicole knelt on the floor in front of the young woman. She grasped one of Allyson's hands hesitantly.

"Trust me on this, Princess. You are stronger than she is." Even Nicole was surprised by the confidence in her voice. Allyson lifted her gaze and stared at her, rapt.

Nicole smiled. "So much for science. Listen to me. There is a force, called gravity, which keeps us on the ground. Even if we climb a tree, eventually we come down." She glanced to make sure Allyson was with her. "Then we have love and hate. Both are more powerful than gravity. But love is the stronger, and its sister, compassion. You care for your brother, right?" Allyson nodded.

"Maybe even more important for tomorrow, you know what's best for Myrridia."

Allyson said, "Aye."

"It's simple. Kill Cecelia with kindness."

Allyson almost laughed. She continued to stare at Nicole, but she was thinking about Nigel Jennings. She had finally realized the implications of what she'd done, succeeding where Edward had failed.

"Be flexible," Nicole broke into her thoughts.

"What?" Allyson asked.

"Don't be rigid, be flexible. Don't be afraid to experiment if it makes sense to you. Go with your instincts, your gut."

Juliana had covered her mouth. She glanced at Helen who also had a hand over her mouth, but hers was to hide a smile. Both women knew that Magical experimentation was anathema to the Church. Helen was now certain that Nicole would be an asset to the others. Did she dare hope that Nicole would choose to remain in Myrridia?

Allyson thought back to her journal. She wondered if she should share it with Nicole. "You are right," she said quietly. "Adapt to whatever she does, and outmaneuver her if possible. Let her wear herself out if all else fails." She looked at Helen, who nodded.

"You can defeat her, my dear. Remember, she is rash and could easily lose control." Helen changed the subject. "Now, how would you make a dramatic entrance? What do you plan to wear?"

Naomi grinned. "I think we need to check her wardrobe. And, I'll show you how to walk with confidence."

The women walked companionably to Allyson's chambers. Allyson dismissed Diana and led them into her dressing room.

"Definitely green and gold," Naomi stated sometime later. "I know blue is the family color, but save it for your brother. Green to match your eyes and the gold suits your coloring. Can you project an aura to match?"

Allyson shook her head, unsure. "I cannot remember if I have ever projected an aura on purpose." She closed her eyes and concentrated. She opened her eyes as Naomi began clapping.

"Well done indeed." Helen smiled, holding a looking-glass up to Allyson. She stared at the glowing aura, green with gold flickering throughout.

"What do the colors signify?" Allyson asked in confusion.

Helen was thoughtful. "I do not know, Allyson. I know when Edward summons light, he can control and change the hues, but I cannot." She paused. "We may have to explore some old Magical texts to discover the answer, or perhaps defer to our resident - scientist? - after she has learned her craft." She glanced at Nicole.

"If I stay, I'm game."

"Do you want us to help you dress and prepare in the morning?" Juliana asked Allyson.

"Please. I have to remember everything you all have told me, and I will need to concentrate on that in the morning. I need all of the help I can get!" Allyson smiled.

"I can help you sleep, if you like," Helen offered.

Allyson met her gaze. "Yes, thank you. Do you mind staying awhile and talking?"

"Of course not." Helen glanced at Nicole. "Can you stay for a little while?"

"Sure."

Helen walked Naomi and Juliana to the door. "Thank you both." She met each one's gaze in turn. "She is as ready as we can make her," she said quietly.

Naomi touched Helen lightly on the shoulder. "It was little enough. Take care of her. She's a great girl. I'll be rooting for her even while I drool watching Sebastian," she said with a smile.

Helen returned the smile. "You have excellent taste, but Nicole's is better," she said cryptically. Juliana raised a curious eyebrow. Nicole couldn't decide if Helen meant Chris or Michael, or perhaps both.

Allyson motioned Nicole and Helen to chairs in the sitting room, then stepped into her bedroom. She returned after several moments and handed her journal to Helen. She looked at Nicole. "This is in the strictest confidence. I could be accused of heresy -" She broke off, biting her lip in consternation.

Helen opened the volume. Nicole started to read over Helen's shoulder; the book was in Latin. "Allyson's Book of Secrets," Helen translated aloud, and turned the page. Staring at the writing, she lifted her gaze to meet Allyson's.

"My dear," she began.

"Aye, Helen, I have written down ideas for changing accepted ritual," Allyson said. "It goes against Church teaching."

Instead of being shocked, Nicole snorted. "Uh-huh. You won't go to Hell just for changing a formula, though the Church hierarchy will make you think you will." She chuckled. "Leave it to a woman." She winked at Allyson conspiratorially. "That's why they don't ordain us, you know. 'Cause we're smarter and men know it."

Helen started laughing; she couldn't help herself. "Your perspective never ceases to amaze me, Nicole. Allyson, your secret is safe with me." She nodded toward Nicole. "My dear, Michael and I hope to change the way the Church controls Magic, and we can use all the help we can find. Nicole may work with us - indeed, I hope she will. Your position may not -"

Allyson shook her head. "Helen, I will do whatever I can, once Robert is wed and has produced an heir or two. Until then, I should likely keep my thoughts in that book rather than acting on them."

"You make a good point."

Helen and Nicole stayed with Allyson until the younger woman finally became drowsy. Helen helped Allyson remove her dress then worked a minor spell to speed her to sleep. She and Nicole maintained a comfortable silence as they returned to their respective apartments, each deep in thought.

Chris and Robert rediscovered they were well matched at chess. Not long after midnight, Robert stood and stretched, yawning. "Let us leave it. We can finish the game another day, if we make it through tomorrow." He gave a tired smile.

Chris stood and gave Robert's shoulder another squeeze. "No need to worry about it now. You need sleep. Do you want me to send Elijah to you? He has progressed far enough to help you with that."

"No, I will be fine, but thank you."

Chris walked Robert to the prince's apartment before heading toward his own room. Robert let himself in and noticed his squire had left a pair of candles burning. Paul himself was asleep in a chair, snoring softly. Robert smiled to himself and exited the room, closing the door quietly.

He climbed to the castle ramparts and stared up at the sky for a while. He prayed quietly, for peace, stability and his sister's safety and sanity. He wished he had more control over his own fate. He shook his head and returned slowly to his chambers, to get some sleep.

Chapter Twelve

Chris woke in the dark hours of the night. He slipped out of bed quietly, without waking Helen. He donned trousers and deerskin slippers and left the room. He knocked quietly on the door of the chamber Elijah shared with Michael. After his second knock, Michael opened the door.

"Sorry to wake you," Chris said.

"No trouble. Do you want Elijah?" Michael turned and started toward the bed.

"No, you actually. I have a sin I need to confess, in case, God forbid, you know." Chris fidgeted as he spoke.

"Oh. Let us go to the chapel, then," Michael said, donning his cassock quietly and bringing his stole and crucifix.

Chris took one of the burning torches and led the way. "I knew I would not get any more sleep until I got this off my chest," he said as they entered the empty chapel.

Michael motioned to a nearby pew. "Unless you prefer the confessional."

"It hardly matters." Chris shrugged. "It is not like this is anonymous."

"Aye. My thought exactly."

Chris knelt and bowed his head, crossing himself. "Bless me, Father, for I have sinned."

Michael sat next to him, inclining his head. "Tell me of your sin, my son, that absolution may be given."

"I have killed a man, Father, and though I did what was best, the deed weighs heavy on my soul. As a physician, I have always respected life, though I know death is inevitable for us all. I have had to face the death of my patients, but I dislike murdering a man. I -" Chris stopped, lowering his head to his clasped hands. "I am not a bad person, I never meant -" His shoulders were shaking. "I feel black and empty inside. Help me, please."

Michael couldn't help comparing Chris to Christian. Had Christian ever stopped to think about the consequences of his actions? Michael crossed himself, refusing to contemplate how many souls were on that conscience. He concentrated on the man, his friend, before him.

"Christ knows a man's heart, Christopher. By His authority, I absolve you of this sin. Your penance is to recompense the man's family. Take and foster Richard's son in Saelym, if the family is willing, and say prayers for Nigel's soul. In nomine Patris, Filius, et Spiritus Sancti, amen." Michael made the sign of the cross over Chris as he recited the familiar Latin.

Chris looked up. "Amen. Thank you, Michael. It is still on my conscience, but I can live with it."

Michael smiled. "May you live with the guilt for a long time indeed."

Robert woke at dawn. He slipped out of bed and went over to the window to stare out at the lightening sky. He shivered in the early morning chill. Shaking his head briefly in an effort to fully awaken, he lit a candle and began dressing. Paul entered the room after a quiet rap on the door. He was carrying a pitcher of water.

Placing the pitcher on the dressing table, he went over to assist Robert.

"I hoped you were still asleep, my lord," he murmured as an apology.

"I would not have minded sleeping the day away, if I could," Robert said. He was trying to lace his leather trousers, but his hands were shaking. He swore in frustration.

Paul gently pushed Robert's hands away and completed the lacing. Directing Robert to raise his arms, he then helped Robert into his surcoat. It was Robert's finest, worn only on special occasions. The velvet was royal blue, and he would use his gold griffin brooch to clasp his matching wool cloak. Paul now smoothed the surcoat and fastened Robert's worn leather belt around his waist.

"You will want your father's sword today," Paul remarked, hoping to distract Robert. He succeeded.

"Oh, yes. So much for a successful entrance, then. I shall likely trip and fall at the unaccustomed weight." Robert tried to keep his tone bantering, but his eyes were solemn. He should have taken time over the past several days to practice with the weapon so he could ably defend himself with it if needed. He shook his head; there was no point in worrying about that now.

Paul offered to fetch the sword and suggested Robert practice walking with it. Robert agreed and asked his squire to bring it to the chapel.

Robert walked quickly to the chapel. He encountered a few servants along the way, but no one else was about. As he hoped, the chapel was deserted; a few candles flickered in the dimness.

Robert knelt in a back pew, praying at first. Then he began clearing his mind of everything except the plans for midday. The thought of dying didn't frighten him as much as the effects his death would have on the kingdom and her people. He didn't hear his sister enter.

He looked up, startled, when she knelt next to him. He stared at her appearance. Instead of the matching blue, Allyson wore a fine silk gown of forest green with threads of gold shimmering throughout. She wore gold and emeralds at her throat and ears, and on her right hand. She radiated a feeling of mature serenity, and Robert felt like a gawky adolescent next to her. Since he had spoken with her late yesterday, she had become an adult.

"What?" she asked.

"I never - I mean, you are beautiful," Robert stammered. Allyson's cheeks turned pink. She put a finger to her lips.

"Tell no one that you noticed. You are my brother, and it would not be seemly for you to think so." Allyson was giggling by the time she finished, shattering the image of maturity.

Robert smiled. "I will not tell anyone." Then his tone grew serious. "Cecelia has nothing on you."

Allyson sobered. "Let us hope not," she said, with a confidence she didn't feel.

Paul entered the chapel. "My lord?" he whispered. Robert and Allyson turned to him. He held out the sword to Robert. Robert took it hesitantly after crossing himself. Allyson stared at the weapon, then looked at her brother. He was solemn, looking far older than his years.

Paul helped him fasten the sword at his waist. Robert stood still for several moments, trying to get a feel for it. He stepped into the aisle and walked toward the altar. As he expected, the sword was larger and heavier than the one he'd worn for the past few years. He was relieved that he didn't seem automatically prone to tripping over it.

In contrast, Sebastian had no intention of dressing for the occasion. He had nothing suitable even if he were so inclined. As a younger son, he'd never expected to inherit the earldom, and as a spy he was seldom expected to dress extravagantly. Nor did he offer to assist Cecelia.

Cecelia had too much pride to ask her brother for help dressing. She had paid dearly for the bolt of purple silk, shot through with silver threads, but she had made it into a fashionable style. She wore silver jewelry, with amethysts and sapphires. She had purchased the jewelry from a Rhennsbury pawnshop and wondered which member of the nobility had been forced to sell it. The fact that purple was traditionally associated with royalty was not wasted on her. It was the color of the Wyckendom ruling family.

"Pride goeth before a fall," Sebastian remarked as she fastened the necklace.

"Pride? I will feel pride after the Claybournes no longer exist. Until then, I am pleased to act as the instrument of their downfall." She checked her hair in the cracked looking-glass. She had braided it then wound it about her head, to mimic a coronet. Her Magical aura would complete the picture.

"I am going to go eat downstairs," Sebastian changed the subject. "Coming?"

Cecelia shot him a Look. "You know better than that. With the Magic I plan to perform today, I must avoid food. After I am victorious, then there will be feasting and celebration."

"As you like." Sebastian let himself out of the chamber. He could never understand the logic of fasting, working Magic to the point of exhaustion, and fainting from hunger afterwards. He figured he would understand it if he had such abilities.

Reginald clamored to accompany his parents. Already tense, Helen sternly told him to be still, that he was staying at the castle. Reginald's face fell, his expression turning sullen.

"Hey, none of that," Chris said, crouching down to Reginald's level. "Is that any way for a defender of ladies to look?" As Reginald looked confused, Chris continued, winking at Helen. "You are responsible for taking care of your sister, young man. Your mother and I have to assist the prince and princess. They need our help."

"But I want to go with you and help them, too," Reginald whined.

"No worries, when you have grown, you will have plenty of chances. As the future Duke of Saelym, you have a duty to keep an eye on your sister. Understood?"

Reginald hung his head but nodded.

"Can he not go with you?" Eleanor pleaded. "I will be good, I promise. He is horrid when he -"

"No." Helen's tone brooked no argument. "If this were a pleasure jaunt, there would be no question of you both accompanying us." In a softer tone, she added, "But if you disobey now, you shall not attend Robert's coronation."

Eleanor nodded solemnly, then went over to Abigail and ducked behind the maid's skirts. Abigail smiled at Helen. "I will see he does not torment her, mistress."

"Thank you, Abigail."

Chris and Helen met Elijah and Naomi as they descended to the courtyard. Grooms were scurrying about, but the activity seemed a controlled chaos. Elijah and Naomi looked tense. Helen took Naomi's hand.

"I lose no matter who wins," Naomi said to her.

"Mayhap not. This is far from finished. Stay with me."

Naomi looked at Helen with surprise. "Won't you be with Chris?"

Helen smiled. "Nay. As a non-participating woman, I will be in the background. Chris, as the Duke of Saelym, will be at Robert's side. We can fret together."

"You've got that right, honey."

"Can I join the worry party?" Nicole asked from behind them.

"Of course," Helen said. "Are you certain you want to come?"

"No. I'd rather stay behind like the coward I am, but I'd worry even more about what was happening. My imagination would be worse than the reality. It's a sick fascination."

"It is friendship and loyalty," Naomi corrected her. "And you're no coward."

"She speaks true," Helen added.

Elijah joined Chris as his friend checked his horse's gear. "Are you ready for this?" he asked Chris quietly.

"As ready as I can be. Sebastian no longer worries me. Cecelia scares me, but there is nothing I can do about her. It all depends on Robert and Allyson." Chris smiled, but it was more of a grimace.

"Sorry you came yet?" Elijah asked lightly.

Chris mounted and looked for Helen. Meeting her gaze for a moment, he saluted her. "No way," he said to Elijah.

A solemn-looking Robert edged his horse over. Elijah reached up and clasped his gloved hand. Robert squeezed back firmly.

"You'll be fine, Your Highness," Elijah said. "Your father may have been in the wrong, but you aren't. Besides, nobody pushes your sister around."

"Lord knows I never got away with it," Robert said, his eyes faraway. "I certainly tried often enough." He flashed a momentary grin.

Elijah patted the horse's rump. "Younger siblings," he said to no one.

"What?" Chris asked.

"Huh? Nothing. Trust me, you wouldn't understand." Elijah chuckled, who then went in search of his own horse, Shaq.

Citizens lined both sides of the street as the royal party traveled to the archery field. A standard-bearer rode at the head of the procession, followed by Robert and Allyson. Chris and Anselm were right behind the pair, as Myrridia's ranking dukes. Anselm had given Chris a verbal vote of confidence as they set out together.

People were cheering, and the sound intensified as they reached the converted practice field. Anselm leaned over to Chris. "Remember this, 'twas Cecelia who insisted on a public meeting."

Chris nodded. "It reminds me of an ancient Chinese curse. 'May you get what you wish for.'" Anselm was puzzled for a moment, and then his eyes twinkled.

Edward, Francis and Hugh Thurstyn were already present. Francis had insisted on appearing, to show the Church's solidarity with the king. Due to his failing health, he had directed the two bishops to attend him. He shook his head at the festive atmosphere of the crowd. Vendors were hawking hot and cold food, ale and mead.

Robert dismounted and handed his horse's reins to a member of his escort. He went over to Allyson and assisted her in alighting. "Wait until you see Cecelia or Sebastian," he directed, then joined Chris, who was surreptitiously helping Anselm off his horse. "Follow me, my lords," Robert said.

The three joined the waiting prelates at one end of the cleared area. Elijah, Helen, Nicole and Naomi found a place to sit on the hastily erected wooden dais near other noble spectators. Helen scanned the field, looking for Cecelia and Sebastian. Juliana joined them, her expression grave.

Cecelia and Sebastian approached the field on foot. Both heard the noise of the crowd. "They will be shouting for me by day's end," Cecelia vowed.

"For your head, more likely," Sebastian muttered. "They may not take kindly to your killing their new king."

Cecelia shushed him. She pushed through the crowd, emerging opposite Robert and his allies. She summoned her aura, discarded her cloak, and stepped toward her enemy. Sebastian was one step behind her. Many in the crowd began hissing and calling foul names. A few threw rotten vegetables. Cecelia ignored them, but scowled as she recognized Lattimore to Robert's right.

Robert schooled his features into a neutral expression. He was angered to see Cecelia dressed in purple, but he was sure the gesture was intended to provoke him. He fought the anger down, knowing he could ill afford the emotion. He had no intention of offering her the slightest advantage.

The Archbishop stepped forward and raised his arms for silence. The crowd quieted. He spoke to them in a frail but stern voice.

"People of Rhennsbury and elsewhere, we have gathered here for a serious purpose. This woman has called upon our young king to answer for grievous crimes committed by his forebears, and he must now answer this challenge. Today's outcome is far from certain. Bear this in mind before you start shouting and celebrating."

The people gathered were now silent. Many had not considered that their king faced a serious threat. Most had come expecting entertainment. Some among the crowd exchanged puzzled or worried glances with their neighbors.

Cecelia stepped forward, her aura shining and visible despite the strong sunlight. Several onlookers gasped. She projected her voice so that all present would hear her.

"Robert Claybourne, you have no right to rule Myrridia." Robert had taken a step forward, but stopped. "You should rescind all claims to the throne. You are incapable of ruling wisely or well. Look at your predecessors - warmongers, butchers of innocent women and children. The man at your right hand has been guilty of the worst excesses. If you insist on being king, face me and embrace your destiny."

It took all of Chris's willpower to keep his features even.

Robert moved again, stopping a couple of yards from Cecelia. He met her accusing gaze with a calm one. "You say '*We*' have no right to rule Myrridia."

Chris and Sebastian smiled at Robert's use of the royal pronoun. "Whom would you suggest instead? Yourself? Or some other? Or perhaps you feel the people of Myrridia deserve no leadership at all? I am not the man my father was, though I have heard that you also are guilty of attempting to harm innocent children." Cecelia paled with anger at the audacity of Robert's accusation. Sebastian inclined his head in approval.

Robert dropped his voice and the people watching leaned forward to catch his words. "We have no intention of conceding the welfare of Myrridia's people to your tender ministrations without a fight." Many cheered until the Archbishop silenced them with a stern look.

Cecelia fought down her rage. "Brave words, princeling. You may want to change them, however." Cecelia raised her left arm and pointed dramatically past Robert. "Observe what happens to Myrridia's most powerful Magician."

A silver-blue bolt of raw Energy erupted from Cecelia's fingertips. It passed between Robert and Chris, missing both by inches. Neither dared move.

Edward had the few moments' warning, but it took all of his focus to deflect the bolt harmlessly into the ground. He was panting with the exertion.

As Cecelia smirked, Edward scowled.

Robert glanced at Edward for a moment, quickly turning back to face his adversary. "It changes naught," he said firmly.

Allyson stepped forward to stand next to Chris. The spectators gasped again. Her own aura shimmered as clearly as Cecelia's, glowing green and gold. Cecelia stared, nonplussed for a moment. Robert noted the change in expression, but didn't look at his sister.

Cecelia crossed her arms. "Hear my complaint, Your Highness, before these witnesses."

Robert nodded; he knew what was coming.

"Six years ago, your father, Reginald Claybourne, and Duke Christian Lattimore, the man beside you, invaded the Earldom of Tippensdown and coldly slaughtered all of the Earl's family who were present. They raped the women and girls old enough to be assaulted, including my younger sister, who was eleven years old." Robert blanched...the rapes were news to him. Seeing Robert's expression, Cecelia smiled slightly, and so continued, "Last Christmas, an attempt was made to end your life and disgrace the Duke of Saelym, in an effort to bring down your father." Her eyes met Chris's, who stared back evenly. "Alas, that attempt failed. The assassin, Gerard, was a longtime associate of my brother, Sebastian, and a good man."

Sebastian kept his features expressionless. He could tell that Cecelia's words were having an effect on the audience, but he was uncertain whether it was in her favor.

Cecelia looked over the spectators, her gaze finally resting on Nicole. "How is your love life, Lady Nicole?" she taunted. Nicole flushed, then stood and stepped forward, spitting at Cecelia's feet.

"Better than you could hope for. I've never admired those who don't fight fairly. You're a bully, Cecelia, and I hope when this farce is over, you rot in Hell." Nicole turned and rejoined Helen and Naomi, her shoulders shaking with reaction. Naomi put an arm around her.

Cecelia turned to face Robert again. Chris locked eyes with Sebastian, who had stepped forward to join Cecelia. Cecelia saw the look and frowned, still displeased with the air of health surrounding the Duke.

Sebastian spoke into the silence. "Your Grace, I would like to request restitution from Saelym for the wrongs perpetrated against my family. I do not hold Robert Claybourne responsible for the acts committed by his father and yourself. As the executioner of Reginald Claybourne, I ask only for King Robert's mercy." Sebastian bowed.

Cecelia stared at him, dumbfounded. Chris crossed the yards separating them and held his right hand out to Sebastian. "Saelym regrets the sins of the past." Many in the crowd began murmuring. "I freely offer -"

As Sebastian shot a look of surprise at "Christian's" prompt and unexpected agreement, Cecelia turned on Chris in a fury.

"How dare you?" she demanded, insulted. "You raped and murdered my mother." She lifted both hands and silver light shot forth, aimed directly at Chris's chest.

Chris stared, shocked into immobility. Sebastian stepped between Chris and Cecelia, his body receiving the force of his sister's attack. His back arched and he fell to the ground, limbs twitching.

The spectators were astounded. Cecelia withdrew her attack as soon as she realized she'd struck her brother instead of her intended target.

Naomi cried out and ran up to Sebastian, who was now unconscious. Chris was on his knees, examining him. As Naomi crouched next to him and brushed some of Sebastian's hair back, Chris said, "He has had a seizure, but he is in no mortal danger."

Chris squeezed her hand and Naomi nodded. He stood and rejoined Robert.

Naomi rose and walked over to Cecelia. She slapped her. "You stupid bitch, what do you think you're doing?" Naomi turned away, returning to Sebastian, and put his head in her lap.

Cecelia was too stunned to react immediately. Recovering, she raised both arms above her head then pointed them forward, straight at Robert. Robert, who had been distracted by Sebastian's actions, returned his attention to Cecelia. He now stared at her, horrified, unable to react. Chris threw protocol to the wind and shoved Robert to the side, knocking the younger man down.

Golden light met silver and exploded. Allyson had not taken her eyes off Cecelia since joining her brother. Green eyes met blue.

"It is you and I, Cecelia," Allyson said in a soft voice.

"So be it, Princess. It makes no difference to me if you die before your brother." Cecelia's aura flared.

Elijah had joined Naomi, checking Sebastian. He stood. "Who can judge between these two women, once they form a Circle, to prevent cheating?" He was worried sick about Allyson's safety. Cecelia glared; Allyson nodded.

Francis said, "'Tis doubtful we can find an impartial witness, Sir Holmes."

"I will do it," Juliana said, stepping forward. "As I am from Esterlyn, I have no more loyalty toward one land than the other. If that is agreeable to you." She directed the last to Allyson and Cecelia.

Cecelia looked the young woman over. Who was she? Cecelia sensed her words were true as spoken. Crossing her arms, she said shortly, "Fine." She had every intention of using illegal spells and doubted either young woman could stop her.

Allyson said, "Aye."

Cecelia glanced at Robert, who had picked himself up and dusted himself off. Chris had given him a look of apology, but Robert was grateful for his quick reflexes. "You may remain outside the Circle, Your Highness, until I finish with your sister. Enjoy the wait." She hoped he would spend the time worrying.

Robert looked about to disagree. Chris spoke quietly into his ear. "She is right. Give no one opportunity to say you gave Allyson an unfair advantage. Just be ready to support her when she is exhausted at the end of this." Chris sensed that Cecelia had already wasted a good deal of energy in the attacks on Edward, himself and Robert. Allyson's odds of victory were increasing. Robert nodded to Cecelia and stepped back.

Juliana glanced from Cecelia to Allyson, then raised her arms and began a prayer to summon protective Energy. "Raphael before us, Gabriel behind us, Michael to our right, Uriel to our left, we beseech thee to protect those within and without as these two maidens do battle in the name of Him most High. Lord God, to Thee belongs the Kingdom, and the Power, and the Glory, 'til the end of days, amen."

Juliana remained focused on her task, unaware of the scowls on Edward and Hugh's faces at her summoning, which differed slightly from the Myrridian Church's form. In calm contrast, Francis observed and listened with approval. Before long, a large half-sphere, shimmering silver and gold, surrounded the three women. The Circle would protect the combatants from interference and protect the spectators from accidental injury.

Robert clasped one of Chris's hands for a moment. Chris squeezed, hoping to reassure the young man. The spectators were hushed.

Inside the Circle, Cecelia looked Allyson over, trying to judge the younger woman's Power. She had been startled to see the aura glowing so brightly around the princess; it indicated she might be more powerful than Cecelia had believed.

"As challenger, I believe the first move is yours," Allyson said, surprised at the calmness of her voice.

Cecelia nodded then raised her arms again. She prayed aloud. "Michael, thy servant requests a weapon worthy of defeating thy enemy." A glowing sword, the blade of which flickered with blue and silver sparks, appeared in her hands. It was a standard spell. She wanted to get an idea of her foe's abilities.

Allyson smiled before summoning a Magical shield, which she maneuvered adeptly, countering Cecelia's thrusts. "Is that the best you can manage?" she asked in a mocking tone, trying to goad Cecelia into losing her temper.

Cecelia's eyes narrowed in anger. "You will lose that confidence ere long, Princess." Allyson's gaze remained challenging.

"I am not afraid of you, Cecelia," she lied. "Do your worst." Cecelia smiled. The cruelty behind that smile left Allyson almost wishing the words unspoken.

Juliana inhaled sharply as she felt the Energies coalescing around Cecelia. The woman seemed to grow taller and her entire body glowed, throwing off the occasional spark.

Allyson bit her lip in consternation; she was unsure if she could control that amount of energy. Her original plan had been to wear Cecelia down and verbally bait her as much as possible. Allyson felt a queasy fear take up residence in her stomach. She prayed for quiet control from her brother, knowing he was unable to aid her from outside the Circle. She raised her arms to symbolize her own gathering of power.

Cecelia released her pent-up rage and hate. It appeared visually before her as an avenging dark angel, who glanced around the Circle, dismissed Juliana's presence and stared at Allyson with undisguised hunger.

Allyson took a few steps back, her back nearly touching the Circle. She knew of no counter to this spell, legal or illegal. She was going to have to improvise, and break Church law.

The entity stepped toward her, its arms outstretched, its expression one of cold welcoming. Allyson wasn't fooled by its expression. It wanted her life or her soul. She thought frantically, sidestepping its approach. It took the entity several moments to turn and relocate her, and she took the time to gather her thoughts into a coherent plan.

Love or compassion, she thought, remembering Nicole's advice of the night before. Cecelia was so full of hate that it would take something equally strong to counter her abilities. Unbidden, Allyson recalled Christian's attempt to rape her a year ago, and she felt a sudden empathy for Cecelia. She smiled and stepped away from her pursuer again, now facing Cecelia across the Circle.

Cecelia could taste her victory. The princess had no defense against her full Powers.

Allyson summoned all of the Power she felt she could control, holding her hands together before her, palms up. "Lord Christ, Thy servant requests Thine aid in her endeavors. I ask only Thy love, to counter her hate. Help her, I beseech Thee." As she spoke, she visualized a white rose, taking the vision from bud to full bloom. Cecelia stared, unsure what would happen next. Allyson was creating a new spell, under extreme pressure!

The flower transformed into a dove, which Allyson flung at the again-approaching entity. "I understand and forgive you, Cecelia," Allyson said.

In a flash, Cecelia's summoning disappeared, without even a trail of smoke. Cecelia fell to her knees, her strength sapped, staring at Allyson in disbelief. Her eyes turned fearful as she tried and failed to summon more power.

"What have you done to me?" she asked, panic-stricken.

"Negated your hate with compassion, temporarily blunting your power," Allyson replied, stepping toward her. "Christian tried to rape me, too, so I understand your feelings."

"Nooo!" Cecelia cried. "I refuse to lose in such a humiliating fashion!" She rose to her feet with difficulty, removing a dagger from her belt.

"Foul!" Juliana shouted, but Allyson had already stepped back warily.

"I shall slay you nonetheless," Cecelia vowed. Allyson stood with her arms at her sides.

"Go on, Cecelia. Strike me down. I refuse to stop you. Slay your unarmed enemy as my father and Christian Lattimore slew your family. 'Tis a pity you cannot assault me first." Allyson didn't move. Juliana marveled at her restraint, but swore she'd throw herself on Cecelia if the woman followed through on her threat.

Cecelia prostrated herself. "A curse on you! You have taken all pleasure from me. Kill me now."

"Nay, let us stop the death, here and now." Allyson stepped toward Cecelia, to assist the other woman in rising. Cecelia's actions had been a feint, and she now slashed at Allyson with the knife. Allyson stepped back. Cecelia rose to a kneeling position, raised her eyes to the top of the Circle, and plunged the knife into her own breast. Her lips moved soundlessly. As her body fell forward, a look of triumph crossed her face.

Allyson exchanged a frightened glance with Juliana before sagging to the ground, her exhaustion taking over. She noted that Juliana looked as worried as she felt. She prayed for Cecelia's soul, crying at her own inability to sway the woman's mind or save her life. Juliana dispersed the Circle. Robert ran to his sister, falling to his knees next to her. She fainted into his arms. Elijah joined them, taking Allyson's pulse and giving Robert a reassuring nod.

Chris helped a weak but conscious Sebastian stagger over to Cecelia. Sebastian knelt and cradled his sister's head. "She took her own life," he said, his voice aching and his eyes bright with unshed tears. "She has damned herself, rather than forgive." Naomi joined him, putting a hand on his shoulder. "Is your offer still available?" he asked her.

"Offer? Yes, of course."

Sebastian looked at Robert. "If Your Majesty will allow it, I would like to leave Myrridia forever, in the company of this woman. 'Tis your choice, and perhaps better than I deserve."

Robert left Allyson to Elijah's ministrations and held out a hand to Sebastian. "Let the killing end here. Go with her and may you one day find peace." Sebastian clasped the proffered hand and bowed his head. "I swear to you, Sebastian Falkes, that I shall appoint a fair-minded man to Tippensdown, to care for her people."

"My thanks," he whispered, his words almost unheard in the cheering that erupted from the spectators.

Chapter Thirteen

As the sky began to lighten on the morning of June first, most of Rhennsbury Castle's residents were already up and attending to their duties. Hot water had been delivered to Robert's chambers, and Paul was assisting him, despite Robert's protestations. He was already nervous and the extra attention just exacerbated it.

Chris rapped on the door before entering and held it open for the servants carrying the coronation garments. He was already dressed in his official finery of black wool trousers, black silk under-tunic, and dark green velvet surcoat displaying Saelym's silver eagle device. He was still bareheaded. He would have brought the ducal coronet with him, but he feared losing it. Paul was toweling Robert dry. Robert's scowl changed to solemnity as he glimpsed the finished clothing. He swallowed.

Anselm arrived as Chris and Paul were finishing lacing Robert's sleeves. Trousers, tunic, and surcoat were white, the velvet surcoat shot through with silver and gold thread work. There was no heraldic device, nor was there one on the heavy brocaded mantle, also white and lined with ermine. Robert managed to look older and younger than his age at the same time.

"Is it too late to back out of this?" he asked Chris and Anselm. "I would rather face Cecelia alone."

"Those are nerves, son," Anselm said, his voice firm and reassuring. "Besides, you are about seventeen years too late. You are sensing the weight of responsibility. 'Twill fade somewhat after today. Why, when you are as old as I am, you will barely notice it anymore."

Chris raised an eyebrow; Robert looked clearly skeptical. Anselm shrugged, but his eyes danced with amusement. "Your Highness, let none say I did not *try* to distract you." He used the honorific Robert was used to, hoping to relax the youth with its familiarity. Let him remain a prince for a while longer; he'd be a king for the rest of his life.

Robert looked grateful. "I am glad I am not supposed to eat. I could not keep anything down. God forbid we have to reschedule all of this were I to mess up these clothes." Paul shushed him and asked him to sit. He toweled Robert's hair to finish drying it then began combing it into a semblance of order.

"You need a trim," he remarked with a smile.

"Too late now," Robert countered.

When Robert stood again, Chris helped Paul drape the mantle across Robert's shoulders. Anselm fastened it with Reginald's griffin brooch. The mantle would be replaced with a royal blue one after Robert swore his oath. The three men stared at Robert momentarily, and Chris could finally appreciate how Elijah had felt the first time that he, Chris, had dressed the part of a duke. The young man radiated kingship.

He smiled at Robert, who was looking increasingly panicked. "You look every inch a king, kid, so fake your way through it. What do you think I do?"

Robert was uncertain at first if he'd heard Chris correctly, then he grinned, and looked more like the youth he still was. Anselm laughed.

* * *

Since Chris was occupied, Reginald decided to be obstinate. He refused to dress in his best tunic. Helen told him he could dress as he pleased, but he would not accompany them. She added that she doubted Colin DeLacey was behaving so poorly, and look how young he was.

Eleanor, receiving finishing touches from Abigail, stuck her tongue out at her brother, then smiled smugly. "Prince Robert will throw you in the dungeon for acting like a baby," she said with five-year-old authority.

"Will not!"

"Will too!"

"Enough!" Helen exclaimed. "Eleanor, sit for a moment, please, and hold your hands the way I have showed you. Reginald." Helen crouched to be at his eye level, taking care with her skirts. "You will get dressed now, or I will send for your father, who is much too busy to be disturbed. Need I remind you how he is when he gets angry?"

Abigail stifled a smile. She couldn't remember Chris ever achieving an expression worthy of Christian in a rage. Eleanor squealed in fright, then giggled as she remembered she would not be the object of her father's wrath.

Chastised, Reginald donned his proper tunic. Helen sighed with relief.

Sebastian had been staying with Elijah and Father Michael, keeping a low profile. He had physically recovered from Cecelia's attack, but his eyes remained haunted. Over the past several days, the three men had taken the time to get to know one another, and a friendship had begun to develop. Elijah was relieved, since he didn't plan to accompany Naomi home that evening, when Angelita Martinez would be contacting them.

"Are you attending the coronation?" Michael asked Sebastian.

"I had not planned on it. I doubt I am invited."

Elijah raised an eyebrow. "You're ditching Naomi, then, so she has to go with me?" He folded his arms in feigned indignation. Michael chuckled.

Sebastian missed Elijah's tone and answered his words. "She would be that disappointed? I did not realize -"

"Naomi is not that fragile," Elijah interrupted. "Compared to her and Mama, *I'm* fragile. I'm kidding you. I'm sure Robert won't mind if you do come."

There was a knock at the door. Michael answered it and ushered in Naomi and Nicole. Helen had called in favors from several noblewomen and obtained finer dresses for them to wear. Naomi looked radiant in cream-colored silk, and Sebastian forgot how to breathe for a moment. Nicole was a cool contrast in green, though she'd muttered to Naomi that she looked like a tree.

Sebastian looked down at his own worn clothes. "I can hardly escort her like this," he said.

"Excuse me," Elijah said as he slipped out. Going across the hall, he rapped at the McCabes' door and let himself in. "Can Sebastian borrow something of Chris's? They're of a similar size," he said to Helen.

"Of course. 'Tis fitting somehow. Chris offered him something from Saelym, though I do not think this is what either had in mind."

"Unh-uh. Thanks." Elijah was still chuckling as he returned to the others. He handed the clothes to Sebastian. "A loan, courtesy of the Duke of Saelym, though he won't know it until he sees you."

Sebastian laughed for the first time in days.

Edward Fitzroy and Hugh Thurstyn assisted Francis McHenry in preparing for the coronation. Edward was prepared to take over for his superior if the Archbishop faltered during the service. Before donning his ceremonial robes, Francis knelt and prayed. He knew he would not live through many more seasons, and he was delighted to be officiating at this event even as he deplored the circumstances leading up to it.

After being helped into his vestments, Francis sat. He would rest until the royal procession arrived. At that time he would join his bishops on the cathedral steps to welcome the entourage. He asked Edward to send Father Ambrose as soon as it was sighted.

Edward and Hugh exchanged worried glances as they walked through the cathedral's sanctuary to take their places at the entrance. They were both concerned with Francis's obviously increasing frailty. They noted there were already a few early arrivals.

The two men agreed to mentally contact the other if they noticed anything amiss with the archbishop. They began greeting the people now arriving.

Juliana dressed quickly with the help of her serving maid. She wore her best gown of muted gold, and a crimson and gold dragon brooch to fasten her ermine-lined crimson cloak. She thought the bright red was a bit overpowering for her features, but she represented Esterlyn today so there was no help for it. Her maid smiled encouragement. "You are beautiful as always, mistress."

Juliana gave an un-princess-like snort but thanked her maid. She now hurried to Allyson's chamber to see if the other princess needed assistance. Allyson was in her finest royal blue silk dress and gold griffin brooch. Diana was arranging her braided hair, as she called for Juliana to enter.

"God, I hate you," Juliana said, slightly out of breath. Allyson raised an eyebrow, sensing Juliana only half meant it. "You can wear all of these bold colors!"

Allyson laughed, prompting Diana to nearly stick her scalp with a pin. "Careful, mistress," she admonished.

"Too bad you are not marrying Robert today, then," Allyson countered with good humor. "White or ivory would suit you."

Juliana laughed in return. "I guess that is my only option to gain you as kin," she said, surprised to realize she was only half-jesting. "I could do worse, I suppose."

"I am sorry Mother is not here," Allyson said quietly. "I guess the nuns would not allow her to leave, though Mother can be stubborn. She will be abbess ere long."

"Would you like me to sit with you? I would hate to see you sitting alone."

"I would like that. Thank you, Juliana."

Juliana inclined her head, then went over to the dressing table and held up various earrings to Allyson's ears, frowning at several before deciding on a sapphire pair. Diana placed Allyson's coronet on her coiled hair to complete the ensemble.

Juliana accompanied Allyson to Rhennsbury Cathedral. Allyson greeted Edward and Hugh with courtesy. Edward had asked her about her confrontation with Cecelia the following day, but Allyson had told him she was not ready to discuss it. Juliana now curtseyed, then followed Allyson into the building.

White candles burned in the wall sconces. Sunlight poured through the eastern-facing stained-glass windows, leaving pools of multicolored light in the aisle. Flowers and more candles were arranged on the altar top.

Allyson stopped several paces from her family's customary pew. Juliana bumped into her and murmured an apology before looking past her. A gray-clad woman was kneeling in prayer. Allyson whispered, "Mother?"

Margaret Claybourne, in nun's garb, stood and turned to face the two young women. The gray habit did little to dull her still-handsome features, though her hair was completely covered. She smiled and held out her hands to her daughter.

"Allyson. I would not miss this. How are you?" The two women embraced lightly, and then Allyson leaned into her mother. "You defeated the Falkes woman, child? Are you all right?" Margaret held her daughter at arm's length, taking in her features, then doing a deeper Reading.

"I will be fine, Mother," she said. "And I truly think that Cecelia defeated herself."

Juliana stepped forward and curtseyed deeply. "Your Majesty," she greeted Margaret.

"Nay, call me Sister now," Margaret said. "And you are from Esterlyn, yes?"

"Princess Juliana DiStephane. 'Tis a pleasure to meet you. I feared I would have to return home without doing so. You are highly regarded there."

"The sisters allowed me this one visit back into the world. I have asked for little since I retired to the convent, though I do have an annoying habit of speaking with the messengers who occasionally pass through. I may no longer be a player, but I sill want to know what is happening in the game." She gave Juliana her full attention. "Dare I hope that a young woman such as you would be willing to marry Robert in the near future?"

"I -" Juliana floundered, blushing. She was rarely speechless, but the older woman's directness had taken her by surprise. Allyson smiled in sympathy. "I cannot say," Juliana finally said, wincing at her lame reply.

Margaret smiled. "You have plenty of time to find a husband suitable to your temperament. I sense strength and fairness in you. An intelligent man will appreciate you."

Allyson giggled. "Of course, the difficulty is finding an intelligent man. The smartest ones enter the Church, though sometimes their plans backfire." Juliana didn't mask her confusion.

Margaret understood her daughter's reference to Edward inviting Chris McCabe to Myrridia. "I hope Edward loses sleep at night because of it," Margaret said. She paused and smiled. "I will have to confess the unkind thought. When I repent it." She gazed at the cathedral's ceiling, feigning piety. "That may be a while. Will you sit with us, Juliana?"

"I wish to sit nowhere else, my lady."

Father Michael led Elijah, Nicole, Naomi and Sebastian to a little-used entrance to the cathedral. Ambrose was waiting for them impatiently, surreptitiously glancing over his shoulder from time to time. Spying them, he looked relieved.

"Hurry," he urged them, "before Edward discovers I am not with him." He held the door open, then gave Michael directions to the sanctuary before hurrying off.

"Poor bastard," Naomi said. "No sex *and* he has to put up with Edward Fitzroy?" Elijah told her to hush, that they were in a religious house even if she wasn't a Catholic. "Sorry," she whispered, then chuckled. Elijah rolled his eyes.

Michael led them to the sanctuary, which was rapidly filling. "Do you want to watch from the upper gallery?" he asked, for Sebastian's benefit.

Elijah shrugged. "Why not? Besides, we may as well make certain there aren't any nasty surprises up there." Sebastian agreed.

"We cannot be too careful," he said. "Robert still has enemies, though he has done naught to provoke anyone yet. Prince Nicholas of Wyckendom, for example, will no doubt try to regain Tippensdown some time in the future, after his father dies."

"Then why doesn't Robert just give it back?" Naomi asked.

"I wish it were so simple," Sebastian said with a smile. "I am the only one with a legitimate claim." His eyes looked haunted again. "For Robert to return it to Wyckendom, without a fight, would imply weakness on his part, regardless of the truth."

"Men are so stupid. It's all macho posturing." Naomi frowned. "Present company excepted," she added belatedly.

"What kind of posturing?" Sebastian asked.

"Macho. You know, chest puffing, strutting around comparing the sizes of -" Naomi stopped as Nicole burst out laughing.

Sebastian raised an eyebrow. "Of what?" he asked.

Nicole flushed as all three men looked at Naomi, who shrugged. Sebastian caught on. "'Tis said that women have a greater sexual appetite than men do."

"Oh, puh-leez," Naomi said. "Don't we have a coronation to watch?"

Chris and Anselm accompanied Robert to the courtyard. Robert wanted to walk off his nervousness, but he was terrified of ruining his garments. Anselm finally helped him relax by reminding the young man that his father had had his turn several years before Robert was born.

"What was it like?" Robert asked, distracted.

"An air of hope normally attends these things. Though I think today may be more hopeful than usual. Here is your mount."

Robert was dismayed to see the white stallion being led to him. "What if I fall off? It is a strange horse." His panic returned.

"'Tis against the law," Anselm said in all seriousness. "You will be traveling at a walk. You have nothing to fear."

Robert let himself be helped into the saddle, and Chris and Anselm draped the mantle behind him. Robert took the reins and patted the horse's neck. The horse snorted but remained still.

"Do not let him know you are nervous," Chris suggested with a grin.

Robert shot him a sharp look, then smiled, realizing the distraction had relaxed him a little. Chris mounted. "We are right behind you."

A short while later, Robert rode out of the castle's main gate, preceded by the castle herald and standard-bearer. As his procession approached the city gate, a cheer went up from those waiting to catch a first glimpse of their king.

The mood of the city was celebratory. Blue and gold banners hung from upper-story windows and common folk lined Rhennsbury's main street from city gate to cathedral steps.

Robert followed the two men in front of him, waving and nodding occasionally. As he dismounted before the cathedral, he thought he saw a familiar face among the onlookers. A young blonde woman was gazing at him, smiling.

"Mary?" Robert breathed. She nodded, dropped a curtsey, and began to back into the crowd.

"Wait a moment, please," Robert called. Several people were looking at each other with surprise. Chris and Anselm joined Robert. Mary stopped retreating, her eyes wide with fear. "There is work for you at the castle," Robert said quietly. "If you wish it." Her eyes welling, she nodded before fleeing.

"What was that all about?" Chris asked.

"A long story," Robert said, thoughtful. He took a deep breath and began mounting the cathedral steps.

The archbishop met him at the top of the steps and clasped his hands. "Welcome, Highness. We can begin when you are ready."

Robert's panic returned. "How about tomorrow?" he asked in a plaintive voice.

"Do you really want to suffer this anticipation again, son?" Francis asked, his expression sympathetic, as they entered the cathedral's foyer.

"Oh. No."

Edward smiled triumphantly as he led Chris into the cathedral entry. "You should have taken my advice and gone home. As Myrridia's most powerful duke, you follow Robert down the aisle carrying the state crown. DeLacey will bear the state sword."

Chris swallowed, then recovered slightly. "Would it not be more fitting for 'Christian' to carry the sword and Anselm the crown?"

"That is up to you, though 'tis an honor I doubt Christian would have foregone. The crown is more symbolic of kingship, and it is the greater honor."

"Considering his opinion of Robert, would he even be here today?" Chris countered. Edward refused to concede the point. Chris shrugged. "I defer to Anselm's age and experience and Christian's reputation as a warrior." It felt right to him.

"As your Grace wishes."

Anselm raised an eyebrow when Hugh Thurstyn made to hand him the crown on a royal blue silk cushion. Robert stared at the sapphire and diamond-encrusted crown, unable to take his eyes off of it. He was feeling overwhelmed.

Chris decided there was no way he would be able to balance the sword on its cushion, walk down that aisle, and avoid dropping the weapon. Throwing protocol aside, he balanced it in his hands, his palms up. "Dear Lord, keep me sure-footed today, for Robert's sake," he prayed.

All stood and faced Francis McHenry as he entered the sanctuary, crozier in hand. Robert was behind him, flanked by

Edward and Hugh. Edward carried the cathedral's Bible. Chris and Anselm were next, followed by Geoffrey Renburg, who carried a royal blue mantle. Robert kept his eyes on the archbishop's back, his face pale, his expression sober.

As Francis reached the altar, he stood and faced the congregation. Robert stopped and knelt at the foot of the steps leading to the altar, his bare head bowed. He knew he was supposed to look like he was praying, but it wasn't an act. He *was* praying. He took a deep breath, then raised his head. Francis met his gaze and nodded once.

"Men and women of Myrridia, Robert Cedric Claybourne has come before you to swear his fealty to you and accept the burden of kingship. Robert, do you come before your people in a state of grace?"

"Yes, Excellency." Robert was surprised at the steadiness in his voice.

"Do you solemnly swear to defend the rights of all of Myrridia's citizens, to the best of your ability?"

"I so swear."

"Do you agree to lead the people, in war and in peace?"

"I do."

"Do you swear to be a caretaker for the people, to assist the Church in maintaining their spiritual lives?"

"I swear it."

"Let us pray." Edward and Hugh had joined Francis at the altar, and the two men provided Magical counterpoint to the Archbishop's words. Robert prostrated himself before the altar, letting the familiar phrases wash over him. He was feeling marginally calmer, but the physical weight of responsibility was daunting.

He didn't realize at first that the Archbishop had stopped speaking. Murmuring a quiet "amen" Robert lifted his head again. The older man held out a hand to help him rise.

"This way, Your Highness." Edward and Hugh removed the heavy white mantle, but Robert barely noticed the change in weight across his shoulders.

He walked with Francis to the Archbishop's throne. Robert knelt before the Archbishop, his hands clasped, his eyes closed. Francis made the sign of the cross over Robert's head, then anointed him with sacred oil. Robert let out a single shuddering breath before opening his eyes. Edward and Hugh draped the royal blue mantle about his shoulders, and Geoffrey clasped it with the griffin brooch, meeting Robert's gaze briefly.

Francis glanced at Chris and Anselm, motioning them forward. Anselm handed the crown to Francis, who placed it on Robert's head. Robert closed his eyes for a moment, then stood slowly. Chris moved before him and handed him the State Sword. "You are doing swell, kid," he whispered, before backing away. Robert met his gaze for a moment in acknowledgment.

Everyone in the cathedral cheered. Raising his hands for silence, Francis said, "I give you your new king. A long and prosperous reign, Your Majesty." He then nodded to Anselm and Chris.

Chris froze. Now what? Edward hadn't coached him beyond this. He wanted to glower at the bishop. Anselm nodded to his family, who joined him, then stepped before Robert and knelt. They exchanged words, and Robert clasped Anselm's hands.

Chris caught on. He met Helen's gaze and nodded. She came forward with Reginald and Eleanor, both of whom gazed at Robert with wide eyes. Chris knelt before Robert. After a momentary pause, he said, "I, Ryan Christopher McCabe and Duke of Saelym, do solemnly swear to be your faithful vassal and servant, now and forever." Surprised blue eyes met steady green ones. Robert almost forgot his own part.

He clasped Chris's hands and said, "I, Robert Cedric Claybourne, King of Myrridia, swear to be your faithful liege lord, through war and peace, famine and prosperity, so shall it be through all of our days, so help me God."

"So help me God," Chris murmured.

Helen sensed a change in Chris. As they walked to their seats, she touched his arm. "I shall never doubt your loyalty again, after using your own name in your pledge. Are you all right?"

"I am fine. I was unable to say the words with his name. It seemed wrong. *I* am the one who is going to stick by Robert, not Christian. I am still Christopher, but I am the Duke, too. I guess I just committed myself to this place for a second time."

"So it would seem."

Juliana and Allyson sat quietly through the coronation and pledging of fealty. Allyson wondered what her fate was to be. She knew Robert would not go back on his word in regard to her marrying - or not - but now her brother would be under increasing pressure to produce heirs. She didn't want to just fade into the background. What she wanted was to run away with Elijah Holmes and combine their Talents or perhaps join Helen, Michael and hopefully Nicole. She firmly hoped Juliana would agree to marry Robert someday. She'd make him a fine queen, a partner as much as a wife.

Juliana watched the coronation with curiosity. She knew her elder brother would face the same situation, hopefully well into the future. She'd arrived in Rhennsbury prepared to dislike both Claybournes and had found herself pleasantly surprised. She raised her opinion of Robert again. He'd seemed quite somber during this entire ritual. He must have the sense to recognize the responsibilities involved. She smiled as she thought about royal blue versus crimson. If she were to marry Robert, she'd be changing one bold color for another. She bit her lip to control the giggle that threatened when she thought of her father's expression if she mentioned such a marriage.

Epilogue

Early that evening, Naomi paced in an unsuccessful attempt to hide her nervousness. Sebastian smiled at her from his seat across the small bedchamber. "I will be fine. I no longer desire to stay here. The past will haunt me. Accompanying you, I will have to look forward."

Naomi nodded, but she had her doubts. She agreed with his assessment of his future in Myrridia, but he had no real idea what her home, and the twenty-first century, was like. She tried to push thoughts of home to the back of her mind.

A quiet knock sounded at the door. Naomi focused her thoughts and opened it. Helen and Elijah were there. "Are you ready?" Helen asked her quietly, studying her face. Helen glanced at Sebastian, who had stood at their entrance. "Michael and Nicole are with Edward in the chapel, preparing, but if you need more time, we can wait."

Naomi shook her head, then looked at Sebastian. "Let's get it over with, then you can all go celebrate with Robert." Sebastian put an arm around her shoulders. He liked the fact that they were nearly of a height.

Robert was exhausted as he prepared to attend the celebratory feast. "Go to your friends, Chris. I will be fine. I just wish..."

"What?"

"I would still ask Sebastian if he wants Tippensdown. I do not understand why Father continued to maintain a garrison there when he could have offered it to a loyal man of his choosing. Do you think Sebastian would take it?"

Chris shook his head. "I doubt he wants it any more. For him it would be filled with too many memories and ghosts." He shivered. "I can ask him, though, if you like."

"Please."

"Helen and I will see you soon."

Chris caught up with the others as they reached the chapel. He tapped Sebastian on the arm. "You, too," he said to Naomi. He told them of Robert's offer. Sebastian looked at Naomi, took her hand, and then shook his head.

"Give Robert my thanks, but tell him the answer is no. It would be too painful for me, and I would not put Naomi through that, if she is even interested. Besides, considering what I did to Reginald, it would make Robert look weak. I have too much respect for him to subject him to the gossip that would occur."

"I figured you would say no, but I told him I would ask anyway. I am sure he will find the proper person for it."

Elijah held the chapel door open for them to file in. "Just so Robert doesn't get any crazy ideas like offering it to me. Can you get thrown into a dungeon for telling the king to go to hell?"

Helen laughed. "For milder words than those, Elijah."

"Maybe I better go home, then, too."

Edward looked up from his meditations at their entrance. Helen had asked him to summon the window since Angelita was expecting them to be in Saelym rather than Rhennsbury. He'd agreed.

Nicole finished lighting candles as Michael knelt to relax his own mind. He'd not worked Magic with Edward for a few years, and he was extremely nervous at the prospect of doing so now.

Elijah hugged Naomi. "Tell Mama I'm well. I may yet decide to come home, you know. In the meantime, take care of Sebastian. He's going to have the worst case of culture shock imaginable," he said with bland understatement.

Naomi punched him in the arm. "You take care of yourself, and Nicole and Chris. And Helen and everybody else."

She hugged Chris now. "Take care of the big lug, will you? He needs looking after."

"Of course," Chris chuckled. "Give your mother my love." He paused, then grinned. "Tell her to feel free to give my savings account to Sebastian, but tell her to keep the interest!" Chris turned to a surprised Sebastian and held out his right hand.

Sebastian clasped it firmly. "I owe you a debt of thanks, for being willing to talk instead of fight. I wish you well where you are going. You are in good hands with Naomi, and you will be in even better ones with her mother."

"Thank you, Chris. You as well, Helen. I am anxious, but I do not dare look back."

Edward had summoned the window he'd opened by accident a year ago. He called on Michael to help him keep it open.

"I suggest you refrain from tarrying. I am having difficulty with this." Edward could see his own concern reflected in Angelita Martinez's face on the other side. Her initial expression had been one of surprised recognition to see him. The window flickered as he spoke.

Elijah hugged his sister again, then Sebastian as well. Sebastian promised to look after Naomi, and with a smile, Elijah wished him good luck. As they walked to the window, Elijah thought it seemed to shrink. He glanced at Nicole, who met his gaze before staring back at the window, her expression unreadable.

Naomi took Sebastian's hand and stepped up to the opening. The window flickered again, shrinking slightly.

"Good-bye," Naomi said quietly, as she and Sebastian stepped through. The window disappeared abruptly.

Edward blinked. He gazed at each person in turn, but his eyes returned to Nicole and Elijah. "I think this window is closed forever. I did not close it, and neither did Senora Martinez."

Nicole went over to Michael. "I agree with Edward," he whispered. "I am sorry, Nicole." She held out her hand to him.

"I think I'd already decided to stay, in my heart, anyway." Michael clasped her hand then gave her a tentative smile and put his arm around her shoulders. "I'll cope," she added. Edward raised an eyebrow, but remained silent.

Elijah continued to stare at the space where the window had been. Chris and Helen joined him on either side, Helen slipping her arm around his waist. "I had plenty of chances," Elijah said quietly. He grinned at Chris. "You're stuck with me now, pal."

Chris groaned in feigned dismay before hugging his friend. "I should have known you would be trouble when we met in med school." He silently wondered if the window's closure was his fault. He'd permanently committed to staying in Myrridia earlier, when swearing fealty to Robert. He shook his head; that didn't make any sense. He'd already committed to staying with Helen months before. Of course, no other explanation made sense, either.

Debra Killeen

About the Author

Debra Killeen pursued a career in pharmacy for fifteen years before moving into the related field of clinical research. While studying pharmacy, Debra maintained a strong interest in history on the side, and while she was transitioning careers, the characters began telling their stories. Eight years later, she's still waiting for them to stop. Debra currently resides in Chapel Hill, NC, where she shares a home with her sister and five wonderful cats. More information is available on the web at www.myrridia.net. Debra can be reached via email at debra.killeen@myrridia.net.
A Prince In Need is her second book in the series, The Myrridian Cycle.
An Unlikely Duke is the first book in the series and here is what Romantic Times Book Reviews had to say:
"...a delightful mixture of time travel with magic and adventure...a good start to a five-part series."

LaVergne, TN USA
18 January 2010
170298LV00004B/24/P